SPINDRIFT

A story of betrayal, redemption, war and revolution!

N H CHAMPKEN

Published by Novel Histories,
Somerset, England, 2020

For my daughter Sarah

ISBN-13: 979-8-6312-8967-3

Copyright © 2020 Neil H Champken

All rights reserved. Note to Readers: This book is written in British English, except where fidelity to other languages or accents is appropriate. You can find out more about this book, our other publications and sign up to our email list by visiting:
https://www.facebook.com/NovelHistories

Contents

Chapter 1	**7**
Chapter 2	**23**
Chapter 3	**40**
Chapter 4	**49**
Chapter 5	**67**
Chapter 6	**78**
Chapter 7	**88**
Chapter 8	**99**
Chapter 9	**115**
Chapter 10	**123**
Chapter 11	**136**
Chapter 12	**146**
Chapter 13	**161**
Chapter 14	**169**
Chapter 15	**178**
Chapter 16	**195**
Chapter 17	**207**
Chapter 18	**216**
Chapter 19	**231**
Acknowledgements	**243**
Map of Aix Roads	**244**
Historial Note	**245**
Map of Douarnenez	**246**
Bibliography	**247**

CHAPTER ONE
Digbeth, Birmingham - 15th March 1809

I had stood and watched as the sweetest wife any man could wish for was lowered into a pauper's grave behind the Digbeth Almshouse. They'd said it was consecrated land but, to me, it was just a patch of neglected earth. Only a few souls attended the funeral, and even the parson scurried away as soon as the rough box hit the damp soil. The two churchers, who had pushed the handcart carrying her poor body, ignored me and busied themselves with shovels. The first spadefuls of wet earth were slapping against the top of her casket when Elisa took my arm and slowly led me away.

Elisa Double didn't know me well, her husband was a work friend of mine, but she was aware of how keenly the loss of my wife had affected me. In the absence of anyone who knew me better, she felt obliged to help as much as she could.

When we reached the filthy courtyard outside the tenement, that Mary and I had called our home, the scene greeting me evoked a raw anger such as I had not felt before. The door to our tiny, ground-floor house stood wide open, and outside there was a horse-cart loaded with our possessions. Emerging from the door, two miscreants carried the oak table her father had given us when we had left Somersetshire two years earlier. They were trouble: they stank of it. They were both burly men, but neither was as tall as me. My step quickened uncontrollably as I advanced upon the man nearest to me. My wife's body was not yet mouldering in the ground, and these bastards were ransacking our home. This was behaviour that couldn't be tolerated and had to be stopped immediately. The man recognised the malicious intent in my eyes, and his Adam's apple bobbed as he swallowed saliva to slake a rapidly drying throat.

"If you pay no rent, you 'ave no tenancy," he shouted as he dropped the table.

Vengeance had me firmly in her vice-like grip, and this sod was about to pay for the misfortune life had heaped upon me. Charging the last few yards, and screaming senselessly, I rained a shower of wild blows on his head. He buckled under the ferocity of the attack, slumping back onto the table, but my rage didn't abate. Each fearful thud of my fists on his skull only served to refresh my anger. At the height of my frenzy, and without warning, a searing pain suddenly demanded attention from every nerve in my body. Near-paralysed, I just managed to turn enough to catch sight of a third man who had not been present before. His features were hidden from me, but he was one of the biggest men I had ever seen. There was an ugly tattoo of a black bear on his bicep and a cruel, rounded cudgel in the ham-like fist that he was raising above me. The first blow had caught me behind the ear and robbed me of movement; the second landed across the top of my head and robbed me of consciousness

I awoke propped against the pigsty in the centre of our dark courtyard. My vision was sketchy, but I could see my long legs, encased in dirty, woollen stockings, stretched out in front of me. For the first few moments I remained motionless, instinctively knowing that any movement would be painful.

"Nathaniel ... Nathaniel Egan, gently does it now."

A female voice whispered in my ear, and I felt my head being moved to examine its wounds. It was Elisa, who must have stayed with me following the attack. My face was dripping with water that she must have splashed onto me from the trough to bring me round.

"Nathaniel, do you know where you are? He dealt you a fearful blow."

"Who was he?" I groaned.

"We don't know his name, but he's one of the new overseers at Chapman's Foundry where you used to work," she replied, starting to dab at my head with a cotton 'kerchief.

"Used to work? What do you mean ... used to work?"

"Chapman has gone, Nathaniel. He had debts, and his creditors have sold the works. You have lost track of time whilst you were nursing your Mary. Robert says that he hasn't seen you at work for weeks."

A hazy semblance of order slowly returned to my thoughts. Josiah Chapman had owned my house. Heavy timbers had been fixed to the door and single window whilst I was unconscious. Whoever had taken over his foundry would need the house to offer to incoming workers. Chapman had never been able to entice enough men to hammer copper or turn his presses, and the offer of accommodation was a good incentive.

"Come home with me," urged Elisa. "Robert will be along presently, and we can work on what is to be done."

She gently coaxed me into her small dwelling in the same 'pudding bag' as my own (NOTE: *A 'Pudding-Bag' was nineteenth-century slang in Birmingham for a collection of tenements built around a courtyard containing communal amenities such as privies or ash pits. The one Egan and the Doubles inhabited also contained pig sties and an open trench which acted as a sewer*). The Doubles' parlour had a floor of beaten earth, and a small fire burning in the cast-iron range dimly lit the room. The family had made an effort to brighten their surroundings, and some tired, dried flowers and childish paintings were pinned to the walls. Elisa ushered me into a high-backed chair by the range and brought me coarse, bitter beer before she started to bathe away the congealed blood caked in my hair. A gaggle of the Doubles' children, all dressed in grubby smocks, suspended their play to come and stare at their beaten neighbour before they were chased away by their mother.

Studying myself in a small looking-glass that was fixed to the wall beside the range, a pair of piercing, green eyes glared back. Much to Mary's annoyance, I was always proud of my looks. Pretty girls would always have an extra glance for me, but now I looked so tired and drawn that I almost couldn't recognise myself. One side of my face was disfigured by an ugly wound, and the week-old bristles that coated my chin made me look well beyond my three-and-twenty years.

Elisa went for more water from the pump, and I sat mesmerised by my reflection until disturbed by Robert Double's voice in the scullery. He had returned from the toy manufactory where we had worked together, and Elisa was relating the tale of the afternoon's events to him in urgent, hushed tones (NOTE: *In the eighteenth and nineteenth centuries all small goods – such as buttons, medals, hinges or buckles - were termed 'toys' in Birmingham*). Robert came and knelt beside my chair. He was a large, heavily set man whose face, and full grey beard, wore the grime of the factory. He was in his early fifties, and I had known him since I had first arrived at Chapman's two years before. He thought of me as something of a young hothead, but I'm sure that he liked me and had tried his best to keep me on the straight and narrow. Much like Elisa, Robert knew how deeply I had felt the loss of Mary and wanted to assist me.

"'Tis a rum do, Nathaniel. To turn you out of your home on the same day as your wife's funeral is the work of evil men," he said, shaking his head gravely. "Josiah Chapman would never 'ave treated you in such a way. He'd 'ave let you stay on longer, Nathaniel. That's for sure."

"What has become of him? Elisa says that he had to sell up?"

Robert nodded. "Rumour be that 'e's in debtors' prison," he said in a resigned tone. "These are bad times. The war is makin' trade more difficult for our masters an' these last few weeks they've been putting men out, not taking them on. There are too many comin' up from the country and there 'aint enough work in the town ... there's a lot o' muttering, Nathaniel, an' I think we're in for some big trouble."

"Why are they turning men away? Chapman could never find enough men to sweat over his damn buttons and medalets."

"Chapman had been strugglin' for many months. His buttons an' trinkets wus doing well enough, but he invested too much in makin' commemorative medals. Do you remember the one for the Battle of Vimeiro? We made 'em for months, but he could never sell enough of 'em. There were other partners, Nathaniel, and they wouldn't wait for 'im to turn the business round. They wanted him out."

"But a manufactory still needs men if they're to make money out of it," I said.

"The new owners 'ave put in one o' those rotary-motion engines to run some new presses. It whistles like a kettle, and by the time you've hammered a blank into shape and started winding down the hand press that monster 'as stamped out a dozen."

Machines had always been of great interest to me, but I wasn't sure what a rotary-motion engine was. There was plenty of talk about the steam engines that had been installed in some of the other large manufactories by Messer's Boulton and Watt. They were both famous men in the town, and I had always thought they were a force for the good. Boulton had built a theatre and had helped to establish Birmingham's General Hospital where I had spent the last few weeks sitting by Mary's deathbed.

"All our presses will be driven by steam, given time. I don't think they will need men soon, and they'll just 'ave children feedin' in the blanks," Double continued.

"Mary and I were forced into town by land enclosures, and there are hundreds of families like us. If there is no work for folk when they get here, what will become of them?"

Robert did not reply, but one glance into his tired eyes said it all: there would be little hope for most of them. The truth of my own situation suddenly flashed into my mind; there was no work for me and now there was no home either. It didn't worry me, it seemed of little consequence if there was work or not. Nothing seemed to be of much importance anymore. God had seen fit to take my wife, and I couldn't understand why. It was beyond me to consider my immediate future, but impulsively my hand plunged into my jacket pocket and drew out the few copper coins that were all I had left in the world.

"You might be best away from here," Robert said. "You're young and can start over again. You don't want to 'ave to go on the parish. You're not to worry for money, everyone who knows you 'as helped out. We knew that you'd taken everythin' due you from the 'Sick and Draw' club, so we've all been collectin' this the last four week."

He proffered a small canvas bag towards me. I took it and spilled out a pound or so in silver coins into the palm of my hand. Emotion unexpectedly took hold of me, and I felt hot tears welling in the corners of my eyes.

The following morning, Robert and I emerged from the narrow gully that led from the pudding-bag onto the wide thoroughfare of Digbeth. On the hill above us, the recently repaired spire of St.Martin's rose majestically above the dilapidated, red brickwork of the huge parish church. The translucent waters of the River Rea glistened in the spring sunlight as we walked past a warren of metalworking shops. The clean water of the river was supposed to be the talisman that kept the work force of Brummagem healthy, but it had not worked for my Mary. Her hacking cough had begun last winter. She had convinced me not to worry and that it would pass, but as the months had gone by, she had deteriorated to such a degree that I had been forced to accept the inevitable. She had consumption: the plague that stalked the back-to-backs and the pudding-bags of the town. The foetid houses, although new, were damp and filth from four hundred furnaces rained down on them every day except the Sabbath. It was unnatural for so many people to live so close together. If only we could have gone away, but she had become so ill so quickly that we had no choice but to stay in Birmingham because of the free hospital. I couldn't afford to look after her anywhere else. Chapman had been extraordinarily good to us: I knew that. He had let me stay in the pudding-bag even when I couldn't go to work because Mary was too ill for me to leave her.

As we trudged over a wooden foot bridge in silence, I couldn't help wishing that I was back in Somersetshire. My memories there were of happier times on the verdant, rolling lands beneath the Quantock Hills around Lilstock, or on the chocolate-brown waters of the Bristol Channel with Father in our little open fishing boat. It had been hard work, true enough, but by a combination of fishing, farming, clerking at the local manor, and a little ironwork, there had always been plenty to eat, and I hadn't been surrounded by filth and illness.

Robert and I were on our way to a tavern to meet a haulier that Robert knew. His name was James Loach, and he plied a regular trade between Birmingham and Bristol. Overnight, Robert had convinced me to seek work away from Birmingham. He knew of my considerable experience of sailing and thought that there was more of a future for me in the merchant service. The war with France had closed so many markets for Birmingham's manufacturers, and there were a growing number of men without employment. Loach traded with merchantmen in the Port of Bristol and had told Robert that I should be able to find a berth there. As soon as the decision was made, it was best to leave as quickly as possible. I had only taken Mary to Birmingham in the hope of finding work building the new machines that were so much talked about. As events unfolded, all that was available was menial work at Chapman's operating a screw-press, and now that

Mary had gone, there was nothing left for me in Birmingham apart from painful memories.

"You could well be lucky, I've heard Loach sayin' that the war 'as made for a scarcity of skilled sailors. Mind you, the Navy press gangs prey on them merchant vessels," Robert said as we turned away from the river and down an alley that would take us towards the parish church (NOTE: *St Martin's church was a focal point of Birmingham in Egan's time. The original medieval building had been dressed in red brick in the seventeenth century to delay its decay*).

"As I understand it, scarcity of skilled men has pushed up their wages. If I could find a good berth for a year or two, I could make enough to be able to go back to Lilstock," I replied.

"Let's talk to Loach afore you get too forward with your plannin'. The last thing you need is to end up impressed into the Navy and none of us 'as any idea 'ow long the war'll last," said Robert, firmly.

We walked into Birmingham's famous cobbled marketplace, that still boasted as its centrepiece a medieval bullring. Being the Sabbath day, all the stalls were empty, and an eerie quiet hung about the place. Taverns were not supposed to serve beer on Sundays, and so I had expected the *Trafalgar Inn* to be as quiet as the market, but as I pushed open the door the saloon was crowded, and we were welcomed by a phalanx of men's backs. A couple of ugly looking bruisers sitting by the door eyed us suspiciously as we walked in but they said nothing.

Several raised voices, shouting in an animated fashion, emanated from the centre of the throng. We edged our way behind the crowd and proceeded to the side of the room: ducking below the angled rafters that jutted out of the walls to support the inn's beams. As our eyes grew accustomed to the murk, we could see that the saloon, which I had visited once before, was host to some sort of meeting. It was obvious from the attitudes of the men that the topic they had gathered to discuss was not of a light-hearted nature.

Two men were seated on one side of a long table at the end of the saloon. Others were seated on benches that had been drawn close to create a kind of auditorium, and twenty or thirty standing men encircled the proceedings. That they were working men was obvious from their apparel and the constant scrape of nailed boots on flagstones. Occasionally, statements from the men on the central table drew cries of encouragement or protest from the congregation, but I could not fathom the purpose of their assembly.

Robert saw Loach sitting alone at a small table in the corner of the room to the left of the long table. The haulier recognised Robert and beckoned us over to join him. He shook both our hands warmly and bade us sit on wooden stools near him. He seemed a decent enough soul, of about five and sixty, clad in coarse, worsted coveralls and a leather waistcoat. He sucked continuously at a long clay pipe that was helping to stoke the fug that surrounded us.

Robert had secured the attention of the serving-maid, and she was pouring 'old and stale' from large ceramic serving jugs for the three of us. Mixing strong, old ale with a lively, young beer was the custom in the area, and the *Trafalgar* was popular because they sold ale from Thomas Salt and Company: one of the finest brewers of Burton-on-Trent.

Taking a long pull on the astringent, black liquid, I felt its deep bitterness and reassuring strength slide its way into my guts. I surveyed the proceedings that were taking place around me. A small, slightly built fellow with permanently knitted brows, shining eyes and an unkempt beard was on his feet behind the long table and speaking in the most strident manner. Sitting next to him was a larger, rounder fellow with a red face.

Leaning over towards Loach and indicating the two men who seemed to be presiding over the meeting with a jerk of my head, I asked, "What goes on here, James? Who are these two characters?"

"The one speaking calls himself Ned Ludd, but nobody believes that to be his real name. *(NOTE: The 'Ned Ludd' whom Egan encountered in The Trafalgar was one of the peripatetic agitators who were starting to circulate the region at the time - all of whom called themselves Ned Ludd. By the winter of 1811 'Luddite' machine wrecking became commonplace throughout the Midlands and the North)*. He's something of a political radical. A fellow told me, before you came in, that he is rumoured to have come from inciting workers to smash mechanical looms in Nottingham," he replied in a hushed tone. "The large man is called George Harris, and he works as a clerk at the great Soho Manufactory run by Mr Boulton and Mr Watt and believes that the new machines will be of benefit to all."

"Well, I'll wager they're both overblown windbags," I replied, accompanying my remark with a wry grin.

"I think they're both trouble," hissed Robert.

"Our labour is being abused," the little fellow with the beard shouted. "We must stand up and fight for our livelihoods. We have given our employers the sweat off our bodies, and how do they repay us? By using fat profits to buy new machines that will drive us all from work, that's how. They don't care about you, Brothers."

Having always held the view that working men would have to fight if they were to gain any advantage in life: I was drawn by the thread of his oratory.

I had heard all sorts of tales of hardship when working as a clerk to the Lilstock Estate. I had spent two days of every week in the estate's office ever since my mother had taught me to read and write at eight years old. Originally, most of my time was spent copying bills of sale and registering the estate's expenditure in ledger books, but with age and experience, my duties expanded to include recording the details of tenant's complaint and disciplinary tribunals. Even though I considered Major Davenport, who owned most of the land locally, a fair man, it always struck me that he decided matters to the estate's advantage. If, for any reason, Major Davenport was away and Hendricks, the scummy bastard of an Estate Steward, resided over the tribunal affairs any sense of fairness was guaranteed to be absent. A sudden increase in volume from the little fellow catapulted me back into the present.

"Was it not the fine industrial gentlemen of this very town that petitioned Parliament not to abandon slavery for want of selling their chains and shackles?" he raged on. "How Christian can that be?"

His face flushed with righteous fervour and his voice rose a full octave as he reached the word 'be'. His speech was greeted with shouts of acclaim and the banging of tankards from some of the men, but the taller, fatter man, who Loach had said was called Harris, rose to his feet frantically waving his arms in the air.

"Calm yourself Ned Ludd," he yelled, "this is supposed to be a debate and not a revolutionary meeting! You'll have the authorities in here unless you rein in your ranting.

"My employer, Mr Boulton, provides very handsomely for his employees. Our houses have their own faucets, and our young 'uns are schooled without charge. Birmingham is fast becoming the workshop of the world, and mechanical progress will provide more work, not less. In these times of great enterprise, working men should support the industrial advances of the age."

Harris lacked Ludd's fervour, but he was an enthusiastic orator, and he spoke, somewhat tryingly, about Mr James Watt's revolutionary steam engines and how his acolyte, William Murdoch, had made fumes from coal that provided light to many big manufactories. He also talked of meetings at Soho House, Mr Boulton's home, held every full moon where luminaries had discussed the burning issues of the day. Apparently, there was a fellow of great education, named Erasmus Darwin, who argued passionately that man had evolved from the apes.

"Aye they're all a lot of lunatics, right enough!"

The cry came from near the grubby window behind my back, and the ensuing laughter stopped Harris in mid sentence.

"That's all as maybe, Mr Harris," yelled Ludd, taking advantage of the break in Harris' speech, "but these great men won't look after those that don't take care of themselves. Men are more important than machines. Industrial experiments and scientific studies are the preserve of the rich and privileged, and have no part of our lives."

"You're sounding like a Jacobin revolutionary, Ned Ludd. You'll find there's strong feeling for Church and King in Brummagem."

It was no surprise to me that it was Robert Double's voice that interjected into the proceedings. Robert's views about anything political were generally supportive of the status quo. His conservative opinions were shared by many of the men, and he received several shouts of support. The fear of invasion from Revolutionary France, a few years earlier, had led to mistrust of any radical politics amongst a large proportion of the men who had worked in the manufactory with me.

"I warned you that trouble was brewin'," Robert muttered under his breath. I disagreed with him, but I had no wish to antagonise him any more than I had to.

"Sometimes, you have to confront what is wrong in life. If we do nothing we'll be trampled on," I replied.

Looking away from Robert, so as not to catch his disapproving look, I noticed that my feet were resting on a grubby newspaper that had been abandoned on the floor. Underneath the darkly inscribed shapes of footprints, that scarred the first page, it proclaimed its title in bold type: 'Cobbett's Weekly Political Register'. I had been in taverns where men had gathered around someone reading aloud from this journal, but I had not studied a copy myself. I carefully wiped it clean and pushed it into one of the deep pockets in my jacket.

"I know my needs, and I need work and paying a fair price for that work." Ludd was back on his feet now and in full flow. "I'm no Frenchman, but were they so wrong to rid 'emselves of an oppressive King? I thought that our own Parliament had put the English Crown in its place a hundred and fifty year ago, but little has changed in the life of any man who has to work for a living," he continued.

"Parliament! That's rich! They'll be no help to us. There are 75,000 souls in Birmingham and no Member of Parliament, and no man in this room could cast a vote for him if there were," shouted the dissenter by the window who had made the joke about lunatics. He was right in what he said; elections simply passed us by in Birmingham. We had no Members of Parliament, and nobody in the *Trafalgar* that morning would be eligible to vote if there were.

"Parliament is only for the nobility and rich landowners," said Harris, who sprang to his feet beside Ludd, vying for attention from the assembly. "We have to look to our employers and their inventors to improve our lot," he bellowed.

"Our employers be damned!" Ludd responded, pushing Harris in an effort to make him sit down. "We must grasp the nettle. Smash their damn machines, brothers, and then they must give the work to us!"

But Harris was not about to sit down, and he grabbed at Ludd's collar as he shouted out, "This is sedition, my friends, pay no heed to this madness___"

The manufactory clerk's speech ended in mid-flow when Ludd slapped the palm of his hand across Harris' mouth, squeezing his nostrils shut with his thumb and forefinger, cutting off his supply of air.

"Those of you that won't listen to me will be joining the queue in Colmore Row for a penny's worth of bread and ox-cheek soup," yelled Ludd.

At this point, a voice started shouting, "By all that's holy, I think this man from Nottingham has some metal. We should take heed of him."

I was shocked to discover that I was on my feet, and the voice was mine.

"Why should we allow ourselves to be treated as pawns in a rich man's game?" I blurted out. Ludd's radicalism had mixed with my own sense of grievance to ferment a heady brew that had just exploded inside me. These men had to fight for their livelihoods and needed encouragement, but also, deep down, I knew that Chapman had treated me fairly, and I wanted revenge on the men who had taken his foundry and thrown me out of my home. Political ardour also distracted from the pain of losing Mary. "Worked to the bone one day and discarded the next. Ned Ludd is right. Let's render their damn machines useless and teach them a lesson that they won't forget," I raged.

By this time, Harris' face had turned bright crimson, and he lashed out wildly with his arms to loosen Ludd's grip on his airways. The two men struggled in a comedic fashion for a few moments before both fell down behind the table, accompanied by shouts and laughter from the on looking crowd.

Robert was tugging strongly at my arm in an attempt to pull me back down onto my stool.

"Have no part in this. You know that working men ain't allowed to be involved in political discussion," he hissed at me, urgently.

My readiness to make my opinions known had got me into trouble before. Major Davenport had sanctioned me countless times in the Lilstock office for supporting the cause of one tenant or another.

"There'll be trouble with the Militia if you keeps bellowing your will at the top o' your lungs an' it'll be trouble we shall all 'ave to pay for," warned Robert, venomously.

Robert's words finally had a sobering effect, and one glance into his eyes was enough to tell how disappointed he was with me, but I couldn't just deny my instincts. Quietly taking my seat once again, I realised that my outburst had set alight the feelings of others involved in the proceedings.

"There's an evil bastard in charge at what was Josiah Chapman's Foundry," a voice shouted from the back of the throng.

"They're beating men to get rid of them since their steam machine arrived an' they're turning them from their homes too," added another, making me smile grimly to myself.

"There are enough of us here, let's go to Chapman's and root out that devilish engine now," the first voice urged. There were roars of approval from some men and shouts of dismay from others, but the suggestion of immediate action prompted everyone to air their views: which they did immediately and as loudly as possible.

"Come away, Nathaniel. There is only trouble to be found here," urged Robert taking hold of my arm and gesturing towards the side of the saloon.

"That man has the right idea," shouted Ludd, pointing in the direction of the mystery rabble-rouser. He was back on his feet now, and Harris was nowhere to be seen, "but we can't go in daylight. Tomorrow night at midnight I say: when the moon's at its lowest."

"Aye, I'm with you Ned Ludd. We should all meet at Chapman's tomorrow night," I shouted, pulling my arm momentarily free from Robert's grasp. I wasn't sure how many of the men heard me because none of them were looking in my direction anymore. Savage arguments had broken out between those who were for dismantling the steam engine and those who were fearful of the consequences. The odd punch was thrown as the fiercest of the protagonists attempted to sway their opponents.

"Listen, listen," I bawled. "Don't fight each other," but none of them seemed interested in what anyone had to say anymore. Robert took a more determined hold of my arm and, this time, Loach was assisting him. There didn't seem to be any point in continuing to shout at these men, and I allowed myself to be led upstairs to the poorly furnished room where Loach was staying.

"You'd better come with me on my wagon, young Nathaniel," said the tranter as he sat me down on a small truckle bed. "I've a feeling there is going to be serious trouble in Birmingham afore long even if Robert succeeds in keepin' you out o' this business tomorrow night. I'll be leavin' early the day a'ter tomorrow for Bewdley, and from there, I'll send my goods to Bristol by barge. I can arrange for 'em to take you an' all. No good will come from stayin' to fight your demons here."

In the excitement of the meeting, I had almost forgotten that Robert and I had gone to the *Trafalgar* to try and find my passage for Bristol. Uproar broke out in the inn below us. Freshly converted radical 'Luddites' were taunting their fellows who were of a more conciliatory nature. The copious amounts of 'old and stale' consumed whilst Ludd and Harris had been speechifying probably accounted for much of their zeal, and it was not long before the sounds of scuffles drifted up through the building.

Leaving the Doubles' home at close to midnight the following day, I headed, once again, towards the River Rea. When I reached the low stone wall that ran along its bank, I turned away from the main thoroughfare and scurried past dozens of courtyard-workshops and smithies that now lay idle. The air still carried the pungent scents of coke furnaces and cooked metal. Approaching the oppressive silhouette of the huge building that had once been Thomas Chapman's manufactory, I could make out the murky shapes of my fellow conspirators lurking beside some nearby stables. Robert and I had argued most of the day about the rights and wrongs of attacking the engine, but I had been unable to make him agree with the course of action I had decided upon. Elisa was petrified of the repercussions and begged me not to go, but my mind was made up. I was consumed by the need to hit back at the men who had thrown me out of my house, perhaps to the point of blindness, but life had dealt with me too harshly to sit back now.

I hadn't been sure if many of last night's social avengers would turn up, but there were about thirty men present, and several of the shadowy figures nodded in recognition as I approached. A muffled greeting came from someone on my left-side and, when I peered into the dark, I saw that it was Thos Bagley: one of my mates from the manufactory. He was a Welshman and just about the oldest worker employed there. I hadn't seen him in the *Trafalgar*, but he was well known for his radical views.

"There 'aint no point in waiting no longer. Let's get it done I say," said a familiar voice. It was Ned Ludd who materialised from the throng, and his sentiments obviously met with the congregation's blessing because they all advanced as one carrying me along with the flow.

When we reached the manufactory's large, wooden, double gates, the cast-iron lock that held them together simply cracked under the pressure of our weight. As we surged into the blackness that was inside, I was immediately struck by a strange smell: the like of which I had never encountered before. There was the familiar coal-dust smell of a furnace, but it was mixed with a

- 20 -

strange oily odour: something like burnt tallow or fat and hot metal. I worked my flint and steel to light one of the small glims that lit the manufactory during dark working hours. As its wick broke into flame, my attention became focused on the towering steam engine that glowered at me in the dim, flickering light. I had seen nothing like it before: a monstrous beam, a huge, spoked, metal wheel and a mess of stays and rods that were all connected to a brass, stove-shaped object that glistened eerily. A small wheel, a little smaller than a cart wheel, with deeply cut teeth was locked to the bottom of the great wheel. This, in turn, was connected to new presses, which I had not seen before, by long substantial iron rods. These must be the new stamp presses Robert had spoken about.

The machine had a disconcerting effect on me; it was a domineering and yet impressively powerful sight. I had always been intrigued by machines and drawn to discover how they worked. I would have loved to have seen this great beast in operation. At home I had helped Father forge a set of gears for the estate's windmill, and nothing gave me more joy than when I saw them all bite together and drive the millstones. To see the great black monster that now stood before me powering a row of button presses would have been like peeking into the future. But no matter how much in awe of the machine I was, a large part of me wanted to destroy it; to strike a blow for the likes of Robert and Elisa Double. What would it mean to them if this engine was responsible for throwing him out of work? What else could he do to make a living?

The others had started to attack the machine with anything that came to hand, and the chimes resonated in the high roof of the manufactory, but I didn't join in the ruckus. I stood alone and watched them. Some of them had jumped the narrow water pit that surrounded the engine and were clambering on to it. Thos Bagley was standing with his feet astride the spokes of the great wheel and swinging a block of wood at the interlocking cog that connected to the wheels hub. His efforts, and everyone else's, were inflicting no damage on the engine whatsoever. By the noise they were making some of them seemed to think their oaths alone could decommission the great engine.

After a few minutes, it was obvious to me that our visit was pointless. We would need heavy tools if we were to dismantle a machine of this size. I have to admit that there was a part of me that was actually a little pleased. Perhaps Harris was right after all and, in the greater scheme of things, the future of men like Robert Double would be better served by working with these machines rather than endless hours of mind-numbing, manual toil. As I struggled with my dilemma, I became aware of a new impetus to the hullabaloo, emanating from behind the engine. In the near darkness, the animated activities of the silhouettes told me that there was fighting.

What nonsense was this? Were they fighting amongst themselves? And then one of the men held up a tallow glim, and I had my answer. The dim pool of light illuminated a huge, black tattooed arm swinging a rounded cudgel. I was transfixed as the evil, ball-shaped weapon swung down on a man's head just as it had on my own. It was him, the bastard who had turned me out of my house! Once again, the full force of vengeance pumped into my veins. This man would pay for his actions! I instinctively ran amongst the nearest row of button presses searching for a suitable weapon when, to my astonishment, the whole scene behind me was suddenly bathed in a harsh light.

At the doorway, a company of militia stood resplendent in their red coats and black, stovepipe shakos. The flames from their tall torches reflected in the steel knives that were fixed to their Brown Bess muskets. Both implements, no doubt, had been manufactured in foundries hereabouts, and now they were to be used in subjugating some of the men who had made them. I felt my testicles tighten as I imagined the awful damage one of those seventeen-inch blades would cause if forced into human flesh. There was a ringing command, and the redcoats marched smartly across the foundry floor with the protestors shrinking away before them. Conveniently isolated, I ducked down behind the nearest press. I knew that a door to a rear courtyard was nearby, and, thankfully, it was in the shadow thrown by the great engine. I examined my conscience momentarily, but I could find little point in standing my ground and being arrested with the others, so I darted for the exit. It was impossible to tell from the ugly cacophony behind me whether any of the soldiers were giving chase, but I knew where there was a break in the courtyard wall and plunged into the ebonite alley beyond.

Little more than five hours later, I sat alongside James Loach as two magnificent shires hauled his heavily laden bulk-cart from the stables behind the *Trafalgar Inn*. I gave him no explanation for my late acceptance of his offer of transport and none was asked for.

CHAPTER TWO
Bewdley, Worcestershire, England - 21st March 1809

REVOLUTIONARIES THWARTED BY THE
MILITIA IN DIGBETH
A detachment of Colonel Pearce's South Warwickshire Militia successfully restrained and arrested fifteen working men who were joined in revolutionary assembly Tuesday last. It is thought they were intent on damaging a steam engine in a Digbeth foundry.

One man escaped and one employee of the manufactory was involved.

As our readers will know, the late Prime Minister Pitt's Combination Act of 1799 strictly forbade working-men from holding any political congress and the miscreants shall go before the Magistrates this week with deportation or enforced naval service the most likely sentence.

Aris's Birmingham Gazette, March 1809

Loach's high-sided cart clattered slowly uphill, swaying gently under the stress of its load and the uncertainty of its construction. The slate chippings covering the track cracked and splintered under the heavy, steel-rimmed wheels as he encouraged his two broad-backed mares to stick to their task. Years on roads like this had obviously taught him affection for the two great beasts.

"Come along, Merrydew, none of your nonsense. Keep to it, Venus, it'll not be too long now, my pet," he cooed gently.

Loach had made an admirable travelling companion. He had not pried into my affairs and had only spoken on our three-day journey when I had addressed him first. However, I sensed that he liked me, and I must concede that the emotion was reciprocal.

There seemed little point in staying in Birmingham after the militia had chased me out of the manufactory. I had made the decision to seek a new life as a merchant seaman and lingering would only give someone the opportunity to betray me as an agitator.

Any hopes that I had of the journey distracting me from my grief were still-born. I fought a constant battle to control my thoughts, but memories of Mary seeped through at unguarded moments. Visions of her smiling face kept appearing in my mind's eye, but she was shrouded in a kind of mist banishing her to a different time. I had known her my whole life, but only really noticed her when she came to work as a maid at Lilstock Manor in her middle teens. Her father owned a few acres and grazed cattle on the same common moorland as mine. Knowing that I'd never see her again bit into me hard, and I couldn't imagine the day when the pain would start to disappear.

The wagon crested the hill on the final day of our journey, and we glimpsed the twin spires of the town of Bewdley which, Loach told me, was the highest navigable point on the River Severn. From there, he would ship the fine, metal goods he had bought from Birmingham down the river by barge all the way to Bristol.

It took a further two hours before Loach coaxed his wagon onto the famous, three-arched bridge that beckoned travellers into the town. We crossed the river and found ourselves in a wide street lined by tall townhouses. Loach turned down an alley, and we emerged onto the riverside quay, pulling up in front of a finely painted sign proclaiming that the site belonged to *Isaiah Finch, Bargemaster and Haulier*. Several men waved greetings to Loach, but Finch, apparently, was not one of them. He went to locate the 'bargemaster and haulier' while I sat on the wagon and drank in the sights of a bustling river port. The impressive bridge dominated the scene, but my attention was attracted to the vessels that still littered the river in the late afternoon. Every cargo imaginable was being carried to and fro upon a myriad of local flat-bottomed boats; while one large 'trow' disgorged imported goods like tobacco and citrus fruits from ocean ports downriver (NOTE: *At the time of Egan's visit the River Severn was considered one of the busiest trade routes in Europe*).

Set back some thirty yards from the quay were rows of hauliers' yards stacked with crates of ironware, pottery and all manner of agricultural goods. Several teams of heavy horses were hard at work lifting cargos from the boats, with the aid of blocks suspended from long, rotating booms overhanging the quayside, and hauling goods to the yards. Above the bustle of the quayside, there was the sound of raucous laughter and foul oaths coming from a gaggle of local women conducting an impromptu market outside the imposing, timbered façade of the *Rest and be Welcome Inn*.

After a short while, Loach appeared with an unprepossessing man who I assumed to be Finch. He was short and thin with thick, dark hair and a pointed, black beard which gave him a Mediterranean countenance. He paid no heed to me at all: which seemed odd considering that I was a potential fee-paying customer. He also avoided looking me directly in the eye, and I must admit that my first impressions of Isaiah Finch were not favourable.

"You'll be alright with Isaiah, Nathaniel, he'll see you to Bristol," Loach said, possibly sensing my reservations.

"I shall aim to keep m'self to m'self, Mr Finch," I said, turning to the bargee. "I wouldn't want to be in your way."

At least this spurred him to address me, "It'll cost you six shillings, and you'll have to buy your own keep," he said in an unpleasant, sibilant voice. "We've no space for travellers so you'll have to fit in where you will."

Six shillings was cheap, I knew that, but in cramped conditions, and with this miserable man for company, it was no great act of kindness either. Nevertheless, I was impatient to complete my journey as quickly as possible, and so I nodded my acceptance to his conditions. With this, Finch turned away and engaged Loach in negotiations concerning his cargo. I wandered over to the noisy market to barter for victuals to take with me.

My transactions took an hour or so, and I had just secured the purchase of half-a-dozen Ashmead's apples (NOTE: *A city clerk from Gloucester named William Ashmead bred the Ashmead's Kernel in the 1760s. Nathaniel Egan had developed a taste for eating them raw at a time when most of his contemporaries only ate cooked apples*) when I noticed Loach leading Merrydew and Venus towards the *Rest and be Welcome.*

"I'll stay at the inn tonight. I'm sure to find a good load when the merchants have been at the Old and Stale," Loach said with a mischievous wink. "You'll need to get to Finch's barge. He won't wait on you. She's called *Elsinore*, painted dark red and moored just beyond his yard. He's a cantankerous sod, but he's always traded fairly by me."

"Many thanks for all your help, James," I said, proffering my hand.

"Good luck to you, Nathaniel," Loach replied, gripping firmly. "Get to Bristol, and don't attempt to fight the whole world by yourself. A good looking, young man like you can make a new start. Try to leave your demons behind you and find some happiness, my boy." With a wave, he turned back to his horses and trudged on.

Daylight was in full retreat when I descended the wooden ladder from the quayside to the Severn trow *Elsinore*. Finch affected the slightest of nods by way of a greeting when I reached the deck. By now, Loach's goods had been stowed in the trow's open hold along with their other cargo, and two crewmen stood idly waiting at the bow.

"We'll make way now that you've arrived," the bargee said sarcastically.

"I'll endeavour to be quicker in future, Mr Finch," I replied with stony civility.

Finch turned away and started barking out commands. Mooring ropes splashed into the water and, following a brief session of frantic arm-waving, Finch casually pushed the trow's beautifully curved, teak tiller over with his left thigh. Two bay work-horses on the larboard bank, one with a rider in the saddle, took the strain on the towrope that hung between them, and the barge left its berth to make its way smoothly towards the centre of the broad River Severn. The huge weight that horses could haul when towing a burden afloat had never ceased to amaze me. In a few minutes we were cracking along at something like three knots.

Elsinore was an expertly designed craft: finely honed for her duties as a cargo vessel, her two open holds occupying nine-tenths of her deck space. A wide bulkhead separated the holds and supported the vessel's single, stumpy mast. Her carvel-built hull lay so low in the brown river that she only had a few inches of freeboard, but she carried brailed canvas gunnels that could be raised in choppy water.

I sat on the bulkhead between the holds, watching as the riverbanks dissolved slowly into darkness. Before long, all I could see was the pathetic smear of light emanating from the bobbing lantern that hung from the lead horse. Stinking fish oil lamps were also burning onboard *Elsinore*: bathing the sailors in a weak yellow light that accorded them murky, rocking shadows. The two crewmen were an ugly looking pair but, at least, they seemed friendlier than Finch. One of them, who I had heard answer to the name of O'Donoghue, came to raise the canvas gunnels. He was a squat, bow-legged animal with the bulk of a bull terrier, the jowls of a spaniel and spoke with a thick West Country burr.

"The horses tow us at a very fair speed," I said, in an effort to strike up a conversation with the man.

"They do well enough, Mister," O'Donoghue said without looking up from his task.

"Will they pull us throughout the night?"

"They'll change team an' rider a few times afore we get far enough downstream to ride the tide alone."

"I didn't realise the tide would be strong enough to carry a fully laden trow this far up the river," I said, my voice betraying my surprise.

"When we get further downstream tide'll carry us quicker 'n they nags," drawled O'Donoghue. "We just need some help from the sails to give us steerage."

"How far downstream do we have to get?"

"Tide'll start affectin' us as soon as we get as far as Tewksbury, an' by the time we're below Gloucester we'll be waitin' for the tide."

"You know the river well. Are you a regular member of Mister Finch's crew?"

"No, he only gave me the nod a few minutes afore we left. He needs extra muscle power for this trip, apparently ..."

O'Donoghue's voice tailed off before he finished his sentence, and he set about concentrated on his task as if I was no longer there. I didn't particularly care. Having ascertained we were successfully underway, I was preoccupied with finding a berth. I had slept little during my wagon trip with Loach. We had regularly stopped to rest the horses, but my mind had been too troubled to let in sleep, and I had spent hours awake listening to Loach's snores. Those nights had now caught up with me, and I was grievously tired. I decided upon a spot under one of the tarpaulins that covered the main hold just by the bulkhead where I was sitting. I gathered my few belongings and settled down on top of stacked rock salt. The eerie whistle of a curlew regaled me as I punched the salt sacks into as compliant a shape as possible and slipped into a grateful sleep.

❖ ❖ ❖

Bright sunlight was assaulting my eyes when consciousness returned. I had no idea how long I had been asleep, but I was chilled to the bone. I had been so tired that I had fallen asleep without sorting out any blankets or even warm clothes. I sat up and beat my arms around me in an effort to stir the circulation: rebuking myself for not finding something warmer to sleep under than a tarpaulin.

The trow was still making steady headway, and my attention was drawn to cheerful voices coming from the towpath. Peering over the canvas gunnel, I saw that the rider and the towing horses had been changed. This new rider was shouting abuse in a jovial manner at a rotund fellow who stood outside a wooden toll-box some twenty yards behind the horses. They were obviously friends and the plump man just laughed in reply. The rider pulled the horses to a halt and turned to wave at O'Donoghue on *Elsinore's* foredeck. O'Donoghue returned the wave and, to my surprise, he lifted the heavy towrope off its cleat and tossed it into the water. The rider jumped down from his mount and pulled in the rope as the trow drifted downstream past him.

"Are we changing the team again?" I called out to O'Donoghue.
"No, tide'll take us from here," he replied, busying himself unfurling the two, small headsails that would fly from the bowsprit and a block on the prow.

Looking down into the murky, brown waters of the Severn there was noticeable movement downstream, but we were already travelling slower than when the horses had been pulling us.

"The ebb is just startin'," said O'Donoghue, walking down the narrow walkway that ran beside the hold. "The current'll run faster the further we gets downstream. We're on the top of springs. Do you know what a springtide is, young 'n'?" he asked, cocking an eyebrow in my direction as he spoke.

"I have spent much of my life fishing the Bristol Channel and know only too well the lunar cycle and the highest and lowest tidewaters that accompany it," I replied.

My pomposity caused me embarrassment the moment the words were out of my mouth, but O'Donoghue's presumption of my ignorance had annoyed me. He just grimaced and walked on.

The next hour was spent breakfasting on hard cheese and Ashmead's Kernel and negotiating with Finch for the loan of two, none too clean, blankets. I knew that they had tea onboard, but Finch said the kettle had boiled while I was asleep, and the only thing I could drink was small beer from the boat's cask.

It was going to be a long day, and, with nothing else to do, I took my newly acquired blankets back to my salt-sack den and settled down to rest. Lying back, something dug uncomfortably into my side. Upon investigation, it was the copy of *Cobbett's Weekly Political Register* from the floor of *The Trafalgar*. I carefully flattened it out, studying the dense type covering its four pages. It was dated over a year ago and consisted mainly of monotonous accounts of what had been said in Parliament, making me wonder why its previous owner had kept it, but then I found the transcription of a speech about land enclosures and took more interest. I warmed to the acerbic additions from the journal's author, one William Cobbett, who was not one for pulling his punches and believed in making free with his opinions. 'It is the chief business of a government to take care that one part of the people does not cause the other part to lead miserable lives,' I read.

My own problems had come to a head two years earlier when my elder brother, David, had turned me off our family's small farm. It hadn't been his fault; the culprit had been an Act of Enclosure which allowed the adjacent estate owner to fence off common lands at Lilstock and grazing to families like mine. This wasn't the act of a government taking care that one part of the people did not cause the other part to lead miserable lives. This was the act of greedy, rich men who used their power in Parliament to line their own pockets and those of men like themselves.

Major Davenport had died a few months before David turned me off the farm. Lilstock Manor had been sold to a man called Viscount Alton, not that anyone ever laid eyes on him, and his retainers had wasted no time in fencing us out. To make matters worse, Hendricks was retained as steward, and he saw to it that I received no work in the estate office. Robbed of grass for our livestock and my clerking income, there simply wasn't enough money to sustain the whole family, and as the youngest son, it fell to me to take my new wife and search for work elsewhere.

The strength of the river's current gradually increased the longer the tide was on the ebb, and with a little help from the sails, Finch had steerageway to guide *Elsinore* downstream. By the time the trow passed the edge of the City of Gloucester, marked by the magnificent tower rising above the cathedral, we were moving at the same pace as when we were towed by the horses. As the speed of the current increased, the water no longer filled the entire channel of the river: revealing bands of exposed mud and occasional clusters of jagged rocks on both sides. The river's banks widened even further as the Severn inscribed wide meanders below Gloucester. Here we encountered boats, similar to Finch's, anchored at the side of the channel: waiting for the next flood tide to take them upstream.

"We'll be lookin' for sound ground to drop anchor, just like they, in an hour or so. Then we can all 'ave a drink for a few hours till the waters change."

I turned to see O'Donoghue standing on the walkway by the side of the hold. The thought had not previously occurred to me that we would have to wait for the tide to change, and I didn't relish the idea of being incarcerated on *Elsinore* for nine hours or so while Finch and his mates drank themselves stupid.

"How far will we get downstream? Can't we moor by the bank?"

The moment I spoke, I could have kicked myself: the channel would narrow exposing more mud the further we rode the tide, and so Finch wouldn't be able to moor by the bank allowing me to get off.

"Don't be soft, lad," chuckled O'Donoghue, continuing about his business.

The trow drifted slowly downriver for another hour until we ceased to make headway, and I heard Finch yelling at O'Donoghue and his mate to put out the anchors. We stopped on the larboard side of the channel: which had by now shrunk to less than a quarter of its former width. We were on the inside of a long, gentle curve in the river, and there were at least fifty yards of glutinous mud between *Elsinore* and the bank. It was not long before the first, faint murmurs of floodwater were gurgling beneath our hull as the tide began to change direction. The river would flood for six hours, and then there would be a period of slack water before the ebb returned and began to carry us in the right direction again.

Finch and his crew settled down on the afterdeck and prepared to eat and drink the day away. I didn't think that they would particularly welcome my company, but I sidled up to the group anyway in the hope that they might be brewing some tea. Surprisingly, Finch offered me some of the crew's meal of dripping puddings that had been procured from a bumboat near Tewkesbury whilst I had been asleep. I accepted without a second thought and gratefully tucked in. It was a long time since a delicacy like a dripping pudding had passed my lips, and every greasy mouthful was bliss. After we had eaten, Finch produced two bottles of very expensive-looking cognac from a secure locker behind the tiller. I suppose he couldn't help but notice my astonished expression as he pulled the cork from one.

"You'll be surprised what a man can glean when he works this river, Mister Passenger," he said in a slightly more courteous tone than he had hitherto employed when addressing me. "Mister O'Donoghue tells me that you wus a fisherman 'afore you wus in Birmingham."

"Aye, I used to fish the Bristol Channel with my father," I replied.

"An' you knows your tides and navigation?"

"That I do. I was fishin' from about the age of six."

"Interesting ...," Finch paused, "but you've never been this far upstream?"

"No. We worked in Bridgwater Bay and downstream, sometimes as far as Lundy Island. We launched our boat from Lilstock beach."

Finch's interest in my sailing credentials subsided as smartly as it had arisen, and he turned his attention to apportioning head-achingly large measures of cognac amongst his crewmen. He didn't offer me a drink, but I had no interest in drunkenness anyway, and withdrew to my salt-sack den in search of a little solitude.

By mid-afternoon, the creamy brown water was roaring against *Elsinore's* hull. I was used to the swift tides in the Bristol Channel, but had never experienced being buffeted at anchor by such a powerful river-race. The three and four foot waves that foamed against the bow took a little getting used to. Lying back and listening to the gushing water, I saw the first bank martins of the year catch flies above the rapidly swelling river. The more I thought about it, the more my resolve strengthened to find a new life in the merchant service. I even allowed the first tentative glimmers of optimism about the future to creep into my mind. The sea is always alluring to those who are not happy with their life on land, and I certainly felt that fate had dealt with me harshly. Intermingled with my feelings of injustice, there was also a sense of some culpability. If I hadn't taken Mary to Birmingham, she would not have become stricken by that dreadful disease. But what else could I have done? I had learnt to work metal in the village forge that my father operated in the workshop behind our outhouse every Saturday. Father had always told me that I had an eye for sketching anything that needed to be made. I had thought, naively perhaps, that I would be able to make good money from similar work for the Birmingham foundries. How wrong I had been! All I had found was mind-numbing labour for me and fatal illness for Mary. Damn Viscount Alton's eyes: if he'd not bought Lilstock estate, I would never have taken Mary away from Somersetshire, and she would still be alive!

Several hours later my spirits lifted a little when I realised that the river was undoubtedly swollen to its maximum capacity once again, and when the ebb began, we could be on our way. Almost as soon as the idea had sprung into my mind, the sounds of stumbling and swearing came from behind me. O'Donoghue and his mate were making their way up the narrow walkway beside the hold. Neither of them seemed too steady on their feet, and O'Donoghue's eyes were hooded as if struggling to cope with the evening sunlight.

"Mister Finch wants t' use the mains'l whilst tides slack. Could you give us a 'and raising 'er?" he drawled, rubbing the back of his neck vigorously, trying to wake himself up.

"I suppose no man can expect his dinner for nothing," I grumbled, getting up and climbing onto the bulwark.

There was precious little wind, but while the river current was stationary, Finch was going to use all his sails to get as far downstream as possible.

"Us'll haul on the halyard, can 'e sweat the line for us?" said O'Donoghue.

O'Donoghue and his mate pulled on the halyard and *Elsinore's* grubby, much repaired mails'l slowly rose into the sky. When the sail was about two thirds of the way up, I jumped and grabbed the halyard as high on the mast as I could, and yanked it towards me. I let my pressure on the line slowly drop and dragged the halyard towards the block at the foot of the mast. The two bargemen took in the slack and cleated the line. We repeated the process several times to get the sail to the top of the mast, it was surprisingly warm work!

Under sail power the trow made sedate progress over the slack tide, but all the time the current gradually quickened beneath us. It was no more than an hour later, just as *Elsinore* was negotiating another wide meander in the Severn, that O'Donoghue sought my assistance again.

"Tis time to get t'sail back down again, Mister Passenger," he announced.

As the trow pointed into the breeze at the apex of the bend, O'Donoghue let off the halyard, and I gathered the sail in great handfuls of canvas, which I turned on top of each other so that they could be retied to the boom.

"Thank you, Mister Passenger. Tis too much trouble keepin' the mains'l up now the river's twistin' like this. It keeps backin' at every curve," he said, with the most fragile note of thanks in his voice, "but tide'll carry us from now on."

"So will this tide carry us as far as Bristol?" I asked eagerly.

"Hold your 'orses, young un," said the broad chested boatman. "This tide'll take us into the Bristol Channel, but we'll have to wait for another 'en to take us up the River Avon an' to the city itself."

O'Donoghue could tell from my expression that I was disappointed by this information.

"Time'll pass quick enough, Mister Passenger," he said, in what was almost a kindly way. "Now, I'll 'ave to take the tiller later so I'm goin' to get me 'ead down fer a couple o' hours." And he was off back down the walkway.

I was woken in the early hours of the following morning by the harsh *'kraaak'* of a heron flying overhead and knew instantly that the trow was no longer afloat. I clambered groggily to my feet. The hazy dawn light was just strong enough for me to see that

Elsinore's bottom sat on the muddy riverbed in a few inches of water. Close by, I could make out the solid black silhouettes of other boats, and in the middle-distance, the vague demarcation between the river bed and the bank. There was movement on the afterdeck, and I turned to see Finch standing at the lip of the hold.

"So you're awake, Mister Passenger," he growled. "I'll say one thing for you, an' that's that you sleeps sound. We've come twenty miles downstream by moonlight, an' you slept through the whole journey."

"I hadn't slept for some days before I came aboard your trow," I replied, by way of an explanation. "Where are we now?"

"We're in the Bristol Channel. They calls this Portishead Pool. Trows an' flat-bottom craft sit out the tide in 'ere an' leave the channel for deeper drafted vessels," he answered.

"How far from Bristol are we?"

"We're only two miles downstream from where the River Avon joins the Channel. We have to come south o' the river so that the next tide will carry us up the Avon an' onto Bristol."

"How long will it take to reach Bristol, Mister Finch?"

"No more than three hours of the next tide will see us up to the harbour gates," he said, showing signs of irritation at being questioned.

"What harbour gates?" I asked, but Finch was walking back towards *Elsinore's* stern and didn't reply.

Making my way to the trow's bow, I stared in the direction where I knew the sea lay and waited for sunrise. As the sky brightened from the east, I caught my first sight of a transformed landscape. As far as I could see across the estuary, the world was made only of mud: incredible, sculpted rivulets of thick, dark mud stretching far into the distance. The once-powerful river had disappeared, to be replaced by a listless, muddy watercourse, about a hundred paces wide, which held a couple of smallish, ocean-rigged ships in the centre of the channel. The diverging coastlines of England and Wales inscribed undulating silhouettes along either bank of the Bristol Channel. Portishead Pool, where *Elsinore* sat, was little more than an indentation on the English side of the Channel. Looking towards the sea, there was no discernable horizon between the slate grey sky and the brown estuary, but my nostrils were full of the rich, intoxicating aroma that can only be found at the edge of an ocean. It was good to smell the sea again after two years of Birmingham's grime and filth! An unexpected quiver of excitement ran through my bones. The coming flood tide would carry me into the historic port of Bristol, where I would turn my back on the first three-and-twenty years of life and make a new beginning for myself.

It took an age before the murky, silt-laden waters of the incoming tide picked up *Elsinore* and carried her into the mouth of the Avon. This new river was much narrower than the Severn, and the flooding tide drove the trow inland at a startling speed. The water rushed upstream at five or six knots, giving Finch enough 'apparent' wind to work the heads'ls and give him steerage for his navigation. The landscape that slipped by consisted of flat, low-lying water meadows, but upriver a massive outcrop of rock, grew larger and larger every minute. Small crestless waves of brown water shot past the trow and broke against the muddy banks as the tide forced more water into the narrow river. After less than an hour, we had left the meadows of the coastal plain behind and the river became surrounded by a dramatic, sheer sided gorge: the sides of which quickly shot up to hundreds of feet. The crevassed, limestone walls of the gorge were about three cables apart, and the people walking near the cliff edge were little more than specks. By now, the tide was touching high water, and *Elsinore* was noticeably slowing down. My brother claimed to have seen a steep-sided ravine several hundred feet high at Cheddar, in the middle of Somersetshire, but until now, I hadn't been sure whether or not to believe him. Ahead of us, the great rock walls of the gorge were tumbling earthwards just as swiftly as they had shot up around us. Even though we were now travelling at no more than a leisurely strolling pace, we had passed the gorge, and there were flat meadows in front of us once again. The river widened into a large pool, and several other working boats were moored to a wooden wharf on the starboard bank. Beyond them stood a high masonry wall curving gently out of view, and a small forest of masts and rigging projecting above it. As *Elsinore* drifted into the pool, I saw two heavy lock gates set into the wall. They were the same design as on the canals in Birmingham but much taller. I walked to the foredeck where O'Donoghue was preparing the anchor cable.

"The 'Floating Harbour' is behind them gates," O'Donoghue said, gesturing towards them with his thumb.

"Floating Harbour, what's that?"

"The Frog prisoners 'ave dug a new path for the tidal river, an' there is a huge new harbour on the other side o' that lock."

"That's incredible!"

"They haven't finished it yet, but when they has people say the harbour will never dry out: not even for ocean going ships," O'Donoghue said, continuing his explanation with uncharacteristic enthusiasm. (NOTE: *The Floating Harbour, built by Gilbert Jessop for the Bristol Dock Company, was operational when Nathaniel Egan was there in March but the official opening was not until two months later*).

"What a thing that is!" I muttered to myself. My head throbbed from just considering the enormity of such an undertaking. How many men must it have taken to dig an alternative channel for a tidal river such as the Avon, and a deep water harbour for ocean going ships?

"Why would they build a harbour all this way up such a small river?" I asked.

"Mister Finch told me it's 'cos it's so far inland. Goods travel much quicker on water than they do in wagons, and this port is much further inland than any other in Great Britain, 'cept for London itself."

"Where else but in England would engineers conspire to cheat the tide?"

"Aye, that's right. Mister Finch says you won't find nothing like it anywhere else in the world."

"How does it work? Do you know?" I asked, but before O'Donoghue could reply Finch yelled an order from the stern.

"Plant the fo'r'ard kedge you idle bastards."

I hurried to help O'Donoghue heave the anchor over the bow, but as I bent down and lifted one side of the kedge, he did nothing; intent on simply staring back down the trow at Finch.

"Come on then," I yelled, carefully stepping over the cable and grimacing under the weight of the anchor.

It seemed to take another couple of seconds to register with O'Donoghue that there was a job to do. Then he grabbed his side and we dropped the kedge into the harbour. It took a few yards forward motion for *Elsinore* to eat up the slack in the cable, and as the anchor began tugging us to a halt, the black lock gates started to open. As they parted, they revealed a long, thin lock which was entirely in shadow from the high stone walls on both sides. Beyond it, there was another pool, completely bathed in bright sunlight. I was so preoccupied with what I could see within the harbour that I was only vaguely aware of a jollyboat being rowed towards *Elsinore*. I turned to look when the small boat bumped alongside the trow's stern.

"The skipper will 'ave to deal wit' the authorities. They'll want to see his cargo papers and such," explained O'Donoghue.

I nodded in reply. I couldn't see the men Finch was talking to in the cockpit, but they were of no real interest to me anyway. I was busy studying the huge lock gates and thinking of the tremendous advantage a port would have over its competitors if it was able to load and unload ships at all times of day. How an earth did the city ever manage to pay for such a venture?

I was utterly lost in thought when suddenly the harbour walls and lock gates span before my eyes. There was a terrifying bulging sensation in my neck and a monstrous pain behind my eyes. In the next instant, I was fighting for breath. In a panic, I flailed out in every direction with my fists. They hit something behind me that was solid and human. O'Donoghue! He had crept up behind me and thrown one of his burly arms around my throat. He was fending off my blows with the other arm, and dragging me away from the gunnel.

"We can't 'ave you leaping overboard just now, my lad," he cried, tightening his vice-like grip.

Consciousness was slipping away from me, and a thick mist descended before my eyes, but I managed to gasp, "Can't breathe ... can't breathe."

The pressure on my throat eased a little, and air sucked back into my lungs. O'Donoghue had grabbed my left wrist and was trying to push my arm up behind my back. Through a mist of confusion and pain, I saw a boy, no more than seventeen, in what looked like a naval uniform. He walked up the hold walkway. Behind him, two evil-looking ruffians also sported naval-like attire, but looked more as if they belonged to the side alleys of Birmingham than a King's ship. Behind them all, on the deck by the hold, I could see Finch grinning, and counting coins from a small leather pouch.

"No hard feelings, young-un but needs must," hissed O'Donoghue, his mouth was so close to my face that I could smell his vile breath.

"What are you doing, you stinking shit?" I gasped, while I tried to swing at him with my free arm.

"Stop that now," said the lad in the long coat with white collar patches. "You're in the King's Navy now, and you shall obey my commands."

"In the Navy? What are you blabbing about, boy?" I yelled back at him in astonishment. "I'm just a passenger on this trow. If I wanted to enlist in the damn Navy I'd go to Portsmouth like everybody else."

"The skipper tells me you're part of his crew and a skilled man to boot. River boatmen are legitimate targets for the Press, and Mr Finch knows it is better to offer one of his men from time to time rather than have us take one from him."

"I'm no boatman. I'm a passenger, I tell you! Don't listen to that vicious bastard!" I screamed, pointing at Finch.

"Now, now, Nathaniel you always knew one of us would have to serve the King," replied Finch in the most horribly ingratiating manner.

"You low-life arsehole, crimp! You've sold me to the press! Did Loach know about this?"

"Mister Loach knows nothing of this business, Nathaniel. This is between you and I, and Mister Midshipman Ebbs here," Finch smarmed in reply.

The two heavily-built seamen came forward and took me from O'Donoghue. They manacled my hands in front of me, and regardless of my struggling, skilfully manhandled me down the hold walkway and to the stern of the trow. I glared at Finch as they dragged me past him.

"How much did you get, Finch? How much is an honest life worth as far as you're concerned?"

Finch didn't reply and just smirked malevolently. When we reached *Elsinore's* stern one of the seamen jumped down into the small boat that was tied there, and the other pushed me so far over the gunnel that I had no choice but to follow his mate. They sat me in the stern sheets, and the young midshipman stepped down from the trow and settled beside me. Without command the two seamen pulled on the oars, and the boat glided in the direction of the lock gates. It had all happened too quickly for me to take it in what had happened, and I slumped in the boat in a kind of daze. I heard Finch and O'Donoghue shouting ironic salutations, and looked up to see their ugly faces grinning triumphantly at me.

"Now see here, Egan. Your name is Egan, is it not?" Ebbs began hurriedly, "I don't doubt those rascals have not played you fair, but you're the King's man now, and there is nothing to be done about it. I have to find men for the fleet, and you're to be one of them." The youth continued animatedly, "You have to tell me now whether you're to be an impressed man or a volunteer?" I gazed at him blankly, understanding none of what was going on.

"Think lively, man! The pressing tender is lying in the pool inside the harbour, and those manacles will have to be off before this boat passes through the lock if you're to be a volunteer!"

"Every man's vision of hell is serving in a King's ship, and you want me to volunteer?" I spat back, venomously.

"You'll have to serve anyway, and an able hand who sails for King George of his own volition receives twelve pounds bounty. As an impressed man you'll only receive the sting of a boatswain's starter."

My mind swam hopelessly with the events of the last ten minutes; my world had been turned upside down yet again. My chance of a new life had been snatched away from me so quickly that I couldn't think straight. But this youngster was trying to do me a favour: or so it seemed. The end of the lock loomed in front of us, and I had no more than a dozen paces in which to make up his mind.

"Yes, I volunteer," I mumbled humbly and presented my hands towards the midshipman. Ebbs had the key in his hand, and the shackles were off as the bow of the boat nosed through the lock and towards the brilliant sunlight of the inner harbour.

"No fanciful notions Mr Egan, both Wellens and Harvey carry loaded pistols," warned Ebbs. The sailor who worked the starboard oar pulled a malicious grin whilst the other stared expressionlessly straight through me.

As the boat cleared the cold shadows, a decrepit two-decked fourth rate ship, flying a naval ensign limply from its mizzen, came into view at the head of the harbour.

"She's no longer in active service; she's the navy's pressing tender for recruits," announced Ebbs, apologetically. "She's in a dreadful state, I know."

A few more lusty strokes from the bulky seamen, and we were sliding alongside. Harvey grasped the main chains, and Ebbs jumped onto the wooden steps that led to the tumblehome and gestured to me to follow.

As he disappeared over the ship's side, I heard him say, "Another volunteer, Quartermaster."

"Ain't the luck with you, Sir," came a caustic reply. "Your third this week!"

CHAPTER THREE
Bristol, 27th March 1809

My dear Father,
Today, I impressed a sturdy, young, river boatman, and managed, with no little difficulty, to explain to him the fiscal benefits of entering naval service as a volunteer. He is a strapping fellow named Egan, and he is remarkably sharp witted for one of his calling. He was the third skilled sailor this week that I had first impressed but then persuaded to accept the King's bounty. I can see no good reason in denying them money, but all three surprised me greatly by their reticence to serve His Majesty. They seem to have no understanding of duty or the honour of serving their country.
  I have been instructed to conduct my recruits to the Royal Dockyard at Portsmouth, and the Press Captain indicated that my first taste of action shall not be long in coming!
  An extract of a letter from Jacob Ebbs to his father the Earl of Hampshire, March 1809

Despite the bright sunshine, I shivered as I stood alone in the waist of the receiving ship. Marines in scarlet uniforms and shining, white cross-belts were positioned at ten-yard intervals along the ship's rail, and the occasional shout of despair emanating from below deck hammered home the dire situation I was in. The prospect of being impressed into a life in the King's service was so appalling I strove, desperately, to banish all thoughts of the future from my mind. I gazed with unseeing eyes across the man-made harbour pool I had found so interesting only a few minutes earlier. However, I had a feeling, deep in my guts, that my predicament would have been even worse had it not been for the existence of Midshipman Ebbs.

He had disappeared below deck as soon as we had come aboard the relic of a warship, and I had been left fretting for what seemed like an age but was in reality, probably no more than a quarter-of-an-hour. A strangely powerful feeling of relief swept over me when his cocked hat appeared at the top of the companion ladder. My mood improved even more when he told me I was not to be confined on the receiving ship that night. The sour smell of overcrowded humanity that was permeating from beneath my feet was turning my stomach, and the prospect of being taken into the ship's bowels had been scaring me shitless.

"I have recruited two other volunteers in recent days as well as yourself, Egan," Ebbs told me. "It seems that we are all to spend the night ashore in Bristol because tomorrow I have to take you, and a wagon-load of brass, to the Royal Dockyard at Portsmouth. As you are all sailors of some experience, they are placing us in a ship immediately."

Ebbs disappeared below again for about half-an-hour, and I watched as a stream of ships was pulled by teams of horses, through the lock and out into the river to wait for the tide. When Ebbs reappeared, he had the ubiquitous Wellens and Harvey with him, and they were leading the other two 'volunteers'. Both of the new recruits wore iron bracelets linked by short lengths of chain around their ankles. Ebbs caught my gaze.

"The Navy has found that many volunteers suffer from a change of heart when their bounty isn't immediately forthcoming," he said by way of explanation. "Your bounty will be added to your pay aboard your first ship. I'm afraid that regulations stipulate that I have to keep you shackled until delivery."

He then nodded towards Wellens, who knelt by my feet and locked a pair of bracelets to my ankles. He then led our whole party towards the ship's entry port. With Wellens and Harvey roughly supporting my arms, the chain between my shackles was just long enough for me to make my way down the ship's side and into the longboat waiting below. Wellens jumped down into the bow, and Harvey sat with Ebbs in the stern sheets and took the tiller. The other two 'volunteers' and I were ordered to sit in the centre of the boat, and our chains jangled as we clambered laboriously over the thwarts. With a word from Ebbs, the boat crew of six seamen pulled us smartly away from the receiving ship.

Shipping was collecting in the pool, and we had to give way to several merchant vessels as we made our way through a series of channels: some of which still had gangs of navigators working at their sides. Eventually, the harbour started to grow wider, and I reckoned that we had reached the old cut of the River Avon itself. In the distance, the outlines of myriad buildings sprawled across the horizon, punctuated by church steeples: this, I decided, must be Bristol. With each oar-stoke pulling us nearer to the city, the vessels in the harbour grew more numerous, and in no time at all, we were in the midst of the busiest stretch of harbour that I have ever seen.

Ships of every description were moored alongside high, stone-built walls, and in some places they were berthed three or four deep. Grand merchantmen intermingled with dirty, South Walian colliers and little coastal traders. The quaysides on both sides of the harbour were alive with bustle and activity as cargos were landed and loaded. The constant streams of people reminded me of the commotion inside one of my mother's beehives. Bodies of all shapes and sizes, many of them laden with some burden, hurried in both directions. Bristol was a vibrant place, full of possibilities, and I should have been here searching out a new life and not being transported into servitude like a common footpad.

The longboat put us ashore on an ancient, stone landing stage in the part of the city where all the tallest buildings huddled most closely together, but the forest of masts and spars continued for a long way down the new harbour. Ebbs led us along the quayside with the air of a man who knew exactly where he was going. We shuffled behind him as quickly as our chains would allow us while Wellens and Harvey brought up the rear. We passed well-dressed city gentlemen picking their way carefully in between the mounds of horse dung, and grubby street peddlers who were verbally jousting with each other for custom. At one point, our little procession had to scatter swiftly as a carter urged his team drunkenly across our path. A young woman in a gaudy red dress and a pimpled face called out, 'Don't worry, my lover. You'll soon be 'ome, and I'll keep it warm for you' as I passed her. I wasn't sure whether she was being cruel or kind, but I didn't have time to ask because Ebbs led us briskly away from the harbourside and into a grand town square which had a huge statue of some luminary on horseback at the middle of it. Gabled roofs and porticoes towered high above me, and many of the houses had four or even five rows of windows stacked on top of one another. Some of these buildings were made of a bright, white stone and their gables were encrusted with decorations and carvings that were as ornate as on any church.

Ebbs led us to a big, black timbered hostelry called the *Hole in the Wall*, which had two marines standing guard over the front door. We stood in a stone-flagged hallway while Ebbs consulted a portly naval officer with a red face. After a short wait, a porter in a dirty, white apron appeared and led us to a small room at the back of the building. I wouldn't describe it as a cell, but the only window was barred and the door carried a heavy lock.

"We are all to stay in here tonight, and our wagon will arrive on the morrow," announced Ebbs. "The innkeeper will bring us victuals, and then, I suggest you get as much rest as possible. There are palliasses stacked in the corner."

After we had eaten, the others started to settle themselves down for the night. I didn't feel tired; I had slept well on the trow and my mind was alive with my troubles. I sat on a wooden bench in front of the small coal fire the inn keeper had lit in the grate and buried my head in my hands. I was disturbed by the sound of footsteps beside me.

"You will be pleased with the news that you are to serve immediately, Egan," Ebbs said brightly as he settled on the bench next to me.

"Is that good news for me?" I asked.

"It is the most excellent news! Some poor devils can remain locked in a receiving ship for months, but you have the opportunity to do your duty almost at once," he replied.

"Do I have any duty other than to God and m'self?" I shot back at him hotly.

"Of course, you do," he said, a little indignantly, obviously shaken by my reply. "You owe duty to your Country and your King."

"My King! He has just had me ripped from a peaceful existence, and is about to enslave me on a man-of-war for the rest of my useful life."

"The trade in slavery has recently been abolished. You may

even find yourself in a King's ship hunting down the evil slavers. Wherever you are deployed, you will be paid fairly and have the honour of serving your King and sharing in his victories, you will be no slave."

"If I have no choice and no freedom then I'm no more than a slave myself," I retorted bitterly.

I had no wish to antagonise him, but my future had been torn away from me, and he couldn't possibly understand how I felt. I was well aware that as a humble rating I had no right to talk to him, a midshipman, in such a disrespectful way, but it was him who had sat next to me, and it was him who had started the conversation.

"We all have a responsibility to protect our homeland, Egan," he said, in a quiet and sympathetic tone. "Look at me; I am also new to the service and have to go where I am told, but I deem it an honour to serve His Majesty."

"It's different for you. You're probably of noble birth and known as Lord something or other. Honour and duty might be in your blood, but your family has probably reaped the rewards," I said angrily.

"Now, now… Let us not quarrel," he replied without demonstrating the slightest irritation at my insubordination. "I do possess a courtesy title, that is true, but my father has arranged with the Admiral that I shall only be known in the Navy by my rank and not my title. However, my determination to serve my country is of my own making: as should yours be."

I knew that I would never be able to find solace in a sense of honour or duty, but Midshipman Ebbs was beginning to impress me. Firstly, he had persuaded me to 'volunteer' so that I received a bounty, and now he was prepared to talk to me as an equal. Most boys his age, if they were granted a little power over other human beings, would have demanded the indulgences their rank afforded them with cruel determination. I wanted to explain to him what had happened to me so that he might better understand my views.

"My wife died of consumption, in the filth and overcrowding of Birmingham, two weeks ago," I blurted out, clumsily.

Ebbs was speechless for a few seconds as he digested my words.

"I'm sorry to hear that, Egan," he said quietly. "What were you doing in Birmingham?"

"I laboured in a manufactory."

"Then what were you doing working that river trow?"

"I wasn't working that trow. It was as I said to you. I was a passenger sold by that lying bastard of a bargee."

"So you have only recently left Birmingham?"

"Aye, my wife was ill for so long they threw me out of work and kicked me out of my house as well. I'd never have been in that hateful town in the first place but for being turned off our grazing lands by the faceless sod of a rich landowner," I explained bitterly: the bile bubbling up inside me.

"So, you are not from Birmingham originally but from farming stock?" asked Ebbs.

I waited a few seconds to let my anger subside before answering, and then I said, "Aye, in Somersetshire. I'm from Lilstock on the Somersetshire coast."

"Lilstock, eh...," he said. He spoke slowly, seemingly lost in thought for a moment, and then he said, "Well, there is nothing that can be done about that now ... You must treat the Navy as a new life and give of your best. I will try to help you as much as I'm able, Nathaniel ... You don't mind if I call you by your Christian name do you?"

"No," I replied, surprised he would even consider using my first name.

"Like yours, the direction of my life has not run a true course either. I had been apprenticed to an engineer, and had no thoughts of naval service until my brother was killed in the Adriatic last winter," Ebbs said.

He went on to explain that he was the youngest son of the Earl of Hampshire and he had been spared the family tradition of naval service because that duty had fallen to his elder brother, Matthew. Following Matthew's death onboard *HMS Glatton*, his father had insisted that family honour be maintained and Jacob, for that was his name, join the Navy.

"Engineering was what I was born to, Nathaniel. As an engineer, my every day was different, and posed me new problems to solve," he enthused. "I didn't want to serve at sea, but I couldn't refuse my father's wishes. He is ill, and I don't think he will be with us too much longer. I couldn't let him die without there being an Ebbs in the Navy. However, now that I am commissioned, I accept my responsibility wholeheartedly, and I shall serve King and Country to the best of my abilities."

We were obviously from completely different positions in

- 45 -

society and held opposing views because of that, but I was finding this pale youth an engaging companion. He was evidently bright and had been well educated, but his greatest asset would seem to be his determination to make the best of whatever life threw at him.

"I'm sorry about your brother's death," I said.

"Matthew I loved, and I feel his loss very keenly," he replied before falling silent for a while. "He was about your age, and I must say you resemble him in a small way." This struck me as a strange comment to make, but I didn't reply. "I had seen little of Matthew over the last three years, but I am finding it difficult to come to terms with the feeling that he is no longer here," he continued. "He had always been a stabilising influence on my thoughts."

Surprisingly, I was beginning to feel some sympathy for Jacob Ebbs. I think I had thought my own pain somehow insulated me from empathising with other people's grief, but now I was learning this was not the case. None-the-less, I was also aware that I didn't want to start talking about the loss of loved ones for fear of upsetting my own fragile equilibrium.

"How did you become apprenticed to an engineer?" I asked, abruptly changing the subject.

"As a boy, I had shown an aptitude for design and was only happy when making something," Ebbs explained. "When I was old enough to leave my tutors, father allowed me to become apprenticed to an engineer called Marc Kingdom Brunel."

"Me…me too," I stammered.

"You were apprenticed to Marc Kingdom Brunel?" Ebbs asked with a shrill note of surprise in his voice.

"No, no … but I too am at my happiest when I'm trying to fathom how something works. My Father worked a forge, and it was my task to produce sketches for him. He was an accomplished craftsman, but sometimes he struggled to visualise an object that had to be made. I have always found it easy to outline my thoughts with a pen. He would have his customers describe their needs, and I would make sketches for him."

"Well, you and I have more common than first meets the eye, Nathaniel Egan," Ebbs said with a smile.

"I have drawn the missing mountings for a dozen ploughshares, and the outlines of endless coulters and mouldboards," I said. "Father and I even managed to make the replacement gears for a windmill, and I have rarely been as proud as when they drove the millstones!"

The eerily sonorous noises of men sleeping were starting to fill our little room, and I think Ebbs and I were the only ones left awake, but I couldn't be sure about Wellens, who was continually tossing and turning on a palliasse by the door. Ebbs showed no signs of tiredness, and I pushed him to tell me more about the time he spent apprenticed to an engineer.

"In many ways, it shall be strange for me to return to His Majesty's Dockyard. Two years ago, Mr Brunel sent me to Portsmouth to study the workings of an impressive suite of machines he had installed," he said.

"Are these machines still there?"

"Indeed, they are. I shall show you when we arrive."

"What are they for?" I asked.

"They are for the manufacture of the countless rigging blocks that are so essential for the operation of every ship," Ebbs explained excitedly. "The machines will be of great interest to you, Nathaniel. They constitute the world's very first manufactory. It is a modern wonder that ten totally unskilled hands can now make 130,000 blocks in one year," he paused for a moment to draw breath. "Previously, it would have taken one hundred skilled men four times as long to make so many," he concluded.

"How are these machines powered?" I asked.

"By an engine driven by steam."

Ebbs tossed the last couple of pieces of coal into the grate, and the fire crackled with renewed energy: splashing a warm glow on both our faces. I was well aware that sitting here discussing machinery was only diverting my brain from the awful reality of my situation. But under the circumstances, what else was there to do? There was nothing to be gained by wallowing in self-pity over Mary's death or my impressment into naval service. I forced myself to keep talking, giving Ebbs a detailed, if meandering, description of the rotary steam engine in Birmingham. I didn't mention the Luddites' attack because I was sure that he would not have understood our sentiments. Instead, I explained how the beam above the engine was connected to a great wheel by a long rod, and how this rod was connected to a mechanism at the wheel's centre.

"That is the 'sun and planets' gear, Nathaniel," explained Ebbs when I had finished. "It must be an old machine, for they have now changed that arrangement for cams. The connecting rod you saw drives a cog around the hub of the flywheel and transfers the up-and-down motion of the beam into a rotary motion. As the flywheel is turned, the teeth around its circumference turn a pinion wheel which would, in turn, drive the machinery in the manufactory."

Ebbs produced a thin charcoal stick and some paper and set about sketching some little pictures to help me understand. He explained himself well, and, after a couple of hours, I felt that I had a firm grip on the workings of the steam beam engine. When he had finished, I thanked him and told him that I thought it was time to try and get some sleep.

"I'm sure that you are right, Nathaniel," he replied, "but before I turn in I wish to pen a note to my sister Sarah so that it can be left for the mail coach in the morning. I am most anxious to tell her I shall be stationed in Portsmouth and that she might visit before we sail."

"Are you as fond of your sister as you were your elder brother?" I asked.

"We are very close, Nathaniel," he replied. "Obviously, we grew up together, but Sarah has a remarkably clear perception of the world, and not being near her is my biggest regret in being called to serve my King."

I was pleased to feel the warmth of my new friend's affection for his sibling, but it also served to rekindle my own unhappy memories of my wife. I had managed to divert my thoughts during the evening, but now I felt the icy grip of despair return and force any optimistic notions out of my mind. I tried not to think of Mary, but I just found myself saddled with the irksome feeling that something was desperately wrong with my world: something I would never be able to put right.

CHAPTER FOUR
Portsmouth Dockyard, 2nd April 1809

My dearest Sarah,
Good news, Dumpling! I am to be stationed in Portsmouth longer than had been first imagined. It is no more than three hours to the Southern Turnpike, so you can be here in an afternoon. Have Stubbings bring you in the four-wheeler. Please come, I miss you and would dearly love to talk with you before I am sent to sea. It can be arranged for you to stay as a guest of the Dockyard Superintendent and his family.

Sometimes, Dumpling, I worry about my courage failing me when I'm eventually called upon to fight. Have no fear, I understand my duty completely and have every intention of handing out a thrashing to the French, but occasionally I worry about letting the family down. As you know, naval service was not my first calling.

How is Father? He was weaker than usual when I left, but I think he was proud he still has a son in His Majesty's service.

If you come, and please do, could you request of Sir John Plumpton, my trustee, the latest fiscal review?

As you know, I had little to do with the estate whilst poor Matthew was alive, but I desire that Sir John believes that I intend to maintain the closest scrutiny of my business affairs from now on.
Extract of a letter from Jacob Ebbs to his sister Sarah,
March 1809

Gingerly, I climbed the sawpit ladder: hampered by a dull ache in the small of the back and painful smarting to the palms of both hands. Since my arrival in His Majesty's Dockyard, my station had been the lower tier of a sawpit where tree trunks were cut into planks. Apart from the constant presence of sawdust in my eyes - I rubbed them on the back of my sleeve as I climbed - my first few days of naval service was much less of an ordeal than I had feared.

At the top of the ladder, the breeze chilled the sweat on my body. I turned to study the ageing little ship careened some fifty paces away on the side of one of the many wet-docks that punctured the harbour's perimeter wharf. She was a transport brig named *Albion* and, much to Ebbs' disgust, both he and I had been assigned to her. Ebbs had dreamed of setting sail in a warship immediately upon our arrival in Portsmouth, and when he had learned he was to serve in a fat, old supply vessel, he had sulked terribly. To make matters even worse for him, it transpired *Albion* was un-seaworthy. She was to be tied over on her beam, half covered with the rickety scaffolding that had been built on the hard next to her, and shipwrights would require a fortnight or more to affect her repairs.

From my point of view, time in the dockyard afforded me the opportunity to catch my breath and consider my predicament. I had decided on the wagon journey down to Portsmouth that spending the rest of my life rotting in His Majesty's Navy was not an option, and that I had to run at the first opportunity. My best chances of getting away would doubtless occur while we were still ashore: my problems were when and how?

Ebbs and I found ourselves both billeted in the same large, characterless barrack block that was, thankfully, more-or-less odour free and sparsely populated. Being a man of rank, Ebbs was granted the luxury of a bed with a canvas screen for privacy, whereas my only allocation was a hammock and a small shelf for the clothing issued to me from the slop chest.

Ebbs' time at the dockyard had been appropriated by the Agent Victualler, and every morning he was rowed to offices in the Weevil Yard on the other side of the harbour. The Navy had recognised that he was a man of education, and was putting him to work procuring, and accounting for in triplicate, *Albion's* chandlery and stores. He didn't return to our barracks until late each evening.

"Something has arisen I just cannot make head or tail of, Nathaniel," he confided in me one night as we walked to the kitchens for supper. "I have seen the requisition sheets, and, when she's seaworthy, *Albion* is to take onboard 1500 casks of powder, but we are only drawing crew rations for one month. To where can we sail and return in one month?"

"We must simply be replenishing ordnance for an isolated squadron somewhere," I replied, with a shrug.

"How irritating it is to be dumped in a dull transport and not a fighting ship," he grumbled to himself as he kicked a loose stone and sent it skittering across the top of the cobbles.

Frankly, I was unconcerned with where *Albion* might be headed. She was a simple supply vessel, and all I hoped was that she wouldn't carry me into any danger. It seemed to me that the longer her repairs took the better. The more time spent familiarising myself with the ways of the yard, the greater the chance some opportunity of escape would present itself. In the meantime, the dockyard food was plentiful, of reasonable quality, and, as long as I pulled hard on my end of the saw, life was just about bearable. Also, being presented with a half-pint of watered gin twice daily went a small way to divert my mind from its worries!

❖ ❖ ❖

Life in His Majesty's Dockyard Portsmouth began in the same way every morning. At daybreak a prim, upright petty officer called Robinson clanged the heavy, cast-iron bell that hung by the dormitory door before strutting about between the hammocks shouting until everybody was on their feet. Usually, Ebbs would have already left for the Weevil before we played out our morose little pantomime, but on this particular morning, my fourth in the yard, the young midshipman appeared from behind his canvas screen. When the maritime martinet had stomped his way to the far end of the room, Ebbs greeted me in the friendly manner that had become our custom when no one could overhear us. He didn't think it proper for a midshipman to be seen to be friendly with an enlisted man, but, to be frank, I hadn't noticed anyone taking much notice when we spoke together.

"Good morning, Nathaniel," he said brightly.

"You appear to be in fine humour this morning," I replied with a nod.

"That I am. I am expecting the arrival of my dear sister very soon."

The rhythmic click of nailed shoes warned us that Boatswain

Robinson was making his return and Ebbs turned away from me.

"All hands," he barked, "and gentlemen, Sir," he added in a softer tone, deferentially knuckling his temple towards Ebbs, "are ordered to assemble immediately upon the hard to witness a punishment parade. So let's be 'aving you, lads. Look lively now."

Robinson was a wiry little sod who looked as fit as a butcher's dog. His smart kit and glazed leather hat, which he wore pulled down over his ears, indicated to me that here was a man who had devoted his life to the Service.

"What's this about, Jacob?" I asked as soon as Robinson had clattered on out of earshot.

"Oh … I heard something about it in the Agent Victualler's office yesterday. There is to be a punishment parade for a poor fellow who is to be 'flogged around the fleet': twenty-five lashes at the side of each ship. A grim business indeed," he murmured as he started to make his way to the door.

"Twenty-five lashes at the side of each ship! There must be thirty ships at Spithead," I hissed as I trotted after him. "What can he possibly have done to deserve that?"

"Attempted desertion," Ebbs replied over his shoulder. "He is one of three runners who were all caught in a tavern somewhere upcountry two weeks since. This fellow is the last to be punished."

This information pulled me up as sharply as if I'd felt the lash of a cat-o'-nine-tails myself. I hung back as Ebbs hurried out of the barracks. My plans for escape would need the most careful consideration. I had no idea that a failed attempt to get away would be met with such savage retribution.

It was too early in the morning for the dockyard's gates to have been opened for the outside labour force, and there were only the hundred or so enlisted seamen that were stationed in the yard gathered along one side of the hard. Two longboats with crews waited at the water's edge, and one of the boats had two capstan bars lashed upright to a forward thwart to make a sort of frame for the condemned man to stand at. I took my place beside Ebbs and dutifully waited as a little procession made its way from the cell block by the main gate and along the harbour side. At their head were two impeccably dressed officers, and behind them a squad of marines. A blue-coated drummer boy, marching to one side of the column, beat out the *'Rogue's March'*. As they passed before us, I saw a fragile, gaunt figure, naked to the waist and bound at the wrists, stumbling along in the midst of the marines.

"They're going to flog that shadow of a man at the side of thirty ships?" I exclaimed to Ebbs as loudly as I dared. "What happened to the other two men?"

Ebbs just looked up at me and gave an almost imperceptible shake of his head.

"They were whipped to death, were they not?" I asked in complete horror.

"I know it is brutal, but they must be punished, Nathaniel ... as a deterrent to others."

I was rendered speechless: unable to conceive of a suitable reply. The fact the Navy was allowed to tear men away from their families and impress them against their will was abhorrent, but to then beat them to death if they transgressed the rules elevated their barbarity to a whole new level.

❖ ❖ ❖

The punishment parade had left my mind in a sour state. After breakfast, I trudged off to the sawpit with my mind caught in a dilemma. The realisation that a gruesome death was the penalty for any attempt to run was a powerful incentive to jettison all thoughts in that direction, but, at the same time, the hateful unfairness of the regime made me more determined to get away. What was certain was that any plans to abscond would have to be based on sound intelligence. By now, the dockyard gates, which were the only way through the high surrounding walls, had been thrown open, and there was a muscular red line of regular troops vetting the credentials of every man who passed through them.

Men of all ages and sizes poured into the yard. The thoroughfares were crowded with hundreds of ship-wrights, carpenters, caulkers, bricklayers, painters, coopers and riggers coming to work (NOTE: *At the time that Egan and Ebbs were stationed in Portsmouth in 1809 the British Naval Dockyards constituted the largest, single commercial enterprise in the world*). It was impossible to believe that amidst such great industry, and amongst such a vast number of men, there didn't exist a relatively safe opportunity to get away.

My fellow sawyer was a dour soul who showed no interest in speaking to me, and whose only concern seemed to be in maintaining the upper station in the sawpit. I had dismissed him as a possible source of information. The majority of the dockyard workers seemed to be stand-offish towards the enlisted men for reasons that were not immediately obvious. However, I had managed to hold a couple of fairly amicable, if trivial, conversations with a caulker whose name was Veale. Following the events of that morning, it was time to grasp the nettle and speed up my researches. To this end, I went in search of Veale on my first break from the sawpit and found him working on the lower tier of the scaffold that encased *Albion's* bulbous bottom.

"Good morning," I shouted, clambering onto the scaffold.

Veale didn't answer, but he gestured recognition by slightly raising a hand.

"A good day for being somewhere else," I said, sidling alongside him.

He was a tall, lean man whose hair, which was greying at the temple, was pulled back into a long, untidy ponytail. He didn't stop hammering hemp strands of oakum into the gaps between planking in the transports hull. He didn't even look in my direction.

"What I wouldn't give to be able to walk out of this yard at sundown like you do," I continued in as conversational a manner as possible.

There was still no reply, but he took a glance over his shoulder to check that no one else was in earshot.

"I have no wish to spend the rest of my life in the King's navy," I said, dropping my voice to a conspiratorial whisper.

"It can't be easy for you impressed blokes," he replied finally, "but this ain't the place to try it. You've no chance of getting out o' this yard."

"But there are so many men coming and going every day __"

"It may look like chaos to you," he interrupted sharply, "but every trade 'as its foremen an' every foreman 'as 'is quartermen. When we get to them gates every tradesman has to vouchsafe his gang. Woe betides the man who tries to smuggle anyone in o' out. He'd spend the rest of the war impressed into the navy hi'self."

Veale turned back to the hull planking and started to hammer much harder than he had before. I knew he thought he was being unnecessarily placed in danger, but I had the bit between my teeth and was determined to push hard for more information.

"But surely amidst so many men, there must be someone who will help me?" I implored.

"I've told you," he hissed back at me with surprising venom.

"The dockyard officers keep everything as tight as a drum 'cause they're as worried about spies and saboteurs getting in as they are about the likes of you gettin' out. I 'as a job an' immunity from impressment as long as I work 'ere, but I'll lose everthin' if I'm seen talkin' to you and then you disappears."

There was nothing else to be said, and an uncomfortable silence fell between the two of us until the scaffolding started to vibrate from the footfall of another man. It was one of the caulking crew who was carrying a pot of hot pitch so that Veale could seal the seams that he had filled with oakum. Veale flashed a glance at me that clearly indicated that our conversation had ended. He may have felt threatened by my questioning, but he started to whistle a nonchalant tune before his mate reached him. A trifle chastised and no better informed, I melted quietly away.

❖ ❖ ❖

Later that morning, Lady Sarah Ebbs arrived in Portsmouth. I was carting off-cut wood from the sawpit, which was to be used as firewood in the officer's residences, when an impressive four-wheeler carrying a young woman swept past me and pulled-up outside the dockyard Mansion House. I knew it was her because about an hour later I saw a gleeful Midshipman Ebbs, who had obviously been summoned from the Weevil, scampering up the mansion steps two at a time.

Returning to the confines of the pit, I thought nothing more of it as I hauled on my end of the double-handed blade. In fact, I had completely forgotten about Ebbs and his sister until he disturbed me during my mid-day meal. I was sitting beside one of the huge dry-docks that surround the 'Great Basin' in the centre of the yard, just finishing a mess of boiled mutton and samphire sauce, when I felt a tap on my shoulder.

"Nathaniel, may I present my sister, Lady Sarah Ebbs," announced a bright-faced Jacob Ebbs with effervescent enthusiasm. He interrupted me with a full mouth, and I awkwardly set aside my wooden tray and stumbled to my feet. "This is my friend and confidant Mr Nathaniel Egan," continued Ebbs, as gaily as if we were at a village fete.

"I'm delighted to meet you, Lady Sarah. I had no idea you would be visiting the yard," I said, making a clumsy sort of half-bow. As I straightened up, I was greeted by two clear blue eyes that were examining me with interest. Sarah Ebbs was a pretty girl about the same age as me with red-brown hair, and the hint of a smile that played around the edge of her mouth.

"It appears that Jacob is not allowed from the confines of the shipyard, and so we must seek our entertainment here, Mr Egan," she replied with the faintest of nods in my direction. She seemed aloof but not as much as I would expect from an Earl's daughter. The only other woman of quality that I had ever seen was Colonel Davenport's daughter, and she had never spoken to me in the four years I worked for her father.

"You have no duties for two hours over dinner, Nathaniel. I thought to show Sarah and yourself the Block-Mill. I'm sure that I mentioned to you that, in a small way, I was involved in its mechanisation," announced Ebbs proudly.

"The Block-Mill! What indeed may the Block-Mill be?" asked Sarah.

"The Navy uses many thousands of wooden pulley-blocks to tension all sorts of rigging and rope work. Up until a few years ago, craftsmen had to cut them by hand, but now we can make them with machines," explained Ebbs.

"And you think a visit to this place is suitable entertainment for your only sister?" asked Sarah.

At first, I thought she was chastising her brother, but I noticed that she ended her question by smiling affectionately at him.

"The machinery in the block-mill was designed by Mister Marc Isambard Brunel, of whom even someone as dim-witted as you, dear sister, may remember was my patron whilst I was an apprentice engineer," replied Ebbs. His face wore a sarcastic grimace as he spoke to his sister, but it was obvious that he was both happy and relaxed to be in her company.

Ebbs led us away from the dry-docks and towards a complex of plain, red-brick buildings that stood alone at the edge of the Great Basin. As we approached them, the air was filled with the strange oily aroma of overheated fat that I had experienced at Chapman's Manufactory.

"Are the machines in the Bock-Mill powered by steam?" I asked.

"They are, Nathaniel. They are powered by an elderly Boulton and Watt engine that, I think you will find, is very similar to the one that you saw in Birmingham. It is also used to pump the water from the dry-docks," replied Ebbs waving his arm behind us in the general direction that we had just come from.

"So this Block-Mill is where you spent your time when you were apprenticed to Mr Brunel, Jacob?" asked Sarah.

"Yes, I was indeed inside this very building for a goodly portion of my time."

We found ourselves standing before a wide, single story shed that sat in the middle of the assortment of adjoined buildings. The shed had two, large, light-blue doors with words 'Block Mill' painted roughly above them. As Ebbs pushed open the left-hand door, the aggressive sounds of fettered steam and the clacking of metal tools working on wood assaulted our ears.

"Goodness gracious, look how many there are!" exclaimed Sarah as we stepped inside.

The shed was filled by three rows of machines that all seemed to be constructed completely of metal. They were driven by leather belts that ran around a spinning shaft fitted in amongst the roof joists, and ran the length of the shed. I had seen horse-driven saws and lathes but this was mechanisation of a totally different order. There were only about a dozen men in the entire shed, and their duties seemed to be no more arduous than collecting half finished blocks from one machine and carrying them to the next.

"There are forty-five machines. Aren't they magnificent?" Ebbs began enthusiastically. "They perform twenty-two different functions from cutting the block shells from an elm log," he said, pointing to a spinning, round saw fixed to a metal bench on his left, "to smoothing the finished article." He waved his hand towards the back of the building. "Most importantly, the quality and consistency of the blocks produced has greatly improved, and less than one-tenth of the number of men is required as when they were made by hand."

The machine next to me constantly drove a chisel backwards and forwards. It was cutting identical holes into the roughly hewn chunks of wood, but the astonishing thing was that somehow the machine fed the blocks under the chisel without assistance, and disengaged itself when each hole was completed!

"Here, let me show you one of our boring engines. They are of the most ingenious design," carried on Ebbs speaking over his shoulder as he almost broke into a trot down the aisle between the machinery. "It drills holes in the elm shells at the beginning of the process, and in all the machines that follow the holes are registered together which ensures the correct alignment."

"Are you interested in mechanics, Mr Egan?" asked Lady Sarah as we walked after her brother.

"I am indeed, Lady Sarah," I said stopping and turning to face her. "I've always been interested in how things worked, and in trying to find ways for them to function better, but I also worry about how machines, such as these, will take work from poor families."

She looked up at me: directly into my eyes.

"That's very philanthropic of you, Mr Egan," she replied thoughtfully. Following a moment's hesitation, her face broke into a warm smile and she said, "I agree with you wholeheartedly that everybody deserves the opportunity to make a reasonable living."

"Don't worry about that, Nathaniel."

The interruption was from Ebbs' ebullient voice.

"The more machines we can invent, the fewer men we shall have to sentence to a life of working drudgery."

Ebbs must have walked back up the aisle to meet us because he was now standing at my side. I felt strangely irritated that he had disrupted my conversation with his sister.

"But it was machines such as these that took my job in Birmingham," I retorted, suddenly a little flustered.

"Yes, machinery threw you out of a job you hated. The skilled men that spent their days cutting endless pulley blocks now work more productively elsewhere in the dockyard," he replied confidently.

"I once heard an orator in Birmingham make a very similar argument," I replied, "but if the manufactory where I worked hadn't installed a steam-engine, I would probably not have ended up impressed into the Navy."

I was aware of the venom that I had attached to the word 'impressed', and I saw a startled look flash across Lady Sarah's eyes as I said it.

"Nathaniel, you volunteered!" Ebbs countered. "Don't you think it more honourable to serve his Majesty than to wind down a screw press all day?"

"It may sound like that to you, but if it is the only work available to …"

I felt anger well up inside me, but I didn't believe that my problems had anything to do with Jacob Ebbs, and I had no wish to upset his sister, so I bit my tongue mid-sentence.

"Please, do not argue!"

Sarah's voice was crisp, and cut through the tension that had suddenly sprung up between us.

"My little sister is right. Come, Nathaniel, let me show you the Boulton and Watt. This one has a flyball governor."

"It has a what?" asked Sarah with a small laugh that restored the equanimity of the situation. "Let us go and see, Mr Egan," she said, and I felt her fingers gently touch my elbow.

The fact Lady Sarah was not only my own age, but that she was prepared to talk to me as an equal left an intriguing tingle of excitement.

Ebbs led us away from the rows of machines towards the far corner of the shed. There was an open doorway, and the nearer we got to it, the greater the hissing sound of steam became. And then we were through the opening, and I saw a working steam-engine for the first time! Its great beam rocked up and down to the beat of the metal piston, as Ebbs had explained to me, and the interlocking gears around the hub drove the great wheel round at speed. I was mesmerised by the ingenious way that the opening and closing of the valves was triggered by the movement of the beam. At the top of the great wheel, a smaller, geared wheel was spinning at great speed and driving the shaft above the machines in the Block-Mill.

The same feeling swept over me that I had experienced on the manufactory floor at Chapman's. This great machine was a magnificent sight, but I couldn't rid myself of the idea that towns, like Birmingham, would have to be packed full with manufactories if they were to provide enough work for all the men who were being turned off the land.

"Now what sort of 'governor' did you say it had?"

Sarah's voice broke my spell as we all stood before the great metal monster.

"A flyball governor," Ebbs replied, pointed at two black metal spheres the size of men's heads that were spinning quickly on a spindle that was being driven by a chain from the engine's driveshaft.

"Well, can you make head or tail of that, Mr Egan?" she said, gesturing at the spinning spheres and smiling at me.

I racked my brains, trying to imagine what its purpose could be before Ebbs had time to explain it to us.

"The faster the engine runs, what is known as kinetic energy forces the two spheres upwards and outwards against gravity," the young midshipman gleefully began his elucidation. "This causes those lever arms to extend, see there," he said, pointing. "It's called Newton's law of centrifugal force and as the arms extend —"

"They close the steam valve on the engine and stop its motion," I almost shouted the instant the idea flashed into my mind.

"Very good, Nathaniel: now you are starting to think like an engineer," congratulated Ebbs. I must admit I was more than a little pleased myself and, at least for the present, my doubts about mechanisation were driven from my mind.

"So if I ever again see two steel balls, both the size of a man's head, I shall comment that they are a 'flyball governor,'" Sarah said with a laugh.

"I hope we have not been boring you, Lady Sarah?" I said.

"No, not at all: I find it quite absorbing," she replied smiling. "I seem to have spent my life trying to make sense of mechanical toys devised by Jacob, and so a visit to the Block-Mill is really not very different!"

❖ ❖ ❖

Ebbs and his sister were afforded an extraordinary amount of freedom over the next week or so. The influence that an Earl can bring to bear on a dockyard superintendent should not be underestimated. Sarah stayed in the Mansion House as a guest of the Superintendent's family, and although Ebbs wasn't allowed outside the yard, he was excused duties so that he could entertain her. Most gratifyingly, from my own point of view, on many afternoons, he somehow succeeded in securing me a few extra hours of liberty so that I could enjoy their company.

I rapidly grew obsessed with these meetings. So much so, that my plans for escape were driven completely from my mind. Lady Sarah Ebbs drew me towards her like a moth to a flame. I wanted to spend as much time with her as possible. She was warm, friendly and considerate. Like her brother, she was sensitive to my point of view, and always listened attentively to what I had to say. It was deeply touching one afternoon, when I saw a tear swell in the corner of her eye as Ebbs was relating the tale of my misfortunes in Birmingham and the circumstances of my 'volunteering'.

"You should have let Nathaniel alone, Jacob. I did not have you listed as a gaoler in any case," she scolded him when he had finished.

"Dear Sister, how febrile your brain is. Of course, I would have let him go if I had known the truth as I do now. But once the bargemaster had offered him for service I would have had to find staunch reason to refuse him."

"...but a man who has had to watch a loved one die? It is my greatest fear with Father ..."

"I didn't know anything of the illness to Nathaniel's wife at the time," said Ebbs, defensively.

"Is your duty so important to you, Little Brother, that you could not act with simple humanity?" There was more than a touch of anger in her voice.

"We all have to do our duty as I know more than most, Sister dear," Ebbs retorted severely fixing Sarah with a steely glare. I had not heard him talk to his sister like this before, and there were a few moments' silence before Sarah changed the subject.

"How did you end up as a manufactory labourer, Nathaniel? You have the demeanour of a more educated man?" she said, wiping the tear from her cheek.

"Mother spent many hours teaching me my numbers and letters, Lady Sarah. She was a churchman's daughter, and my brother and I could both read and write before we were ten years old. I was sent to clerk at the estate office at Lilstock on my eleventh birthday."

"Please ... just call me Sarah. You were an estate's clerk at eleven. That can not have been easy?"

"The work was simple enough, Sarah, but many of the cases of injustice were difficult to stomach. It wasn't easy to simply record proceedings when I didn't think that what was being decided was fair."

"I can imagine that you found it difficult to deal with all the affairs of an estate office. I know you to be a compassionate man because of what you said about machines robbing men of work in the Block Mill," she said.

"You should be careful when you question Nathaniel, Sister. He has something of the 'Leveller' principle within him," interrupted Ebbs with a nervous grin at his sister that was designed to wash away any remnant of his previous harshness.

"Has your mother's efforts at education turned you into a radical, Mr Egan?" Sarah asked playfully, her mien now completely restored to its usual composure.

"I don't know about that," I said, "but I'm afraid that my learning couldn't protect my family from the greedy land grabbing made legal by the Lilstock Enclosure Act."

"The Lilstock Enclosure Act!" Sarah slid a glance towards her brother as she spoke. "Your family were moved from the land?"

"Not my family, only Mary and myself. Father owns his land, but there simply wasn't enough to sustain us all after the common grazing was taken away from us. So, I had to seek work in the town."

This statement was met with a few moments' silence, and then Sarah asked, "With your interest in mechanics, could you not have found better-paid employment?"

"I had high hopes of finding work as some sort of engineer, Sarah, but the pay for apprenticing was even lower than working the presses. For workmen there are no guilds in Birmingham, and any sort of training is hard to come by."

"It must have been very difficult for you," she said sympathetically.

"This war makes matters even worse. Manufacturers who lose trade from the continent lay off their men pretty sharpish (NOTE: *Bonaparte introduced the Continental System in 1806 in an attempt to blockade Britain and restrict her trading power. Britain responded with the Orders in Council which required all shipping to proceed only via British ports. As a result European trade was effectively strangled, and Britain's workforce suffered greatly. Egan's time in Birmingham would have coincided with Thomas Attwood's campaign to have the Orders rescinded that was eventually successful in 1812).* I had been hoping to be able to move on, but when Mary fell ill, we had to stay in Birmingham," I said.

Later that night, I sat alone outside the barracks, and watched the warm lamplight that spilled from the windows of the Mansion House dining room. I couldn't really say why I was sitting there, but my guess would be that I was hoping to catch sight of Sarah Ebbs. She didn't come to the window, but I saw her brother glance out. This caused a strange and unexpected jealousy to bubble up inside me. What could it possibly matter to me if I wasn't allowed to dine with this girl? I had only known her a few days, but she was starting to monopolise my thoughts. She was a link with the real world: a reminder of what a normal life might have to offer. I was realistic enough to understand that a rich, educated young woman from a landowning family would never become romantically entangled with a pauper like me, and anyhow, my loyalty to the memory of Mary was too strong to allow any amorous desires to brew up. As I sat there, day-dreaming of fanciful events that might transport me into that dining room, a thin sea fog drifted in from the bay and started to soak into my clothes. I knew I was doing myself no good by sitting there, but I couldn't tear myself away and it was only when I began to shake from cold that I disconsolately dragged myself back inside the barracks.

❖ ❖ ❖

I could hear shouting, but I had no idea where the noise was emanating from.

"Get on your feet ... on your feet, you useless scroat," a voice scolded.

I felt, as much as saw, a dark shape block out the light. I threw up my hands and shouted out, "What do you want? Get away from me," but the voice carried on ranting, and a grotesque black animal wearing a naval uniform appeared before me. Its huge, ugly features cracked into a sickening leer, and it pushed its awful, pustulent snout to within a few inches of my face. It had a gigantic body, but its wizened, hideously elongated legs dissolved in some sort of swirling, primordial mist beneath it. I struck out as hard as I could with my fist, but in the next instant, an excruciating pain exploded in my back as something hard hit me from behind.

"Get on your feet, you useless scroat," said the voice again.

I opened my eyes to see Boatswain Robinson's face quizzically peering down at me. I was lying on the deck beneath my hammock, and he was holding his lantern just above my head so that he could inspect what he saw.

"Twenty years I've been in the King's Navy, an' I don't believe I 'ave ever seen a more useless scroat than you! You can't lie abed when your first ship has received her orders."

"What's that, Bo'sun?" I mumbled, still scrabbling to regain reality.

"*Albion* has been ordered to leave dock, on this morning's

tide," he barked back, "an' you're a goin' wi' her. Now grab yer kit an' get outside."

"But ... she's still lashed over on her side __"

"Not no more she ain't. Now move!"

Confusion reigned. My life had slipped into a comfortable cocoon for the last few days, and the realisation that my service in the navy was about to begin for real was hard to comprehend. Robinson gave me one final volley of, "Get on your feet, you useless scroat," and strutted off.

Pushing my scant belongings into a canvas sack, I stumbled out of the dark barracks to be greeted by the grey dawn of a damp and dismal day. Robinson was proved correct and *Albion's* makeshift scaffolding had disappeared, and her dumpy hull sat upright and moored to the wharf. The lock gates to the dock were completely open, and I could see that the tide was very nearly full.

Within the hour, *Albion* was swinging from a heavy cable running through the top of a huge, blue mooring buoy, about one hundred and fifty paces off the mole that flanked the northern end of the dockyard. Dark clouds obscured the rising sun, and the mole was occasionally obscured by blustery rain showers.

Under Robinson's direction, the dozen or so of us crewmen onboard had raised a jib and main stays'l to aid the two crews that laboured in the longboats that pulled us out. No sooner had the little brig settled on her mooring, with her bow to windward, than Ebbs clambered over the side followed by several seamen bearing his sea chest. He looked harassed, and his uncharacteristically disarrayed uniform indicated that he had readied himself in some haste.

"Quartermaster ... Quartermaster Robinson, where are you, man?" he shouted the moment he reached the deck. "Don't let those boat crews go. We have to report to the ordnance hulk off Weevil Yard directly, and we shall need them to take us in. There are six more crewmen coming aboard: organise their stations, if you please."

Despite his flustered appearance, the young man delivered his instructions with commendable authority.

"I fear there shall be no more recreation for us, Nathaniel," he whispered to me as he hurried past. "We must take on our cargo of powder, and our new captain's arrival is imminent. I fear events are taking place very quickly. I only received my orders an hour ago, and we shall be at sea tonight."

"Shall I not see Sarah again?"

It was the first thought that came to mind, and to me, seemed the only question of any importance.

"I fear not," he replied, with great surprise. For a moment, he stopped and eyed me curiously. "I have just given her the same news that I have given you, and consequently she is readying herself for the journey home," he said in a measured tone.

He scurried away, leaving me alone at the starboard rail. Of course, it was obvious we would be sent to sea soon, but somehow I had managed to block it from my mind. The awful reality of my life had been masked by the presence of Sarah Ebbs at the dockyard, and now this comfort was to be ripped away. The flats of my hands started to beat uncontrollably on the rail. I was hitting the rail so hard that they started to hurt, but I carried on regardless. When finally my hands would take no more punishment, I buried my face in my smarting palms, and just managed to stifle an anguished scream. Peering out through my fingers at a squally shower that blew across the harbour, my heart gave a little leap. There was a small figure in a gingham cloak and blue bonnet standing alone on the mole. I rubbed my eyes and stared through the watery haze. The girl raised her right hand and gave a little wave. It must be Sarah! Had she come to see me? A surge of enthusiasm rushed through me, and I jumped into the air and waved vigorously. I wanted to shout, but I knew she would not be able to hear me. Why had she come? Had she come to see me, or was she hoping to catch a glimpse of her brother? I ran along the starboard side to get as close to her as possible, but a dirty, grey, sheet of rain swept across the harbour, and to my horror, the small figure on the mole dissolved into the mist. I stood transfixed, waiting for the misty rain to clear when my trance was broken by a coarse oath barked in my ear.

"Look lively, you useless scroat." It was Robinson. "We are to make sail, and I need you with me at the halyards."

I dragged on the halyard Robinson had thrust into my hands, but my only concern was scouring the haze that concealed the Mole. I was desperate to catch another sight of the girl in the blue bonnet, but visibility was deteriorating, and the cloud seemingly grew thicker by the minute. Emerging from that grey smear of rain was further confirmation that my life was about to change. Steadily approaching us was a pinnace rowed by ten seamen, with an officer in her stern-sheets. He wore the single gold epaulette of a commander on his left shoulder, and I knew that I would not see Lady Sarah again because our new captain was about to take charge of his ship, and in the next few hours, *Albion* would be at sea.

CHAPTER FIVE
Off Rochefort, France - 9th April 1809

Great excitement and joy! There is to be an attack on the French fleet in the mouth of the River Charente. I am uncertain as to the role our little ship will play, but I am assured by Commander Parnell, our Captain, that we shall at least bear witness to everything that happens.

I'm told that the Frogs escaped from Brest in a gale nearly two months ago. They have built themselves a bolt hole on the River Charente near Rochefort, but Lord Cochrane is to winkle them out and Admiral Gambier's fleet shall gobble them up!
The entry from Midshipman Jacob Ebbs' diary for 10th April 1809

As *Albion* drew closer to the French coast in the last of the day's light, the inky silhouettes of about a dozen vessels stood out from the dark landmass in the distance. It was not an impressive flotilla, and as we closed, it was noticeable that they were largely ancient merchant ships. I was studying them and wondering why the Navy was collecting a transport convoy so near the Atlantic coast of France, when my attention was distracted by shouts from the little afterdeck behind me.

"Signal to the frigate, Mister Ebbs, if you please. Have her brought into the wind, Quartermaster."

Upon hearing Captain Parnell's orders, I scoured the dark shapes once again and noticed that one ship was far more impressive than the others. In fact, she was a handsome cruiser of at least forty guns. The final embers of the dying sun reflected from the gilt that decorated her stern windows and beneath them, picked out in dark gothic letters on a golden scroll, was the word *Imperieuse*.

I had heard of *HMS Imperieuse*. She was Sir Thomas Cochrane's ship, and stories of Lord Cochrane, as he was commonly known, had been rife among the workforce at Portsmouth dockyard. He had sailed into Plymouth four years earlier with six-foot, golden candlesticks swinging from his main topgallant yard. He had earned more prize money in one year than any other commander past or present. There were tales of his able-hands being paid more than the commissioned officers of similar sized ships. *Imperieuse* was crewed, so they said, entirely by volunteers. If an individual is to make the decision to risk his life and limb in the King's Navy, it is only sensible to do so in a ship that offers the chance of fiscal reward. For my part, I was happy to be assigned to a fat, old supply vessel that would be kept well away from any fighting. I had not asked to be part of this war, after all.

There was a splash as our number one bower was let free, and a minute-or-two later I could feel the momentum of the old transport check beneath my bare feet. *Albion* rode to her anchor before falling back into position a cable's length astern of the frigate. Staring into the darkness, the brooding contours of what looked like a long, low island no more than a mile from our larboard side became increasingly apparent to me: its rocky outline being a shade darker than the French mainland that sat behind it. To the south of us, a little further away than the island, I could just make out against the dusky sky the masts and yards of a squadron of men-of-war. I couldn't see any colours, but they must be English for them to tolerate the closeness of Cochrane and his motley flotilla.

What could we possibly be doing here? At Portsmouth we had been packed to the gunnels with casks of black powder, so it stood to reason that we must be on some kind of supply mission, but what could it be? My musings were interrupted by Midshipman Ebbs when he bustled along the starboard rail.

"Look lively, Egan," he chirruped. "The Captain's called for a late crew supper and that uncouth fellow, Capel, has developed a habit of stealing any unclaimed rations. We're going to have trouble with him I fancy."

Jas Capel (NOTE: *Jas was a common nineteenth century diminutive for James*) was a mountainous man who had been among the final group of seamen to join us at Portsmouth. He was coarse and aggressive, and I did everything possible to avoid his company.

"What are we doing here, Jacob?" I asked. "If we're supplyin' ordinance, why are we anchored within spitting distance of the French coast? We have no troops in France."

The young midshipman glanced around the deck and then hissed under his breath, "Nathaniel, you must call me Sir or Mister Ebbs onboard. I can't be seen to have friends among the crew."

"Yes, yes, but what are we doing here!"

"All that I can tell you is that eleven ships-of-the-line and a dozen smaller warships under the command of Lord Gambier are near the Ile D'Oleron to the south of us."

"Eleven ships-of-the-line! Shit! They must be planning an attack, but what can our part in it be?" Ebbs didn't reply, and I was shocked into silence by the size of the fleet. "Well at least we won't be in the firing line," I concluded a few moments later, largely to console myself.

"No matter what we are asked to do, we must exercise our duty with pride, Nathaniel."

"I don't see why. King George has done precious little for me: apart from enslave me!"

Ebbs blanched. "Don't say such things you'll have us both hanged. Now be a good fellow, and get your supper and be back on deck for your watch by eight bells," he said and scurried off.

❖ ❖ ❖

The following morning, the sounds of great industry coming from the hold of the little ship woke me. Climbing the companionway to the deck, I was greeted by a beautifully bright April morning. There was a brisk breeze blowing onto the French coast, and a warm sun on my back. The scene had changed a great deal from when I had climbed into my hammock. The size of our flotilla had grown considerably, and *Albion's* leeward side was now packed with small boats and supply vessels like piglets clustering around a sow. Hammers and wood saws chimed out, accompanied by the yells of carpenters' mates. Large details of hands were hauling manfully on blocks, that ran from our yards, bringing an unfinished tree trunk onboard. There were many things I had not been able to fathom since I had so courteously been invited to serve his Majesty, but this was the oddest yet!

Amid the commotion on deck, one figure demanded my attention. He was tall, taller even than me, and wore the blue frock-coat with two gold epaulettes of a Post Captain. From his half-boots to his cocked hat his attire was immaculate. His long, distinctive red hair framed an angular face with sharp features and cold, blue eyes. This could only be Cochrane himself: the man Bonaparte called 'The Sea Wolf'. He was engaged in a good deal of shouting whilst also being in urgent conversation with Commander Parnell. I felt a tug at my elbow. It was Ebbs.

"I'd get back below. This is no place to be idle", he hissed. "The man's a slave driver."

"Is that Cochrane?"

"Who else would it be?" retorted Ebbs with some asperity. "You're still not on watch, so get off the deck before he finds work for you."

"What's he about?" I asked, but Ebbs was already on the move. He stopped and took a pace back towards me. In a hushed voice he said, "He's turning us into a floating bomb!"

❖ ❖ ❖

The whole day was spent hauling on ropes or hacking at huge timbers with an adze until my hands were raw, and I gratefully clambered into my hammock at the end of the watch. The confounded hammering and shouting continued on deck throughout the night, but at least the other hammocks slung in the forecastle belonged to members of the larboard watch, and so I wasn't bedevilled by their snores. However, sleep wouldn't come and I lay awake endlessly turning. I was worried, deeply worried. Being conscripted into a war that had nothing to do with me was bad enough, but finding myself aboard Captain Cochrane's 'new weapon' introduced a different terror into my life. After that bastard bargee had presented me to the press in Bristol, life on a naval transport was about the best option that could be hoped for. At least, I wouldn't be in the direct line of fire, and the constant loading and disgorging of cargo might provide some opportunity for escape. Now, I found myself preparing to sail towards a secure French anchorage sitting on top of 1500 casks of powder with the possibility of any stray shell dispatching me back to my maker in an instant. Panic started to take a grip of me. Pinpricks of sweat were beginning to break out down my back. Someone let out a deep groan of desperation, and it was a few seconds before I realised that it had been me. Shaking myself violently, I tried to master my thoughts, attempting to force other subjects into my mind, but they stubbornly refused to obey. The gargantuan explosion, which the future must surely hold for me, was all I could think about. Fear steadily continued to mount until I was reduced to a petrified torpor. All I could do was watch the ebony shadows rock up and down the dark hull planking, and eventually, when anxiety had left me completely drained, I slept.

I awoke to find the ship quiet once again, apart from the ever-present groaning of timbers and humming of hemp rope. I climbed the companion to the deck, and could see the litter of small boats had returned to their respective ships. Two roughly planed tree trunks stretched incongruously across the deck. They braced the whole ship, and were scarphed to both the frame timbers and lodging knees. The casks of powder, which we had loaded in Portsmouth, were firmly wedged into the forward hold and nearly rose to the level of the deck. Any gaps between them had been tightly filled with sand bags, I presumed to offer greater resistance to the blast, and on top of our cargo had been scattered hand grenades and off-cuts of scrap iron.

It seemed most of *Albion's* crew had left and I could only see about a dozen men still onboard. A cocked hat bobbing up and down behind the belfry was a giveaway that Ebbs was still here. I could also see Capel and Robinson, but the others I didn't recognise.

The weather had changed from the previous day. A westerly wind was now blowing at something like a force five on Francis Beaufort's new scale, and a deep swell was starting to run into the French coast. Robinson's bosun's call summoned the crew to the afterdeck, where we mustered around Captain Parnell. He was a calm man in his early thirties, who had given us all the impression that he was a genial and sympathetic officer, but his address demonstrated that he also possessed steely determination.

"The chance to serve our country has arrived for all of us," he began slowly, sending a cold chill through my body. "There is a French fleet bottled up in yonder Roads. They escaped from Brest in a gale nearly two months ago. They must not reach open sea again. On tonight's flood tide, we shall take *Albion* into the mouth of the River Charente, and, with the aid of the fireships you see gathering around you, we will cause such damage and panic that the Frogs shall fall easy prey to Lord Gambier's fleet."

The Commander's eyes rested on each man in turn as he spoke, and there was a ripple of murmurs as the men had their suspicions confirmed.

"They have built a heavy boom of chain and wood across the channel to protect themselves. We shall, under Lord Cochrane's direction, take *Albion* tight to this boom and blast it apart to facilitate the action. This attack is entirely of His Lordship's invention, and nothing like it has ever been attempted before. Nobody can predict the exact nature of the explosions, so when you are given the order get to the pinnace with all possible haste.

"Following the attack you will all have to row like the very devil to reach safety against this swell and the tide," he continued. "To this end, we have selected the youngest, biggest crew available to us. The Frogs regard fireships as barbaric instruments of war, and they are bound to think likewise of explosion vessels. They have vowed to hang any of us they catch. If that fate should befall any of you, tell the Crapauds you're victualling crew from yonder barges," he swept his hand towards the small fleet of supply vessels that lay gathered in the distance behind Gambier's war ships. "Now let us join together in prayer."

❖ ❖ ❖

It was late afternoon when Cochrane's gig bumped gently alongside *Albion's* old, round-bellied hull. The hemp rigging was singing in the still-freshening wind as he was piped aboard by a small side party that included Ebbs and me.

"Good afternoon, William," Cochrane said cordially to Parnell as he stepped on deck. "Is everybody aware of their duties? Lord Gambier has finally given his consent so we attack as soon as it's dark and the flood is underway. With luck the Frogs will not be expecting us in this swell."

As the two officers walked aft towards *Albion's* little cabin, I shot an anxious glance at Ebbs. I wanted to talk to him, but he only raised his eyebrows quizzically in response. This was it! The attack was about to start and fear was eating into my guts, but his wide-eyed expression told me he was more excited than scared.

Ebbs dismissed the side party, but, before I could speak, he walked smartly towards where the ship's boats were stationed for'ard of the mizzen mast, and I followed in silence. Half a dozen men were gathered there, and Ebbs gave the order to swing out the pinnace so it could be towed behind us in readiness for our getaway when the time came. (NOTE: *Ship's pinnaces were open boats, of various sizes, primarily designed for rowing but could also be sailed. Albion's pinnace was 20ft long, could rig two lateen sails and comfortably sit a dozen oarsmen, double-banked*).

As dusk began to close around us, Bo'sun Robinson ordered me aloft to the main topmast to make sail. We were finally on our way, and I felt as sick as a dog! The spittle in my mouth dried to nothing as I stripped the gaskets from the canvas and readied the clewlines. From my station high on the yard, I could make out fortifications on the little rocky island that defended the northern end of the French boom. There were probably cannon hidden behind the crenulations, and they would be opening up in a matter of minutes. Despite the sound of the wind, I could hear blood pumping hard in my ears.

We advanced in line. Behind *Albion* there were three more 'explosion' ships similar to our own, and then a host of fireships. I knew that they were fireships because I had watched them being prepared. Huge holes had been knocked through their hulls to facilitate the rush of air once they were set alight. Ebbs had told me there would also be trails of gunpowder criss-crossed on their decks that had been doused in resin and turpentine. Up above, their rigging and sails would have been covered in tar, and, finally, grappling hooks were hung from their yards to attach them to any prey they drifted against. Some of the fireships also had frames fitted to their yardarms that supported strange, slim cylinders, about five or six feet in length, and attached to long bamboo poles. They were the brand new weapons known as *rockets (NOTE: William Congreve of the Royal Artillery developed the idea of military rockets after they were used against British troops in India. He had formed two rocket companies in 1809, and Cochrane was among the first Naval Commanders to see a future for rockets. Congreve was with Gambier's fleet at Aix Roads*).

If the fireships made it into the anchorage, the only escape for the tightly packed French ships would be into the estuary shallows where they would run aground and be easy prey for the English warships that would follow us down the Roads.

Once the tops'l was set and *Albion* was underway, there was little to do apart from fret. The little ship was now sailing her final course. The crew congregated at the bow, and a quarter-moon struggled to light the ocean before us. Ebbs and I stood a few yards away from the others. All we could see ahead were the tiny pinpricks of light from lanterns on the French ships, and the occasional foaming of waves as they broke over the distant boom. All of a sudden, there was the crack of a small explosion, and an eerie blue light was splashed about our world.

"They can't see us, and they're trying to find us with flares," said Ebbs who was now plainly stimulated by the situation.

The dull crump of cannon being fired came from the fortifications on the little island that Ebbs had told me was called the Ile d'Aix. Strange glowing trails followed the shot and inscribed arcs through the sky: the French were heating their shot in furnaces to increase its range. I made every effort to control my fear but Ebbs must have sensed my anxiety.

"I heard Cochrane describe our course to the Captain, Nathaniel," he said. "As long as we stay to the starboard side of the channel they can't reach us. He was on blockade duty here in '07."

As if to substantiate his claim, the ocean offered up a splash half a cable's length to larboard.

"One lucky shot amidships and we'd be chatting with St.Peter not each other," I stammered as I felt a shiver run the length of my spine. "Shall we survive this night, Jacob?"

"Of course we shall. Tonight will be a great victory!" replied Ebbs effervescent with excitement.

Despite the swell, the darkness and the cannon, *Albion* successfully led the flotilla into Aix Roads. Two brig-sloops had been sent ahead of us to anchor on either side of the estuary's shoals. Now, they uncovered their lights, and I saw the three white lamps and one red displayed on the yardarm of *HMS Redpole* on our larboard side, and the three white and one green of *HMS Lyra* to our starboard. In front of them, I could clearly see white horses breaking over the boom. Beyond that, the rigging of the first line of French ships was etched black in the dark sky. Orange and yellow flashes appeared from the depths of the blackness followed, half a second later, by the dull boom of cannon. The batteries on the Ile d'Aix had been too far away to be a threat, but the bow chasers of the battleships were a different matter. Within moments, there was the foreboding slap of metal shot piercing canvas above my head. I hoped beyond hope, that Cochrane wouldn't dare to take the ship any closer with his crew onboard; *Albion* was no more than three hundred paces from the boom. It could only be a matter of time, before a lucky ball lodged in the powder below and we were all blown apart.

"All hands to the pinnace!" Cochrane yelled. "Tie off the helm, Mister Robinson. I shall kindle the portfires. Prepare to row for your lives, lads!"

Nobody was quicker to react than me, and I was over the side the very second the order came out of His Lordship's mouth. I gratefully slithered down the rope netting, that had been draped over the ships side, and was seated in the boat before the next man appeared over the rail.

When a face did appear, it belonged to Capel who, like me, had obviously been waiting for the order. As he reached the boat, he screamed at everyone behind him to hurry themselves, and in the next few seconds the whole crew, bar Cochrane, had scrambled down the netting.

"Come on, come on! Where is he?" groaned Capel who was now seated in the middle of the pinnace.

"Belay that!" growled Boatswain Robinson, "or you'll feel my starter."

Robinson was a simple man, but he understood that discipline would be imperative to maintaining order in the boat as we sat at *Albion's* side riding the deep swell.

Commander Parnell played his part in calming nerves. 'Steady lads'. His voice reverberated authoritatively from the stern of the boat. 'We'll be gone from here in a few seconds'. He looked the picture of calmness in his best frock uniform. He could be waiting to be taken to dine somewhere in the fleet.

"Get your oars to pass," he ordered. "Ship oars."

I could hardly bear the tension, and was convinced I would piss myself at any moment. The ocean's cold, impenetrable blackness surrounded me and seemed to offer nothing but imminent obliteration. I felt as if I was sitting alone in a wilderness even though my shipmates were only inches away. The seconds ticked by like hours, and Cochrane only had fifteen minutes of slow match to play with. Suddenly, a breathless future Peer of the Realm appeared above us. He swung a leg over the gunnel, and, with the accompaniment of a cacophony of shouts of encouragement from the crew below, he hurried down the ship's side.

"Make way lads!" he shouted as his sea boot hit the pinnace's for'ard decking.

Relief broke over me like a jet of icy seawater from the deck pump. At least my poor hide would remain intact for a few more hours. The pinnace leapt across the water faster than I had ever felt a rowed boat move before. At each pull of the oars the finely made, carvel hull surged away from the *Albion's* side.

"Rest on your oars!"

Cochrane's order cracked through my mind like a lash. The crew had been so intent on their task that they were unable to stop rowing immediately. Some were already beginning the next stroke before their brains could obey the command causing the boat to slue in an ugly fashion across the swell.

"Quiet lads," Cochrane snapped raising his hand to signal silence. The wind whistled in our ears and the swell hissed beneath us, but from the direction of the *Albion* came the unmistakable sound of a dog's bark.

"We've left the ship's mascot on board," declared Cochrane. There was an awful pause and then he continued, "We'll have to go back. She is one of God's creatures, and she has put her trust in us and so we'll not forsake her. Put the tiller over, Mister Parnell."

There were cries of disbelief within the boat, which only stimulated the boatswain to make free with his rope's end. My mind refused to take this new information on board. We couldn't seriously be risking a dozen lives for the sake of a dog! Had everyone gone insane? I felt Robinson's rope crack across my shoulder, and I realised I had stopped rowing. His starter had the desired effect and I pulled on my oar with all my strength. If I was to have a chance of survival speed was essential. The pinnace curved neatly back towards the pregnant vessel, and Cochrane leapt expertly from the bow onto the netting. As he disappeared over the rail, I could visualise the nightmarish situation of a frightened dog scampering away from His Lordship. The larboard oarsmen had boated their oars and were hanging onto the side of the floating bomb. We all stared into the darkness above, anxiously awaiting the reappearance of our Commodore. I thought I saw him reappear at the rail virtually every second. My palms started to sweat, and it was impossible to sit still on the thwart.

Was it to end here? Blown to smithereens whilst bobbing about in a ship's tender rescuing a fox terrier!

At last! Cochrane's behind appeared above me. He clambered down towards us. "We still have five minutes to stand clear," he said as he fought with his free hand to control the squirming brown and white dog. I was struck by the playfulness of the terrier we were all risking our lives for. What a terrific game she must have thought it was!

"Make way," ordered Parnell from the stern sheets.

I lowered my blade gratefully into the water and pulled frantically on the oar. When I bent a second time, my panic began to subside. Bending to my oar the third time, the night sky was split asunder as *Albion* erupted into a mountain of vivid, red flame. The fuse had burnt out early in the wind, and the sound emanating from the conflagration was like nothing heard before by mankind. It was like the Almighty clapping heaven and hell together. The sea convulsed as if hit by a tidal wave, and our boat was lifted up like a cork and dropped into a vast trough. The power of the explosion rendered me paralysed with fear and unable to assist in anyway, but I saw Parnell react instantly and throw his weight against the tiller, so that the pinnace rode the wall of water bow-on. The air above me was alive with the explosions of shells and bore a huge cargo of burning timbers, shrapnel and flame. I could see the fearful debris arc thirty feet above us because it lit the sky as brightly as a summer's day. Ahead of us, the sea exploded into life as the awesome shower of wood and iron crashed down. It was like a broadside from the entire home fleet landing in the water not fifty yards away.

As I clung to the side of the boat, I heard Cochrane shout, 'If we hadn't returned for the dog we'd all have perished under that, Mister Parnell' as he fought to maintain his balance and retain the now terrified dog in the dancing pinnace.

"God save us that we're a nation of animal lovers, My Lord," yelled Parnell in reply.

CHAPTER SIX
The Atlantic Coast of France - 12th April 1809

Of the fleet of fifteen French men-of-war skulking in Aix Roads on the morning of the 12th, five were burnt and several others extensively damaged following the daring attack led by Captain Lord Thomas Cochrane. A ninety foot boom of log and chain that had been anchored to the sea bed was blown apart by a number of 'explosion' vessels which were the invention of Lord Cochrane. This idea had originally been most strenuously opposed by the commander of the fleet, Admiral Lord Gambier, as too barbaric.

The Morning Chronicle, 19th April 1809

My mind was as convulsed as the ocean that boiled around me. A heady concoction of adrenalin and fear left me incapable of clear thinking. I clung desperately to the gunwale of the pitching pinnace, begging for the tumultuous waves to abate. My fingers dug so deeply into the boat's timbers my nails were bleeding, and my mouth was in such need of spittle that the dryness was torturous.

Even though the terror of the explosion had reduced my brain to mush, I knew, in the single instant of that tremendous, brilliant flash, that if I survived this ordeal it was imperative to run from the Navy. Giving fate the option of another roll of the dice and another perilous situation was not an option. As it was, we had been unbelievably lucky; a few seconds earlier and we would have died under the debris of the explosion, a few seconds later and we would have been scattered over the ocean in a million pieces. This war was not of my concern, I had not asked to be part of it. Why should I sacrifice my life because George wanted to play 'king of the castle' with Bonaparte?

What remained of *Albion* was still afloat: burning brightly astern of us. Weak moonlight highlighted the billowing clouds of sulphurous smoke that issued from inside her, and hid the French fleet from view.

The wild yawing of the pinnace eventually began to subside, and, with it, the muscle-clenching tension began to ebb from inside me. My fear quickly transformed into disbelief, and then into anger. I kept thinking that this simply shouldn't be happening to me. What was I doing clinging to a boat on a rampant ocean surrounded by fire and destruction? I felt the pinnace surge forward, and realised the crewmen around me were beginning to pull on their oars. The smoke that screened us from the guns of the French fleet was only temporary, and I bent my back with the rest of them.

The boat, powered by strong muscles, ploughed ahead into the Atlantic swell towards *Imperieuse*. The light from the flames cast eerie black shadows on the lee side of each wave we rode over, and the body-aching work of pulling against the tide was made ten times harder by nervous exhaustion. The mental torture of waiting for the explosion to happen had sucked the energy out of my body. The boat crew all worked in silence except for one man behind me who was constantly cursing beneath his breath. At each stroke I asked myself, how can I get away from His Majesty's Navy?

We laboriously made our way past a line of fireships with their gaping air holes and their rigging dripping with tar. They were making their way down to the breach we had made, and some of their crews were beginning to climb into boats. Amidst the darkened bowels of the nearest ship, a flame roared into life as the floating incendiary was primed for the destructive task ahead of it. Behind us a second terrific explosion rent the air as another of Cochrane's explosion vessels reached the anchorage.

Eventually, after what seemed a lifetime we came close enough to make out the welcoming, golden curves of the figurehead affixed to *Imperieuse's* stem. We all craved rest and the final hundred yards seemed interminable. I was desperate for the dull thump of the pinnace against the hull of the frigate that would herald an end to the agonising work that tortured my muscles. But instead of finding sanctuary at the frigate's side, I became suddenly aware of an orange aura emanating from somewhere ahead of us. Twisting my head to look over my shoulder, I saw a fireship already fully aflame. Her crew must have panicked and set her alight at least a mile before their release point. She was still some way off, but the westerly winds, which were now slowly veering west-northwest, were driving her, unmistakably, towards the stern of the frigate. Cochrane had seen the danger and was standing on a thwart scouring the ocean for her crew's boat.

"I'll have someone's guts for this," he fumed. As he spoke, a rocket shot from one of the fireship's yards illuminating an erratic, jerky flight path that reminded me of a frightened snipe breaking cover on a Somerset moor. It crashed into the sea no more than a cable's length from our starboard bow. "Mister Ebbs, put Mister Parnell and I aboard the flagship, and take the pinnace to tow that rogue ship out of harm's way."

The shoulders of every man aboard slumped at the prospect of more back-aching toil. The voice behind me growled angrily and none too quietly this time. At the same time, it dawned upon me that these circumstances could work in my favour: this could well turn out to be the opportunity to run that I had been hoping for. With the officers gone there would be ten men aboard a boat commanded only by a boy and the Bo'sun. We were surrounded by burning shipping, and if we were not seen again who was to say what had happened to us? There was no reason to think the other members of the crew were any more loyal than I was. All impressed men dreamt of running, didn't they? I was sure that they would go along with a mutiny: all that had to be done was to seed the idea amongst them.

My first problem was what to do with Ebbs? He was my friend, perhaps my only friend! He would have to be coerced to come with us, but if he refused I had to stay strong and see this thing through. My mind was beginning to race, there should be no trouble in a twenty foot pinnace crossing the English Channel, the two masts were stowed beneath the thwarts after all, but what if we were stopped? A ship's boat heading for England with no officers on board would look suspicious, and discovery would almost certainly mean death. I'd often heard it said that bravery was a response to fear. I didn't feel brave, but my desire to get away was so overwhelming that I was able rid my mind of all thoughts of the possible consequences. My plotting was interrupted when the pinnace finally bumped alongside *Impérieuse* beneath her tumblehome. Cochrane and Parnell leapt onto the large, block steps that ran down her hull.

"Carry on, Mister Ebbs," instructed Cochrane as he climbed up to his ship.

Ebbs was preoccupied with preparing for his new task, and, as he ordered the boat to pull away, he was blissfully unaware of the resentful looks being exchanged amongst his crew. As we dragged on our oars and steadily pulled away from the frigate, a malignant silence settled over the pinnace. Another rocket darted from the fireship adding a splash of brilliance to the pale moonlight above us. I looked into each of the crewman's faces in front of me. I was convinced they were angry enough to support my plan, but what was the best way to activate it? I glanced round to see who the angry man was who sat behind me. It was Jas Capel. I hated Capel, but in this situation he could well turn out to be a powerful ally. As my next pull on my oar reached completion, I turned and muttered to him, "This could be our chance."

"What do you mean?"

"To run!" I hissed.

I reached forward to take another stroke but let the blade of my oar rise above the water and merely lent back on my thwart.

"There's ten of us in a boat pulling away from the fleet," I whispered over my shoulder. Capel was resting on his oar, like me, and I could smell his foul breath as he replied.

"Aye, an' only a lad and one petty officer to stop us."

I felt a tingle of excitement at his answer. "Will the others join in?" I asked sotto voce.

"Croskell and Rayment are my mates an' they'll do as I says," answered Capel.

"Do you know any more of them?"

"I knows Mawgan, that's the surly looking bastard with a beard in the stern, to be a good 'un. I'm sure he'll back us: that makes five. That's enough!"

"What about the Midshipman?" I hissed.

"To hell with the little bastard," said Capel, and with that, apparently, our conspiracy was settled. Capel stood up and turned to Ebbs who sat in the stern sheets. "Why should we 'ave to go,

Sir?" he yelled at Ebbs who was ferreting under the thwart for a grappling iron and line to take the burning ship under tow. He looked up at Capel, but he was so astonished at this affront to his authority that he said nothing.

"We wuz nearly all blown to kingdom come, and we've just pulled back against a runnin' tide. We're all but done-in, an' draggin' that ship is too much I say," Capel carried on.

It was exactly what I had wanted to happen, but wished Capel had waited until we had found out how many men were with us before he had taken action. Nevertheless, I had started this evil tide running and now I would have to sail before it.

Finally, Ebbs grasped the situation and he bawled back, "Belay that talk, Capel!" with as much authority as he could muster in his young voice. "If we don't divert that fire ship the frigate could be set ablaze."

"He's right! Capel's bloody right."

The words had shot out of my mouth involuntarily. This was it: now I'd committed myself to mutiny!

Ebbs stood up and stared back at me in stunned silence.

"What did you say, Egan? That sounded all but mutinous to me," he said slowly.

The look on his face made me feel sick with guilt, and made my head begin to swim. I had no wish to betray him, but there was no other choice left. My mind was made up. I was running, and I was starting right now.

"We're takin' the boat, Mister Ebbs, and striking back for England. You should come with us," I found myself shouting back.

"Are you quite mad, Egan? You'll do as you're told," the boy yelled ignoring my suggestion. "Another word out of you and you'll feel Mister Robinson's rope's end."

His face was flushed with anger, and I could see that his fingers were trembling.

"You stow it, Egan, or I'll belt you proper." I heard Robinson growl from the bow behind me. "An' you Capel, take your seat and shut your mouth."

The crew had all stopped rowing and were twisting in their seats, captivated by the unfolding drama. Were they all with us, or had I just pronounced my own death sentence? Glancing up at Capel, I could see he was not about to obey Robinson's order. Ebbs was glowering at us, and the Bo'sun was commanding men to get out of his way as he came down the boat, but then there was a shout from one of the larboard crewmen.

"With your permission, Sir. The wind is backin' and the fireship is heading further north."

We all looked, and the ship's course had indeed altered slightly. It was no longer bound directly for *Imperieuse*. She was also noticeably slowing down as more of her sail disappeared in the flames.

"Let's keep pullin' towards her, mates. We don't want anyone from the frigate thinkin' anything is amiss," growled Capel, as he sat back to his oar.

"You don't want anybody to think what, Capel?" barked Ebbs, but Capel didn't reply and began to row.

I started to pull at my oar and a couple of the others joined in with me.

"Belay rowing!" yelled the Midshipman as he pushed his way into the middle of the boat. "Capel, what do you mean? Why don't you want anyone seeing us from the frigate," he demanded, but Capel ignored him and those of us who were pulling belligerently stuck to our oars.

"This is mutiny!" Ebbs screamed.

By now Robinson had reached Ebbs' side, and it was him that attempted to restore order.

"By God, you'll do as the officer orders, or I'll see you all swingin' from a yardarm," he yelled.

"Stick to your guns, Jas."

I turned to see where the encouragement came from, and it was Croskell, the bow oar. Capel had been right to count on his support.

"You can't get away with this, you fools. The penalty for running from the enemy is death," Robinson growled letting his starter swing provocatively from his hand. "What do you think your doin'?"

"I think the situation is clear to everybody except a fool like you, Robinson," I bawled, glaring up at him but still pulling on my oar.

The white heat of the moment had shredded all my inhibitions, but it was heartening to hear a couple of shouts of approval from behind me. The boat crew were going along with the mutiny, and the quicker we could take control the safer we would be. But I knew that Robinson would do everything he could to stop us.

There was uncontrolled anger in his eyes as he swung back viciously with his knotted rope's end, but Capel was quickly on his feet and grabbed his arm before he could strike a downward blow.

"Steady on there, Robbo! What do you want to do that for? You ain't a bad sort. A bit thick for sure, but you could still come with us. You might be useful," said Capel.

"You're going nowhere, Capel! Now sit back down before any more damage is done. If you all return to your duties, I shall overlook this as a moment's madness, but if there's any more of this nonsense I'll report you all for sedition," snapped Ebbs.

"I can't do this anymore, Jacob. I've got to get away!" I shouted.

I used his Christian name without thinking. Ebbs' eyes widened to the size of saucers and stared back at me dumbstruck, the harsh shadows thrown from the flames on the fireship seemingly accentuating his disbelief.

"I would never have thought this of you Egan. Don't be a fool! You will be hunted down like dogs if you run from a battle. You must contemplate the dishonour, and the shame upon your eternal soul," he screamed.

"Who's to tell that we've run from a battle, Mr Ebbs?" interjected Capel, uttering each word with menacing relish.

Robinson made a grab for him and said, "Capel, I'm arresting you for mutiny and ___"

"You ain't arrestin' anyone, you lackey," spat Capel, who then produced a short, hand-fashioned knife from the back of his waistband. He drove it deep into Robinson's stomach and ripped it in an upward motion towards his chest. I was still seated on the thwart as blood spurted from the wound, splattering over my neck and shoulder. Capel swung one of his gigantic fists at the Bo'sun's head, and sent him tumbling over the starboard gunwale still grasping the awful wound in his gut. His head sickeningly snapped back as his face smashed against my oar, and he splashed into the water. Ebbs tried to draw the short, curved sword that hung at his left hip, but Mawgan reached forward and grabbed his arm.

"Egan, get that man back aboard!" Ebbs shouted.

"Egan, you leave him where he be," grunted Capel.

I stumbled mechanically to my feet, but it was too late to make a grab for Robinson who was drifting face down away from the boat. I stood before Ebbs, feeling wretched as we both swayed to the ocean's motion. Events had accelerated much quicker than I had imagined. My plan had not included murder and Capel had no cause to butcher Robinson, but even this couldn't deflect from my decision to run. Not that my certainty made it any easier to look Ebbs in the eye. Betrayal and disbelief were etched on his young features, and I felt worthless as I stared back at him.

"Turn this boat around and retrieve Mr Robinson," Ebbs shouted to the boat in general, but his confidence had deserted him and he delivered his order without conviction. He sounded like a young boy pleading for another helping of pudding.

"Stow it, Your Majesty, you ain't in command of this boat an' there's nothing you can do for Robinson anyhow," growled Capel.

"What's our plan, Jas?" asked Mawgan, who was still pinning Ebbs' sword arm behind his back.

We hadn't thought far enough ahead to have a plan, and Capel turned to me with an enquiring expression written plainly across his ugly face. I was at a loss what to say, but then, over his shoulder, I saw a way out.

"Look, behind the burning ship," I shouted. "They're victualling barges. One of them sailing back to England would arouse no suspicion."

Capel's face lit up.

"That's it. We'll take one o' they," he said gleefully. "There won't be no more than a couple of men an' a boy on 'em ..." He paused and scanned the gaggle of seamen around him. "I takes it that we are all in this thing together, or are there others who want to go the same way as Robbo?" he said grimly.

There was a ripple of affirmative answers, but one or two of the voices were less enthusiastic than others. Capel was a dangerous man, and no one was likely to voice a challenge to him when he was in this mood.

"What to do with you? That's the problem," said Capel as he turned to Ebbs, and yanked the sword from the midshipman's scabbard. "Do you want to come with us, and seek a living away from the King's service?"

"I'd rather die than associate with muck like you, Capel," replied Ebbs.

"That's easily arranged, Lord High 'n Mighty," roared Capel, raising the cutting edge of the curved navy hanger to Ebbs' throat.

"No!" I screamed and leapt in front of Capel, pushing him away from Ebbs. My mind raced for an explanation Capel might accept. "If we murder an officer it'll go against us if we're caught," I said glancing at Ebbs, but he just glared back at me in cold defiance.

"If we don't cut up the privileged little shit, he'll sing out chapter an' verse on us," interjected Croskell, who, along with the rest of the crew, had moved into the middle of the boat.

"Look, there's *Redpole*," I blurted out pointing at the distinctive line of three white lights and one red that had marked our channel to Aix Roads. "When we get near the victualling barges we can throw him overboard, and the tide will help him swim down to her."

I glanced again at my erstwhile friend, and this time imagined that I could detect faintest manifestation of gratitude in his expression.

"I've not got the stomach for more killin'," said Mawgan.

"Egan might be right," added Croskell. "There ain't no point in gutting an officer if we don't 'ave to. If he does reach the light vessel, they'll have to stay on their station for hours, and won't be able to signal till morning even if they wanted to."

"Right then, first we 'ave to get a line on that fireship or the frigate will be wondering what's going on. We'd better all get back to the oars," barked Capel. The crew seemed to have accepted him as their leader. "We'll just tow 'er a couple of points farther north and let 'er go," he shouted.

Mawgan sat Ebbs down in the middle of the thwart that faced me. He was trembling either from shock or outrage, or possibly a mixture of the two.

"Judas!"

He almost spat the word at me.

"Jacob, this war has nothing to do with ___ "

The voice he used to interrupt me was mangled with emotion, "I have never encountered a betrayal as callous as yours, Nathaniel."

"My betrayal isn't of you, Jacob, but of King George and his Navy. If you remember, I didn't ask to be here," I replied.

"But you murdered the Bo'sun without remorse."

"I just have to get away. I'm sorry for Robinson, but there was nothing I could do about that."

Ebbs' clammed up, his unseeing eyes stared straight into mine and the fireship illuminating his dispirited face as we crested each wave.

It didn't take us long to reach the burning ship, and Capel hit the cat's head with his first throw of the grappling iron. A few minutes of agonising effort at our oars dragged the nose of the ship round, until she was set squarely in front of the wind.

"Right lads, that'll do," growled Capel, and we gratefully rested. "Cut the line and we'll go an' take a look at who's on board that victualling ship," he said, pointing at a sloop that sat in the shallows someway behind *HMS Redpole*.

As we approached the murky shape of the supply-sloop off our larboard side, Midshipman Jacob Ebbs, shorn of his scabbard, jacket and boots, leapt over the starboard gunwale of the pinnace, and was swallowed up by the dark Atlantic swell as he swam for his life.

CHAPTER SEVEN
The Bay of Biscay - 16th April 1809

My Lords, I wish to bring to your attention, once again, the plague of desertion that afflicts His Majesty's navy. The problem escalates within my own squadron as each year of war passes. As I am sure you are aware, our beloved Lord Nelson wrote that, 'Whenever a large convoy assembles at Portsmouth and our fleet is in port not less than 1000 men desert'.

If I were to anchor anywhere within reasonable reach of landfall, I would have to expect to lose a dozen swimmers from every ship, each night.

I would humbly suggest to your Lordships that we consider releasing impressed men after, let us say, fifteen years service in the hope that they would find more appetite for their duty.

Extract of a letter to the Sea Lords from Captain Jeremiah Blythe, 1808

It was four days since we had made our escape from Basque Roads, and my taut nerves were beginning to relax. With my mind no longer preoccupied with my immediate survival, memories of my Mary were seeping back into my consciousness: where they mingled with my guilt over the betrayal of Jacob Ebbs. My depressed mien was, however, countered by the reappearance of a comforting, if unexpected, glimmer of optimism. I stood at the tiller of *Brixham Belle*, the fat, single masted supply sloop we had commandeered, and felt that the future was back under my own control. A warm sun was high in the sky and a brisk wind beat on my face as the ungainly sloop rolled down the back of each swell. I was heading back towards England, a free man once again.

Brixham Belle had not been built for speed or comfort but for girth and capacious holds. Her bluff bows smashed through the waves rather than riding over them, and she was making very slow, uncomfortable progress in the westerly seas. We were tacking out into the ocean, away from the French coast and hopefully away from the attendant British naval blockade. The other nine mutineers were clustered in front of me, squabbling like children about when it would be safe to turn towards the Western Approaches. Capel, who was keen to make all our decisions for us, was demonstrating that he had no knowledge of the sea whatsoever.

"We 'ave gone out too far by now ... we'll miss England completely if we stay at this. We should 'ave turned north two days ago," he barked.

"You'd 'ave us broken up on Ushant, Jas," Mawgan replied laughing. "It's plain to see that you are no sailor."

"No, I 'aint," shot back Capel with a malevolent gleam in his eye, "an' don't you take the piss, or I'll slice you up like I did for Robinson."

"Calm yourself, Jas. I 'aint funnin' you. We're nigh on four hundred miles out now an' a course of north-northeast should be safe enough," said Mawgan. He had been checking the charts below and taking noon sights with the sextant over the last few days, and so I was content to trust his navigation.

"Do you think we'll still be far enough out to avoid the blockade?" I shouted from my position at the tiller.

Mawgan heard my question and turned to look at me. "I think we should be, Nat. We'll 'ave to take our chance sometime."

"Shall I bear away then?" I asked tentatively.

Several voices shouted in agreement, but I noticed that Mawgan waited for a nod from Capel before he raised his hand in acknowledgement.

Shouting a warning, I swung the tiller across causing *Brixham Belle* to sluggishly turn her bows away from the wind. Mawgan set the crew to easing sheets and the hemp stays groaned as the pressure relaxed on our sails. The heavy boom whistled out across our starboard beam and flicked playfully above the Atlantic waves. I kept *Belle* turning, and watched the big compass in the binnacle in front of me tick round to settle on north-northeast. Mawgan had the sheets run back in, and the patched, red mainsail shaped into a smooth, deep curve.

The sloop's master had been of no assistance to us whatsoever since we had clambered aboard his vessel in Aix Roads. He was a small man, of late middle-age and he spent most of his time sitting sullenly at the taff rail. I knew that his name was George Stayham because it was written on the log book. His crew comprised of one very slow-witted, young man who spoke only occasionally, and when he did he suffered a stutter so disabling that he was unable to articulate more than two or three words at a time. The pair of them sat behind me, watching in silence as I brought the tiller amidships and *Brixham Belle* settled onto Mawgan's new course.

"Sail ahead!"

The cry from the bow caught me by surprise. There was a flurry of activity as everyone, saving Stayham, the boy and myself, ran forward to take a look. I knew full well that it would be at least half an hour before they would be able to discern any detail of the newcomer above the horizon, and so I lent against the tiller and waited for someone to come and tell me what they could see. Presently, Capel made his way back to the cockpit, and steadied himself against one of the backstays.

"She be a cutter. Could be a King's ship, but she looks a little small and we can't make out no colours," he grunted. "Is there some signal we should make if she's a Royal Navy vessel?" he said turning to Stayham.

"You cowards should make whatever signal what you think best," replied Stayham defiantly, without so much as a glance at his interrogator. It didn't seem to me that this was his brightest course of action, and I could have predicted Capel's response.

"Well if you're going to be of no use to me, I think it best to slit your gizzard and dump you over the side!" bellowed Capel, glowering at the old seaman.

"No, no… there is no signal. The King's Navy don't treat merchant supply vessels with any respect," said Stayham apologetically, which stuck me as the more sensible approach.

"When we gets close by, we'll all hide in the hold and take the fool with us. You stay on deck with the old sea dog," instructed Capel. "If he speaks out o' turn, I'll lacerate his idiot."

I couldn't help but notice anxiety flash into Stayham's eyes when the boy was mentioned and guessed that he was his son.

Nothing happened quickly aboard *Brixham Belle*, and it was a full hour before I could clearly make out the clean lines of the little cutter. Her lines were as pretty as you like: with a straight bow and a long counter stern. She was painted a medium grey, which was not a popular colour among naval officers, and as Capel had suspected she flew no ensign. She was heading straight for us, but her progress was a little erratic and her rig was sloppily trimmed: not making full use of the following wind. Capel ushered the men and the boy below deck. He adopted a position on the hold companion where he could see Stayham and me but was hidden himself. As the two vessels closed upon each other, I could clearly make out damage to the cutter's sides, and what looked like shot holes in her fore-sails. She stood a little way off us, and then slowly turned to windward and hove-to. I saw life on the cutter for the first time as a figure struggled to stand up-right by her stern rail.

"Ahoy, sloop there!" the man shouted. "Are you English?"

Brixham Belle flew a dowdy union flag from her gaff, but this was obviously a man who took no chances.

"Aye, supply sloop *Brixham Belle*, late of Captain Lord Cochrane's squadron, and making passage for England," I bellowed in reply.

"I've come to ask your help, Sir. This is pilot cutter *Peggy Ann*. We've been attacked by privateers and I fear my crewman is mortally injured."

I looked at Capel and said quietly, "He sounds in trouble. We should help him."

"It could be some sort o' trick."

"They're genuine shot holes in his sails and he's English," I replied.

Capel craned his neck over the raised edge of the hold, "Would I be right in thinkin' that that would be a fairly swift craft?" he asked.

"She certainly looks it, Jas. Are we going over there?"

He nodded his consent, and I shouted, "We'll come across," towards the cutter.

Capel instructed Croskell to take care of the Stayhams, and to keep the rest of the men below deck. We boarded *Belle's* little landing tender that we had been towing behind us, and I pulled the short way to the cutter. I left Capel hanging onto the main chains and clambered up the side. As my head rose above the gunwale, I saw that her deck was in some disarray. A prone figure lay forward of the mast, and the man who was making a show of helping me over the side seemed dazed and unsteady on his feet.

"A schooner attacked us a few hours ago ...," he said, hesitantly. "They were shouting at us to heave-to, but I didn't like the look of them. They had guns ... six-pounders I think ... and they started firing at us as we went past... Josh, that's my crewman," the fellow gesticulated towards the figure on the deck, "caught one in the chest and I ran forward to help him, but she gybed and I was flattened by the boom." He paused for a second or two and gulped in a few mouthfuls of air. "It was all I could do to turn us south ... I didn't think they'd follow us towards France ... knowin' that the Navy would be there."

"Who were they?" I asked, watching Capel climb onto the deck and kneel over the crewman.

"From their accents, I'd say they were Welsh," said the shaken sailor. I glanced at Capel who pulled an ugly grimace and shook his head in response to my unspoken question, and then he slipped, uninvited and unseen by the sailor, below deck.

"My name is Samuel Barkas, and I'm a Bristol Channel pilot by trade," the fellow continued.

I introduced myself and asked, "What were you doing so far south?"

"I was searching for merchant shippin' in need of pilotage, and I stopped a fisherman to ask if they 'ad seen any likely vessels," replied Barkas. He was swaying slowly from side to side and clinging firmly to the rail to keep himself upright.

"Was it a French fisherman?" interjected Capel sarcastically from the little coach house door that stood on the cutter's afterdeck. "It smells like a Froggie distillery down 'ere. I think a shot has broached some of your contraband, Mister Pilot!"

Barkas looked up at me a little sheepishly. "The fisherman was French," he said apologetically. "I was loading brandy from him; that's how the schooner crept up on us... but I don't think you two tars are that innocent either!"

He pointed unsteadily at the stern of *Brixham Belle*, where a cluster of men were standing on the deck. "I don't think the King's Navy puts ten men in a supply vessel!" he said accusingly.

"Bloody Croskell, never could do what I tells him," hissed Capel between his teeth.

"I need to lie down," Barkas said, turning towards me. As his hand left the rail, he staggered and I reached out to support him. He put his hand on my arm, and his weight slumped against me. "Could you help me down the companionway?" he asked. "Perhaps your friend would be good enough to wrap Josh in a hammock?"

It took me some little time to help him to a small cabin at the rear of the cutter. When we finally got there, it was so cramped that it wasn't easy to manoeuvre him onto the cot suspended from a deck beam. He was a well-built man of about forty, and when I lowered him down, I could see congealed blood on the back of his head. He had obviously taken a huge blow from the boom when it had swung out of control across the boat. Finding a basin, I filled it with water from a small cask in the corner of the cabin. Easing him onto his side, I began a rudimentary attempt at bathing his wound. As I was engaged in my doctoring, I was aware of Capel clambering back over the cutter's side and wondered what he was up to.

"The men who attacked you, were they privateers?" I asked after a short while.

"No, Welsh free-traders I reckon. They do fair enough trade runnin' contraband home, but discovered 'tis cheaper to steal somebody else's goods than buy your own," replied Barkas in a resigned voice, but my efforts seemed to be reviving him a little. "There's a bottle in the locker yonder," he said pointing. "Can I have a drink?"

Pouring him a healthy measure, I asked, "Did you know the Frenchmen you were buying from?"

"Aye, Jean and Emile Goriau. They sell cognac in the Scillies, an' I reckon the Welshmen got wind of their business, an' decided to muscle in on it." The combination of strong spirit and lying down definitely perked him up because he now seemed quite keen to talk. "I'd met up with Jean and Emile south of St.Agnes, and we had seen a schooner hull down on the horizon. We headed southwest for that day and the following night an' thought we had got rid of 'em, but they attacked us when we were loading at first-light. I don't think the Frenchmen knew anything about it but they may 'ave," he said thoughtfully.

"It sounds like a precarious living. Apart from being attacked by rival gangs, aren't you frightened of being caught by the Navy?" I asked.

"The Navy's got its hands full. What with the blockade and all. Besides, I'm too small a fish for some cruiser captain to bother with. I did see a squadron of men-of-war heading south a week or so ago. Is that where you've run from?" he said, putting down his glass and lying back on his cot.

"We've left our squadron off Rochefort," I replied. There seemed little point in denying the obvious. "We took that old sloop," I indicated towards *Brixham Belle* with my head. "I'd not asked to serve in the King's Navy and when I was forced to sail a floating bomb straight for the French fleet, I knew that I had to get away."

"You don't have to explain yer self to me," Barkas said, turning his head to look at me. "I don't think King George should be fightin' the French at all, and I'm not one for payin' his new income tax or import duties which fund his folly."

"You don't think that we should try to resist Bonaparte at all?" I asked.

"I thinks the danger of invasion is well passed, and the likes o' you an' I have far more in common with a workin' Frenchman than we do with the hoity-toity bastards that decided we should be fightin' Bonaparte."

His words sent a surge of relief surge through my body.

"King George has done nothing for me, and I feel no guilt for running from his ship, but I betrayed a good friend to do so and for that I feel a burning guilt," I said.

"Don't, lad. I've sailed for the King myself, and I know how the desperation for liberty builds up inside a man," said Barkas with a little of the heat leaving his voice.

I had not doubted my decision to run from Aix Roads, but I hadn't had time to examine my emotions since the mutiny. Talking to Barkas, my thoughts just tumbled out of my mouth without me having to think about them.

"If a man decides he wants to fight in the Navy, is well paid and has some knowledge of when he may leave that is one thing, but to enslave a man against his will; that is a different thing entirely."

"If Englishmen could vote, an' had a stake in their own country they might be more inclined to fight for it," replied Barkas displaying a note of revolutionary fervour.

Our debate was interrupted by the sound of the tender bumping against the cutter's hull. Within a minute or two, there was the rasp of boots on the companion ladder, and I knew that there was more than one newcomer because of the accompanying sound of bare feet on the deck above us. A few moments later, the cabin door opened and Capel's ugly face appeared.

"I've been over to *Brixham Belle*, and I've brought Croskell and Mawgan back over 'ere with me," he said.

"Did you take care of poor Josh for me?" asked Barkas.

"It so 'appens that I did, old man," Capel replied unpleasantly. Barkas looked at me and raised his eyebrows, but he didn't reply.

"Why have you brought Croskell and Mawgan on board?" I asked.

"It struck me that that bastard Stayham would dob us in it given half a chance," he said. "Besides, if anyone's lookin' for us they'll be searchin' for ten men, so I reckon we'll all be safer if we split up. This little beauty will speed us 'ome a fair sight quicker than that old tub!"

On hearing this Barkas lay flat on his cot and shut his eyes.

"I'm sure Mister Smuggler 'ere can get us safely ashore when the time comes," Capel concluded with a hint of menace in his voice.

❖   ❖   ❖

Hoping that he would sleep, I left Barkas alone, and didn't return to the little cabin until about five hours later, as dusk was gathering around us. It was difficult to know what to say to him. It was important he didn't think that I had only played the Good Samaritan to gain his trust whilst secretly plotting with Capel to take over his boat. I was already smarting with guilt from my betrayal of Ebbs, and had no desire to load myself with more reasons for self-loathing. However, I knew that delivering a believable explanation of what I was doing sailing with a man like Capel would be no easy task.

It was with some trepidation that I pushed open the cabin door, *Peggy Ann* was well stocked with victuals, and I took some hard bread and a hunk of cheese as a peace offering.

"Are you awake, Samuel?" I asked. His body stirred and he turned his face towards me but didn't reply. "How are you feeling?"

"I've a head like I've ne'r felt afore," he groaned, "an' I feel like I need to sleep for a day or two."

"I had no idea Capel was going to invite himself onboard. He had said nothing to me," I blurted out, as soon as I sat down by his cot.

"Calm yourself, Nathaniel," Barkas said, raising a placatory hand. "I've had plenty of experience of 'is sort. Now, tell me 'ow are you doin' with *Peggy Ann*?"

I was caught unawares by his acceptance of the situation, and it took me a few moments to redirect my thoughts. "I've spent the last few hours at her tiller," I eventually replied. "She's a real beauty."

"I can feel her movements lyin' here. You done well for someone who don't know her. She takes some handlin' does *Peggy Ann*," he said slowly. "Who's that up there now?"

"That's Mawgan."

"He's doin' alright, but he hasn't got the feel for her that you 'ad."

"He was a quartermaster's mate in the Navy. He's set us a course for the Severn Estuary. What do you think of that, Samuel?" I asked, gently.

"Aye, that's well and good. I want to get back into the Bristol Channel." He paused for a moment and looked at me quizzically, before he asked, "Is that big bugger in control?"

"Jas Capel has appointed himself as the leader of our band of mutineers___" I started to explain.

"Can he sail?" Barkas interrupted.

"No. Capel's just a bully boy. He cut up a petty officer that we could have left alone___" Barkas held up his hand to stop me once more.

"So 'e won't want to keep *Peggy* after he's got back to England then?"

"No ... all their talk is of what to do when they get back on dry land."

"Now listen to me, Nathaniel," he propped himself up on his elbow and looked straight into my eyes. "You strike me as a fellow a body could trust."

"What's the matter, Samuel?"

"I think I could be lying in this cot for some time before my 'ead clears, and I need someone to sail *Peggy Ann* for me."

"Well, we have to do that if we want to get back to England," I said. "Mawgan is useful about the sextant, and Croskell can helm well enough."

"I know they *can* sail her home. What I mean is that I need somebody I could trust to be up on deck for me. I don't know these men from Adam, and this is the second vessel they've taken. I want you to make sure they go ashore and leave me my boat." His voice rose as he spoke, and it was obvious that he had been lying awake fretting over the future of his cutter. "From my point of view, I would be better to ally myself with someone who I think would be prepared to give her back in a couple of day's time, an' I trust you more than I do Capel and those others."

I found myself saying, "You can put your faith in me, Samuel." After my betrayal of Ebbs I was glad of a chance to reclaim some self-respect. "I'll do everything possible to make sure that we all disappear when we make England, and you can go back about your business unmolested."

"Why not stay with me?"

"What do you mean, Samuel?"

"Why not stay aboard with me after we put those other bastards ashore? I can keep you safe. I was one of the lucky few who were paid-off durin' the Peace of Amiens. My ship was old an' she was due to be broken up anyway. I started workin' as a pilot, an' they rewarded me with an 'Admiralty Protection'." (NOTE: *The Treaty of Amiens was signed in March 1802 and suspended hostilities between France and the United Kingdom for a little over one year. Egan was a teenager at the time, and remembered the celebrations that had been held at his home in Lilstock. Barkas received his 'Admiralty Protection' from the Press because Channel pilots belonged to one of the exempt professions that were deemed necessary to sustain Britain's overseas trade*).

"You're safe from the Press? ... safe from naval service?"

"Aye, I've a passport for life, and the right to keep two crewmen on this vessel. So I'm askin' you to stay with me and sail in safety, if not in honesty!"

It was astonishing to be made such a generous offer by somebody I had known so briefly. I was so shocked that my response was to stare back at him with my mouth wide open.

"Well, what do you think?" he demanded, after a moment or two.

All my instincts were screaming at me that this was a proposition to leap at, I had no other plans to consider, and nowhere else to go when we reached England. Barkas was a decent man, and I sensed that we could coexist quite happily. Even if it didn't work out, I would be no worse off than now.

"Thank-you, Samuel. I don't know what to say ... I am honoured that you should ask me sail with you in *Peggy Ann*," I finally blurted out, when the gift of speech returned to me. "I think we can sail her to good effect, but how do we guard against future attacks from the Welsh pirates?"

"Don't worry about them, Nat. They won't catch Samuel Barkas out again. I can promise you that! In future, we'll be goin' about our business in far more surreptitious ways. The question is can I rely on you?"

"You may depend on me, Samuel." I proffered my hand and he shook it firmly.

"You can depend on both of us!"

Both of our heads corkscrewed round, to see Capel standing at the cabin door.

"What a spectacular cover for a couple o' mutineer's, eh? Sailin'under a King's Passport."

Obviously, I had left the door open, and he had taken it upon himself to follow me and eavesdrop on our conversation.

"We shall just be puttin' Croskell and Mawgan ashore when we reach England: that's what I say," he continued, with his widest grin displaying a nearly full set of stained, misshapen teeth, "and then we'll put back to sea as a threesome!"

CHAPTER EIGHT
The Bristol Channel - 18th April 1809

"All manner of corruption, intimidation, violence and murder are perpetrated daily in the execution of smuggling around our shores. It is difficult to fathom the enormity of the so-called 'free-trade', but we suppose smuggling to be a highly organised enterprise aided and supported by the coastal populace and gentry alike. As everyone present is well aware, all trade with France is most stringently prohibited, and yet the consumption of brandy throughout the kingdom has escalated astonishingly. I am well aware, that many members of this house drink brandy apparently without conscience. They are robbing the exchequer of desperately needed funds to fight the upstart Emperor, and ask yourselves this; where does Bonaparte glean his information of British ships and British defences if it is not from the smuggler?"

Chancellor Spencer Perceval speaking in the House of Commons, 1807

Peggy Ann was dancing across the familiar, chocolaty waves of the Bristol Channel, and my spirit danced with her. The sky was bright, the wind steady, and I was starting to feel that my life had a future after all. The only cloud on my immediate horizon was the prospect of a continued association with Jas Capel.

Barkas had announced this morning that we would be setting Croskell and Mawgan ashore later in the day. They were both on the foredeck chatting with Capel, and seemed elated at the prospect of returning to home soil with their ordeal in the navy behind them.

Barkas' health had made a sterling recovery, and he was sitting next to me at the tiller instructing in the intimate nuances of *Peggy Ann's* handling. She was a playful vessel and it was a joy to sail her along the dune-fringed coast-line of Somersetshire. Mastering *Peggy Ann's* capabilities was all part of immersing myself in my new role in life: the role of a smuggler.

The one problem was Barkas' steadfast refusal to explain his plans for Capel. There was no obvious reason for letting him stay with us. Why had he made no attempt to get rid of him? Whenever I tried to question him about it, he was either evasive or just changed the subject. Was he scared of Capel, like we all were, or did he have some task or secret vocation for the huge, repulsive bastard?

I was familiar with this part of the Channel, and understood the huge tides that result from the ocean being funnelled between the West Country and Wales. The massive tidal range creates thousands of acres of brown, mud laden sea, and on falling tides shifting sands can create navigational problems for the unwary (NOTE: *The Bristol Channel and Severn Estuary have the second largest tidal range in the world. The water can rise and fall in excess of 50 feet between high and low water on a spring tide*).

"We'll be landing the brandy and your friends about a mile further up the coast," Barkas said suddenly and without preamble.

"This is a difficult coast to put Croskell and Mawgan ashore, Samuel," I said, eying the miles of mud and sand that fronted the coastline, "but I will feel safer with them on land. Your passport is only good for two, if the Preventive officers stop us …"

"Don't fret; there are no Preventive boats in the Channel."

"How on earth do you know that?" I asked.

"Because of the flag on St. Mary's church at Berrow… yonder," replied Barkas, pointing. About a mile away over the silt laden waters, I could just see the square tower of the church sitting snugly behind a vast bed of swaying reeds.

"There is no flag on the church," I said.

"Exactly," said Barkas triumphantly, "but there was an hour ago. My brother lives in Berrow, and will have seen the Preventive cutter go down the channel. As soon as we hove into view, he hauled down the flag of St.George to let me know that the coast is clear."

"That's a very trim little system, Samuel."

"Aye, that it is! We'll come ashore just before the church tower, so you can start to ease your sheets, Nat."

Slack-water was fast approaching, and the tidal push beneath us was losing its impetus. Nevertheless, the wind alone was strong enough to make manoeuvring *Peggy Ann* towards the Berrow Church an easy task. As we moved nearer to the beach, I could see that it was studded with rows of squat, black posts which ran into the water and gave testimony to the local, herring stake-fishery. Most of the posts were loaded with nets, but there was only one figure silhouetted in front of the low dunes that lay between the muddy beach and flat, green salt-marsh behind them.

"That'll be my brother," Barkas said. "Now hold your course firm and head straight for 'im. Don't wander to either side or you'll have us stuck."

Peggy Ann only drew one and a half fathoms, but her bottom was touching the sand a full cable-length short of the beach. We were even some way shy of where the posts and nets disappeared under the water. A small flock of Green Plovers flew up from the marsh, displaying the bold black and white markings on their under wings, and shouting their plaintive *'peewit'* cries above our heads.

"You're not goin' to get much closer, Nat, turn her into the wind and we'll get the sails down," Barkas instructed. "One last nautical task for you buggers before you begin your new lives as lubbers …," he shouted to Croskell and Mawgan as he left the cockpit and headed for the halyards at the mast.

Within quarter of an hour, *Peggy-Ann* was anchored, nose to wind with her sails neatly furled, and Barkas was giving instructions to Croskell and Mawgan.

"I need you to row the brandy ashore. I only managed to get seven tubs onboard before those Welsh bastards attacked me and one of 'em is broached, so put three in the boat and row 'em over to my brother."

Capel and I launched *Peggy-Ann's* little tender and brought it round to the starboard shrouds, where I tied off the painter. Croskell and Mawgan climbed down into the tender to make her ready to go ashore.

"Then, I want one of ye to come back for the other three and m'self," Barkas shouted down to the little boat.

"You're going ashore, Samuel?"

I was aware that there was an element of surprise in my voice, but he'd not mentioned that he was leaving *Peggy-Ann* himself, and I suddenly felt insecure.

"There are matters I need discuss with my brother. I need to know what shippin' 'as passed while I've been away," he replied in an off-hand sort of way.

Mistrust of Barkas crept into my mind for the first time. Was he going ashore to turn us in? I dismissed the thought almost as quickly as it had appeared. If we were to sail together, we had to trust each other, and he had to go ashore at some point. Unfortunately, Capel didn't have the wit to think twice.

"How do we know you 'aint coming back with a troop of dragoons, an' a couple of extra sovereigns in your pocket?" he roared.

What an arsehole Capel was! His outburst could ruin my future on *Peggy-Ann*.

"Of course, of course, Samuel … we understand," I said submissively to Barkas, in an attempt to reassure him, but Capel was having none of it.

"You speak for yourself, Egan."

The great shit was about to start sounding off. His nostrils began to flare as he poked his ugly face in my direction: a sure indication that he was getting riled.

"I'd like to know what he ___"

"We have to trust him," I shouted back at Capel before he could get really worked up. "We don't have any other choice." I felt my bile for him rise, but I had to try and make him understand. "He has brought us home, and is offering us a future on this boat. Why would he betray us now, you stupid bastard? Can't you think before you speak?"

The venom in my words came as a shock, even to me, and I immediately wished that I had spoken with more care.

"Don't speak to me like that," Capel growled at me, very slowly.

He wasn't accustomed to taking abuse from anyone, and little flecks of spittle flew out of the corners of his mouth as he spoke. I felt the colour drain from my face; I was scared. Capel was the sort who would attack first and ask questions later. It was with great relief that Barkas' voice interrupt us.

"Compose yourselves, the pair of ye," he shouted forcefully. There was fire in his words that I'd not heard before, and Capel attended to what he said. "There'll be no fightin' 'tween you two. If you're to work with me, you'll 'ave to accept what I say." He spoke with stern authority and his face was etched with determination. "I'll not sell you out whilst I'm ashore, and I'll depend on you to take good charge of my boat. We're safely back in English waters now, an' I can promise you that you'll not be bothered 'ere." He then spoke in a kindlier tone. "Why not just rest up? There are 'ooks and line in the locker at the back of the cabin. Catch some fish, treat yourself to a good feed and drink some brandy."

I looked across at Capel. His eyes still held their malevolent gleam, but he seemed to have understood what Barkas had said. For an instant, I had a strange feeling that I had come across him somewhere else: before he ever appeared aboard *Albion*. The atmosphere between us wasn't healthy, but luckily Mawgan's head appeared above the rail and broke the spell.

"We're ready for they tubs now," he announced in a jocular fashion.

"I'll fetch them for you," I said, glad of a reason to get out of the range of Capel's glares.

It only took a few minutes to roll the wooden tubs to the companion and manhandle them up the ladder. At Lilstock Manor, cider and beer were stored in hogsheads and firkins, and I had never seen casks as small as the ones used by the French distillers (NOTE: *Bonaparte was so desperate for gold to pay his troops that he specifically built distilleries close to the Channel ports to supply English smugglers with contraband. Spirits were packed into specifically designed small 'tubs' so that could easily be handled by one man and therefore, quickly moved or concealed*). Capel's brawny arms were strong enough to pass the tubs down to Croskell whilst Mawgan steadied the tender against *Peggy-Ann's* side, and there was no need to rig a whip.

"Pull straight for my brother." Barkas instructed Croskell and Mawgan. "He will mark the deepest channel, and 'e will lead you across the harder ground as you wade ashore. Pay attention to 'im for this mud can swallow up an unwary man!"

"Fear not, we'll keep a true course," Mawgan assured Barkas, and gave him a strange sort of nod which I took to signify his thanks. He then turned to Capel, "You take care, Jas. Don't buy yersen' more trouble than you 'ave to."

He nonchalantly waved towards me, and pushed the bow of the tender away from the cutter and towards the beach. As they started to pull towards the square church tower at Berrow, Barkas touched me on the shoulder and said, "We'll need to set the shoring posts."

Peggy-Ann's shoring posts were large timbers with flat 'feet' attached to the bottom. We set them on the cutter's side so that as the tide dropped the boat would be left standing up on the mud and not roll onto her side. *Peggy-Ann* had solid lugs built into her sides, and the timbers had to be manhandled over the side and slid through them. Barkas and I started to struggle with the nine foot posts with Capel just watching us, seemingly still in a malicious sulk.

"Look lively, Jas," Barkas snapped at him with annoyance. I was shocked by how confident he had become in ordering Capel about, but slightly to my surprise, the giant slowly came to our aid without argument. His strength made light work of our task, and both posts were in position within half-an-hour. By which time, we could already see Mawgan starting to pull away from the beach on his return journey to collect Barkas and the last three tubs of cognac.

Capel disappeared down the companion to collect the brandy, and Barkas turned to me, "I should be back by the next tide, Nathaniel. I'd give that bastard Capel a little space to settle down. Don't try to get 'im to do any work; I want you both to be alive when I return!" I wasn't sure whether he was joking or not, but he didn't allow me any time to mull it over before he delivered more advice."If you set about that broached cask be sure to add plenty of water. That brandy is at least four times the strength of what you're used to. Drink more than a cupful and it'll kill you for sure."

"Why do they make the spirit so strong?" I asked.

"To save space, Nat. We don't want to be luggin' around more weight than we 'ave to, and we can water it down when we get it ashore. The Frenchies are so desperate for English golden guineas that they make everythin' easy for us."

Before long we could hear the clatter of Mawgan clumsily boating oars and the tender bumped alongside. Barkas climbed over the side, and within a few minutes they were on their way back to the shore.

"You're taking a big risk with our lives trustin' him as much as you do," Capel growled in my ear as we watched the little boat work its way towards the beach.

"We have to trust Samuel. Neither of us have too many prospects ashore do we? Trust is a valuable commodity, Jas," I replied.

"Aye, I'd say that it was. A shame that that young Midshipman's trust in you came to naught!" he replied, adding a mocking laugh. His reminder of my betrayal stung badly and I felt another rush of anger. However, one glance at Capel's size and remembering how scared I had been when abusing him earlier, I quickly composed myself. Chastised, I said nothing and busied myself tidying a halyard that lay uncoiled on the deck. The tide steadily ebbed, until finally *Peggy-Ann* settled on the sand, heeling to her starboard side but secure against her shoring-posts.

❖   ❖   ❖

The next tide flooded and ebbed, without any sign of Barkas' return. *Peggy-Ann* was left to sit alone on the desolate acres of sand and mud that filled Bridgwater Bay. I entertained myself preparing a long-line from the hooks and tackle that were in the cabin locker. Capel was equally busy, taking full advantage of the broken brandy cask to remove himself from the sane world with liberally watered jugs of brandy. While he had still been able to speak, he had bored me with an endless litany of anecdotes about the unfortunates he had bullied or assaulted in the past, but eventually the stupefying benefits of very strong liquor came to my aid leaving him sprawling on the deck, thankfully, speechless.

I baited and threw out my long-line, and sat astride the bowsprit drinking in the peace and waiting for the tide to deliver me a fish for breakfast. It was late evening and the pink sky went through a hundred transformations as the sun dipped behind the bulky silhouette that was Steep Holm Island. A lone fulmar petrel glided past the larboard rail on stiff wings and glanced curiously at the beached cutter. I fetched a blanket and threw it over Capel, and headed for my bunk below.

At dawn, I pulled in my line and was rewarded with a couple of more than acceptable codling. The tide was approaching high water, and *Peggy-Ann* was gently lifting off the bottom. I was busily gutting my breakfast when I became aware that Capel was awake.

"Where is the bastard then?" he growled at me from where he lay on the deck.

"Well, obviously he's been delayed," I replied. "It wouldn't be a crime for a man to spend time with his brother."

"It wouldn't be no crime to report a couple of mutineers either," he said sarcastically. He had propped himself up on his left elbow, and even the diffuse light of the early morning was evidently causing him pain and he kept his eyes narrowed to little more than slits. "'Next tide' is what 'e said, an' 'e still 'aint here on the second. If he doesn't show on this 'un, I reckon we should bugger off and leave him where he be."

"I'll get you a drink, Jas, and then you can go back to sleep."

I wasn't about to entertain any thoughts of sailing *Peggy-Ann* with Capel alone. If Barkas didn't return, I would be over the side.

"Water, Egan... I need water bad," Capel bellowed at me, still keeping his eyes nearly closed. "Don't fetch no more brandy."

I filled a leather cup from the water cask and took it too him. He gulped the water down in seconds, and so I took the jug from his side and filled that as well. As often happens, when a man has drunk heavily of spirits, a draught of water in the morning can return him to inebriation. Capel just swore a couple of oaths and fell back flat on the deck again with a thud. I was glad. I didn't need to spend a morning listening to his drivel, but it was irksome Barkas hadn't returned on that second tide.

Capel couldn't be right could he? Had it been Barkas' plan to keep us sitting here while he fetched the soldiers? Finch had lied to me, why not Barkas? He would have been able to guess that I wouldn't sail *Peggy-Ann* away with Capel and so he knew his boat was safe. Was that why he had let Capel stay and taken Mawgan and Croskell ashore when both of them were better sailors than Capel? None of these were very comforting thoughts, and suddenly the Bristol Channel felt a very lonely place. If only Mary was with me! I tried my damnedest to convince myself that my trust was safe in Barkas, but my insecurity wouldn't disappear. In order to distract my mind, I took my cod below to the stove.

After eating, I tried to pass the time by leafing through some of Barkas' books that were jammed onto a small shelf in his cabin. There was a copy of *The Rights of Man* by Tom Paine. It was not a book that I had read, but I had heard it being quoted in arguments by radical hotheads, like Thos Bagley, back in the

Birmingham manufactory (NOTE: *Tom Paine, a Norfolk man, wrote 'The Rights of Man' largely in support of the French Revolution in 1791. Paine was dismissive of hereditary government, and argued for equal political rights for all men. He was anxious that his work should be read by ordinary working families, and he withdrew his copyright to facilitate the production of cheap editions. By the time of his death in 1809 more than 1,500,000 copies had been sold throughout Europe and at least 250,000 in Britain*). My eyes scanned the dense type, but it was difficult to concentrate. My mind was constantly re-examining Barkas' continuing absence. It was a struggle to assimilate Paine's arduous text, and I found myself reading and re-reading the same paragraphs. I must have sat there for two or three hours, over which time I read no more than five or six pages. Eventually, Paine's views on a just society beat me, and I fell asleep on the cabin bench.

When I awoke, the sun was high in the sky and streaming through the cabin skylight. The flood waters were once again lapping at *Peggy-Ann's* hull, and I was aware of Capel clumping about on the deck above me, when he shouted out.

"Oi, Egan, I think your mate's on 'is way back."

Barkas was coming back! The most immediate problem in my life was solved! A mixture of relief and joy flooded over me. I ran to the companion and leapt up the ladder, to check that the oaf on deck had got it right.

On the far side of the beach, there were two figures dragging a small boat towards the water that was inching its way across the sand. I couldn't make out Barkas for certain but the taller of the two men certainly looked like him.

"I told you, Jas," I said excitedly. "Samuel Barkas is a man of his word."

"I ain't sure that's 'im?" grunted Capel.

"It'll be him, it has to be him."

The pair on the beach dragged the boat a little past the dark line in the mud that marked the last high-water mark, and sat down on the gunnel to wait for the tide to reach them. Then the taller man stood up, looked in our direction and began to wave.

"That's Barkas alright!" I shouted out.

Capel actually looked a little disappointed that Barkas was making his return.

"I'm going to the head," he growled, skulking off in the

direction of the bow.

In about three-quarters-of-an-hour, an animated Samuel Barkas appeared at the cutter's side.

"Nathaniel, that's our quarry, the West Indiaman I've been waiting for!" he shouted, excitedly pointing to the square sails of a merchantman that had appeared three or four miles downstream of us. He threw me the painter and scrambled up *Peggy-Ann's* side.

"I didn't know you were waiting for a ship. Are you her pilot?" I asked.

"I thought I'd missed her. No later than the beginning of April is what Rawlins wrote me," Barkas said, totally preoccupied with his own thoughts and ignoring my question.

I tried again, "Samuel, who's Rawlins?"

Barkas ignored my question a second time, and trotted down *Peggy-Ann's* deck to the cockpit and started scrabbling around for something: I followed.

"Where's my glass?" he groaned.

I had been keeping his glass in a locker on the back of the coach-house, and I handed it to him.

Barkas grabbed it eagerly and studied the merchantman for some time, expertly steadying himself on practised sea legs as the cutter rolled to meet the now vigorously flooding water. Presently, he lowered the glass and announced, "She's Rawlins' ship, alright. That's the *Admiral Blake* from Jamaica. They must be three weeks late at least."

"Who's Rawlins?" I asked again.

"He's the First Lieutenant. Now we'll have cargo worth landing!" said Barkas, enthusiastically.

"Help me raise some sail, Nathaniel. We can go and meet them now there is enough water."

❖ ❖ ❖

Tentatively, I put *Peggy Ann* as close to the West Indiaman as I dared. The officers on board obviously recognised the little cutter because they came to the quarter-deck rail to wave down to Barkas, who grinned back at them. The wind blew away any attempts at conversation and they were reduced to communicating through sign language. Barkas made signals which implied the passing of something between the vessels, and a smartly dressed, bearded man on the quarter-deck nodded his understanding. Within minutes a block appeared at the end of their main-course yard, and a line was slung down to us where it fell with a clatter across the coach roof.

"What are they sending down, Samuel?"

"Tobacco, Nathaniel. Bales of beautiful dried leaves from King George's erstwhile colonies in America."

There was no time for further questions before he was issuing instructions and the first bale of tobacco appeared above my head.

"Jas, go down to the forward hold, and Nat, can you have the hatch up and we'll stow 'em as they arrive."

Barkas put some tension on the line, and the first tobacco bale ran down to us. I leapt forward and undid the slings as it hit the deck. The tobacco, which smelled like newly cured grass at the bottom of a hayrick, was wrapped in tarpaulin, and was about the size of a healthy corn-stook, but only half the weight.

"Pack these below, Jas," I yelled to Capel, and tossed the bale through the small hatch on the fore deck. It was a surprise to see his head dutifully disappear from the opening as he obeyed my command without comment. Twenty or so bales smacked down on our deck in the next few minutes, I lost exact count in the frantic activity. Leaning back against the starboard shrouds, I looked at Barkas. He was wearing a beaming smile and rubbing his hands with delight.

"That's worth a pretty penny, Nathaniel," he said, as he put the last bale through the deck hatch for Capel to store below. "We've just taken on board a good year's money for the ordinary hard-working soul."

"How can that be?"

"In Bristol the tax duty is three times the cost of the tobacco. Rawlins and the other officers receive part of their pay by way of cargo space. I split the proceeds with Master Rawlins and we all buy ourselves an easier life."

"Another trim system, Samuel. You seem to have developed a very tidy scheme."

"This is only one o' my contrivances, but I can't work 'em alone, Nathaniel. I needs a trustworthy man to work with me. Are you certain that I can count on you?"

"I've thought of little else while you were ashore, and I have no other pressing engagements," I replied with a grin. "I think we work well together."

- 109 -

"Good. Now listen up. I don't want Capel to know all my business, so keep what I've told you about the money to yourself."

"Are you sure you're happy to keep Capel ____" Barkas waved away my question as he always did when asked about Capel.

"I need to be aboard the *Admiral Blake* to keep up appearances as her pilot. That's part of my arrangement with them. Are you happy to take charge of *Peggy-Ann*?"

"I am, Samuel."

"Good. Now I will drop you a tow because nobody will have any interest in a pilot cutter being towed by a merchantman. We'll 'ead straight up King Road, which is the main channel, and I'll let you go somewhere near Portishead Point. You'll 'ave to take 'er from there."

"Will there be enough water?"

"There'll still be plenty for you, but we'll 'ave to anchor the merchantman in King Road and sit out the next tide. You keep on until Firefly rocks, there's a bell there to let you know where they are, and then head inland to Portishead Pool. Do you know it?"

"I have been there," I assured him.

"That's the best place to sit out a tide."

"When shall I see you again?"

"On the next tide, I'll take the *Admiral Blake* into the mouth of the Avon and upriver as far as Pill where they'll take on a river pilot. I'll hitch a ride back to Portishead with some carter or other, and I'll be on the old wharf behind the pool a few hours before tomorrow evening's high water. Now, is that oaf Capel sober enough yet to row me across?"

❖   ❖   ❖

It was a strange experience to sit on the mud in Portishead Pool again. It seemed an age ago that I had been there on Finch's trow *Elsinore*. In truth, the term 'pool' is something of an exaggeration. It is no more than an indentation in the coastline, but it was packed with river traders of one sort or another all waiting for the tide to change. Just as it had been when Finch's trow lay there.

Not relishing another prolonged spell alone onboard with Capel, I hid in the cabin throughout the day, leafing through *The Rights of Man*, but regularly visiting the deck to check the old wharf, that lined the coastline behind, to see if Barkas had appeared. On this occasion, he was as good as his word and he was standing on the old wall about three hours before high water.

As soon as there was enough water to carry the jolly boat to shore, I went to fetch Barkas. Having not spoken to Capel for a few hours, I had no idea what state he was in. Knowing he had been busy empting the broached brandy cask, I guessed he would be unaware of my leaving. He hadn't questioned me about any of Barkas' business schemes the whole time we had been sat in the pool, and so it had been easy for me not to betray any confidences. However, it had obviously been playing on Barkas' mind and it was his first question when he climbed into the little boat.

"Did Jas bend your ear while I was away?"

"I've hardly had a peep out of him apart from farts and belches."

"Good, I was fairly sure that open cask would keep he quiet," replied Barkas.

"Samuel, what are we going to do with our cargo? *Peggy-Ann* has a rich smell of tobacco about her that I should think would be of great interest to any passing Preventative Officer."

Sitting on a boat stuffed full of contraband, for nigh on twenty four hours, in such a crowded anchorage, had been playing on my mind. I had no idea what the punishments were for smuggling, but as a mutineer I could not afford any sort of brush with the authorities. Barkas' passport might protect us from the Press, but would hold no sway with the Customs Service.

"Don't you worry about that, Nat. I should think most of our cargo shall be gone afore this tide turns."

With Barkas safely aboard the jolly boat, I slowly picked our way through the busy anchorage: pushing the oars rather than pulling so that I could see our path back to *Peggy-Ann*. It was a tedious journey because we had to change direction every few yards to negotiate the fore and aft anchor cables of the trading boats. As we passed each vessel, as like as not, a head would pop over the side to have a word with Barkas or just nod a greeting.

"Have you anything aboard, Samuel?" shouted one thin fellow from the side of a two-masted river barge.

"Aye, finest Virginia," Barkas replied with a grin.

There were similar exchanges between Samuel and countless other boatmen as we made our way across the anchorage.

"I think I see what you mean about unloading our cargo before we leave this pool," I said.

"Aye. They'll all be over to *Peggy-Ann* in the next hour or so, Nat," replied Barkas, "and with the next tide our American leaves will be on their way to many of the river ports on the Severn and Wye, and the King's war chest shall be no fuller."

The water level was rising all the time, and so was the number of small boats that were moving about in the anchorage. The rivermen were starting to ready themselves to continue their journeys on the new tide, even as the day's light was beginning to fade. We rounded the stern of a long, green barge and *Peggy-Ann* came into sight. There were already a couple of small boats alongside, and Capel, who would have had no idea of what was going on, was arguing with a sailor who was standing up in one of them.

"I knew he'd be useful one day," said Barkas with a grin. "No one will mess with our cargo with that huge bastard on board!"

Capel and I spent the next two hours loading tobacco into the boats that came alongside. Barkas had hung two, small, red lanterns in our shrouds as soon as he had climbed aboard, and this was, as it turned out, his signal that he was open for business. It seemed as if every vessel's tender in the pool paid a visit to *Peggy-Ann* that dusk. Barkas would negotiate each transaction in his cabin, and we would just hear the chink of coins dropped into a wooden box, and Barkas yelling how may bales to give the customer.

For boatmen who were unable to pay for complete bales, Barkas weighed out portions of tobacco on a primitive scale that he had hung from a nail in the lodging knee of his dimly lit cabin. Every few minutes, a boatman would appear from the cabin with a bundle of leaves for Capel and me to wrap up tightly in tarpaulin, and every quarter-of-an-hour or so Barkas would shout for us to bring him another bale from the hold. Some of the men who came aboard didn't have enough money for contraband and brought nets of bread or sacks of vegetables to trade with. Barkas was happy to accommodate all, but I was amazed that he was prepared to conduct his trade so openly. It was still bothering me that he seemed totally blasé about the activities of the Preventative Service. Even a one-eyed officer, should be aware of the stream of small boats visiting *Peggy-Ann*.

"Aren't you worried about customs officers seeing what we're up to?" I asked him, when our torrent of customers finally came to an end.

"There's only one officer in Portishead, and he's only a lowly

Tide Waiter," Barkas replied.

"Well, aren't you worried about him?"

"Old Thomas Elliot is fat and lazy, Nat. I've known him for years. I gave him half-a-crown when I was waitin' for you on the wharf, and told him to spend it in *The Black Horse*," replied Barkas with a laugh.

"Don't worry about Preventative Men, Egan, you sap. Just concentrate your mind on how much money is in 'is wooden box," said Capel, kneeling down to pour himself a generous measure of brandy and water from his jug.

"That's Samuel's money, Jas," I replied.

"Aye, that's right it's my money," snapped Barkas. "What I don't need for more cargo, I'm givin' to Josh's widow. It's not her fault those Welsh pirates killed him, and she'll have nothin' right now."

"That's a really decent act, Samuel," I said, remembering the little purse of silver that Robert Double had given me in Birmingham.

"I dare-as-say that there'll be five shillin' in it for each of you."

"Five shillings 'aint much for the graft we been doin'," said Capel.

"It's twenty times what His Majesty would pay you for haulin' his rope, and it's what I say you'll get," said Barkas sharply.

Capel didn't reply immediately, but fixed Barkas with a malicious stare. He put down his jug and rose slowly to his feet clenching and unclenching his fists. My heart started to thump more rapidly as I watched them.

"I should get more than five shillings," Capel growled.

Barkas lent forward against the coachroof and his hand slid into a hidden, hinged locker to the left of the door. He produced an impressive flintlock, duelling pistol with delicate ivory inlay on its stock and an ornately engraved barrel. He nonchalantly blew non-existent dust from the weapon, and without looking at Capel, he said in a pleasant voice, "If you sail with me you take my orders, an' accept the living I offer you."

Capel stood stock-still for several seconds, and I stopped sucking air into my lungs. I was convinced he was about to explode, but his malevolent expression slowly transformed into something approaching a thin, wry smile. He shrugged his huge shoulders and bent down to pick up his grog; before taking a long pull and turning to survey the barges that were starting to leave the pool. The confrontation over, thankfully, I could breath easily again.

The river had reached high water, and like the tide our flow of customers, had run slack: the boatmen and our merchandise were on their way upstream.

"Now that we 'ave established our chain of command, we 'ad better ready ourselves because as soon as this tide starts to fall I intends to ride it seaward," said Barkas.

CHAPTER NINE
Off Land's End, Cornwall – 12th June 1809

"We think this trade in slaves must go on. That is the verdict of our oracle and the priests. They say that your country, however great, can never stop a trade ordained by God himself."
                    King of Bonny (West Africa) to Hugh Crow,
                          a Liverpool slave trade captain, 1807

Peggy-Ann had been heading southwest towards the Isles of Scilly for two days. Land's End was a few miles off our larboard side, and its craggy outline hove into view as we rose up on each swell: only to disappear again as we slipped into the following trough. The water had gradually changed colour from the murky brown of the Bristol Channel into the vivid ultramarine of the ocean. The strong westerly, that we were beating into, healed the cutter forty degrees to starboard. *Peggy-Ann's* gaff mains'l was drawn as tight as a drum skin, and the waves were beating a slow, monotonous rhythm as their crests slapped against the taught canvas.

It was nearly two months ago that I had first clambered over *Peggy-Ann's* side, and the grime from town life had finally worked its way clear from my lungs. I was now comfortably ensconced as a channel pilot's mate and Barkas and I had become something like friends. We were seated together in the stern sheets either side of the tiller. We seemed to have formed an unspoken alliance against Capel, who was standing on the companionway ladder gutting mackerel into a bucket on the deck, but Barkas was still refusing to confide in me why he allowed him to stay onboard.

While he worked, Capel was bragging about some odious act of wanton violence he had committed somewhere; I had long lost the thread of his tale. Barkas glanced in my direction and raised his eyebrows to signify his disinterest. When Capel mounted the ladder to toss the bucket full of fish entrails to the raucous, gaggle of herring gulls that tracked our wake, Barkas was quick to commandeer the conversation.

"We shall reach the island of St Mary's by early mornin' if this weather holds," he said. "We may 'ave to cruise the other islands for a day or two but the Goriaus will be there soon enough."

"The Goriau brothers are the French fishermen who were supplying you with cognac when you were attacked back in April?" I asked.

I seemed to remember that had been their name, but had avoided quizzing Barkas about the attack because he was still angry about the death of his crewman, Josh.

"Aye, that's as it was, Nat. They supply me with French spirit from time to time, but we had only loaded seven tubs and I 'ad given them guineas enough for twenty five. We shall 'ave to go an' rectify my account."

"Never trust a Frog."

Capel's contribution to our discourse drifted behind him as he disappeared below to put the gutted mackerel in *Peggy-Ann's* cast iron stove that sat in the tiny saloon. He may be of little use as a sailor or a companion, I thought to myself, but at least he was adept at baking fish.

"Do you think the Goriaus will still have the cognac after all this time?"

"I don't know, Nat. I have no knowledge of what 'appened after those pirates opened fire. Josh was killed and I was knocked flat. They may 'ave got away and stashed the contraband or they may 'ave been boarded. Or they may 'ave 'ad trouble with the Navy. They ain't keen on 'em smuggling!"

"The war makes life hard for everyone," I commented sarcastically.

"I shouldn't think King George misses too many meals," replied Barkas, "but look on the bright side, Nat," he added with a grin, "the price for free-trade brandy 'as risen astronomically!"

"Farmer George only remembers his meals because Mrs King spoons them into his mouth for him!" I said. (NOTE: *By 1809*

Egan would have heard rumours of King George's madness. The King's illness could well have been exacerbated by the arsenic in the powders that were used to medicate him. In the following year, the Prince of Wales replaced his father and ruled as Regent).

The insensitivity of my insult made me feel a touch guilty, but it also served to turn my thoughts to my stomach. Happily, the smell of cooking fish was already mingling deliciously with the ocean air, and I knew that I wouldn't have to wait too long to be fed.

To avoid the unwanted possibility of a merchantman interrupting out trip by requesting Barkas' services as a pilot, we were flying the thin, yellow pendant from our gaff which the cutters normally flew only when they had already placed their master onboard a ship. I was watching the pendant flick and jerk in the strengthening wind, when a tiny, black storm petrel skimmed the water's surface behind us which is, as every seaman knows, a sure sign that bad weather was on its way.

Capel's ugly bulk materialised at the companion hatch, and proffered two wooden squares containing baked mackerel and potatoes towards me. Barkas and I were both ravenous, and within minutes we were shouting to Capel for more.

His face appeared at the hatch again. "There ain't no more," he grunted. "I can't spend my entire life cooking for you two bastards."

"You can take a watch at the helm, Jas. That'll occupy you for a few hours," Barkas replied.

Capel was no seaman, but as long as we set a course for him, he could helm the cutter passably well.

"I don't mind if I do. There ain't nothin' else to entertain me and neither of you two wants to speak to me," groused Capel.

"Of course we do," I said cheerfully. "I distinctly remember asking for more food not more than a minute ago!"

Barkas pulled the log-reel from the stern locker, and then stood up to make room for Capel to sit by the tiller. He slipped a small sandglass, which I knew to be a fourteen second glass, from inside the reel, and threw the wooden log out behind us. He let the log line run out as the sand flowed through the glass, and he counted the knots, which were tied in the line, as they slipped through his fingers.

"Six knots ...come on, Nat. Let's see where we be on the chart," he said.

We made our way down the companion ladder into the saloon and then into Barkas' cabin. There was so little room, with us both inside, that I caught my brow on the nail that had held the scales at Portishead Pool. The evening light fought its way through grimy, leaded lights that were built into three sides of the hull. Spread out on the desk and weighted with assorted metal objects was his chart of the North Cornish coastline. The chart was yellowing and dog eared and had the printers mark for *'Mount and Page'* displayed at the top. The area of ocean above Cornwall had been covered with another sheet of paper, and on here there was a ragged row of marks, made with one of the new graphite pencils, running down the chart mimicking the coastline, but a few inches away from it.

"That's a record of our progress," said Barkas, gesturing at the pencil marks as he slumped into a chair. "I log our compass course and speed every three hours."

Navigation on paper was a new discipline as far as I was concerned. Father and I had spent many days fishing in the Bristol Channel. We would take the odd reading across the compass to check our position against prominent features on land, but we just relied on local knowledge that had been passed down through generations of fishermen.

"I don't want to approach the Scillies in darkness, Nat. There are reefs 'round those islands that 'ave wrecked at least a thousand ships," Barkas continued.

He took up a plane-scale and set it alongside the course marked on the chart. Then he opened a pair of brass dividers so that they reached from the scale to an etching of the points of a compass that he had pasted on the side of his chart. He slid one end of the dividers along the scale until the other point indicated our course on the compass rose.

"We've been sailin' southwest by west for three hours. The log tells us our speed is about six knots," Barkas said looking up at me. "I 'ave to make adjustments for the tide, but we should be … about 'ere." He made another mark on the paper, and joined it to the others with the aid of the scale. "If we stay on this course through the night, we may just find ourselves snagged on rocks around the Eastern Isles afore first light."

He decided to change our course by three-points in a more southerly direction to buy ourselves more time, and ensure that we didn't near the islands before daybreak. Climbing the companion to tell Capel, I was greeted by the sombre yellows of a juvenile sunset on the western horizon, and the first drops from a rain squall. I told him to steer south by south-west, and tossed him one of the capacious, tarpaulin boat-cloaks that hung by the coach roof door.

When I returned to the cabin, Barkas had rolled up his chart and was settling into his chair with a half-pint jug of watered cognac before him.

"Come 'n have a drink, Nat," he said. "You'll 'ave to sit on the cot."

He pulled off his boots and poured us both a generous measure. The strength of the rain was increasing and it started to drum on the deck. It was accompanied by the roaring of the sea against the oak planking of our hull as *Peggy-Ann* forced her way to windward. There was such a cacophony in the cabin that it was impossible to hear what he said, and I had to ask him to repeat himself.

"I'll wager that you find this sort of sailing preferable to serving His Majesty," he almost shouted, before he took a heavy pull on his glass of spirit.

"I should say that was right, Samuel. I saw no future in naval slavery."

Barkas took the glass away from his lips, and stared at me momentarily, before he put it down on his desk.

"Nay lad, don't confuse slavery with 'The Service'," he said, with determination. "To pluck you from your life and put you in a King's ship was cruel, but I 'ave seen the unspeakable evil of the transatlantic slave trade."

"You, Samuel?"

"Aye, I served on a Bristol Slaver before abolition. I saw sights so abhorrent that when a navel vessel hove-us-to, I was the first man to volunteer for the King just to get off that devil ship." (NOTE: *His Majesty's ships would systematically stop British trading vessels, including slavers, to 'recruit' able seamen. The fittest men would be chosen and offered a bounty to volunteer for navel service. A refusal would result in them being impressed without the bounty; exactly the situation that Egan had found himself in at Bristol*).

"But why has the trade in men from foreign countries been abolished, but the slavery of Englishman apparently acceptable?"

"Impressment 'aint right, Nat; I 'aint sayin' that it is, but slavery is an evil sin, far greater than any other. I've seen things on a slave ship that you can't even begin to comprehend."

"Explain it to me, Samuel, if you can, but I don't see how it can possibly be regarded as just to take a man from his family, against his will, and force him to serve in a King's ship where he could be blown into a thousand pieces any day."

I knew, of course, that English ships had carried Africans to the Americas and the Sugar Islands, but I actually knew very little about the slave trade. It's a subject that was discussed by workers in Birmingham, especially when it was abolished two years ago, but the consensus of their opinion seemed to have been that the radicals should concentrate on improving the plight of starving families at home.

"Men and women were shackled 'and and foot ... and stacked in racks, no more than two feet high on ... on ... the orlop deck."

Barkas' voice cracked with emotion and he kept pausing to compose himself. It was difficult to hear him above the racket in the cabin and I urged him again to speak up.

"They were secured in their positions by iron 'oops across their necks ... a clearer vision of hell a man will never see ..." he went on. "The poor bastards lay in their own excrement for days on end until we wus ordered to pump sea water over them. Plenty were ill ... real ill ... I knew that 'undreds of them wouldn't even survive the voyage let alone life on the..."

The images in Barkas' mind got the better of him, and he slowly shook his head and stopped talking.

"I had no idea what went on ... It is unfathomable how human beings can inflict such suffering on their fellow creatures, Samuel," I said.

Listening to Barkas made me re-examine all that I had ever been told about the slave trade. As a child in Lilstock, I remembered a plaque hanging in the church that carried the image of a black man kneeling in chains. Our parson had encouraged his congregation to sign a petition for a man named Clarkson, who was touring the county. None of it had made any sense to me at the time, but I now realised it was all part of the great campaign to end the trade in slaves. It had seemed so alien to my life in Somersetshire at the time, but the sight of this hard, resilient seaman slumped in front of me, silent and in obvious distress from what he had witnessed, gave me a new perspective. I actually felt fortunate for the first time since I had been forced away from Lilstock.

"It strikes me that powerful men exploit souls, less well off than themselves, all over the world, Samuel," I said.

"You ain't wrong, Nat," he replied, "but slavery has been a blight upon the world from the time of the ancient Greeks an' before. The Moors of North Africa 'ave been enslavin' Europeans for centuries."

"Tell me, Samuel, how did the traders procure the slaves for their ships? Presumably, the tribesmen were too fierce to be simply plucked off the beach?"

Barkas looked up at me sharply.

"I don't want to talk of these things no more, Nat," he said.

"Please, Samuel," I implored.

He sat hunched over his desk for a few minutes in silence, and then slowly began his explanation.

"Our Captain was an oily bastard, happy to do the biddin' of rich men in Bristol. He'd been tradin' off the West Coast of Africa for years, and knew full well which tribal leaders wanted to 'ave dealing's with him an' which didn't. He bought slaves from a man called the King o' Bonny; who was the ruler in the region we frequented. Bonny bought the poor, forsaken souls from the huge slave markets in Africa's interior." I fancy I might have seen Barkas quickly wipe a tear from the corner of his eye as he spoke. "He kept them corralled in a fort near the coast until European traders came to buy 'em."

"What did you use to trade with?"

"I only landed there the once, Nat," Barkas said pointedly, "but we 'ad all sorts of manufactured metal goods with us, but what the King o' Bonny wanted most o' all wus guns. Guns made him powerful, and power made him wealthy …," he hesitated again. "That's enough now, Nat. I won't talk of it no more," he said firmly.

"I can't work out why we accept such double standards?" I said to myself as much as to Barkas. "In Portsmouth they told me the Navy had sent ships to chase slaving vessels across the oceans to free the slaves, but the men who were sailing those ships had been enslaved themselves!" (NOTE: *Following the abolition of slavery in 1807 the West African Squadron was instigated to hunt down slaving vessels. The ships were returned, under prize crews, to African ports where the slaves were released and the vessels sold off. During Egan's time in Portsmouth the squadron consisted of only one ship and one sloop*).

"Listen, Nathaniel, you've not had the best luck, but we can manage a better life for you now. We'll sail a bit close t' the wind sometimes, but we'll make our living easy and you'll not go 'ungry," Barkas said with an air of finality. We spoke no more, supped French spirit and retreated into our thoughts. The little cabin had gone almost dark when Capel started shouting oaths from the cockpit above us, and I went out to relieve him of the tiller.

CHAPTER TEN
St. Agnes, Isles of Scilly, Cornwall – 17th June 1809

It is our intention to establish a new revenue force, as soon as is practicable, to be known as the Preventive Waterguard. It is the opinion of this Board that, now that the threat of invasion seems to be behind us, the Sea Fencibles are no longer a body of men that it is desirable for us to maintain. Whilst they may have afforded our coasts some protection against French invasion barges, it is doubtful that they pose any deterrent to the smuggler. In fact, some District Commanders regard the Fencibles under their orders as little more than smugglers and wreckers themselves.

The Customs Board, London, 1809

Marc Goriau was a stout, capable-looking fisherman in his middle years. He had a round, open face and yellow hair that stuck out from beneath a woollen cap like clumps of barley straw. Barkas pointed him out, to Capel and me, as we approached a group of men seated outside a whitewashed cottage on the edge of a hamlet in the centre of the island of St. Agnes.

"He seems happy enough with 'is self," Barkas muttered under his breath.

There was no way of guessing how the impending meeting between these two former allies would go: was it to be a violent argument or a friendly reunion? Barkas made a perfunctory gesture with his hand, which I interpreted as his signal for us to follow him, and he took off with determined strides down the path.

We had arrived on St. Mary's, the biggest of the Scilly Islands, two days earlier, but had found no sign of the Goriau brothers or their boat. Barkas had questioned every seaman we encountered in the port of Hugh Town until eventually he had found a pilchard fisherman who had seen, what he thought might be, a French ketch beached on St. Agnes.

Barkas had insisted on investigating immediately, and we had left St. Mary's the same afternoon. His agitation had visibly increased as we had approached the rocky outcrops that surrounded St. Agnes. We dropped anchor amidst a cluster of local fishing boats in a cove on the north side of the island. As we prepared to go ashore, Barkas surprised both Capel and me, by announcing that he was taking only the idiot giant with him and that I was to stay onboard *Peggy-Ann* as an anchor watch.

"I should be with you as well, Samuel. We can watch the wind and come back if there is any danger to *Peggy-Ann*," I protested. If Barkas was expecting a problem with Goriau my gut reaction was that I should be at his side.

"There may be unpleasantness," Barkas replied.

"Why ...? Why should he cause trouble?" I asked.

"I ain't sure, Nat. I've always 'ad Marc Goriau down as an honest man, but part of me reckons that they knew somethin' about that pirate attack."

"You expect fightin' and you suddenly want me along wit' you," Capel chipped in indignantly.

"You mean you suspect that they rigged the pirate attack just to rob you?" I asked Barkas, ignoring Capel's remark.

"I think that could be the case, Nat," Barkas told me grimly.

"But that would mean that they killed Josh."

"Exactly ...," Barkas had replied.

A grim aura seemed to have settled around Barkas; gone was the compassionate fellow of a few days ago, who had not been able to speak of the dreadful sights he had experienced on a slave ship. He now gave me every impression that he was ready to administer whatever justice he saw fit.

Despite the possibility of fighting, I was determined to stay with Barkas. If it had been the Royal Navy we had encountered and not his cutter when we sailed *Brixham Belle* away from Basque Roads, I could now well be dead!

"We should all be in this together," I insisted.

"Shame that midshipman couldn't depend on you the same way," Capel snorted dismissively at me.

Capel's gibe hit home: stirring up my latent guilt. I was left to brood over the truth in what he said, and took no further part in the conversation.

"Will you be takin' your pistol, Sea Dog?" Capel asked Barkas.

"No, we don't know if they're guilty. If we arrive bristlin' with weapons it may provoke violence before I know the true story."

Nevertheless, I noticed the huge apology-for-a-man fingering the back of his belt where he kept hidden the short knife that I had seen him kill Robinson with.

"On your head be it, Nat. We'll all go ashore," Barkas finally announced.

We left *Peggy-Ann* together, and began our stomp around the island of St. Agnes. When Barkas pointed out Goriau in front of the whitewashed cottage, I felt a swarm of butterflies take to the wing in the pit of my stomach. I stood and watched for several seconds, with some trepidation, as Barkas marched purposely down the path; Capel keeping step with him. I found myself trotting after them, and caught up just as a young woman appeared from inside the cottage carrying a tray of pottery mugs. She was greeted enthusiastically by the gathering, and I realised that the whitewashed cottage doubled as the island's beer house.

We were only a few yards away when Goriau spotted Barkas and cried out, "Samuel, *mon ami*. I have been seeking you for *beaucoup, beaucoup de jour*."

The Frenchman shot up from the small cask he was sitting on and galloped towards us. His pleasure seemed genuine enough to me, but Barkas stood his ground and made no effort to greet him. Goriau, wearing a broad grin, threw his arms wide and attempted to embrace the Englishman, but Barkas held out his hand to keep him at a distance. Goriau's face fell; he was either astonished by Barkas' reaction or an accomplished play actor.

"Samuel, what is it that is wrong? *N'êtes-vous pas* pleased to see me? I was not being sure what has happened to you following the attack."

He stopped talking, and eyed Capel and then me.

"*Ou est*, Josh?" he asked hesitantly.

"Josh is dead. He stopped one of the balls that those bastard pirates fired at us," Barkas replied in an icy tone.

"I am sorry, *très, très* sorry. I have no *idée*," replied the Frenchman, whose face contorted into, what convinced me as, genuine remorse. "We turned and ran, as did you when the cannons they started," he continued in an earnest fashion, while looking directly into Barkas' eyes. "They holed our side and overhaul us, Samuel. They come aboard and steal our *contrebande* ... your *contrebande*."

"Evil bastards," muttered Barkas. "So, you have lost all my money?"

"*Oui*."

The expression on Goriau's face had obviously gone someway to persuading Barkas of his innocence because his voice became noticeably friendlier.

"Did Jean and yourself escape unscathed?" he asked gently.

"*Qui* Samuel. We didn't resist the men who boarded. They were many times too many."

"Did they take everything?"

"Everything, Samuel, everything is gone."

"Stinkin' Welsh bastards!" Barkas fumed.

"Yes, *Gallois* ... that is what we had thought also," Goriau said.

"What do you mean, *thought*?" Barkas asked his voice ringing with astonishment.

"We have not any way to be paying for more *contrebande*, and had to return to *beaucoup heures* of the fishing."

"What has this to do with anything?" Barkas asked.

"About *deux semaines* past, we were caught in a gale some way from our home port of Concarneau. We were blown into the *Baie du* Douarnenez as the night is coming, and so we take up refuge in that port." Goriau hesitated for dramatic effect and then went on, "When we come in, we see that this same schooner is alongside the quay. What is more, Samuel, she is flying *un drapeau tricolore*!"

"I'll be buggered! We know that they 'aint Frenchmen an' I'm sure they wuz sportin' a British ensign when they attacked you Marc."

Barkas' doubts about Goriau seemed to have slipped away. The butterflies in my stomach were beginning to settle, confident that the threat of confrontation was now passed. The Frenchman continued his story.

"That is not all. The night is much black, but as far as I see they are unloading tubs of cognac, and they carry them into a warehouse in the harbour."

Barkas' face was the picture of astonishment.

"They were unloading contraband *in* France?"

"Samuel, I check this warehouse in the morning and it has the name of *Adolphe Absolon* above the door."

Barkas didn't reply but just slowly shook his head in bewilderment and waited for Goriau to explain himself.

"That same name is on the warehouse in Concarneau where I had bought the cargo we had taken from us."

Both men fell silent as they considered the Frenchman's news. I broke the silence, the idea just popped into my head.

"The Welsh pirates must be working with the French."

They both turned to look at me.

"French merchants sell Marc the contraband, and then tip-the-wink to this schooner to recapture it and return it for resale," I explained.

"You could be right," Barkas said thoughtfully.

"But I don't understand why the British blockading ships don't grab her?" I said.

"I reckon that their skipper takes great trouble to avoid the Navy," said Barkas, "there isn't really a blockade at Douarnenez an' even if they are spotted, she's a big schooner an' pretty fast with it. She could get away to windward of any nosey frigate, an' the navy might just mistake her for a dispatch boat."

"They fly *un drapeau Anglais* when they attack Frenchmen and *un drapeau tricolore* when they attack the Englishman," Goriau interjected. "If smugglers, such as us, were stopped by a French ship we would not trust this merchant again, would we?"

"I'm thinking that you've put yer finger on it, Marc. They want to keep us all smugglin' so that we can be robbed again in the future. The bastards are soaking up the free trade from both ends," fumed Barkas.

"Where is this place, Douarnenez?" I asked.

"The Bay of Douarnenez is on the west coast of Brittany, and away from the main smugglin' ports of the English channel," Barkas answered.

"It has a very large *baie*, the English they do not bother with it too much," explained Goriau.

"If you do see English ships, do they stop you fishermen?" I asked.

"*Non*, the British Navy don't bother the fishermen."

"Not even to check for contraband?"

"*Non*, they do not search us. Even *bateaux* the size of that schooner can slip in and out of ports that have no blockade," he added.

"Then why can't we slip in there and get even with them!" I announced, triumphantly.

There was silence for a few moments, and then Barkas replied, wearing a scornful expression, "We can't take on an armed schooner, Nathaniel."

"No, but we might be able to tackle an unarmed warehouse, and take back what was stolen for you," I replied.

The deep frown lifted from Barkas' countenance, and the broad grin, that he flashed in my direction, conveyed that he liked the idea. Goriau seemed impressed as well, and it dawned upon him that he didn't know who I was.

"*Qui est votre ami*, Samuel?" he asked.

"Marc, this is Nathaniel. He is my new crewman, now that Josh is dead," Barkas announced.

"...and the other one?" the Frenchman enquired.

We all turned expecting to see Capel, but the great slug had become bored with the conversation, presumably when it was evident that there was no longer any chance of fighting, and he was disappearing into the little whitewashed cottage.

"We should follow *peut-être*?" Goriau suggested. "There are men I want you to meet."

"Aye, you're right enough, Marc, I needs a drink," said Barkas.

As we walked towards the cottage, I studied the group of men sitting outside, and noticed for the first time that some of them were clad in blue tunics: very similar to what Bo'sun Robinson had worn. I grabbed Barkas' arm and pulled him back.

"Samuel, they're naval men, and don't forget that I'm a mutineer," I hissed in his ear.

He let out a booming laugh, and replied, "Don't fear them, my friend, they're Sea Fencibles. In the King's pay, true enough, but I doubt there's an 'onest man amongst 'em."

"Sea Fencibles?"

"They're a maritime militia recruited from local sailors and fishermen to protect the south coast against invasion. You're not familiar with them because they don't recruit 'em as far as Somersetshire."

"And they're Marc's friends?" I asked quietly.

"I reckon so."

❖ ❖ ❖

The gathering in the beer house turned out to be quite a raucous affair. It struck me, that most of the male population of St.Agnes must have been in that smoky, little parlour. I questioned myself, as to how so many men could afford to waste a whole working afternoon drinking?

Being newcomers, we aroused a great deal of interest from the islanders who were all keen to know our business. Initially, their inquisitiveness was something of an ordeal, but I forced myself to chat to whoever spoke to me and to keep a smile on my lips. My problem was that I had been unable to push Capel's taunt, about my betrayal of Ebbs, from my brain. Drinking beer wasn't helping. It was the first I had drunk for some time, and after an hour-or-so the dark and very bitter ale was starting to slide down a little too easily. The intoxicants stirred up everything that was supposed to stay safely locked-up in the back of my mind. I became overcome by a sense of guilt: guilt because I should still be mourning my wife, guilt for the mutiny, guilt for Capel's murder of Robinson and guilt because I had let my friend be thrown into the sea.

Luckily for me, alcohol can dull as well as stimulate a troubled mind, depending upon the dosage, and the more I drank the easier it became for me to return my torments to the submerged state. By the time my sixth or seventh pot of the black brew had disappeared, I became totally at ease with myself. It was strange to feel so comfortable in the middle of an alien little island with a bunch of men I had never met before, but perhaps that was part of the reason why?

Leaning against the knobbly, clay-plastered wall of the parlour, I watched a couple of fishermen engaged in a very vocal, arm-wrestling contest on one of the nearby tables when Marc Goriau sidled up beside me.

"I used to supply cognac regular to *des îles Scilly*. I supply many of these men here," he said, waving his finger vaguely across the room.

"You mean they're all smugglers? I thought they were Fencibles?" I replied under my breath.

"Being a Fencible gives them very much advantage," said Marc. "True, they are supposed to be assisting in the catching of *contrebandiers*, but it also mean that they have knowledge of where the Revenue men are!"

"But where can they sell their goods?"

"Mainly they row for the mainland in small gigs with no sail," Goriau replied.

"Rather them than me," I said.

"Indeed, I would not row an open *bateau* over six leagues of angry sea."

"Don't they have trouble from the Revenue cutters?" I asked.

"With no sail they are not ... how do you say? ... dependant upon the wind. If they see the Revenue they row straight for the wind where no sailing *bateau* can follow," Goriau explained.

"It's still a risky business," I said.

"Of course ... but it is not always easy to see *un petit bateau*, with not a sail, in amongst the waves, *non*? As well, they have many cousins in Cornwall, who are Fencibles *de la mer*, who let them know when the Revenue *bateaux* are gone," Goriau said, adding a wink.

At this point, Samuel Barkas walked up to join us in the company of a smallish, weaselly man with a shiny, bald head.

"Frenchie!" the newcomer exclaimed loudly and embraced Goriau.

"Nathaniel, you should meet Bill, he's petty officer of Fencibles an' Marc's old friend." Barkas had to shout above the noise of their reunion.

"Keep it down!" a voice yelled from a table behind us. "Some of us is tryin' t' find out what's goin' on in the world."

It was an elderly man with a long, grey beard who spoke. He was seated at a table with a group of seamen of similar age, they were all listening to the man in the corner who was reading from a battered looking edition of *Cobbett's Political Register*. I guessed that the reader was the only literate one among them.

"Sorry, don't mind us," Barkas said to the little assembly, and raised a hand in apology.

"William Vowles at your service, Nat," the weasel said to me in a quieter voice, and extended a grubby paw. He was comfortably shy of middle age, and he wore a sharp, enquiring expression. "Just call I, Bill. I'm the senior naval officer residin' on the island of St. Agnes," he said, puffing out his chest a little. I couldn't tell if he was proud of his responsibility or whether he regarded it as a huge joke. "I'm responsible for the activities of most o' these reprobates, but then if you know Goriau, you'll know what we gets up to," he concluded with a chuckle.

"Pleased to know you," I said, shaking his hand.

"Samuel 'ere, tells I that you 'ave a plan to take back the goods he an' Frenchie 'ad stolen?" Vowles said.

"Do you think me mad?"

"Well ... we generally waits for someone like Frenchie 'ere," Vowles said, indicating Goriau, "t' bring goods out to us, but a few English boats 'ave been inside French 'arbours afore." (NOTE: *The year following Egan and Barkas' adventures, Bonaparte began to positively encourage English smugglers into French ports. Gravelines became known as 'the City of Smugglers', and housed hundreds of English free-traders in especially constructed compounds*).

"I was thinking we could use Marc's boat. She's French. Why should they suspect her?" I suggested.

"*Esprit du Breese* is careened near Wingletang Bay. She has, as you say, a bare bottom," Goriau said dejectedly.

"Are you still repairin' her from the attack?" Barkas asked Goriau.

"*Oui*, it will only take ... maybe *vingt jours* to have her ready *pour la mer*."

"It would be better to go with no moon, an' that means in the next week," said Vowles.

"It would be as nothing to make *Peggy Ann* appear French," chipped in Goriau.

"Aye, just steal 'er registration number for a start!" said Vowles.

"What is this 'registration number' that you speak of?" I asked him.

"The fishermen in each region of France 'ave a letter, and each individual boat carries a number. The authorities pretend that they can check 'em all and tax each catch that's brought in, but I doubt if they can," explained Vowles.

"So we paint the Goriaus' number on the side of *Peggy-Ann*?"

"I reckon so. An' we 'ang a few herrin' nets about and have a pile of fish on deck," Barkas added with obvious enthusiasm. "With a Frenchman shoutin' excuses to the harbour master for usin' his dock ... that should be the end of it!"

Barkas' voice tailed off as his attention was grabbed by some commotion behind me.

He lent forward and murmured in my ear, "We 'ave to get 'im out of here, sharpish like, before 'e starts trouble."

"Who?" I asked, and as soon as the word was out of my mouth I knew. I saw Capel. His eyes were bulging out of his stupid, red face and the veins on his forehead looked fit to burst. He was stumbling after a robust-looking Scillonian woman, who was holding the torn bodice of her dress across her breast. She turned and started to scream a stream of invective at him. Capel raised a clenched fist and the nearest local man to him grabbed his arm. The drunken shit lashed out sideways with his other hand. In taking rapid evasive action, the fisherman crashed into the table of men who were reading the newspaper. The amiable ambiance of the parlour was shattered in a couple of seconds. In the next instant, Capel was in the grip of several burley Scillonians, and Barkas was diving into the middle of the mêlée.

"We're sorry, my friends, we're sorry ...," he shouted, pushing his body in-between Capel and the largest of his captors. "We're goin' this very minute ...," he said, holding up his hands in appeasement. "Please forgive 'im. We've been at sea too long. It won't 'appen again."

Bill Vowles rushed to the woman, whom he must have known, and threw a protective arm around her. She seemed receptive to his ministrations and her shouting stopped. Meanwhile, Barkas had taken hold of Capel's collar and was prising him away from the seamen. Luckily, neither Capel nor his captors offered any resistance; it's difficult to tell with someone as idiotic as Capel, but I think he realised his safest exit was to allow Barkas to drag him away while he feigned complete inebriation. He certainly played his role magnificently, letting his head bob up and down and grunting unintelligibly. He even produced a stream of saliva that dribbled from the corner of his slack mouth.

Positioning myself between the Scillonians and Barkas and Capel, I started mumbling apologies as we all backed away towards the door. What happened to Capel was of no concern, but we had to get him out of there before he ruined everything for us. We would need help from the Scillonians if we were to make our preparations to sail to France. Capel was a liability; why did Barkas insist on keeping him with us? I would gladly have let the Fencibles deal with him, but I had to make sure Barkas got out of there in one piece.

Capel's charade was working, and the local men held back. Goriau was talking to them and they seemed to be assuaged by grovelling. Barkas kicked open the door behind me, and pulled Capel out of the beer house. I ran out after them.

As I had suspected, by the time we had gone a little way down the grassy path, Capel miraculously recovered his wits enough to walk unaided. He turned to look at us and a sickly smile broke across his face. He let out an odiously licentious cackle which was the final straw for Barkas and he exploded in anger. He started screaming in Capel's face that he could have caused us all to be seriously hurt or thrown off the island. Astonishingly, Capel seemed to accept responsibility for his stupidity and hung his head like a naughty child, keeping his mouth shut. I couldn't stand to look at the hateful bastard any longer and pushed on alone towards the cove where *Peggy-Ann* lay at anchor.

I passed a group of women who were packing pilchards tightly under weights into hogsheads and collecting the 'lamp' oil through wooden taps. They all spoke to me and seemed at ease with visiting seamen. They wouldn't be that friendly if they knew the behaviour of one of the men that followed behind me, I thought to myself.

❖ ❖ ❖

Our task for the next few days was to disguise *Peggy-Ann* as best we could for our foray into enemy waters. Vowles was taking a personal interest in our adventure and he was ever-present as our preparations took shape. It was Vowles who had made sure we had careened at the best place: which was the causeway between St. Agnes and the adjoining little island of Gugh. And Vowles who took responsibility for procuring everything we needed. He was also willing to summon a couple of Fencibles whenever we required extra hands. Capel's indiscretion at the beer house was never spoken of, but it was noticeable that Vowles and the *Turks* treated him coolly (NOTE: *Vowles had explained to Egan that in the Scillies all the inhabitants of St.Agnes were known as Turks. Supposedly because of their swarthy appearance which was said to be derived from shipwrecked Turkish sailors who had settled on the island).*

By the third day, I was slapping thick, black paint over the hull to mimic the French fishing boats, and Barkas was nearby on top of a ladder painstakingly inscribing the Goriaus' registration in white characters. The ocean-motion, that any seaman feels for his first few days on dry land, was still affecting me, but it felt good to be ashore. I had slept the previous two nights in Vowles' cottage and his family were making me welcome. It felt as if life had become ordinary again and my mind drifted back to happier days. Memories of Mary and our early married days in Somersetshire successfully swamped recollections of that tumultuous explosion and the bloody mutiny that followed. I also found that reminiscences of Sarah Ebbs appeared in my head. What did she think of me now? Had Jacob survived his swim? Had he told his sister of my betrayal of him? I thought fondly of her; the knowledge that kind people walked the earth gave me a warm feeling.

St.Agnes had a rugged, isolated feel that made me feel strangely safe. This was probably because the administrative island of the Scillies was St. Mary's and it, and all the attendant authorities, was over a mile away across the Sound to the north of us. St Agnes felt wonderfully free from outside interference.

I hadn't visited the southern half of the island, where the Goriaus' boat lay, but I was told that it was a rocky wasteland, exposed to the ferocity of Atlantic gales. By contrast, on the eastern side, where *Peggy-Ann* was careened, the island was generously coated with vegetation and flowers. Some of the plants were unfamiliar to me, and the flowers I did recognise seemed to be unseasonably early. There were also some large baskets of potatoes, left at the edge of a paddock, that were at least a month before their time.

The local people took a keen interest in our activities, especially when the French registration numbers appeared on *Peggy-Ann's* bow. The sharper individuals among them realised we were planning to visit France, and there was little point in trying to keep our escapade secret. Everyone on St.Agnes was either involved in smuggling or knew somebody who was, and the attack on Barkas and Goriau was unanimously condemned. We received nothing but wholehearted support for our plan of retribution.

By the evening of the fourth day, our preparations were complete, and Vowles insisted on marking our imminent departure with an impromptu gathering at his cottage. It was a low-key affair but everyone we had met turned up. A couple of fishermen brought half-a-dozen boxes of fresh halibut and ling, so that we could claim to be a fishing boat if we were stopped. They were full of advice about how to make *Peggy-Ann* behave like a fishing vessel but I reckoned that Goriau knew it all already. Everyone was sitting about eating toasted sardines off the fire when Marc Goriau arrived with his brother. Jean Goriau was to be the fourth member of our crew, and it was the first time I had met him. He was the antithesis of his brother: slightly built and reticent to the point of being shy. We talked together for a little while but I didn't manage to learn much about him: his English was nowhere near as good as Marc's. As the fire died down, people started drifting away leaving only Vowles, the Goriaus, Barkas and myself in the little parlour. Vowles produced a bottle of wine which he claimed to be Bordeaux, but we had no way of knowing.

"To a safe journey for my friends," Vowles said, raising the bottle to his lips.

"Thanks to you, Bill, everything is prepared proper, an' I reckons we can look forward to an' uneventful trip," replied Barkas.

I hoped he was right. We passed the bottle around until it was empty.

CHAPTER ELEVEN
Douarnenez Bay, North Western France
– 23rd June 1809

The British no longer leave a port of the Mediterranean or of the ocean which is not sealed. Their divisions spread across all our coastal points from Dunkerque to Bayonne, from Spain to Sicily... In mockery, starting last year, the English frigates cruising our coast fly the colours of France under the Spanish flag. The English feel so comfortable and at home that their ships drop anchor in all security in the harbour of the Basques, under Groix, at Belle-Ile. They set their moorings at Quiberon and the Bay of Douarnenez has taken the name 'Bay of the English'.

Julien de la Gravière, Admiral of France, 1809

Barkas had predicted that our trip to the French coast would be uneventful and he was proved correct. From St.Agnes we sailed south by southwest for a day and night, in the hope of staying far enough out to sea to avoid the British warships we knew would be blockading Brest. We changed course late on the second morning and approached Douarnenez Bay from the south, reaching across an obliging westerly for the rest of that day. We saw no sign of the blockade, and a gorgeous orange sun was dropping towards the horizon on our western quarter when we passed the rocky headland that marked the southern jaw of the huge bay.

Douarnenez Bay is a great expanse of water, more or less

enclosed by two long tongues of land that jut into the Atlantic. I had never seen anything comparable to it in England, but Barkas said that the estuary of the River Fal was nearly as impressive. The coastline looked similar to what I had recently seen in Cornwall, and this made my first impressions of the land of my enemies quite amicable. A mile or two ahead of us were a couple of fishing boats riding home on the end of the flood tide and others were entering the bay from the north. Their sail-plans, at least at distance, looked similar to ours, which was encouraging. In fact, the whole enterprise was starting to feel surprisingly comfortable. I had been apprehensive about entering enemy waters, but the further we progressed unmolested the more assured I became that we would be able carry out our expedition successfully.

We followed the southern coastline of the bay about half-a-mile from the shore. There were no people or dwellings on the mainland, but several hundred yards from the headland we sailed past what resembled the remains of a gun battery. The heavy masonry structure had no age to it but the walls were pock marked with the indentations of shells and large sections of it had been knocked to the ground.

"Your navy is not for bothering to maintain a blockade of the *Baie de* Douarnenez. They knocked out the batteries some years ago, so that occasionally their ships can use *La Baie* to hide from a gale," explained Goriau. "The port of Douarnenez itself still has some *batteries défensive*."

Peggy-Ann hugged the edge of the bay for a further hour or so. The prevailing westerly had lost a little of its force but we were helped on our way by the steady off-shore breeze that picked up as the night progressed. The dusk was starting to deposit a grey haze in the sky, and the first pin-pricks of bright light stood out from their surroundings as folk on the mainland lit their evening lanterns. By now the tide had run slack, and the fishing boats in the bay were starting to cluster as they neared the town of Douarnenez in the south eastern corner of the bay. Barkas told Capel and me that we should all go below and leave the two Frenchmen alone on deck. It was only a short while after we had clambered down the companionway that Marc started shouting in French and I knew one of the fishing boats was nearby.

"Goriau is tellin' 'em that we 'ave damage to our rudder and need to make repairs, I think," said Barkas, who was the only one amongst us who claimed to understand any French. "The Frog fishermen are tellin' 'em to 'ead for town and tie up in the river. They say there shall be shipwrights there in the mornin'. I'll tell you, this couldn't 'ave been easier. They're sendin' us exactly where we want to go!"

"Don't count your chickens too soon, Samuel," I warned.

My confidence was running high, but there was no point in us becoming too cocksure. I was standing on the steps underneath the coach-house roof and through the little windows that looked out over *Peggy-Ann's* deck, Douarnenez was just a cluster of tiny lights in the distance: no more threatening than any Somerset fishing-village. We knew the privateers' warehouse was situated on the quay beside the Pouldavid River, which ran through the centre of the town, and that's where the French fishermen were sending us. Marc Goriau had told us that a newer wharf had been built to the east of the town which is where the fishing boats would be heading.

"This is perfect, Nat. I'll wager that the town quay will be quiet at this hour," continued Barkas.

"Will Marc know how to get us to the right place?" I asked.

"Aye, he knows well enough … but if he didn't," Barkas chuckled. "Some Crapaud is telling 'im right now … we're in luck; there are lantern buoys for 'im to follow an' a light on the island marking the mouth o' the river."

"Island? What island?"

"Leave it to Marc, 'e knows these waters. 'E give me a chart afore we left, it's in my cabin. I'll go an' get it."

"Frogs ain't likely to be no match for us," piped up Capel for no reason that was readily apparent.

"We're not going to join in the war, Jas. We're only going to take some brandy from a warehouse," I told him irascibly.

To avoid the possibility of any further conversation with Capel, I concentrated on staring out of the window and searching for the lighted steerage buoy. After a few minutes a dull smudge of light appeared on the water ahead of us, slowly growing bigger and bigger. Eventually, the lantern that swung on top of the buoy disappeared from view beneath *Peggy's* larboard bow. Yellow triangles of reflected lamp-light on the water were broken into a hundred pieces by our bow-wave as we slid through the pallid pool of brightness surrounding the buoy. My attention was drawn to the next marker, which was still well ahead of us, but in the diminishing dusk light seemed to be shining much brighter and much higher up than the last one. As we drew a little closer, I could make out the dark shapes of buildings and trees that seemed to be beneath the light. It must be burning from the top of some sort of tower or beacon, but an ever-growing number of twinkling lanterns in the distance told me that the town was still some way off, and so the buildings must be situated on the island that the French fishermen had mentioned.

Barkas had spread Goriau's chart on the little galley table besides *Peggy-Ann's* iron oven and was studying it assiduously.

"It's called Île Tristan," he said, as I took a seat on the bench next to him. "There's a long channel runnin' down the side o' the island an' into the river where the quayside is," he said, tracing the channel with a grubby finger along the left-hand side of the island. The Île Tristan was a small, oval island about half-a-mile from the mouth of the Pouldavid River (See Map).

"An' over 'ere is the battery that defends it," said Barkas, tapping his finger on a diagrammatic representation of guns marked at a settlement named Tréboul on the mainland, behind the island.

"I'm glad Marc has navigated that channel before," I said. "It looks pretty treacherous to me."

"Don't be fooled by no French chart, it's probably a lot wider than it looks!" replied Barkas.

It seemed an age before we were abreast the island but it cannot have been very long because there was still enough light to see that the navigation lamp, an impressively large one, was burning on top of a crenulated tower. The channel ahead of us was marked with a row of tree branches sticking out of the water, that Goriau kept on our starboard side. This channel was, as Barkas predicted, much wider than it had appeared on the French chart, but it would be much trickier to navigate in less water and the tide was just showing signs of being on the turn. On the mainland to my right there was another stone gun emplacement identical in design to the one by the mouth of the bay. But this one was intact and the dull, black muzzles of half-a-dozen heavy guns jutted beyond the walls, protecting the channel we were sailing in and the mouth of the river beyond.

I knew from the chart that Île Tristan was about two cables long, and as we slid past the densely wooded island, the tide was definitely starting to run against us. By the time we were half way down its length, the sea level had already receded a foot or so down the steep sides of the island, and jagged, weed covered rocks were starting to reveal themselves at the channel's edge. When we reached the southern end of the island, I could look into the broad mouth of the Pouldavid River and see the town of Douarnenez on its eastern bank. There was a substantial seawall protecting the coastline on that side of the river mouth, and the last navigational light swung from a stanchion at the point where the seawall turned the corner and became the river quay. Further down the coast, and built on top of the seawall, there was another gun battery pointing out into the bay.

South of the island and stretching almost to the river mouth, there was a shallow shelf to the larboard side of the channel. Even in the dusk light, I could see the dark shapes of rocks not far beneath the surface. Where they showed themselves above the water, the shrinking tide angrily boiled white froth around them. It was plain there would be no crossing these shallows, even at high water. However, as we approached the river mouth the shelf ended forty or fifty yards short of the seawall, and the water rushed through a gap, created by a deeper channel, that ran from the river and into the bay on the other side of the Île Tristan.

Peggy-Ann was nosing forward gently now, and we were within the mouth of the Pouldavid River itself. The western bank opposite the town was well wooded, like the island, and on that side of the river there was no quayside but only a rather pleasant sandy beach that ran into the water, and a long line of sturdy mooring posts that stood some twenty yards or so beyond the main channel.

Barkas' third prediction turned out to be also true, and the harbour was deserted when the Goriaus eventually tied up to the river quay. I watched from my window, as Marc jumped ashore and went in search of the Harbour Master to report our landing. Barkas, Capel and me all sat tight and waited for his return, while his brother stayed on deck so that he could deflect any port official that might be nosing about. By the time Marc returned, it was truly dark, and the ebbing tide was gurgling against the hull.

"I find the *petit devil* of a Harbour Master," he announced from the hatchway above us. "He smells bad of sweat, and is half-way down his first *bouteille*. He cares of nothing except that if we land fish, we pay a tax. *La ville* is under curfew 'till half an hour before Mass in the morning, but fishermen are exempt because of the night tide. No one will bother us here, I think. Come, we have much to do."

Barkas and Capel followed the Frenchman, but I wanted to take my time. I had never left England before, and the prospect of stepping onto foreign land was something to be savoured. This was the perfect expedition: not too dangerous, but with more than a frisson of excitement!

It was disappointing that there was not even a distant enemy soldier to be seen when I poked my head above the hatch. In fact, there was nobody on the quay at all, and the only movement came from the row of battered, brass oil lanterns that hung from posts along the quayside, and swung gently in the wind. Their dim illumination spread as far as a row of dark, square buildings set back some forty or fifty yards from the quayside. The occasional faint shout from the fishermen on the dock to the east of us drifted on the air, but the centre of the little town was ghostly quiet.

"We want to load a goodly cargo and be gone as soon as the next flood tide gives us enough water," said Barkas, as we gathered together on the afterdeck. "The tides droppin' quick, so we 'ave a full seven or eight hours before the river's full enough for us to leave. Take your time and act quiet and careful," he said, looking Capel straight in the eye. "Which warehouse were the Welsh bastards using, Marc?"

"Don't worry, I know it. It has a sign of black and white. I will take you there now. *Je pense que* we leave Jean on the boat, so he can fetch us if any person is making trouble."

"Aye, I agree," replied Barkas. "There may be some kind of curfew watch about so we need to keep our wits about us."

Leaving Jean behind, the rest of us started cautiously down the deserted quayside keeping out of the pools of yellow light that radiated from the lanterns. We passed a couple of large, stone-built buildings which evidently housed shipwrights because of the boat carcasses that sat outside. As we crept past them, the same odd oily, burnt aroma emanated from inside that I remembered from Chapman's Foundry. Beyond the shipwright's workshops, the buildings were much bigger and made of wood. They were trading warehouses, two or three stories high and had their owner's names and the nature of their businesses painted on the walls. After a couple of minutes, Goriau slowed his pace until we were all creeping along the quay.

"This one is it," he hissed, stopping outside a featureless building. I could just make out barn-like doors down an unlit alley to the side of the warehouse, and above our heads swung a wooden sign. It had once been painted white with black lettering but the sign writer's craft had been ravaged by time and most of the paint had flaked off. Only the largest letters were still legible and they read *'Adolphe Absolon et Fils, Esprit Marchands'*.

We looked at each other for a moment before Barkas, who we all naturally looked to for leadership, touched Capel on the shoulder and gestured that he should follow him. He walked purposefully down the alley but stopped at the door and put his ear close to it. Goriau and I cautiously followed after them, and reached the door just as Barkas was trying the latch. To our surprise the inner-bar lifted and the door opened. A gloomy light emanated from the back of the building, and Barkas pushed Capel in front of him as they went in. Goriau and I hung back outside the door, glancing a little nervously at each other, and we both visibly jumped when we heard a voice raise a challenge from inside.

"*Qui est-ce*? Is that you, Evan?" demanded a voice heavily laden with a Welsh accent.

Capel replied, 'No it ain't,' and I could tell from the sudden exertion in his voice that he had started running.

No one had considered the possibility of a night-watchman. I forced myself to go through the doorway, and saw a very startled Welshman staggering to his feet. In his panic, he stumbled against a wooden crate and half lost his footing. In the next instant Capel had his huge hands around the man's throat, and was forcing him backwards behind one of the wooden lattice partitions that divided the interior of the warehouse. Barkas was close behind them and he too disappeared from view. The scream of pain that followed sent a testicle-tightening chill through the length of my body. I ran across the stone floor not knowing what to expect. When I reached the partition, a gruesome mêlée was underway. Capel had a fearsome grip on the Welshman's windpipe with his left hand, and he seemed to be fending off Barkas with his right. The Welshman's eyes showed larger whites than I had ever seen before, save for a bullock that had not been slain by the first stroke from the butcher's cleaver. His face was deep crimson and the blood vessels in his neck were as fat as the stems of creeping ivy. He was striking out wildly for his assailant's eyes as he fought for his life, but Capel was too strong and his arm too long. With a violent shove the huge man shucked Barkas away from him and the seaman fell on his backside. In that instant, Capel grabbed the stumpy home made blade from the back of his belt.

"No," I screamed, as the knife slash across the petrified Welshman's neck: first from right to left and then back again. I rushed forward, I don't know what I thought to achieve, but stopped as the unfortunate night-watchman crumpled mechanically onto his knees. His wildly staring eyes fixed for a few moments on his murderer before he fell forward making a horrible slapping sound as his face hit the stone flags. Capel contemptuously stood over him, and shook the excess blood from his hand as if its presence somehow offended him.

My hostility towards Capel erupted! "You utter bastard ... you stupid, hateful bastard," I yelled at him. He turned a malevolent but slightly quizzical gaze onto me and Barkas, who had just struggled to his feet, leapt between us.

"Leave it, Nat," he shouted. "'E shouldn't 'ave done it, but it's too late to remedy that now. Remember that these are the bastards that killed Josh."

"That's still no reason to needlessly butcher the man! We could have tied him up. We've got to sit tight in this town for hours, how are we gonna hide that?" I yelled, sweeping my hand in the direction of the night-watchman.

"He could 'ave seen the boat, and anyway, 'e saw me. It's safer that 'e's dead," growled Capel, and I swear there was a thin smile on his lips.

The Welshman's body gave a little jerk as it lay in a spreading pool of blood, and I assumed that he was now dead. Barkas pulled me away and I could feel that he was shaking.

"Nat, you go search up top," he ordered. "We'll take whatever is most valuable. I can see that there's plenty o' cognac, but take your time an' see if you can find any silk or lace, they always fetch a good price."

Biting back my anger, I decided that it was best to control myself and do as bidden. There was a rough, wooden ladder nearby that led to a mezzanine that covered three-quarters of the warehouse. The light from the night watchman's lamp just penetrated the murk on this upper-floor where it merged with the pale moonlight that ghosted through the partially glazed windows that lined one wall. There were piles of goods in untidy stacks all around me. Strangely each pile had prices chalked on boards that lay beside them. At the top there were prices in francs and decimes and beside them there were prices in English guineas: presumably

- 143 -

a 'sell on' price which seemed to make the silver franc worth something similar to a golden guinea!

One pile of casks was simply marked *'Hollands'*. This was the rich, cheap gin that was still popular in England's towns. The casks were small and could easily be managed by one man - like the ones we had unloaded from *Peggy Ann* when we had put Croskell and Mawgan ashore. There were also bales of cloth (I didn't know what kind, but not silk), scarves, ladies gloves and even some cases of glassware but mostly it was cognac. There was row after row of cognac or *'Nantz'* as the chalk signs described it. Goriau had told us that Bonaparte had built several distilleries near Nantes to supply the 'free-trade' with cheap spirit, and this was just one of the warehouses where the French smugglers came to buy it.

"There is no silk or lace, Samuel," I called down the ladder.

"Quiet," he hissed back. "Keep your voice low. The night watchman may be dead but we don't know who else might be about. Come down 'ere and help us load cognac."

When I got back to ground level, Capel was disappearing out of the door with a cask under each arm. The sight of him was abhorrent, and as I met Barkas at the bottom of the stairs, my expression betrayed my loathing.

"Come on, Nat. We 'ave to forget what 'as happened and get away from here. These tubs seem to be the best quality," he said, waving his hand towards a neat stack of casks behind the ladder. "Take a couple t' the boat."

Making my way to the door, I saw that some packing cases had been pulled around the night-watchman's body and stacked high against the lattice partition. I didn't want to look too closely, but I fancied that a little pool of dark blood was beginning to seep out from beneath the timber boxes.

The four of us scurried up and down the quayside as quietly as possible, carrying tubs of spirit to *Peggy Ann*. It took us about an hour-and-a-half to ferry fifty-five or sixty of the small casks to the cutter and stow them below deck, and in all that time we saw nobody. *Peggy's* guts were three-quarters full, when Barkas decided we had enough on board.

"That'll do," he said, taking hold of my arm to stop me heading back up the quayside to the warehouse. "I don't want her so full she'll not sail. Take the weight off your feet, Nat. We'll 'ave a few hours wait before there's enough water to take

Peggy-Ann out o' here."

I felt suddenly exhausted and slumped down on the coach house roof, but Barkas pointed me towards the companionway.

"We'd better all stay out o' sight," he said. "I can't believe there 'aint goin' to be some sort of patrol along at some time tonight."

"What about the body? We'll be done for if someone finds that."

"Relax, Nat," Barkas replied calmly. "The curfew don't end 'till eight o'clock, an' we'll be on our way afore then."

I wished I could share Barkas' composure. Glancing across the river and in what little moonlight there was, I could see the river had dropped to barely a quarter of the width it had been when we came in. In the milky light, the water looked as black and as solid as polished jet stone with the uncovered sandbanks, that surrounded it, shimmering with an eerie luminescence. The row of stout mooring posts that I had seen on our way into the river were now clear of the water, and stood broodingly in the sand like giant, black sentinels.

The prospect of spending the next five hours in a cramped cabin with four other men was nauseating, but the knowledge that one of them was going to be Capel made it a hundred times worse. How I hated him! Climbing onto the companion ladder, I could see the bastard making his way down the quayside with a tub under one arm and a wooden box full of bottles under the other.

I made my way into the little cabin, followed by Barkas and Jean Goriau. There was only one chair and so I selected Barkas' kit box in the corner and sat down. I reasoned that Barkas would take his chair and Capel and the Goriaus would have to sit on the cot. At least, if I had to bear the pain of sitting in a tiny cabin with a detestable man, he would have to sit as far away from me as possible.

"What is it that you have there, Jas?" I heard Marc ask Capel at the top of the companion ladder.

"Well, there 'aint much point sittin' in a boat full o' spirit if there 'aint none to drink is there, Frenchie. So I brought us a few bottles."

Just the sound of his voice made my tensions rise. I heard the blood pumping through my ears, and knew the next few hours were going to be a severe trial. I kicked off my boots and pushed myself further into my corner. I knew there was no chance of finding sleep but I shut my eyes and prepared to wait out my torment.

CHAPTER TWELVE
*The Brittany Coast, North Western France
– 24th June 1809*

It is my contention that the cutter, which is a vessel of native British design, is insufficiently employed within His Majesty's Senior Service. The Excise Service has made excellent use of the speed, manoeuvrability and windward capabilities of cutters; all of whose capabilities are derived from a comparatively large rig, counterbalanced by a deep draught. There can be no more than 40 cutters currently registered to the Navy roster, but I have witnessed first-hand the flexibility these craft provide on the West Indies Station. A 70ft cutter of about 100 tons can comfortably serve ten 18-pounder carronades, or indeed fewer longer guns, and operate as excellent support vessels to squadrons on blockade duties.
        Post-Captain Cornelius Carroll writing to the Portsmouth Gazette, October 1806

By first light, we were punching back into the westerly that had been our benefactor the previous evening. *Peggy-Ann* was being buffeted by the kind of steep waves that are often found over shallow waters near a coastline. My comrades were flushed with their success and a couple of bottles were doing the rounds of the cockpit. Capel and Barkas had started their drinking during the night and the Frenchmen had joined in when we had successfully navigated the harbour exit and reached the relative safety of Douarnenez Bay. Barkas' behaviour was the most shocking; anyone would think he had rooked the Bank of England the way he was shouting. I didn't exactly begrudge any of them their joy, but I couldn't participate. To my mind, we were still far from safe, and any spirits that I had to share with Jas Capel would have turned sour in my mouth. Why had that arse-hole had to gut the night-watchman? Everything had been going so well until that moment and now all I was left with was the image of a dying man crumpling onto a cold, stone floor.

The previous night's incarceration in *Peggy's* tiny cabin had been an interminable ordeal; the longest night of my life. I had cursed the name of Viscount Alton a score of times for instigating the chain of events that caused me to have to endure it. Sleep had been quite out of the question because of Capel's braying voice, bragging about how he had 'seen to' the night watchman when 'none of us could'. Feigning sleep in my corner, I railed at my own inability to do anything about him. My loathing for the man was so intense that I felt nauseous sitting close to him. Inexplicably, the others seemed to have accepted what he had done as some sort of necessity. Was it ridiculous of me to hate him so much?

The sound of floodwaters gurgling against the hull had come as a blessed relief in the predawn, and I had got out of the cabin and away from Capel as soon as Barkas had given the word that it was time to leave.

The lanterns along the quayside had burnt out during the night, but the early dawn haze revealed no signs of life onshore. It took our combined muscle to shove *Peggy's* prow far enough away from the quayside to catch the breeze in our jib. It was still a few hours shy of the town's curfew ending when we made the best use of the early morning breeze to beat back up the channel beside the Île Tristan.

Barkas hadn't opted to hug the coastline but had instead set a course deep into the bay before coming onto a long starboard tack that took us beyond the southern headland. The odd ribald cry from the cockpit had convinced me to stay away from the others, and I settled on the foredeck and stared at the grey murk that filled the horizon in front of me. The sun was on its way up but it was struggling to penetrate the cloud blowing in from the Atlantic. A single fulmar, accustomed to finding an easy meal by following fishing boats, rode the wind abeam of us and I was watching the bird's effortless display of flying skill when I became aware of a figure lurching along the starboard side towards me. It was Capel! My heart took a dive. Why couldn't the bastard leave me alone? I just wanted to avoid him until we made it back to Scilly and then, I promised myself, I would never climb aboard the same boat as him again.

"What you doin' sittin' by yer self," he said, in the thick speech of a drunkard as he slumped onto the deck next to me. "We got away wit' it! So why don't ya' have a drink wit' me."

"I don't need a drink, Jas. There is still much to do, can't you just leave me alone?" I replied, in as placatory a manner as possible.

"Tetchy git 'aint ya'," he slurred. "I know you wus upset that I had to kill that fella." His evil smirk was portentous of the brandy-fuelled hubris that was to follow. "Someone had to kill 'im. 'E knew what we was about an' it's only 'cos I was man enough to do it that we're all safe an' sound now," he said.

Even by his standards of stupidity Capel was sailing into uncharted water; I think he genuinely believed he had done something heroic, which warranted my congratulations. He pushed his ugly face far too close to mine, jutting out his jaw in a weird manifestation of what I can only interpret as indignation. Revulsion and anger rose within me with equal measure, but my mind was still clear enough to apply a firm brake to my emotions. Even in his current state of inebriation, Capel was a dangerous man, and I felt the familiar tremble in the muscles of my right arm that I often felt when the prospect of danger was close by. I needed to get rid of him and quickly, but I had no idea how. Then a flash of inspiration hit me and I shot onto my feet.

"A ship! A ship coming over the horizon," I yelled at him, pointing frantically into the grey void ahead of us.

"Wha… I can't see nothin'," mumbled the idiot, stumbling forward in an effort to clamber to his feet.

"Quick, tell Samuel. We are in imminent danger," I said, pushing him in the direction of the cockpit.

He ignored my attempts to send him sternward, and using a shroud to steady himself against the action of the swell, stared in the direction I had pointed.

"There 'aint no ship," he started, screwing up his eyes in an effort to see a sail that I knew he would not find.

"There, there!" I yelled at him, waving my arm vaguely in front of him. "Tell Samuel now! We'll have to reset all the heads'ls."

I knew that the prospect of hauling on lines would see Capel off and rushed forward to pull the coiled tail of the jib sheet from its cleat. That was enough and thankfully he shuffled off back down the deck.

Alone again, I replaced the sheet and took a couple of deep breaths as my anger subsided. Billowing towers of cloud were building in the western sky, underscored with the kind of thick, grey miasma that can foretell only of bad weather. The darkness over the water rendered the horizon almost undetectable as the sky and the sea melded together. Barkas and Goriau appeared at my shoulder.

"Jas say that you have seen *un bateau*," said Marc, straining his eyes to study the murky filth ahead.

"Well ... I may have, I'm not sur___"

"Did you see anythin', Nat?" interrupted Barkas, "or were you just sayin' that to get rid of 'im?"

He was grinning as he spoke. At least my ruse to rid myself of Capel hadn't disturbed Barkas' high spirits.

"Capel's a liability," I hissed. "Samuel, when we get back to Scilly we'll have to put him aboard a boat for the mainland."

"You're right enough, I reckon," replied Barkas, "but we can't foist him on someone else, we'll 'ave to take 'im oursel___"

Barkas stopped mid-sentence and we all exchanged looks because to the north of us came the unmistakeable, dull rumble of heavy guns.

"Nathaniel did see *un bateau*!" exclaimed a wide-eyed Goriau.

"Now don't you two start getting' any peril-some notions," Barkas said nonchalantly. "That'll be the British blockade takin' exception to some Frenchman. They're miles away an' I don't reckon they'll give us any bother but we'll stay on this starboard tack for an hour or so an' give 'em plenty o' sea room."

My arm muscles began to tremble again. It was almost as if by lying to Capel I had brought the Navy down upon us. The thought of being stopped by British warships in a boat stuffed full of contraband alerted all my instincts of self-preservation but Barkas' confidence went some way to reassuring me.

"We're headin' straight for a fogbank, looks like," he said. "If the Navy are about they'll 'ave a hell of a job findin' us in that lot."

Despite Barkas' confidence, the mood aboard *Peggy-Ann*

changed radically. The brandy bottles were dispatched over the side, and my crewmates became instantly quiet and watchful. We pushed on towards the dank weather ahead of us which had suddenly become all the more inviting. The first fine, traces of sea fog were already streaming around us in long, translucent trails and much denser drifts lay ahead. After about quarter-of-an-hour, we were inside the comforting shroud of a fogbank that was so thick that I could hardly see from the bow to the stern. A few minutes more and we burst out into a patch of clear water again, but the next bank was only a cable length further on. We continued like this for some time, slipping in and out of drifting banks of fog. Usually, the areas between them were filled with finer, translucent veils of vapour, but occasionally we found ourselves in clear air with a view on one side or the other. We broke into one clear patch of water, much wider than any of the others, and I was at the starboard shrouds watching the French coastline slip under the horizon when Marc Goriau shouted the warning that we all dreaded from the larboard rail.

"*Regardez! Un bateau.*"

I ran to the other side of the boat.

"Where away?" Barkas shouted from the tiller.

Goriau was pointing north, and all our eyes turned to see the crisp white sail that was bearing down on us. He was on a broad reach, no more than two miles away and was swiftly making water on us.

"I don't believe it ... it's a British naval cutter," shouted Barkas. I stared stupefied at the newcomer; amazed that no one had noticed her before. At that distance, she looked quite beautiful; trim and sleek as she flew across the water. Her sail plan was similar to *Peggy-Ann's*, but I knew she was, in fact, much bigger and that she presented a very real threat to my life. Looking for leadership, we had all instinctively gathered around Barkas at the tiller.

"Where did she come from?" I asked, of nobody in particular.

"Never mind where he came from, if he catches us he'll stretch our necks, Egan," squawked Capel.

"The British, you hang smugglers?" asked Marc.

"We're mutineers!" yelled back Capel.

"They'll never know you wus mutineers," said Barkas, "but one thing is certain, they'll take our cargo, and they'll take *Peggy-Ann!*"

"We 'ave to lose 'em in the next bank o' fog," Capel shouted, frantically. He was losing his self control and demonstrating the panic I was desperately fighting to control.

Barkas remained impassive: God bless him. He ignored Capel and after studying the situation for a few moments he said, "We should shake out them reefs; with all *Peggy's* clothes on we can give 'em a good race to the next fogbank."

I had quite forgotten that in an effort to make *Peggy-Ann* look more like a fishing boat, we had shortened our mains'l and taken much of our bowsprit inboard before we left St. Agnes. Now we were in need of every inch of canvas we could carry. The good thing was that there was no time to worry about the advancing cutter: we had a lot of work to do and we had to do it quickly! Barkas pointed the cutter into the wind and I shook the reef out of the flapping mains'l while Marc, Jean and Capel hauled on the gaff halyards. The two Frenchmen and I then ran to the foredeck where we let off both fores'l sheets and dragged out the bowsprit. Capel had collected the number one jib from its station beside the main shrouds, and we feverishly worked to bend it on. The moment we had the big sail at the top of the forestay Barkas pushed the tiller away, and *Peggy-Ann* leapt back into life. Her bow picked up and she rode a little higher towards the wind than before.

"Harden everythin' up and we'll race 'em to the next fogbank," commanded Barkas.

The sanctuary of the next fogbank was fully two cable lengths ahead and even with all our canvas out the cutter was still gaining on us. Their sails transformed into narrower triangles as they sheeted-in and turned on to the same course as us and the size of his fores'l grew steadily as they gained on us. She was probably about a hundred foot long, well over a hundred tons and much bigger than the Excise cutters that I'd seen in the Bristol Channel while fishing with my father. I could now make out the white ensign that flew from the back of his gaff and knew that our pursuer was in deadly earnest.

Capel obviously saw the ensign at the same moment as me, and he grabbed for the halyard that flew a little tricolour from our starboard backstay.

"Leave it," commanded Barkas.

"But he'll think we're Frogs," protested Capel.

"That's what I want him to think," Barkas shouted back. "We might trick 'im into waiting for us. If 'e thinks we're Frogs 'e'll

- 151 -

expect us to turn under the cover of the fog an' try an' run back to France."

Ever since this escapade had begun, I had been more scared of running into the Royal Navy than of sailing into a French port. Barkas was probably right that the chances of anyone on board the cutter recognising Capel and I as mutineers was minimal, but we were obviously smuggling and because we had Frenchmen with us, they might even treat us as spies.

There was a puff of white smoke from the bow of the cutter and half a second later it was accompanied by the dull thud of a gun being fired. I waited but saw no splash.

"He's started firing," I shouted to Barkas who was at the tiller skilfully guiding *Peggy-Ann* across the face of each swell to keep as much wind in our sails as possible.

"He'll only have a little gun in the bow. That will be 'is warnin' shot telling us to heave-to. He'll have to tack if 'e wants to give us a broadside and if 'e does we'll be in that fog," he shouted back.

I was confident in Barkas' seamanship and the dark haven of the fog bank ahead was tantalisingly close. The first wisps of mist were around us already, and soon the cutter would lose clear sight of us. Looking straight ahead, there were only fifty yards of water beyond the bowsprit before everything was enveloped in the inviting grey abyss. The cutter was still more than a cable length behind us, but his jib twitched and then crumpled as the wind disappeared from it. His bow went down and his mains'l swung across the deck: He was coming about!

"He's going to fire on us before we reach the fog," I warned. Four guns became visible as the cutter turned and as I spoke white smoke belched from each of them. My mouth instantly went painfully dry and I worked my jaw frantically trying to produce saliva as I waited those few moments as the shot made its way towards us. He couldn't hit us from there while he was making a turn, could he?

"He's a hopeful one, he is," quipped Barkas.

First, there were two splashes well short of us, but they were followed by two more which were only thirty yards off our starboard side. The wisps of fog around were rapidly turning into dense drifts, and Barkas bore off the wind a little to head into the thickest of them. The naval cutter was obscured from view by the time I heard the thumping of her next broadside. Clinging to the gunwale, I held my breath and waited for something to happen. There was a splash not fifteen yards away from me and some droplets of water landed on the deck by my feet. In the next instant, there was a sickening crunch at our bow and the awful sound of splintering wood.

"It's only the forward rail," yelled Barkas. "Lady Luck is by our side."

Air gushed back into my empty lungs as *Peggy-Ann* pitched on into the sanctity of the fog, her speed unaffected by the hit.

"Ready about," commanded Barkas. "We'll tack: he's bound to try another shot but we'll just 'ave to hope 'e guesses the wrong way."

In the next few minutes there was another crash of guns, but they sounded a little further off this time, and there were no telltale splashes. We were now encased in a shroud of fog, and reassuringly I could see no more than thirty yards in any direction.

Peggy-Ann was a fast boat, and it was distressing to think the Navy's cutter could run her down so easily, but with an extra forty feet in length and thirty-odd crewmen, she could manage much more sail than we ever could. But for the moment I just clung to the knowledge that every yard increased our safety.

"How long do you think the fog can hold, Samuel?" I asked.

"I think we're safe for a couple o' hours," he said. "As long as it keeps driftin' in from the west I'll keep headin' that way."

"*Pensez-vous que* he will wait for us to return to the coast *de la* France?" asked Marc.

"I think I would 'ide in the fog outside Douarnenez Bay if I were 'im. If they saw us come out o' there they will be expecting us to try an' get back in," reasoned Barkas.

The oakum tell-tales flying from our stays showed that the wind was still blowing steadily from the west and Barkas regularly tacked across the breeze, hopefully putting more miles between the cutter and us.

Our encounter with the Navy shook my shipmates to the core, and *Peggy-Ann's* deck fell completely quiet. Even the arse-hole Capel managed to keep his mouth shut, and every face wore the same anxious, watchful expression, that I'm sure my own did. But the longer we stayed cocooned inside the thick morass of sea fog confidence started to slowly seep back inside us all. I was more circumspect than the others, but there was a tiny glow of optimism somewhere deep in my stomach. After about half-an-hour, Marc

Goriau felt safe enough to let out a piercing yell that he followed with a few relief laden oaths in both English and French. When the weight of raw fear is lifted from men, they often feel the need to dispel their tension through talking, and it was no surprise to me that Capel became the most garrulous.

"The Navy 'ad me goin' there for a minute," he said, slapping at his chest above his heart with the flat of his hand and laughing. "Who's to join me in a little drink?" He positioned himself on the top of the coach house roof and had a bottle in his hand. "We'll be alright from now on, trust me. That were a close shave that were…Come on, help me sup this bottle."

Astonishingly, Marc and Jean took up his invitation and made their way to the coach house and sat down beside him. Marc took a long pull on the bottle while Capel just continued to babble stupid rubbish. No matter how relieved I felt, I was no more inclined to listen to his drivel and moved down the boat to stand at the rail by Barkas.

"Do you want a spell away from the tiller, Samuel?" I asked.

"I'd better stay here for another hour or so longer," he replied. "I'd like ye to go for'ard, Nat, and keep a sharp eye amidships. I 'aint sure that we can rely on they," he nodded towards the trio of drinkers on the coach roof. "Fog like this can have a habit of clearing very quickly."

A little reluctantly, I took up a position by the mast and stared into the grey nothingness that insulated us completely from the outside world. Standing here it was impossible not to hear Capel's loathsome voice engaged in conversation with Marc.

"How was it that you ever become *un matelot*?" I heard Goriau asking him.

"Eh? … Not by choice … I were forced into it," answered Capel. "I was framed by some flea-ridden bastards in Birmingham. I wus an overseer for a button maker and I 'eard a whisper that some Luddites were plottin' to attack our foundry."

For the first time in my life, I was spellbound by every word Jas Capel had to say.

"What are Luddites?" enquired Goriau.

"Low-life revolutionaries. They was tryin' to stir up trouble amongst the workers an' get 'em to break up our steam engine."

"But were not these workers your *camarades*?"

"They were no comrades of mine, Marc. I was paid to keep the foundry runnin'. If them bastards 'ad smashed the machine

I'd 'ave been out of a job. As it was, I laid in wait for 'em and cracked a few 'eads before the militia showed up."

I clung to the rail by the starboard shrouds to steady myself: my head was spinning from his revelation. My arm was shaking, but this time not from fear but naked, uncontrollable anger. Capel was the bastard who had wielded the cudgel in the foundry, which meant he was also the whoreson who had turned me out of my home the day Mary was buried! Forcing myself to stare rigidly into the fog, I realised I had reached the very limit of my self-restraint. If I so much as looked at Capel now, I knew that I would simply fly at him and he was much too big for that. This had to be done right: what was needed was self-control and a weapon. My fingernails were digging deeper and deeper into the timber of the side rail. Here was a man I detested before hearing his execrable story, but listening to him made my hatred grow into a visceral monster that consumed me in the same way the need to run had consumed me after the explosion on *Albion*.

"I understand not what these Luddites have to do with your becoming of *un matelot*?" continued Goriau.

"All soldiers are dullards," Capel snarled. "They arrested me along wit' the bleedin' revolutionaries. Them Luddites 'ad put their 'eads together and concocted a story that convinced the magistrate that I was one of 'em. Stupid old toff convicted me of 'Political Congress' and sentenced me to naval service."

For his part, Capel was oblivious to the effect his tale was having, but he had still more fuel to stoke the avenging fire that had been set alight inside me.

"I got even with them bastards though," His sickening voice continued. "They put 'alf a dozen of us in the same cell an' I was wit' this little old Welsh git who wouldn't leave me alone. 'E was no more than five foot tall an' 'e kept tellin' me that fate was punishing me for my sins. I can remember 'is face as clear as I can see yours now. 'E had ginger and grey tufts of beard all over 'is chin and not a hair on 'is head."

His description could only be of my old friend Thos Bagley; he was just the pugnacious sort who would persist with baiting Capel in a prison cell.

"When everyone was asleep I smacked the old git in the guts."

"But for why to do this?" asked Goriau incredulously.

"He was one o' they. He 'ad conspired against me with the rest of 'em. Anyway, 'is bald 'ead shot bolt upright and 'e stared into my eyes for a second an' then 'e folded up, dead like. In the mornin' the guard reasoned 'is heart had stopped in the night. If only they knew 'eh? 'E won't be harassin' Jas Capel no more."

And then the evil bastard let out the disdainful laugh that was the final straw. In that second, it became obvious it was my responsibility to exterminate him. I couldn't explain why this task was mine and mine alone, but I can only surmise my hatred was so intense it had taken control of my mind. In fact, my brain was so deranged with loathing that everything on the deck took on an unreal, almost dreamlike, appearance. For some reason, which I could not explain, I found myself drawn slowly towards the coach-house door in front of the cockpit. I walked purposefully behind Capel and the Goriaus without so much as glancing in their direction. I took a few steps down the companion and ducked my head out of sight.

My hands slid across the polished panelling to the left of the door. It was as if they were no longer under my control. My fingers frantically explored every groove and crevice in the wood, searching for something. Suddenly, a sprung catch gave way, and my hands pushed into the secret locker that subconsciously I knew had to be there. Quickly, I found the smooth butt of the duelling pistol Barkas had produced only a week before. Groping around a little further led to the discovery of a powder horn. I guessed that Barkas wouldn't keep his emergency firearm unloaded and so I quickly filled the priming pan with powder, snapped down the wind guard and shoved the pistol into my waistband and hid it with my jacket.

When I stepped from the companion and back onto the deck, my thoughts were a little more ordered: I had my weapon now and was in control of proceedings. The dreamlike haze had left my vision, but my determination to exterminate Capel was as clear as before.

The westerly wind had increased a little, and it was now strong enough to sting my left cheek. The fogbank that had encased us so tightly was starting to drift apart. To avoid seeing Capel, I concentrated my attention over the larboard rail and saw wide stretches of rolling ocean that would have been hidden under a blanket of fog only a few moments before.

I had never considered killing a man before, but Capel no longer qualified as human: he was an obscenity, and I was going to extirpate him. It flashed through my mind that my resolve might desert me as I actually pointed the gun at its target, but I didn't allow myself to dwell on the thought. He had slaughtered Quartermaster Robinson, the night watchman and Thos Bagley out of sheer blood lust, and now I was going to avenge them. I forced myself to look at him so as to concentrate my mind. He was still sitting on the front of the coach house in between the two Frenchmen with his back towards me. I moved forward, keeping my eyes fixed on the back of his head. The look on my face would have betrayed everything if he turned round, but he didn't and just carried on yakking to the Goriaus. I was getting very close, but my mind was in such a fevered state that I couldn't take in what they were saying. I was reaching down to my waistband and fingering the butt of the pistol, when *Peggy-Ann* heeled violently to a strong gust and I stumbled sideways. I had to balance myself with a hand to the coach house roof. Jean Goriau stood up and moved for'ard, as if he was going to check on the for's'ls. For a few seconds, Capel's life was spared, but I steadied myself and locked my eyes on the back of his skull, waiting for the gust to abate before drawing the pistol.

In that instant, my murderous plan was quite literally blown asunder. There was a thunderous rumble of powder and a flash so bright that I will remember it until the day that I die. *Peggy-Ann* shuddered as she was shunted sideways through the water and her starboard side exploded into a million splinters. Jean Goriau emitted an awful, piercing cry from somewhere near the bow. I was thrown flat onto the deck beside the coach house and the first thing I heard was Barkas yelling: "It's the bloody Navy. They've found us in the fog. Help me on the tiller, Nat."

When I lifted my head above the coach house, I saw Marc run screaming towards where his brother had been. I was completely shaken out of my executioner's trance and climbed to my feet and started for the cockpit. Unbelievably, the glowing white sails of the naval cutter were emerging from the fog no more than thirty yards away from us. She was on a starboard reach and heading behind our stern. How had they found us? I clearly saw a seaman on their foredeck, bringing a swivel gun to bear on *Peggy-Ann* and instinctively threw myself back onto the deck. The gun fired. It sounded puny in comparison to the broadside that had preceded it, but the deathly rattle of grapeshot peppering our deck was muscular enough. Raising my head above what was left of the rail, the cutter swept majestically past us and disappeared once again into the mist beyond. I surveyed the damage behind me and saw Barkas lying in the cockpit. Struggling to my feet, I made to run towards him but stopped almost immediately. I didn't have to go to him. I could tell from where I stood that the mutilated body with the fearful grimace on its face had no chance of being alive. The deck around him had been torn and gouged by the two-ounce lead shot that had been packed into the gun.

"*Mon frère, mon frère. Où est mon frère?*" Goriau wailed behind me. Instinctively, I started to move towards him, not that I thought there was anything I could do to help, when I heard another command.

"Get back to the tiller, Egan."

For those few seconds, I had entirely forgotten about Capel's existence but when he spoke to me the full weight of my hatred gushed back into my brain.

"There's no point in the navy catchin' all o' us. Get to the tiller an' try an' make 'em follow you. I'm headin' back into that sea fog."

He was dragging *Peggy-Ann's* tiny tender to the larboard rail.

"Get on with it you little shit," he yelled at me over his shoulder.

"Jean … Jean," Goriau whimpered from the foredeck.

I don't know which was more appalling: the deaths of Barkas and Jean, or Capel's belief I would be prepared to sacrifice myself in an attempt to draw the Navy away from him while he made his escape. I watched motionless as he manfully tipped the little boat over the side. A task only someone of Capel's gargantuan size could have achieved unaided. He had stripped away his shirt, and I clearly saw the black bear tattoo I had first seen outside my house in Birmingham.

Peggy-Ann couldn't have been sailed even if I had any intention of doing so. At least one of the balls from the cutter's broadside had broached our hull, and we were taking in water. She was starting to list and even with the mains'l still full we were only crabbing across the swell and hardly making any headway. The gaps in the swirling fogbanks off our starboard side were widening but the murk was as dense as ever to larboard and behind us. There was no sign of the cutter, but he would be turning into the wind behind us. It would only take her a few minutes to reappear and when she did her guns would be reloaded and primed for firing.

I supposed that Capel was right and there was a chance that one man could row unseen into the thickest of the fog, from where he might possibly affect an escape. He slung some oars into the tender and swung his legs onto the rail as he prepared to jump down. Walking up behind him, I pulled the pistol out of my waistband and pointed the muzzle at the back of his head. A cold bead of sweat began to trickle down my temple and my heart was thumping against my ribs. My hand shook as I tried to aim the gun steadily at his skull. For an instant, I didn't think I would be able to go through with it, but the thought of Capel surviving to needlessly murder again was enough to spur me on, and I squeezed the trigger. I didn't have the stomach to witness the consequences of my actions and turned my head away. The powder in the priming pan fizzed and the pistol kicked in my hand. At that instant, I joined the ranks of the world's murderers, and there was a moment's silence before Capel's bulk slapped over the rail and then splashed into the ocean. I had killed for the first time and felt nothing inside at all.

I tossed the pistol into the water and turned my attention to Marc. There was no sign of his brother, and the Frenchman was sobbing uncontrollably and running frantically from one gunwale to the other.

"We must turn *le bateau*. *Mon petit frère* has disappeared."

"Marc ... he has gone," I said as gently as possible.

"I promised *ma mere* to look after him."

"I must drop our ensign or well have another broadside from that cutter."

"*Non ... non*, you will help me tack *le bateau* ..."

Goriau grabbed hold of me and started to push me towards the cockpit. I just managed to hold my ground, but he almost had me over. I seized handfuls of his jerkin and swung him backwards by his shoulders until he was pinned against the mast.

"If we don't haul down our colours you and I will die as well as Barkas and your brother," I screamed at him my mouth only inches away from his face.

It didn't matter how close I got to him or how loud I shouted: he wasn't able to hear. But he did stop fighting me and just whispered pitifully, "Help me to turn, help me turn."

I knew the naval cutter would reappear any second, and I left Goriau and hauled down the French tricolour that was flying from our gaff. I pulled it to halfway down the mains'l where I was sure it would indicate our submission. Goriau had followed me down the boat and was standing open-mouthed over Barkas' carcass. I wanted it to be clear to the Navy that we had given up, and I didn't want them to see anyone near our tiller.

"We must leave the tiller unattended, Marc," I commanded, but without any real conviction he would obey me.

"Help me turn, help me turn," he started again.

There wasn't time to coax him away from the stern and so I enveloped him in a bear hug and tried to walk him up the deck. He started to shout and struggle, and it was all I could do to hold onto him, even though I was much bigger than he was. He managed to get one of his arms free and landed a couple of blows on the side of my head. He was starting to rant and scream, and his rolling eyes indicated he had lost all control. A stream of nonesensible drivel was coming from his mouth and he was working himself into a wild frenzy. Where was the bloody Navy? I wanted them to arrive now and put an end to this. The outcome of impending recapture was enough for me to contend with, without having to fight a maddened friend. And then she reappeared! As if in answer to my pleading, the cutter burst out of the fog bank behind us: a gleaming predator bearing down on her prey. I felt a surge of relief but at the same time prayed that gun smoke didn't belch from her side.

The emotions of the last few minutes had left my mind blank, and my struggles with Goriau had sapped the last of my strength. I was hanging on to him as tightly as possible and watching the cutter over his shoulder, when my knees involuntarily sagged beneath me. My eyes widened in disbelief, and I let go of the demented Frenchmen as the cutter drew close by. Standing at the bow in the uniform of a naval lieutenant and staring straight at me was the unmistakable figure of Jacob Ebbs!

CHAPTER THIRTEEN
The Brittany Coast – 24th June 1809

My Dearest Jacob,
Your letter gave me the most dreadful fright. The thought of my little brother in the hands of mutineers was almost more than I could bear. It was painful to read, but I thank the Lord they saw fit to grant you your chance with providence and cast you into the sea. They could so easily have robbed you of your life, which I think would have brought an end to my own.
Turning to matters more pleasant, do you have any news of your friend Mr Egan? I have to admit that I enjoyed his society at Portsmouth. Is it known whether he survived the battle?
A letter from Lady Sarah Ebbs to her brother Jacob, dispatched on 3rd May 1809

A wave of disbelief ran through me: what was *he* doing here? I could only stare, in the hope that any second I would realise my mistake, and the smartly dressed lieutenant standing on the approaching cutter would turn out to be someone who merely resembled Jacob Ezekiel Ebbs ... but that realisation did not happen!

Marc Goriau continued his tormented ranting, but my mind was overloaded assimilating Ebbs' reincarnation, and I let my hold of him drop. The Navy cutter started to spill wind to lose speed, and inscribed a graceful arc behind us. She turned smartly to windward and hove-to about fifty yards distant. Ebbs remained motionless at the rail the whole time, and I'd swear that the intensity of his glare was boring holes into my head.

The reappearance of the cutter was a significant enough event to penetrate Goriau's grief and drag him back into the here and now. His eyes still shone with tears, but at least his words started to make sense again.

"We are *un Anglais et un Français* together. We must say *tout de suite* that we are contrebandiers and not spies, or they may hang us. I will say I am a monarchist, and that I *répugne* Buonaparte," he said in a surprisingly intelligible way.

"He knows ... he knows ... who I am."

It was my turn to make little sense. Goriau, momentarily silenced by my reply, flashed his eyes frantically from me to the naval officer who stood at the cutters rail.

"*Qui est-il*? Do you know him?" he asked.

"What? ... Yes, I know him," I replied distractedly.

"Then who shall I tell that I am?"

I was too stunned to be able to offer any advice and could only stare at Ebbs in silence.

"Nathaniel, who is he?" hissed Goriau, urgently.

I heard him, but he sounded as distant to me as I must have to him only a few minutes before.

The cutter launched a boat, and five men climbed into her and started to pull towards us.

"I must know, Nathaniel. I must know what I am to say?" pleaded Goriau.

I desperately wanted to help him, but I just couldn't make myself speak; although, I had no idea how to advise him even if I could.

Peggy-Ann's starboard side was so low in the water by now that the cutter's crewmen took their jollyboat round our bow to the larboard side, and Goriau and I watched a sprightly but hefty quartermaster swing himself over the rail.

"Let's be 'aving you then. It looks as though you're for goin' down, so look lively or we'll all be swimming. Is you Frenchies or Englishmen?" he barked, as soon as his feet landed on the deck.

Goriau was waiting for me to take the initiative, I felt compelled to say something but all I could do was raise my hands in a submissive gesture. The petty officer glared at us suspiciously, but then turned his attention to the seamen who were following him over the side.

"Get below, Bo'sun. Let's see what they are so keen not to talk about. Clavey, search the cabin, and bring me any charts an' the log if there is one," he commanded before turning his attention back to us. "So what's it to be then? Frenchmen or Englishmen?"

I ignored his questions, but my mind was beginning to return from its befuddled fog. Should I make an effort to rush and fetch Barkas' passport before the seaman had time to rifle through the papers in the cabin? But then I thought, that presenting an 'Immunity from Impressement' paper to Ebbs, who was more aware than anyone of my service history, was not likely to prove a winning course of action.

"We are *contrebandiers*." I heard Goriau blurt out. "*Je suis* French."

Without any lead from me, he had evidently decided honesty afforded him the greatest safety, and his accent made any attempt at feigning Englishness pointless.

"Good, so they can speak. Is you a Froggie too?" the Quartermaster snapped, poking me in the ribs.

"The err... the Lieutenant ... at the rail," I struggled to find my words. "Is ... is his name Ebbs?"

"Yes, Lieutenant Ebbs is in command here. I'll take it that you're English then?" the quartermaster barked back.

Hearing Ebbs' identity confirmed robbed me of my ability to answer but my silence didn't antagonise him for long because the bo'sun shouted from the hatchway.

"Bull's-eye, Mr Yule! There are tubs 'n tubs o' spirits down 'ere!"

This news immediately galvanised Quartermaster Yule into action.

"Quick, lads let's salvage all that us can," he shouted. "Dobbs, you watch these two. Take no nonsense from 'em. You can shoot if you 'ave to but set 'em to work helpin' us load this contraband."

The bo'sun started to heave the tubs of cognac onto *Peggy-Ann's* deck, which was by now quite steep. They rolled down to what was left of our starboard rail. Yule and his sailors had to wait for a swell to lift *Peggy* before they could carry the cognac up the incline of the deck, and pass them down into their boat that was secured to our larboard chains.

Within the half hour, we were all sitting in the boat with ten tubs of cognac stacked in front of us, watching as *Peggy-Ann* starting to slip beneath the waves.

The short pull to the cutter was an anxious, gut-churning

experience. What could I expect from a meeting with Jacob? Did he hate me? Was I to die as a mutineer after all? Or had he forgiven me? All said and done, I had kept Capel from killing him. Guilt, over my part in the mutiny, had gnawed at my mind ever since that night at Aix Roads and now I was to learn the consequences of my actions. It was with some difficulty, and trembling muscles in my arm, that I hauled myself up the side of the cutter, but when I climbed over the rail Jacob Ebbs was nowhere to be seen!

❖ ❖ ❖

Goriau and I were left to stand alone on the deck. Yule had disappeared below, presumably to report to Ebbs, and the boat crew busied themselves with unloading the cognac and returning the jollyboat to her station. The rest of the cutter's men were hauling the larboard battery of four, nine-pound cannon inboard and stowing powder cartridges and shot below. Ebbs had obviously left his guns serviceable until he was absolutely certain we were not going to put up a fight. Or perhaps, he was hoping for an opportunity for another broadside? Had he wanted to take his revenge on me by blowing what was left of *Peggy* out of the water? My preoccupation with Ebbs and my own fate was total until I caught sight of Goriau from the corner of my eye. Fresh tears were running down his cheeks, and I turned to see *Peggy-Ann's* mast was listing drunkenly. Her hull must be nearly full with water by now and she would soon be on her way to the bottom. I managed to push aside my obsession with Ebbs and consider Goriau for a moment. *Peggy-Ann's* sinking must feel to him like the funeral of the brother he hadn't seen die. It also flashed through my mind, that I would miss Samuel Barkas.

I forced out the words; "Lord God, please accept their souls."

Goriau turned and made the slightest of smiles to signify that he appreciated my sentiment.

"Captain 'ill see you both now."

It was Yule, the quartermaster, who spoke. He was standing behind us but neither of us had noticed his reappearance on deck.

"Did he ... did he say anything about me?" I asked falteringly.

"No, why should he?"

Yule shrugged as he spoke, and pointed towards the companionway. He led us to one of the two cabins below-deck and rapped on the door. It was a familiar voice, but much sterner than I remembered, that granted our entry. Yule gestured towards the door handle, so I turned it and walked quickly into the cabin. I was determined to discover what Ebbs intended to do with me straight away but he didn't make things easy for me. He sat stoically behind a small desk concentrating on an almanac that lay open before him, and didn't look up.

"Jacob ... it is me, Nathaniel," I blurted out, directly.

He didn't respond for a few moments, and then he slowly lifted his eyes to meet mine and snapped back coldly, "You will address me as Sir. I command His Majesty's cutter *Theseus* and I will be spoken to with due respect."

His reply sent a chill slithering down my spine. Any lingering hope that he might still regard himself as my friend immediately extinguished.

"Do I enter you two onto the log as fishermen or smugglers?" he asked in a disinterested voice.

"I am Marc Goriau a *pêcheur français, Monsieur*," started Goriau. "I am a Royalist and I hate Bonaparte."

I had no idea what the true colour of Goriau's politics may be, but I didn't think his protestation would cut any ice with Ebbs.

"You won't be the first Frenchie who has served His Majesty's Royal Navy and I dare say you'll not be the last. Whether you are loyal to the white cockade or the tricolour is no concern of mine," Ebbs said, spitefully, before turning his attention back to me.

"Under what name shall I enter you?"

Was this a hint of assistance? He knew full well what my name was, but he would also know that entering a mutineers name onto a ship's book was tantamount to signing his death warrant.

"Nathaniel ...," I said, desperately searching a vacant mind for a surname, "... Smith?" I suggested.

It was the best I could come up with at that moment, but if Ebbs was intending to help me any further than hiding my identity he gave me no way of knowing and just growled, 'Very well, you are dismissed'.

Goriau did as we were bidden and shuffled towards the door, but I held my position in front of his desk. I had to at least try to find out what Ebbs had planned for me. If I left that cabin without knowing what the future held for me, anxiety would tear me apart.

"Jacob, what happened at Aix Roads after the explosion was nothing __"

Ebbs shot to his feet.

"Get out before I have Mr Yule flay your back for insubordination," he yelled.

Yule took a firm grip on my arm. I stared into Ebbs' eyes for a second or two. There was only anger and indignation in them and not a glimmer of kinship.

"Come along, Smith," Yule said, as he pulled me roughly towards the cabin door.

When we reached the companion he asked, "Does Mister Ebbs know you? What's your talk of Aix Roads?"

Yule's face wore an earnest expression and Goriau's a bemused one. I wanted to clear-up my abrupt name change for Goriau before he said the wrong thing, and I knew that the quartermaster would require some sort of explanation. Lying seemed the best option.

"We knew each other before either of us was in the Navy."

"Mister Ebbs has only been wit' the squadron a few month', and he 'as been a good-humoured young officer in all his dealings. I've never even seen him angry afore. You recognised 'im when he was standing at the rail didn't you?" Yule replied.

"Yes, I feel he's deeply disappointed to find me smuggling," I said, glancing at the Frenchman. His almost imperceptible nod reassuring me that he understood at least enough to keep quiet, and Yule seemed to accept my explanation, and turned his attention to finding us work.

❖ ❖ ❖

It was strange, but I had had a feeling that Yule was a decent man almost as soon as I met him. He was keen to put us to work because he needed to know whether Goriau and I would be useful additions to his crew, but I also think he wanted to keep us busy so that we wouldn't have time to dwell over our new predicament. He must have seen many men's lives ruptured by naval impressment and had found it the best policy to keep them occupied.

It hadn't been long after *Peggy-Ann* had gone under that *Theseus* had hauled her sheets and set a northerly course. Straightaway, Yule had stationed me at the mainsheet, and sent Goriau to the cutter's huge tiller. He called for slight changes to the course, and watched attentively to see how we managed. It is easy for a seaman to gauge another's abilities by giving him control of an unfamiliar vessel, and within a couple of hours he seemed satisfied we were both the experienced sailors that we had professed to be.

Yule's policy of working us hard turned out to be effective insomuch that I didn't have time to fret about my future, but the events of the day caught up with me in a sudden rush. It was still only mid afternoon, and the day had seen me become a murderer, witness the death of two friends and be impressed into the Navy for the second time. I was totally drained of energy, and my mind activated a simple safety valve to protect itself from further punishment. It was just like the steam governor on Watt's engine letting excess pressure out of the mechanism: my legs gave way, and I crumpled onto the deck. Many martinet petty-officers would have deemed this dereliction of duty, but I was vaguely aware that it was Yule who helped me to my feet and called over Goriau to take me below as he dismissed us from the deck.

I stumbled down the companion behind Goriau as if I was a blind man. We both had to bend almost double to make our way to the crew quarters beneath the fo'castle. Most of the crew were on deck and there were only a handful of men below. I have no recollection of climbing, or being put, into my hammock, but my head was instantly full of dreams. I can't readily recollect what they were about, but I do know Jas Capel's ghost-like face featured in them somewhere and that I suffered no guilt over his death whatsoever.

❖   ❖   ❖

There were twenty-three men onboard *Theseus*, and they gave every impression of being a dedicated and competent crew. It was apparent Yule took great pride in sailing the cutter well, and it has to be said, she was an absolute beauty. Fresh from a Medway shipyard, she still smelt of planed timber that had not yet been impregnated by the odours of the ocean. A combination of the new canvas above and the un-fouled hull beneath meant that she could gambol along at twelve knots or more when the wind obliged.

Late in the afternoon of my second day aboard *Theseus*, the tops'ls of a ship appeared above the horizon. We were headed straight for her. With the rest of the crew showing no interest in her sighting, I reckoned that we were keeping a rendezvous. She slowly grew above the curvature of the earth, until all three masts were clearly visible. From the cut of her sails she looked like a British frigate, but I couldn't be sure. Yule was standing at the rail nearby.

"Who is she, Mr Yule," I asked, courteously touching a knuckle to my temple.

"That is 'is Majesty's twenty gun frigate *Tiger* under the command of Captain Pearson," he replied. "He patrols the Breton coast from the Bay of Douarnenez to Belle Isle an' *Theseus* reports to 'im, an' ferries his dispatches to the fleet. Not that much happens on our beat … apart from apprehending the odd smuggler," he said, with a grin, and then excused himself a little sheepishly, "Beggin' yer pardon, Smith."

A seaman nearby was bending coloured signal flags onto a halyard. I knew each flag equated to a number, but had no idea what message this particular combination referred to. Within a few moments of our signal, a reply appeared at the frigate's main mast. The ship's courses were then brailed-up, and the main tops'l shivered and lost its shape. The crew were bracing the big sails onto the other tack.

"She's heavin'-to," said Yule. "Bring the boat alongside, Smith, an' take Goriau to 'elp you."

When *Theseus* was within a cable of the frigate Yule backed our fors'ls and brought the cutter to a halt. Unhitching the jollyboat from its towing position astern, Goriau and I dragged the boat around our leeward side and up to the tumblehome, taking great care that her painter was cleated-off somewhere at all times.

Yule was standing by the tumblehome with the gate open when Ebbs appeared on deck. It was the first time I'd seen him since our interview when I came aboard. A crew of half-a-dozen went over the side and secured the boat. Ebbs strode towards the tumblehome gate and nodded at Yule. He didn't so much as glance in my direction, even though he had to brush past me to reach the wooden steps that led down to the boat.

The swell was lively and the substantial, clinker built boat bounced gamely amidst the white caps as she was pulled towards *Tiger*. I stared at Ebb's back as it receded into the gathering dusk and tried, once again, to guess his thoughts.

CHAPTER FOURTEEN
The Western Approaches – 26th June 1809

Stories have become legend that relate to the Isle of Man's impregnability whilst it was a stronghold for contraband traders during the last century. Unfortunately, for the people of our south western coasts the powerful smuggling families from that island simply upped sticks and moved their evil enterprises to Ireland and Wales. From there they operate with apparent immunity from the changes implemented to the Revenue Service following the 1801 Act of Union.
From 'A Voyage around our Islands' by B.W. Teal, 1806

I don't know how long I had been asleep, but I was woken by a boat thumping against the hull only a few feet away from where Goriau and I lay in our hammocks. A voice shouted 'send down Smith an' the Frenchie,' from the other side of the oak planking, and a few minutes later, Yule appeared below deck with a foully smoking lantern in his hand.

"You two 'ad better look lively; I've never known Captain Pearson to bother with new recruits afore."

I wearily climbed to the deck, my head still heavy with sleep and went to the rail. For some reason, I half expected to see Ebbs in the jollyboat waiting for us but in his place in the stern sheets sat a red-coated officer of marines. The boat crew were accompanied by two 'lobsters' with their muskets.

My achingly tired mind immediately cranked up its gears and started to run away with possibilities. What had Ebbs reported to

Pearson? Had he told him about the mutiny? Were they summoning me to my death?

In what seemed no more than a few minutes, Goriau and I found ourselves standing before the small, but elegantly decorated, stern windows of the King's frigate *Tiger*. Ebbs and Pearson were pouring over a chart that was spread out on a table to the larboard side of the Captain's cabin. My toes fidgeted on the deck and my arm muscles trembled as we waited for the two officers to acknowledge our arrival. Eventually, Pearson took a couple of steps towards us. He was a young man to have attained the rank of Post Captain, probably only a few years older than me, but the florid stains to the skin around his nose and cheeks indicated that he had already developed an unhealthy affection for potent drink.

"You were a few miles south of Ushant when my cutter sank you. Are you familiar with the waters around the Bay of Douarnenez?" he snapped. He had the irritating, clipped accent and arrogant manner of some of the gentry that had annoyed me so much during my time in the Lilstock Estate Office. I took an instant dislike to him.

"I had never ventured into French water or a French port before, Sir," I replied, submissively.

"What about you?" he said, turning to Goriau.

"My brothers and I are *pêcheurs* …were *pêcheurs* … from Concarneau, *Monsieur*. We are familiar with *Baie de Douarnenez*."

"Fishermen be damned. Ebbs here tells me that you are smugglers!"

This statement did offer some solace. If Ebbs had described me as a smuggler, he obviously hadn't told him about my involvement in the mutiny.

"We 'ad to sell cognac to our *amis Anglais* to make a living, *Monsieur*."

"I couldn't give a damn about your fiscal situation. Did you regularly sail the waters south of Ushant?"

"*Non*, not regular, *Monsieur*. Occasionally we do this."

"And did you encounter a schooner that was sometimes flying an English ensign and sailing with apparent impunity in the waters surrounding Douarnenez Bay?"

"*Qui*, we did."

"You did!" Pearson and Ebbs spoke in near unison.

"We see a black schooner that fly both the flag of the English or *le drapeau tricolour* depending on who was nearby," said Goriau.

"As you thought, Mister Ebbs," announced Pearson triumphantly.

"Yes, Sir. A privateer hiding behind our colours as a *rouse de guerre*," replied Ebbs.

"I'm sure that this is the ship we saw a mile or two from the mouth of Douarnenez Bay," he said, taking Ebbs by the arm and leading the young lieutenant back toward the chart table. "They were flying a red ensign about here ...," Pearson jabbed his finger at the chart. "We hove-to and signalled for them to stop but they ignored us."

His speech was a little muffled but I could make out what he was saying.

"They headed straight up the bay and directly for Douarnenez port. I chased them until the town's coastal guns opened up, but I saw that the French let them sail straight into the harbour."

I heard Ebbs' reply more clearly, "They must be Frenchmen, Sir. Or why would the Frogs allow then into the harbour?"

"By your leave, Sir" I interrupted.

They both turned and stared at me, apparently astonished by my effrontery.

"Well, what is it?" snapped Ebbs, taking a pace back towards Goriau and me.

"We don't know her nationality, Sir, but there are certainly Welshmen aboard that schooner. They're not privateers, Sir ... their more like pirates. They prey on the 'free trade' boats: both French and English," I explained.

"Free traders be damned! Smugglers you mean," interjected Pearson, with a snort of derision. "Why on earth would they confine themselves to such an activity?"

"They sell goods from one port to Frenchmen, and then follow them to see where they pass it on to English smugglers. They then take it back from one or the other, and re-sell the same goods from a different port. They double their money at no risk to themselves, Sir," I explained.

Pearson glanced at Ebbs, thoughtfully rubbing a predominant cleft in the centre of his chin.

"What do you think, Mister Ebbs?"

"It could be possible, Sir."

"They attacked Marc," I said, gesturing towards Goriau, "and his brother as they were supplying Barkas, that's the skipper of the cutter you sank, with cognac. Barkas' crewman was killed, and they boarded Marc's boat and took his cargo, Sir," I continued, doggedly. "We know that they operate from a warehouse in Douarnenez."

"How do you know they operate from a warehouse in Douarnenez?" asked Ebbs, sharply.

"We've been inside it."

"Inside it! How?" exclaimed Ebbs.

"We had gone to Douarnenez to avenge their attacks on Barkas and Marc," I replied steadily. "They trade from a warehouse on the river quay that is stuffed with goods for trading with the English smugglers. We helped ourselves, Sir."

"And nobody stopped you?" asked Pearson.

"No, we were able to get into and out of the harbour unchallenged, Sir."

"They took your contraband but then they let you go?" Pearson enquired, looking earnestly at Goriau.

"*Qui*, they did."

"So the schooner is armed, but if we can catch her low in the water then she could well be stuffed with contraband?" Pearson mused, still rubbing his chin. "I shouldn't wonder that they don't drop off large consignments on the Scillies."

"Or if there are Welshmen aboard, it could be that they run straight to the Bristol Channel, Sir. From there they can run contraband into all the western ports of England and Ireland," Ebbs replied.

"I'm damn sure this is the schooner I saw," said Pearson, largely talking to himself. "French and Welsh privateers ... she would make a pretty prize."

"You say that you came and went from Douarnenez unopposed?" Ebbs asked me.

"That's where our cognac came from, Sir."

"Which would explain why your cutter had French registration numbers painted at its bow?" asked Ebbs.

"An English pilot cutter doesn't look too much like a French fishing vessel either with or without registration numbers," Pearson interposed.

"No, Sir. I quite agree, but I am intrigued to know how their subterfuge worked," said Ebbs

"We masked our sail plan as best we could, and it was dark the entire time we were in the port. We also had two Frenchman aboard who could shout in the right language, Sir, and we didn't think anyone would be looking too closely," I explained, anxious to be as helpful as possible. I had no idea what the future held for me, but attempting to revive my friendship with Ebbs couldn't harm my chances of survival.

"Are you considering sending in our boats to cut out that schooner, Mister Ebbs?" Pearson asked.

"Not necessarily our boats, Sir. But if we captured a local fishing boat we could take our men right into the harbour undetected," Ebbs said.

"I fear, that unfortunately, the Frogs ain't stupid," moaned Pearson in reply. "All the fishermen keep an eye on each other, if we were to grab one they would make sure that the authorities knew about it pretty damn quick. The batteries around the town would be looking out for your commandeered boat."

"I 'ave *un bateau*," interrupted Goriau.

The effect of his statement was like dropping a handful of gunpowder into a fire.

"A French fishing boat? Superb! Where is she? How many men will she carry?"

Questions tumbled out of Pearson staccato fashion, as thoughts flashed into his mind.

"She lies in the *Illes de Scillies*. We could 'ave *quarante ou cinquante* men below deck for a little time, *Monsieur*," replied the Frenchman.

"*Theseus* has to report to the Admiral which would give us the opportunity to collect this Frenchman's boat. We could be back here in a few days, Sir," Ebbs said to Pearson enthusiastically. "On which island does your boat lie?" he asked, turning to Goriau.

Goriau stared back at Ebbs in a strangely confrontational manner. For a few moments he remained silent, and then he replied in a slow but determined voice, "I cannot say to you unless you agree to release Nathaniel and me from your Navy after we 'ave taken you into the *Baie de* Douarnenez."

"What?" Pearson erupted.

Goriau's demand took me completely unawares, and like the two naval officers, I was left dumbfounded.

"Nathaniel and I 'ave the *knowledges* that you need. We 'ave travelled the channel into Douarnenez harbour, and we 'ave been on the town quays *la nuit*."

Pearson was shaking with rage. He gave every impression of fighting for breath, and his face turned to the most vivid puce colour that I have ever seen on human flesh.

"Preposterous," he yelled after a couple of moments. "I'll not be dictated to by an impressed Frog. I've a good mind to thrash the information from you."

"Even should you discover *mon bateau* you will not know which *navigations* to make or which harbour the schooner lies. My family has paid heavily of this devil war. You 'ave just killed *mon frère*, and I will never take you into Douarnenez, *Monsieur*, without this assurance."

He spoke evenly and the way he held his nerve in the face of Pearson's outrage was deeply impressive. For his part, the captain looked fit to explode. I feared he was about to scream some dreadful retribution at us when Ebbs' calm voice cooled the impending storm.

"Perhaps we should give the matter careful thought, Sir," he said. "I believe them when they say that they have sailed into and out of the Bay unharmed. The brandy they had on board supports their story. If they can do it once they can do it again, and that could be of great benefit to us. The Admiral should have reached Scilly by now, so it isn't even necessary for us to change our plans."

"*Mon bateau* may still be requiring a little work to make her ready for ____ "

"Shut up." Pearson cut Goriau short. "Marine," he bellowed, and the cabin door opened instantly. "Take these men back topsides to wait," he ordered. "I can't think with them in here."

❖   ❖   ❖

"Where on earth did you get the idea to barter for our freedom like that?" I blurted out the moment the marine left us alone. "Don't get me wrong," I said, holding up my hands to give myself time to qualify my question. "I think it a superb ruse, but it can't possibly work … can it?"

"We 'ave to try. I 'ave not years to devote to Buonaparte's war. I would rather die than spend the rest of my life serving in your Navy."

I hadn't known Goriau long enough to be totally familiar with his character, but there was no doubting his sincerity over this matter. He had the bit firmly clamped between his teeth and he was not going to back down from his ultimatum. From my point of view, the plan had a chance of working, and consequently, it would have my wholehearted support. Also, I had an inkling of an idea that there was still hope for some support from Ebb's: even if he wasn't prepared to show it yet. If he was not going to grant me another chance, why hadn't he already exposed me to Pearson as a mutineer and had done with it?

"Do you think that if they question enough fishermen in the Scillies they will be able to find your boat, and renege on any agreement that they make with us?"

"You 'ave to remember that *Capitaine* Pearson will be anxious not to waste any time. His ship could be ordered elsewhere at any time," Goriau replied. "You should not underestimate the loyalty of the men on St.Agnes, but even if they find *mon bateau* they will be needing us to navigate the channel and get to the *river quai*."

"Yes. They need you but do they need me?"

"You have no need to worry about my loyalty to you," the Frenchman replied firmly.

"Yes, yes ... you're right. I'm sorry. I was so taken unawares by your plan that it's difficult to think straight," I muttered.

"Pardon, you also are right," Goriau said. "It was difficult for me to think past the grief of losing *mon frère*."

I was so preoccupied with the Frenchman's demands on the Navy, that the demise of *Peggy-Ann* had temporarily been forgotten.

"I know that you and Samuel Barkas were *amis*," Goriau continued, "but Jean and I were very close ...," his voice tailed off and his eyes were glossy with tears once again. His iron determination of a few minutes ago seemed to have completely left him as he slumped back against the shrouds.

"There is nothing anyone can say that will ease your loss, Marc," I said. "I lost my wife only three months ago. The pain envelops me like a fog, but for the time being we must try to think clearly."

"I am also sorry, Nathaniel," Goriau answered. "You are right. Let us think only of how we get away from here."

"If we take the sailors into Douarnenez and they do let us free what would you do then? The authorities would be able to trace the boat to you, and I don't think they would be happy to see you in France again."

"The only family I had left was Jean. Royalist *mercenaries* killed *mon père*, and *ma mère* died shortly afterwards of a broken heart. I will go to *les Îles de Scillies* and continue to smuggle *contrebande*."

"How shall we get your boat out of the bay again?"

"I do not know, Nathaniel, but if we cannot it is better to lose *le bateau* than lose our lives to this war. One day France will regain its senses and the Corsican murderer shall be guillotined!"

"So much for liberty, equality and fraternity!"

"Buonaparte has usurped the revolutionary ideals we all struggled for!"

"You were a revolutionary?"

"As a young man, I attack the feudal estates of the *Aristos* but when Buonaparte crown himself *Empereur* he create *une nouvelle aristocratie* __"

Goriau was interrupted when the quarterdeck door behind us suddenly opened with a bang and Lieutenant Ebbs strode towards us.

"He'll go along with it!" he announced triumphantly.

This was the young man who I had known before speaking now. He wore an unmistakeable smile of elation on his face and the familiar gleam was back in his eyes. Was he pleased because a way out for me had appeared? I had to test him farther.

"You mean he has agreed to set us free if we can ferry your men into Douarnenez harbour, Jacob?" I asked enthusiastically.

"Address my correctly, Smith! The situation changes nothing between us!" snapped Ebbs.

The return of his previous persona was instant. The authoritarian Lieutenant was back, but at least he had lifted the curtain a fraction and shown a glimpse of his former self. His high spirits must be due to the sudden improvement in my prospects: mustn't they?

"What *garantie* can you offer, Monsieur?" Goriau said, breaking the silence that suddenly fell between Ebbs and myself.

"The word of a British officer should be enough for an impressed man," replied Ebb's testily.

Goriau stuck to his task, "What if something should become of you, Monsieur. Do we have the word of *Capitaine* Pearson?"

"The captain has considered your plan, and as you are not

entered upon the ships' books, he is prepared to treat you as commandeered pilots. You will be eligible for release from duty following your mission. You may depend upon his assurances. Now, we need to go straight to your boat and set to work immediately."

"Nathaniel and I need to drink cognac and *dormir* before we can do anything else," Goriau said imperiously. "Bring me a paper with your signature that confirms our agreement, and I will tell you on which of the island *mon bateau* is lying, Monsieur."

Ebbs stared at the Frenchman in silence, his cheeks starting to fill with colour. He was smarting with embarrassment at being dictated to by a Frenchman. For a moment, I thought that Goriau had pushed him too hard and that he was going to burst into a rage. Then he seemed to take a grip of himself, and simply said "very well", turned smartly on his heal, walked away and disappeared through the quarterdeck door.

CHAPTER FIFTEEN
St. Mary's Road, Iles of Scilly – 28th June 1809

It is the intention of this Board that all necessary surveys and preparations be instigated, with the utmost urgency, for the purpose of building a breakwater between St.Agnes and Samson in the Isles of Scilly.
   It is the objective of their Lordships to partially block Broad Sound and create a safe anchorage in St.Mary's Roadstead for His Majesty's ships under the protection of Star Castle. This is to provide the Channel Fleet with an alternative victualling base for ships blockading the western coasts of France.
A letter from the Navy Board to the Office of Admiralty Survey, 1809

Quartermaster Yule and I, along with ten of *Theseus'* crew, were gathered on top of the low cliff that sat behind the small, natural harbour at the north-eastern corner of the island of St.Agnes. The scene in the roadstead to the north of us, had changed radically since I had been here three days earlier. Four ships of the line and three frigates now lay anchored in a column, and I could just make out the pennant of a Rear Admiral flying from the biggest of them. Vowles' peaceful fiefdom, free from Admiralty interference, had become a thing of the past.

Our voyage from the Western Approaches had been a wild,

wet affair, but the weather had eased the moment we entered St.Mary's Road which ran through the middle of the Scilly archipelago. During the two days of our crossing, I had not seen Ebbs at all, and he can hardly have left his cabin. He had, however, appeared on deck, in a cleaned and brushed frock coat, the moment *Theseus* dropped anchor. He had engaged Yule in a brief conversation, and then called for the jollyboat so that he could report his arrival to the flagship.

We were on St.Agnes because Goriau had told Pearson and Ebbs, once they had furnished him with written assurances that his plan would be honoured, that his boat, *Esprit du Breeze*, lay there. Their acceptance made me feel far more at ease. If I could survive another trip to Douarnenez then I would taste freedom once again! However, Ebbs' refusal to speak or explain his intentions as regards me was unnerving to say the least.

Before leaving *Theseus*, Ebbs had obviously instructed Yule to organise a landing party, and at around midday the quartermaster ordered me into a longboat that had been sent from the squadron. I had expected to find Goriau in the boat, and was surprised to discover the Frenchman had been left on board the cutter. Alongside me in the longboat were *Theseus'* carpenter, two carpenter's mates, four marines, three seamen and Yule: as well as the boat's crew who were tugging us towards the rugged little island.

We had landed on the stone steps that are built into the modest mole protecting Porth Conger, the island's small, natural harbour. From where I now sat, on top of the low cliff that surrounded the inlet, I could see the anchorage behind the sandbar, between St.Agnes and Gugh, where we had careened *Peggy-Ann* a few days earlier.

Finding myself here, back amidst familiar surroundings, made me think of happier times; memories of afternoons spent with Sarah Ebbs in Portsmouth or being a free man aboard Barkas' boat, drifted into my mind. Those days seemed to belong to a different age. Delving even further back, I tried to remember living a trouble-free life with a beautiful wife in Somerset, but that memory was so distant it didn't feel as if it could be true.

"We're to wait 'ere for Mister Ebbs."

It was Yule's voice that broke into my thoughts. He had sat down next to me whilst I was daydreaming. I nodded in reply and continued staring into the rocky harbour beneath us.

"Do you know the officer in charge o' Fencibles on this island? I'll be needin' somewhere to quarter the men," said Yule.

"Aye, I know him Mister Yule. His name is Vowles, he's a good man," I replied, withdrawing from my memories.

"I've sent a man to find 'im," Yule said, luxuriantly stretching out his legs on the spiky grass and setting himself at ease.

The quartermaster and I had spoken several times during our passage from France. He had convinced me that my original assessment of him had been correct, and that he was a decent man: someone who took his duty seriously, but treated his men with consideration.

After a few moments he asked conversationally, "Smuggling must 'ave been lucrative for you?"

"You cut short my career before I could find out," I replied.

"Was that your cutter? She was a trim boat: the sort o' vessel I'd like for m'self one day."

"No not mine. That was the skipper's bones your swivel gun spread across the deck."

"I'm sorry for him, but smugglin' be a dangerous game," Yule replied, shrugging his shoulders. "It just so 'appened, that Lady Luck were shinnin' on you an' the Frog that day."

"She was shining none too brightly then; we were sunk and two men died!"

"Aye, Mister Ebbs might 'ave sunk the pair of you an' all, but now 'e tells me that you are to be free men again after this malarkey is over."

Yule's confirmation that Ebbs has confided to him the details of our agreement was good news. Nevertheless, the tone of his voice told me he didn't agree with the decision.

"It's the sort o' mission that only Captain Pearson would 'ave consented to," he grumbled.

"Why do you say that about Pearson?"

"Captain Pearson." Yule corrected me, but without malice.

"Why do you say that about Captain Pearson?" I repeated my question dutifully.

"He's a vigilant seaman right enough, but the talk amongst the squadron is that he enjoys the bottle a little too much," Yule said. "When he's drunk he gambles ... badly. They say that he's left his markers all over the Portsmouth tables."

This went a long way to explaining why Pearson had accepted Goriau's outrageous artifice. If he was in debt, he would be desperate for prize money. If Goriau could guide Ebbs and his men into Douarnenez, and they succeeded in cutting out the rogue schooner, he would gain a prize without risking his ship.

"I'm not to go lookin' for the Frenchman's boat until Mister Ebbs returns."

"How long will he be?" I asked.

"He'll 'ave to wait for orders to take back to *Tiger*."

"Will the Admiral have to approve their plan for the attack on Douarnenez?"

"I ain't sure that Mister Ebbs is going to tell him!" Yule replied, clearly bemused. "But he tells me that I 'ave to repair your mate's fishing boat."

"I don't think there will be much work left to do to get *Esprit du Breeze* seaworthy," I answered, trying to placate him. It was in my interest to have Yule in support of the plan. "The hands you have brought will have her in order in a day or so."

I glanced at *Tiger's* carpenter and his two mates, who sat on the tussocky, salt-soaked grass that topped the low cliffs, surrounded by bundles of tools.

"I can understand why Captain Pearson would want a harebrained plan such as this to succeed, but how did you persuade him that Goriau an' you can slip in and out o' Douarnenez 'arbour?" Yule asked, displaying an exasperated expression.

"Well, because we already have!"

Yule's face was the picture of surprise! All signs of his former scepticism disappeared, and he stared at me in silence for a moment or two.

"You mean that you 'ad just come out of the 'arbour itself when we stopped you?" he asked aghast.

"Aye, the Frogs weren't a problem. If it wasn't for the Navy …"

"Well I'll be," Yule said, shaking his head. "That explains why Mister Ebbs 'as kept the Frenchman on board *Theseus*."

The reason why Ebbs had wanted me on the island, and left Goriau on the cutter, had been troubling me. Goriau was far more important to the mission than me: I knew that. They couldn't afford to lose him, and I had been sent to St.Agnes because of my local knowledge: it was fortuitous that they had no idea how scant that was!

"Mister Ebbs is guarding against the possibility of the Frog running. 'E obviously 'as friends on the island, and any mission without him at the tiller would be scuppered afore it began," said Yule as if to confirm my thoughts.

"I also 'ave instructions to detail one of the marines to stay close to you every minute you're ashore, Smith," Yule said, fixing me with a deliberate stare. "I'm tellin' you, for your own good, because I 'ave to tell 'im to shoot first and ask questions later, should there be the slightest chance of you abscondin'."

❖ ❖ ❖

Yule may have sent a man to look for 'the officer in charge of Fensibles', but I knew it would not be long before Vowles' curiosity drew him to the party of strangers that had appeared at his harbour. I remembered him joking about being the senior naval figure on St.Agnes, but deep down he enjoyed exerting what power he had as the petty officer of Sea Fencibles. Sure enough, within half-an-hour of our arrival his unmistakable figure came loping towards us from the direction of the village, accompanied by a couple of fellows that I recognised as Fencibles. They made an incongruous trio, dressed in a mixture of naval slops, and the traditional fisherman's make-and-mend garments. Yule, who was still sitting beside me, was eying them with suspicion as they approached us.

"It's the local sea militia, Mister Yule," I told him. "That's Vowles in front, may I speak to him?"

"No you may not," Yule replied firmly. "Marine Gardiner … stay close," he commanded one of the lobsters, with a nod in my direction, as he stood up and stepped towards the newcomers. Vowles spoke first.

"A'ternoon, Gen'lemen. Fencible Petty Officer Vowles jus' makin' sure we aint bein' invaded," he quipped. "I saw you come from the cutter and … well blow me! Is that you, Nat'?"

"Nathaniel Smith is currently servin' His Britannic Majesty, an' I 'ave orders not to let him fraternise with the locals," Yule announced sententiously. His voice was so pompous that it evoked a couple of sniggers among *Theseus'* crewmen.

I could see from Vowles' reaction to my unexpected name change that he was taken aback, but luckily, he said nothing. Our eyes met. In that instant, I was aware of the doubts flooding his mind. Had I been on the level with him when on the island before, or was I a Navy stool pigeon? Was I here with naval ratings to expose him and his men as smugglers? I was desperate to reassure him, but had no idea how. I made a gesture of helplessness, by turning my open palms skyward, and indicated towards Gardiner with my head. Vowles couldn't think I was a naval sneak if I was under guard: could he? He didn't react in any way, and just looked away from me and back at Yule.

"And what brings ye to St.Agnes?" he asked Yule.

"You're in charge of the Sea Fencibles on this island?" Yule replied, ignoring the question.

"That I am. St.Agnes 'ill be safe while my lads are alert."

"I am Quartermaster Yule of His Majesty's Cutter *Theseus*. I understand that there is a French vessel careened on your island."

This wasn't an easy conversation for Vowles. Firstly, he had to question everything he thought he knew about me, and then a Petty Officer was potentially accusing him of harbouring an enemy vessel.

"There ain't no Frenchie on St.Agnes," he said hesitantly, "not that I knows about, Sir?"

He was looking at Yule warily and thinking on his feet. I knew that if he tried to lie he would end up in deep waters, and so I shook my head, as vigorously as I dared, behind Yule's back. Luckily, Vowles took notice and caught on immediately.

"Unless you're meaning the fisherman driven onto the beach at Wingletang Bay a couple o' weeks back," he corrected himself boldly.

"So the Admiralty are happy that Fencibles let French vessels land on St.Agnes are they?" Yule replied sarcastically.

Uncertainty crept across Vowles' eyes, and he glanced in my direction.

"The Goriau's beached in a terrible storm ____ " I started to lie.

"Quiet, Smith," Yule growled.

Yule was reasserting his authority, but my brief intersession had been long enough for Vowles to gain his composure and climb back into the saddle.

"Not hostile Frenchies they don't, Sir," he began with a note of indignation in his voice. "But 'onest fishermen in peril, that's a different matter. It's our duty as God fearin' men to let them on our beaches. An' I happen to know, that them brothers hate the Corsican upstart."

Vowles darted another sly glace in my direction as he spoke. I ached to be able to explain myself to him, but at least he had looked to me for support under Yule's interrogation and I took that for a good sign.

"I'm not so sure that you all 'aint smugglers together," said Yule.

"That we're not, Mister Quartermaster."

Vowles raised the indignation in his voice a notch. "I've 'ad that French boat under guard ever since it arrived," he said. I knew he was lying. "We weren't to know what reason Nathanial and Mister Barkas took out their pilot cutter. You've no call to say me and my lads is smugglin'."

"Oh, very well, I suppose I shall 'ave to trust your word," Yule answered begrudgingly.

Vowles' shoulders dropped a little from relief.

"As the man in charge, we shall need your help anyways," the quartermaster continued.

"Anythin' for 'is Majesty's Navy," Vowles replied confidently.

"We shall be no more than two days," Yule said. "I shall need shelter and victuals for twelve men." He stepped away from me and took Vowles by the arm. They walked along the cliff top, and I could no longer hear what was said.

As they were talking, one of the fencibles slipped back towards the village. Doubtless he would be on his way to pass the word that the Navy was here, so that any incriminating casks and bottles might be speedily tidied from sight. Also, they would have to station one of the fensibles by *Esprit du Breeze* now that Vowles had boasted about having her under guard. As he was talking, Yule raised an arm and pointed towards the moored warships. Following the direction indicated, I saw Ebbs' boat was leaving the flagship and starting to make its way back towards St.Agnes.

❖ ❖ ❖

Vowles billeted us that night in the comparative comfort of an old boathouse sat on the flat land behind Porth Conger. The decrepit wooden structure had been built half a cable's length from the coast to protect its contents from the ravages of the severest winter storms. Deep gouges in the beaten earth floor indicated that some boats, presumably big, smuggling gigs, had been hastily removed before we arrived. (NOTE: *Gigs, crewed by six rowers and a cox, were traditionally used to ferry Scillonian pilots to merchant vessels. In 1808 gigs were limited to crews of four rowers because the Government considered that larger crews were primarily employed in smuggling. Six or eight men were capable of rowing into the eye of the wind faster than the revenue cutters could sail to catch them. For this reason revenue officers - and theoretically Fensibles like Vowles - were made responsible for burning gigs with berths for more than four oarsmen*). A fire had been lit in the stone-lined pit that was used to heat the boathouse in winter. We didn't really need a fire in June but *Theseus'* sailors seemed to be enjoying the novelty of it, and a steady stream of local people brought fuel and provisions to the house. They were curious to see the King's sailors who had arrived on their island, and several extraneous Scillonians seemed to accompany each delivery. Vowles had obviously spread the news of my return, and I caught several odd glances on inquisitive faces that appeared at the door.

Sitting in the corner of the boathouse, with my silent red-coated minder beside me, I watched Ebbs chatting amiably with a couple of his crewmen. On his return from the flagship earlier that afternoon, he had ordered me to lead him, Yule and the carpenter across the island to the Goriaus' boat.

He had not spoken to me on the walk to Willywicks Bay or on the way back. Any questions he had were directed through Yule. What was his game? Was he to be my friend or my enemy? He hadn't named me as a mutineer and, presumably, he had had a hand in persuading Pearson to accept Goriau's ultimatum, but it had been three days now. Surely he could explain his intentions by now? The silent treatment made me nervous, but it was also beginning to make me angry.

As I pondered Ebbs' behaviour, Vowles came into the boathouse: he was my other problem. Some of the looks I was receiving from locals were far too hostile for comfort. What had he said to them? They would be wondering what had happened to Barkas and Goriau; perhaps he had told them that I had turned them over to the Navy? I needed to talk to him, but Marine Gardener, who was a simple soul, took his orders extremely seriously. He had delivered a painful rabbit punch when I tried to pass the most innocent of pleasantries with a fishwife, who I recognised, laying out food on a makeshift table near us.

I managed to catch Vowles' eye when he glanced in my direction and gave him a little nod. He responded with the slightest of winks. Gardiner needed to be distracted just long enough to for me to be able to explain myself to Vowles.

The crewmen and a few local men were starting to congregate at the table, and plates of food were disappearing as quickly as the women were bringing them. A small, fat man with his hair in a greased queue was tapping a beer cask on one end of the table.

"Let's get at the victuals, Smith," Gardiner announced enthusiastically.

"I'll not bother," I replied. Disappointment flooded across Gardiner's face and I hoped that the lure of food would be too great for him.

As luck would have it, the fat man hammered the wooden tap home into the cask and a plume of ale shot into the air, much of it landing on Gardiner's back.

"Sorry, M' hansom," the fat man said laughing, "'ere you deserve the first draught." And he proffered a heavy pottery beaker in Gardiner's direction.

"I be guardin' this man," the marine replied, "I shouldn't be takin' a drink."

Nevertheless, I saw his hand reach out impulsively before he managed to control it.

"Go on!" the fat man urged, "one won't 'urt."

I had not seen this fat fellow before, but he glanced at me as he spoke, and made a sort of encouraging gesture with his eyebrows.

"Yes go on, Gardiner," I urged, with all the sociability I could muster, "and I'll take a pot as well."

Our cajoling worked and Gardiner had gulped down half his tankard by the time the fat man had filled one for me. I took a deep draught. It was similar to the dark and deeply bitter beer that I remembered drinking in the beer house a few days ago, but I smiled enthusiastically and asked, "Is this your own beer?"

"The wife makes it. Scilly don't grow the finest barley but we do the best us can," the fat man replied, nonchalantly slopping more ale from a jug into Gardiner's tankard as he spoke. I had no idea who my new ally was, but everything made more sense when Vowles materialised behind his shoulder. He was grinning and had a bottle in his hand.

"You lookin' arter our guests, Georgie?" he said, sidling up to our little group. "Why ain't these fellows eatin'? I'll get a right earful from my missus if any o' these victuals go to waste."

"I 'as to stay with Smith," announced Gardiner but in a more relaxed way than he had spoken before. "Why don't you come to the table with I?" he continued, looking at me.

"I'm not hungry but you fill a plate. I've nowhere to go."

"I got m' orders an' they're to stay b'you."

"Are you from Somerset?" Vowles asked the Marine.

I hadn't noticed Gardiner's accent before, but now that Vowles pointed it out it was a clear giveaway.

"That I be. An' I likes a drink and decent victuals as much as the next man. If only we can get to the table before those greedy bastards gobble 'em all up," Gardiner whined.

"We have something in common then. I'm from Somerset as well: Lilstock on the Bristol Channel," I said, feigning an interest in engaging Gardiner in a conversation that I knew he would regard as a violation of his orders.

"Oh ... I wuz livin' in Evercreech afore I joined up," Gardiner replied in a distracted sort of way. "Now, why can't we get to the trough like everyone else?"

"If you ain't hungry perhaps you'd enjoy a glug o' this," Vowles said, proffering me his bottle which stank of strong spirit.

"Aye I would," I replied, taking a long pull on the bottle. Its fiery heat took my breath away, but I continued with the charade. "We can eat later; let's have a drink, Mucker," I said, pushing the bottle into Gardiner's hand. His determination to resist the demon drink dissolved and he swung the bottle to his lips.

"That's the way, my friend," Georgie, the fat man, enthused. "Now let's go an' find you some scran."

"I suppose it'll be alright," the marine mumbled.

"My missus has brought a pig an' brawn pie that you would die for," Georgie said.

"You stand 'ere an' no fraternizin' with the locals," Gardiner said to me sternly, but Georgie was playing his role perfectly.

"Don't worry about his nonsense," he said, putting his arm around Gardiner. The lure of food was too much for a half drunk marine, and he let himself be led to the table.

"The Navy sank *Peggy-Ann* and killed Samuel Barkas," I blurted out, the moment Gardiner was out of earshot. Vowles took a step back and stared at me, aghast.

"And what happened t' you?" he asked, when he had gathered himself.

"I've been impressed into the Navy again, but this time it'll be alright __ "

- 187 -

I was speaking as quickly as I could, when Vowles interrupted me.

"What do you mean, it'll be alright? An' why ave you got a silly name?"

"I didn't want them to be able to trace my record."

"An' where are Marc and Jean?"

"Jean died in the attack, Marc's still on the cutter."

I wanted to explain the whole situation to Vowles before Gardiner intervened, but he looked disturbed by the news of Jean Goriau's death. I had to wait for the news to sink in; I had no way of knowing how friendly they had been.

"Was Barkas' boat full of contraband?" Vowles asked, after a moment or two.

"Yes, yes. The Navy took some of it before she went under."

"Are they holdin' Marc on the cutter so that you don't run?"

"I guess that's part of it."

"I wuz shocked when I saw you wit' the Navy at the Porth Conger, I 'ave to admit it. I 'ad you down as a wrong 'un an' we'd all 'ave our Fencible money taken away for suspicion o' smugglin'."

Relief surged through me: Vowles believed me!

"I know how it must have looked to you."

"The Lieutenant said that they gonna be usin' Marc's boat to get 'em into Douarnenez harbour. Ain't that what you just done in *Peggy-Ann*?" Vowles asked, suddenly speaking more softly as if it had just occurred to him not to be overheard.

"Exactly, that's why they think we can do it again. Goriau made them agree to set us free if we succeed."

"What?" he hissed, a little too loudly. "Your tellin' me, the Navy 'as impressed you, caught you smugglin' red 'anded, and now their gonna make you free men if you leads 'em into Douarnenez 'arbour?"

"Aye, the Captain in command is desperate for prize money," I whispered. "He has given us his word and a written passport."

Vowles stood for a moment shaking his head.

"I don't trust 'em, Nat. I just don't trust 'em," he said. "I don't think you should go through wit' it. I just can't see 'em letting you come back. What would 'appen to this captain if, for some reason, someone started wavin' this paper agreement of yorn around the Admiralty?"

"I have to go through with it. I don't have any choice. I know the Lieutenant from my time in Portsmouth and I trust him."

Vowles hesitated for a moment before replying.

"There's no moon tomorrow night, and some o' the lads are takin' two o' the bigger gigs to the mainland. There's too much contraband on the island, and far too many naval vessels in the roadstead."

"Could they fit me in?"

"Aye, o' course they could, an' I'm sure ye can get away from this boathouse."

"But how can I run to the mainland and leave Marc?"

My mind sprang into life. This was a new whiff of freedom, but what was my best course of action?

"Marc'll be alright. They don't need you. They need 'im for their plan 'cos he can speak French and 'e knows the town."

"Let me think on it —"

"Smith!"

It was Yule's voice that came from close behind my left ear.

"I 'ope you and Mister Vowles are only talking pleasantries because the Lieutenant's got his eye on you," he hissed.

Looking across the boathouse, I saw that Yule was right, and Ebbs was glaring at us.

"We wus only catchin' up, Mister Yule. No 'arm done," Vowles said apologetically. "Yule wants me to 'elp with the work on the Frog ketch so I'll see you tomorrow," he whispered to me, as he knuckled his brow towards the quartermaster and slunk away towards the throng of men around the food.

❖   ❖   ❖

Vowles' offer of escape robbed me of any chance to sleep that night. My mind churned over the pros and cons of the two options, as I continuously rolled from side to side. Electing to follow Vowles' plan would involve an arduous, and potentially dangerous, crossing, but I would be a free man as soon as the gigs pushed off from the beach tomorrow night. On the negative side of the ledger, there was always the chance of running into the Navy. If I was impressed for a third time, there would be no chance of discharge until I was too frail to pull on a halyard. Yet, on the other hand, if I stayed on St.Agnes, putting my faith in Pearson and Ebbs, I would have to endure the possibility of heavy fighting in Douarnenez harbour. However, survival would mean freedom from the Navy forever, and possession of a written passport to prove it!

I also had to factor in what was best for Marc Goriau and how my decision would affect him? He had stood by me, making sure I was included in his pact with Pearson, and so I owed it to him to see it through: or did I? Perhaps he would expect me to run if a better opportunity arose? As Vowles had said, he was far more valuable to Pearson and Ebbs on the voyage to Douarnenez than I. And then there was Ebbs himself; was I capable of betraying him again? If only he'd speak to me, I'd know what he expected. Had he stuck his neck out with Pearson so that I should have this chance to redeem myself? Or was it like Vowles suspected; that the Navy had no intention of honouring their pact with Goriau, and Ebbs was simply reluctant to lie to me? Did I even care which of them was let down? I was having no problems finding the questions, but was not being so successful with finding the answers. I was still wrestling with them when Yule started shouting to his slumbering workforce that it was time for the day's labour to begin.

Grabbing a hasty breakfast, from the tables near the fire, I became aware of a hung-over Gardiner stumbling about after me. Within the half hour, we traipsed out of the boathouse, and I latched on to the end of the untidy crocodile of grumbling men with my marine shadow beside me.

Vowles was already at Willywicks Bay when we arrived. He had a couple of *Turk* tradesmen with him and they were unloading finished timbers from a horse drawn wagon. I tried to catch his eye but he seemed to be making a point of not looking at me. The hazy light of dawn afforded me my first opportunity to examine *Esprit du Breese* properly; it had been very nearly dark the previous evening. She lay on her side a good way up from the last high-tide mark. The Goriaus had obviously brought her in on a spring tide, and had intended a major refit before being interrupted by our trip to Douarnenez. There were several jagged holes left by the shot from the rogue schooner. Generally, her hull was in quite poor condition. The pitch and paint that covered the wood had been scraped back in places and sections of the carvel planking had been removed entirely.

I stood at the back of the little group of crewmen who had gathered at the side of the careened vessel, while Yule and Ebbs surveyed her and allocated work. Vowles was only a few yards away and could easily have engineered some pretext to speak to me. The fact that he didn't did nothing to help me make up my mind. I was beginning to harbour hopes that he had shelved his plans for helping me to escape which would mean there wasn't a decision to be made. Shortly, Yule came to my brain's rescue by finding something for my hands to do.

"I can't believe that we're doin' this," he growled, as he approached. "Smith, I want you to strip back all the timbers port side o' the stem and remove anythin' that ain't at least half way sound."

"Only half-way sound, Quartermaster?" I asked.

"This ain't no bleedin' boat yard. I just wants this tub to float for another few days not another winter," he said, handing me a quarter-sized wooden mallet and chisel.

I set about my task with enthusiasm, trying to divert my mind from thinking about Vowles and his escape plan, but it was of little use. Within a short while, my mind was churning over much travelled ground and stuck once again in its familiar quagmire. Every few minutes, I found myself involuntarily glancing around to see where Vowles was but he was never close by. Was he avoiding me on purpose?

The hazy dawn was rapidly transforming into a bright, windy morning. I was hacking away at some fairly ancient French planking, consumed by my problem, when Ebbs materialised at my side. He reached out and forced one of his thumb nails into the trenails (NOTE: *Trenails are round, oak pegs used by shipwrights to hold carvel planking in position*) that held a timber to the futtock nearest the stem.

"These will have to do. We can't replace them all," he announced haughtily without looking at me.

It was the closest he had stood to me since we had been in the cabin on *Tiger*. It was an opportunity that was just too tempting to pass up.

"I reckon she'll be sound enough to make my last voyage, Sir," I blurted out.

My boldness shocked me, and it certainly had the same affect on Ebbs who turned and stared at me open mouthed.

Fear of the unknown drove me on to get an answer, "I shall be out of the Navy after the trip to Douarnenez won't I, Sir?" I persisted, but he just fixed me with an exasperated stare before stalking away and disappearing around the bow. I slung down my chisel and swung a punch at the soft timbers in front of me. Why wouldn't he speak to me?

"Calm down boy."

The soothing voice came from behind me, and I turned to see that it was Vowles.

"What did 'e want?" he asked, jerking his head in the direction that Ebbs had just gone.

"If only I knew, Bill," I replied philosophically.

"Is you up for tonight?" he asked nonchalantly as if it was the most simple of questions.

I found myself replying, 'Aye, Bill' without a second thought. The rights and wrongs of both plans were still bouncing around my head. I didn't think I would ever be able to make a decision. In the absence of any verification from Ebbs, I was simply allowing Vowles to direct my actions.

"The gigs'll be 'idden in that copse to the north west o' us," he said, pointing across the barren, rock-strewn landscape towards a collection of tiny, wind-bent oak trees about a quarter-mile away. "We'll be ready to go a couple o' hours a'ter midnight."

"How shall I get away from the boathouse tonight?"

"You'll just 'ave to come when the others is asleep. The marines is working as 'ard as the others, an' I can't see the Lieutenant insisting on a sentry standin' all night. If he does, I'll think of a way to move 'im," Vowles said, glancing over his shoulder. "I'd best push off."

He gave me a final nod and stumped off in the direction of the village. His instructions couldn't have been clearer, but rather than solving my dilemma, the moment he was out of sight, I started worrying about if it was fair to leave without speaking to Goriau, or if I was betraying Ebbs.

It goes without saying that nothing else was in my mind for the rest of the day. I still had doubts when Ebbs re-appeared to check our work in the evening. A dozen seamen and Vowles' *Turks* were making short work of the repairs and *Esprit du Breese* would be seaworthy again in another day or so. Ebbs announced that he was satisfied, and we packed our tools into the wagon as the dusk was beginning to gather in the clear Atlantic sky above us.

❖ ❖ ❖

I had a fraught time of it in the boathouse that night. After a meal of herring and potatoes the *Turks* headed home, and the crewmen from *Theseus'* gathered around the beer barrel. I drank a couple of pots with them and then settled down on the pile of hay that was my bed. Gardiner was far less watchful than he had been the previous evening. I listened attentively for Ebbs leaving instructions for pickets to stand throughout the night, but I heard nothing. I lay still, feigning sleep, until Yule ordering the men abed. I still had my doubts about whether this was the right decision, but I had told Vowles that I was coming to the copse and steeled myself to stand by my word.

When everything was quiet, apart from snores, I pushed off my blanket and slowly rose to my feet. The boathouse was lit only by the dying embers of the fire, but as far as I could tell everyone was asleep. I picked my way slowly past the sleeping bodies and towards the door at the side. My toe collided with the raised stones at the foot of the door, and I had to cling to the wall for a few moments, suffering the pain in silence. I had reached the door unnoticed and felt a surge of self congratulation. I may not be able to make a decision but I could outwit my naval gaolers! Reaching for the latch on the door, I heard a sound from the front of the building. I froze: my mind suddenly alive with possibilities. Perhaps it was Vowles coming to collect me? Or possibly there was a sentry after all? My heart pumped fast and I had to wait several moments for it to calm down and my head to clear. I stood motionless by the wall listening intently: there was nothing. The longer I waited, the more I was convinced that no one was about, and once again confidence started to flow through my veins. Allowing myself the luxury of believing it was only the breeze that had disturbed some of the boathouse's old timbers, I lifted the latch and crept outside.

For a moment, I waited for a challenge: nothing came. The sky was bright with thousands of tiny stars in beautiful swirls and patterns. It struck me as odd, to be looking into the heavens at such a fraught moment, but it had the effect of calming me. With new resolve, I trotted in the direction Vowles had pointed out. After a few strides, my foot caught under a stout bramble stem and I hit the ground with a thump. I lay still and listened for a few moments. There was the sound of a footfall behind me! Or was there? I lay still, straining my ears, but heard nothing else. Climbing to my feet, I told myself to be more careful. As Vowles has said, it was a moonless night, and seeing my way was going to be hard. Slowly, I felt my way through the clumps of spiky, salt-grass. I was getting close to a little oak wood now and could just make out the black shapes of individual trees against the minutely lighter tone of the ocean.

"Nathaniel Egan!"

My head corkscrewed round but there was nothing to be seen.

"Tell me that you are not about to betray me again, Nathaniel."

When the voice spoke a second time, I recognised it as Ebbs'.

"Jacob, where ... where are you?" I mumbled.

The sounds of crunching of grass came from out of the blackness.

"I followed you from the boathouse."

Behind me there was only a lightless void. I didn't know where he was until I became aware of his breathing. He couldn't be more than a few feet away from me.

"Don't tell me where you are going, I don't wish to know. Do your new acquaintances have to pay as high a price for your friendship as I had to?" His voice was cracking from his attempts to control his anger, but the odd word was rendered in a near hysterical higher pitch.

"Jacob, I ..."

I had no idea of what to say to him and my words simply dried up.

"If a man's word is worthless, then that man is worthless," he yelled in my face and disappeared back into the darkness.

CHAPTER SIXTEEN
*Seven Leagues West-Southwest of Ushant
– 8th July 1809*

The slithering creature that is Buonaparte should be dismissed as the lowest form of life on God's earth. He has besmirched every principle of fraternity and equality that the Revolution in France once claimed to own.

He creates grandiose titles for himself to justify his tyranny over the French peasantry, and he even has the audacity to invent a crown to put on his own head.

Here is a man who once taught that the word of God was the enemy of revolution, but now that he has proclaimed himself Emperor he announces that his birthday is to become a religious feast day (the Feast of St. Napoleon – 15th August).
     An extract transcribed from an open address by
     Orator Thomas Hughes, Birmingham Bull Ring 1806

After Ebbs berated me in that dark hinterland behind the boathouse at Porth Conger, I experienced an instant, and complete, change of heart. My uncertainties disappeared, my mind made up for me. Deep down, I believed that I owed too much to Jacob Ebbs to run out on him again.

Somehow, after he had gone, I stumbled to the wood to keep my rendezvous with Vowles, and told him that I was going to Douarnenez with the Navy. Back at the boathouse, with the responsibility of making a decision finally lifted from my shoulders, I actually fell asleep!

When I awoke, there was no sign of Ebbs, and I was told that he had left to rejoin *Theseus*. I didn't set eyes upon him again for nearly two weeks, and there was no way of knowing if he knew I had stayed on St.Agnes or not.

It took longer than expected for *Esprit du Breese's* new timbers to swell, and it was a full ten days before she became watertight. With the help of the *Turks* we were able to float her onto a spring tide. Yule knew where to rendezvous with *Tiger* and *Theseus*, and two days later, we joined the little flotilla late in the evening, about twenty miles west of the French Atlantic coast.

Pearson and Ebbs were obviously waiting for us, and as soon as we had backed our fores'l the frigate's launch and longboat started rowing across supplies for our expedition. Lanterns were hung from our standing rigging, and under Yule's direction, bulging nets of small arms, powder and provisions were swung onboard. The frigate's boats then started to ferry boatfuls of men over to *Esprit*. Swathed in an eerie, rocking lamplight our deck quickly became crowded with men, and Yule frantically set about imposing some sort of order to the chaos.

Ebbs and Marc Goriau arrived with the final boatload. I had half expected Ebbs to display some sort of surprise when he saw me aboard, but if he did notice me in the near darkness, he did nothing to reveal it. He hurried off, taking Goriau with him, on a tour of the boat, and about an hour later he gave the order to pull in the fore sheets. We were on our way towards Douarnenez!

Goriau and I took up positions next to each other at the larboard beam rail and watched the dark shapes that were *Tiger* and *Theseus* slowly disappearing into the dark ocean behind us.

"We should be staying closely together at all times, *mon ami*," Goriau whispered conspiratorially. "When we land the Lieutenant near the schooner *noir*, you and I shall head straight backwards *à la mer*."

"Are you convinced that they'll let us leave after the landing?"

"Of course, we have *un accord*."

"I think there will be fierce fighting when they try to cut out the schooner, Marc. I'm not so sure we will have the opportunity to leave," I replied.

"The fighting is not concerning us; we have *un accord* to get *les Anglais* into the harbour *secrètement*. No more than this," Goriau hissed firmly.

If only I could be as sure as Goriau that that was all Ebbs had planned for us. The familiar, prickly sensations of fear and anxiety were creeping back into the pit of my stomach. What would happen when we reached Douarnenez? Would Ebbs really let us sail away as soon as we had landed his men? Would he need to keep *Esprit* in reserve in case he failed to take the schooner? His refusal to speak to me suggested he had more demanding roles in mind, for Goriau and me, than mere ferrymen. Nevertheless, it was comforting to have an ally like Goriau at my side, especially now that he was far more positive about our immediate future than I was. The broken man, who had lost his grip on the world when his brother was killed, had well and truly disappeared.

Sailing *Esprit du Breese* with so many men littering her deck was no easy task, but at least Ebbs had the luxury of skilled men near to every rope and halyard. His voice rang out from close behind us.

"Raise a steerage lantern to the mainmast head, Mister Yule."

We turned to see Ebbs standing a couple of paces for'ard of the wheel, and I could sense Goriau's body tense. I guessed that he abhorred having someone else giving orders aboard his boat.

"That's as it should be for a fishing vessel working French water is it not, Monsieur Goriau?"

Hearing Ebbs' display of manners made me smile to myself. The Navy had commandeered Goriau's boat, but convention dictated he should still be addressed as the ship's master, and therefore a gentleman. The Frenchman wasn't interested in the niceties of naval etiquette, and only raised a disinterested hand as an affirmative reply.

I watched intently as the young Lieutenant organised his crew for the short voyage to Douarnenez. A small vessel with such a large number of men on board would need authoritative leadership. Ebbs' personality had changed since we had been together at Aix Roads. He had always been full of confidence and keen to succeed, but his ambition was tempered by his obvious humanity. He seemed to have become far more of the traditional, authoritarian cliché of a naval officer in the months I had not known him. But I still sensed that the men he commanded not only obeyed him but respected him as well. I just wasn't sure whether the philanthropic youth I had once sailed with still existed under that hard, efficient exterior.

❖   ❖   ❖

Despite her excessive human cargo, *Esprit* bucked gainfully into the fresh easterly that had sprang up the following late evening. The men on deck instinctively shuffled towards her windward side as she heeled, in an effort to give a little more stability. It was cold in the wind, but Yule had told us that we would all have to go below as soon as we came within eye-glass range of the French coast, and I was determined to stay on deck for as long as possible. I was as reluctant to cram into the fish-hold, with sixty odd others, as I was to experience the inevitable fighting that would take place after we landed. Even with the deck hatches open it was going to be hot and asphyxiating down there, but at least transferring the men's weight below the waterline would make *Esprit* travel a little smoother.

When we had completed her renovations on St.Agnes we had been told not to load *Esprit* with her full compliment of rock ballast around the keel, and now it became apparent why. With this many men onboard, as well as the ballast, she would have sat too low in the water to make headway: especially to windward.

"Monsieur Goriau, the gaff-uphaul will not tighten the mains'l. Could I request you to lend your assistance?"

It was Ebbs voice and there was enough light from the waxing gibbous moon to see Goriau, who was still beside me, react with a grimace.

"Will you *aidez-moi* with English for the sailors, Nathaniel?" he said, touching my arm. Nodding my acquiescence, we started to pick our way for'ard through the men sitting on the deck.

"*Merci*, Monsieur Goriau," Ebbs called after us.

"We shall have to be straight to the wind," Goriau shouted back to him.

With the pressure off the sails it only took the Frenchman a minute or two to demonstrate to the seamen waiting at the mast how the topping lift worked the block at the masthead to tighten the mains'l gaff. He also had to shuffle his way down the deck to show them the outhaul at the clew end of the boom that also tightened the sail (NOTE: *Goriau's boat served as both fishing boat and coaster, and employed a different arrangement of tackle for adjusting the shape and size of the mainsail to what Egan was used to on a fishing boat in the Bristol Channel. The gaff rig particularly lent itself to fishing because changes to the mains'l can be made quickly, and by few hands, to regulate the speed of the boat when towing nets or long lines).*

"If he cannot sail *mon bateaux* why does he not step away and leave her to me?" Goriau grumbled, as we made our way back to where we had come from.

As if to substantiate Goriau's point, no sooner had we resumed our position at the rail, and Ebb's was calling for more advice. This time he spoke in French, and I had no idea what he wanted, but Goriau stumped off astern to talk to him. I was left alone to scan the horizon in front of us. The French coast was no more than a fat, dull, grey line straddling the horizon, illuminated by the hazy moonlight that leaked through the clouds above it. We were much too far away to be able to estimate where the Bay of Douarnenez lay, but the sea ahead of us was empty. I found myself mulling over how Goriau and I would cope if it transpired that we were given the opportunity to take *Esprit* out of Douarnenez. With so little ballast left below we were going to have a hell of job sailing to windward. I didn't have long to contemplate this problem, because my concentration was disturbed by a sudden commotion behind me. Crewmen were pulling what appeared to be old clothes out of a bale that had appeared on the deck.

"Mister Ludlow. Please see that those clothes are distributed in an orderly fashion," yelled Ebbs, from near the tiller where he was still talking to Goriau.

"Aye aye, Sir," came the reply as I saw the youthful shape of Midshipman Ludlow pushing his way through the group of sailors holding a lantern above his head.

"Now see here you lot, unhand that clothing and stand away from those bales, all of you. Lively now!"

I hadn't been aware that Edward Ludlow was aboard. He was little more than a boy, but I had watched him on *Tiger*, and he was an honest, likeable youngster with a shock of thick, red hair. He was the junior, and so I guessed that the midshipman's mess had all drawn lots to see who would have the honour of serving as Ebbs' second-in-command. He swiftly restored order and nominated two men to distribute the clothing.

"Now do try and employ a little common sense, you two. The biggest garments to the biggest men: top coats and trousers for the marines, and top coats alone for the seamen."

Yule appeared at the rail by my side and cast his eye over the proceedings.

"A right load o' old rubbish," he commented quietly to nobody in particular.

"What's this all about, Mister Yule?" I asked.

He turned to me: "Mister Ebbs gave me ten shillings which I gave to your mate Vowles for old clothes to disguise the landing party when we first arrive in Douarnenez. They'll be carryin' weapons an''ll need top coats to conceal 'em. Trouble is wit' this lot of old garbage is the French 'ill think they're bein' attacked by ship full of footpads and street beggars!"

There were guffaws of laughter from the sailors behind us. One bright spark was sticking his head straight through a huge hole in the back of a black coat. Yule was right to condemn the quality of Vowles' offerings. They were mainly old fisherman's cast-offs: knitted and oiled smocks, tarpaulins and alike. The rows of men, who had been sitting on the deck, were standing up trying on what was allotted to them. For fishermen to dismiss a garment as beyond repair meant, quite simply, that it was beyond repair, and these were the rags that Vowles had collected up from the back of boat sheds and dog boxes to be sold to Yule. Not even my anxiety over impending danger in Douarnenez, could subdue the comedic absurdity of seeing fighting-men prancing about in stinking, torn and much mended attire like so many small children. I laughed out loud and even caught the trace of a smile on Yule's lips.

"They may look shockin' but at least they didn't look as if they have anything to do wit' the King's Navy," he said.

The humour of the situation disappeared when one of the crewmen, who had been tasked to allot the clothing, tossed a filthy looking long, woollen coat in my direction.

"I thought that Goriau and I would be staying aboard *Esprit*, Sir," I asked Yule anxiously.

"Don't ask me Smith," he replied. "I don't get told nothin'."

❖ ❖ ❖

I had dozed intermittently, but not really slept, over the last hour or so. I was glad of the woollen overcoat, even if it did stink of ancient pilchards, and pulled it tightly around my neck as I stretched my legs which were stiff from inactivity and cold. The first pale suggestions of the oncoming dawn were evident in the forms of clouds directly above me, but the steerage light, swinging from the end of the gaff, still bore testament to the darkness around it. I was sitting with my back to the windward rail and my feet firmly wedged against a deck cleat, to counter *Esprit's* yawing, when Ebbs ordered Midshipman Ludlow to start moving the men below deck. We must be very near the Bay of Douarnenez, and Ebbs would be worrying about prying French telescopes scanning our deck. Ludlow appeared silhouetted by the dim glow of the binnacle lamp. He was standing at the top of the companion, and the crewmen were filing past him on their way below deck.

Yule and Goriau were walking towards me, and I climbed to my feet to talk to them. Looking out over the side, and through the surrounding greyness, there was a pin-prick of light, some way off, in the darkness. I stared intently at it. It was definitely there! The longer I concentrated on it the clearer it became.

"Don't worry *mon ami*. It is the lamp of steerage from a *bateau de pêche* making for Douarnenez harbour," said Goriau, reading my thoughts as he and Yule came alongside me.

"Why is there only one of them coming home on a June tide?" I asked.

Yule made a sort of derogatory snorting sound and said: "This be a Sunday morning tide!"

He spoke as if this simple explanation should be enough for me to understand his meaning, but I had no idea what he was referring to.

"Well?" I said.

"A good Catholic don't go out to fish a Saturday night tide when 'e 'as Mass in the mornin'," he said exasperatedly.

"Oh," I replied. My father would never fish on a Sunday, but if the tide was right he'd fish Saturday night and come home on the Sabbath's flood. "I thought the Revolution had scared all the god fearing men out of France?"

"Bonaparte may have usurped our Revolution, but he is, as you say, a wily fox enough to give the people back their religion," said Goriau.

"Smith, you'd better be making your way below now!" Ebbs' voice rang out clearly from the stern. "And you as well if you please, Mister Yule."

Dutifully, I made my way up the deck after nodding a farewell at the Frenchman. There was a little knot of men waiting to mount the companion, and Ebbs was standing a few yards away by the mizzen shrouds.

"Shall I be staying on board *Esprit* when we get into harbour Sir," I asked.

"Get below, Smith," the young Lieutenant hissed back, even in the poor light I could see the annoyance on his face.

"But Monsieur Goriau and I shall need to plan our __."

"Get below, Smith," he snapped again, and turned his back to signify that our exchange had ended.

Heat rushed into my cheeks; I wasn't sure whether it was embarrassment or anger. Why couldn't Ebbs just give me a clue as to my future? I stepped towards the companion way and was glad that the sailors had all gone below. I reached the ladder at the same time as Yule, who was scanning the deck, and I stopped for a moment and did the same. Ebbs, Goriau and Ludlow were the only ones left topsides.

"They're the only ones who speaks Frog," Yule murmured, answering my question before it had been asked.

"Where do I fit into all this?" I asked.

"He'll tell us in 'is own sweet time," the Quartermaster replied. "I don't expect he knows 'is self yet."

The first thing that hit me, as I climbed down the ladder, was the heat below deck. *Esprit du Breese's* hold was fully forty feet long and her beam wider than most English vessels of a similar size, but sixty men packed together generated heat quickly, and it would not be long before the air soured. The gentle washes of hazy light that illuminated two clumps of seamen's heads told me that both hatches were open, but it was obvious that this number of men couldn't stay down here for long. There was a hum of voices in the hold, but Yule silenced them as he climbed down the companionway.

"Keep your mouths shut! All o' you. Unless you want to meet your maker afore we've 'ad that schooner," he growled. "It's getting' light an' we'll be approachin' the harbour in the next 'alf hour."

The wind was veering to the south, and *Esprit's* movement felt steadier as she reached across the waves. On the higher - windward - side of the hold a massive man with a completely bald head and a bulging, red neck was distributing weapons. To his left a small man held a lantern to illuminate the proceedings, and at his feet the bald man had one of the landing nets full of powder and arms that I had seen swayed aboard *Esprit* that afternoon.

"Come on boys. I got pistols an' cutlasses for everyone an' there be some dandy tomahawks for those that want 'em," bulging neck shouted.

He hardly had room to pull cutlasses and boarding axes out of the nets and pass them out amongst the men. I could see the black, high stock of a Royal Marine tunic poking out above his woollen overcoat, and I recognised him as one of *Tiger's* marine sergeants.

"Sergeant Walters, do that quietly," Yule hissed at him. "See that all the seamen are armed, and that the marines are supplied wit' the requisite quantities of powder and shot."

I hung back by the ladder and didn't push myself forward to claim any weapons. Why did I need arms? I had no idea of what was expected of me?

Many of the men were beginning to get excited by the possibility of a fight, and Yule had to keep hissing at them to keep quiet. The man directly in front of me gave his mate a punch in the arm, and they grimaced at each other grotesquely as they locked fists together in some sort of confidence-building ritual. There were whispered statements of violent intent all around me. As their heady malevolence fermented deeper, my own confidence was leaking away. Why wouldn't Ebbs tell me what was to happen? The thought of being sent ashore with a cutlass in my hand, to slash indiscriminately at Frenchmen I had no quarrel with, was making the muscles in my right arm tremble. I had felt enough revulsion for the pirates who had attacked Barkas and Goriau to consider carrying arms against them, but the King's war with France was none of my concern.

For a brief moment, the vision of the back of Jas Capel's head flashed into my mind, and I could feel my finger on the cold metal of the pistol's trigger. Once again, I smelt the fizzing priming powder in the pan and felt the weapon explode in my hand. The memory of his execution washed over me with no trace of emotion, but imagining the atrocities that I might witness in the next few hours was a horrifying prospect.

The sun must have been truly up by now because beams of light danced brightly on tops of the heads that were under the hatchways. The mood within the hold grew more sanguineous by the minute. It felt like waiting for a tightly corked jar of scrumpy, that had been left by a fire, to blow out its sides. As their blood fever grew, the men became increasingly boisterous, and started to push their way towards the companion as if they couldn't wait to get ashore. How could they face the prospect of losing their lives with such eagerness? There must be some men in this fish hold that felt the same anxieties as me? If there were, none of them were letting it show. The prospect of fighting seemed to have carried their brains clean away. The more agitated they became the more they sweated, and a kind of foetid steam was rising above the sea of bodies. Most of the men around me were Sergeant Walters' Marines, and the overcoats they wore to cover their red woollen tunics were making them sweat even more profusely than the others. The air grew danker by the second, and the stench that hung around me will live in my memory for the rest of my life.

I felt a sharp pain as my ribs were crushed against the hull planking by the men continuing to push towards the companion ladder. It felt as if each breath of air was fighting its way inside me, desperately trying to inflate my lungs. Out of the open hatchway above the companionway, there were benign, fluffy white clouds that seemed totally alien to my predicament. Something snapped inside me! Wildly swinging my elbows at the heads of the men who were pinning me against the hull, I hoisted myself onto their backs and scrambled towards the companion ladder. Fearsome oaths emanated from beneath me, and I was half expecting the sharp pain from some sort of blade but nothing came. Planting my left foot against something hard, I have no idea whether it was a head or a torso, I made a determined leap for the ladder. The smooth wooden rungs felt cold and slippery, and I realised that my palms were greasy with sweat. The first whiff of clean air was irresistible, and I hauled myself up the ladder until my head was nearly level with the hatchway. No retribution followed from the men below, and I felt more under control, clinging to the ladder by myself.

I craned my neck, in an attempt to see where we were. As I did so, I could hear Goriau explaining to Ebbs about the channel that ran from the mouth of the river, south of the island, and into the bay beyond. *Esprit* fortuitously rolled on the swell, and I caught a glimpse of the high, crenulated stone tower, that I had seen before, and knew we were no more than a few minutes away from the harbour wall!

"Get your head down, Smith!"

It was Ebbs' voice. His face, wearing an exasperated expression, appeared framed by the hatchway above me. He reached out with a foot, and planted it roughly on my forehead, forcing me downwards. I quickly retreated a couple of rungs, but could go no further because a marine had climbed the companion beneath me. Ducking my head, I just clung on where I was.

"Everybody stays below until I say otherwise," Ebbs hissed down the companionway.

It couldn't possibly be long now before I learnt what Ebbs expected of me. There was another muscle spasm in my right arm, and my mind grappled with the possibilities for my immediate future! It occurred to me that the schooner might not be here. Perhaps it had slipped out to sea without Pearson noticing, and we would just have to turn round and head back to *Tiger*.

There was an outbreak of activity above my head, the pounding of running feet and the squeaking of hemp rope in wooden blocks. Goriau was shouting instructions to the others, but he spoke in French and I couldn't understand him. I felt *Esprit's* bow turning through the wind. We must be tacking inside the River.

Ebbs' face appeared above me again. He was beckoning furiously at me and I clambered up the top few rungs of the companion. As my head rose above the deck, he bent towards me and whispered sternly in my ear.

"Get on deck, Smith: you and the next two men. Look lively now. We're going to turn downwind and come alongside. Get to the fore deck, and help Mister Ludlow with the fors'ls."

Jumping onto the deck, I ran to where the red-haired midshipman was unhitching the jib sheet on the starboard side.

"Let the stays'l fly Smith, and help me sheet in on the larboard side," Ludlow hissed at me.

The briefest of glances around the scene that greeted me from the deck, told me we were about eighty or ninety yards into the mouth of the River Pouldavid, close to the western bank; near the line of stout mooring posts I'd seen on my previous visit with Barkas. There were several vessels moored alongside the stone-laid quay wall on the opposite side of the river, but there was still plenty of room for us. There were no crewmen to be seen on any of the ships and the quayside was deserted.

Esprit's mizzen gaff had been dropped to its boom, and as

Goriau, who was at the tiller, put her bow through the wind, the loose-footed sails above our heads flapped viciously. The main course gaff had been dropped limply across the big sail, cutting the working sail area by half and keeping *Esprit's* momentum to a minimum. As soon as we felt the wind bear on the opposite side of the bow, Ludlow and I started heaving on the sheets. *Esprit* shivered 'in irons' for a few seconds, and then slowly began to make headway across the wind. Ebbs let the main boom drop at the throat, and the two crewmen with him hauled it into the centre of the boat.

"Ease your sheet again, Smith," Ludlow ordered. "We just want to keep her movin' slow."

Goriau was neatly manoeuvring *Esprit* through 180 degrees, and we were now beginning to run downwind, back towards the mouth of the river, under the power of the two fors'ls. We were past the centre of the wide river, but still some way off the quayside that ran the length of the eastern bank. Goriau groped his way towards an empty expanse of quay wall that lay behind two moored vessels, gauging our speed against the distance we had to cover and selecting his angle of approach.

"Get ready to let your sheet fly and then drop the halyard," said Ludlow.

As he spoke, Ebbs was making his way towards us.

"Go back below, Smith," he said, as quietly as he could when he reached me. "We shall have to speak French if anyone hails us from the shore."

Before climbing down the companionway, I glanced across at the two vessels moored at the quayside. The first, which we were just about abreast of, was a raggedy looking, old brig and the second, about a hundred yards down the quayside, was an impressive looking, black schooner. I estimated her length at over 150 feet and weight at about 400 tons. She was heavily laden and sat low in the water.

I reached the companionway at the same time as one of the marines who had been helping Ebbs, and we both turned when we heard a growl emanating from the tiller behind us.

"*Merde*," Goriau said, his eyes transfixed on the black schooner. "*Il est le bateau diable!*"

So, I was out of luck, and the pirate ship was here after all!

"Methinks, we 'ave found our quarry," the marine whispered in my ear as I made my way down the ladder.

CHAPTER SEVENTEEN
Douarnenez Quayside, France – 9th July 1809

William Symington, a Scottish engineer, has successfully demonstrated the potential for nautical steam power. His boat, The Charlotte Dundas, *towed two loaded barges upon the Forth and Clyde Canal last month. The steamboat towed its burthen for an impressive 18½ miles in 9½ hours.*
Aris's Birmingham Gazette, April 1803

All that could be heard from the deck above was Goriau's voice barking staccato commands in French and the corresponding clatter of footsteps. The men around me in the packed hold were silent except for the dull hum created by their collective breathing. My hearing was at a heightened state: as it can be when the rest of your senses tell you nothing. *Esprit du Breese* crept forward very slowly towards the quay wall. Goriau would have sent Ebbs and Ludlow to throw fenders over the side, and they would be preparing to put a line ashore. There was a dull thud, and then another, as *Esprit's* larboard quarter bumped against the quay wall. We had arrived, and I had no idea what was about to happen to me or what my role would be!

Some high boots appeared on the companion ladder and they were followed by the young Lieutenant.

"Right men," he said in a forced whisper. "We're alongside and there is no activity on the quay whatsoever, thank heavens. I want the marines on deck first. Five of you to go with Sergeant

Walters, and make sure nobody disturbs us from the direction of the battery on the sea wall."

"Very good, Sir," Yule snapped in obedience. "Let's 'ave the first five Marines up the companion. The rest of you stand back."

"I want five more on the quayside, in amongst the warehouses. Keep your weapons out of sight, all of you," Ebbs continued. "The rest stay here but for God's sake stay quiet, and be ready for action if you should hear musketry." He made as to climb back up the ladder, but he turned and looked at me, "and see that Smith is armed, Mister Yule" he snapped, before he disappeared.

The marines dutifully filed by and followed Ebbs up the companionway. Earlier, I had been hoping the rogue schooner wouldn't be here, or that I might be left on board *Esprit du Breese* to help Goriau sail her out of the bay when we had delivered the Navy. Those two possibilities disappeared when Ebb's ordered that I should be armed! When the prospect of danger is very close, it is much crueller to be left worrying about what might happen than to be actually involved: I tried to tell myself.

At least, there was no shouting or shooting from the quay, and so we were not yet discovered. The empty sensation in the pit of my stomach grew when Yule appeared at my side. He was carrying a heavy, naval pistol and a short cutlass in a dark leather scabbard.

"'Ere," he said, "you'd better take these."

Marc Goriau came down the companion and stood on the second or third rung, above my head. "*Monsieur* Yule …? *Monsieur* Ebbs wants you to bring up your *hommes*," he hissed.

I took the pistol from Yule and pushed it into my belt.

"Is it loaded," I asked.

He nodded as he passed me the cutlass, I climbed the ladder and stuck my head back out into the fresh French air.

The scene that greeted me on the quayside was not dissimilar from the last time I was here: except that on this occasion it was in daylight. The wharf was deserted, apart from the five marines who were skulking in one of the alleyways between the warehouses. We were lying a little further up the quay than where we had tied up *Peggy-Ann*, but I could still see the flaking, black and white sign for *Adolphe Absolon et Fils*, and there was that same strange aroma of overheated tallow in the air.

Looking up the quay to the sea wall, I could see Ludlow and

his group congregated around a hand cart that had been left not far from the battery. Their muskets were nowhere to be seen, I guessed they were concealed among the fish boxes on the cart.

What could be seen of the little town of Douarnenez, stretching out behind the banks of the river, had an eerie abandoned feel. Yule must be right and the Catholic faithful would all be called to worship. Goriau was the only Frenchman in sight. There were a couple of silhouettes a few hundred yards down river, and a wispy spiral of smoke reached into the sky from the river, but I couldn't make out where it came from.

The schooner was moored no more than fifty yards behind *Esprit du Breese*. Unlike *Esprit*, whose bow pointed seaward, the schooner was moored facing down river. On either side of the grotesquely carved dolphin, that served as her figurehead, was the name *Liberté*. I instantly questioned how we were going to turn the vessel, and sail it out of that river, without rowing it away from the quay by longboat.

Ebbs stood on the quay, gesticulating to Yule. He held up ten fingers and thumbs and beckoned frantically. Yule selected ten of the remaining marines and wordlessly dispatched them to climb over the rail and join the Lieutenant. As Yule himself made to climb the rail, Ebbs waved him back, and indicated that we should all lie down. Positioning myself beside the bowsprit, I had a good view through the rail as events unfolded, and could also scan the quayside for the inevitable arrival of some sort of Frog opposition: but none materialised.

Ebbs, holding his finger to his mouth, led the marines onboard *Liberté*. It felt bizarre to be lying flat on my stomach, watching an act of war unfold in silence. It was like watching a troupe of travelling mummers, back in Lilstock, except with the added elements of fear and anxiety. The schooner's deck was higher than *Esprit's*, but I could see the top half of Ebbs' body. He issued instructions by hand signal, and three men, armed with pistols, moved towards the fore deck. Three more disappeared astern, presumably to guard hatchways. Ebbs summoned the remaining marines to follow him, and he headed for the high coach roof midway down the schooners' deck which, I guessed, would house the main companionway. When he reached it, he drew his pistol, signalled to the men on the fore deck with a downward motion, and they all disappeared from view. I strained my ears, but there was nothing; not a sound came from the schooner. They must have overpowered whoever was on board with ease or else there would have been firing. One man couldn't bear the tension any better than me, and he stood up and climbed a couple of steps up the fore mast ratlines, to get a better vantage point, before Yule grabbed his foot and pulled him down.

"What could yus see?" the quartermaster hissed, when he had chastised him with a couple of soundless punches.

"Nothin', Mr Yule. Nothin' at all," was his reply.

The minutes ticked by without producing any activity, and then Ebbs reappeared on the schooners' deck. He climbed over the side, jumped onto the quay and trotted towards *Esprit du Breese*. We all crowded to the rail, behind Yule, to hear what he had to say.

"We've secured the schooner, Quartermaster," he said, his face flushed with excitement. "There are half a dozen of them on board but, unbelievably, only two of them were awake."

"Where's the rest of the crew, Sir?" Yule asked his commanding officer.

"They tell me they stayed in the town last night and are due back any moment, but I don't believe a word of it. They were too scared of us for me to believe their comrades are due back anytime soon. The holds are stuffed with tradable goods, but they can't have been planning to leave on the next tide. If the schooner's departure is not imminent, my guess is that the crew'll be spread across the taverns and bordellos of the area."

"What do you want us to do, Mister Ebbs?"

Yule had the eager expression of a small boy on his face as he spoke.

"Mister Yule, you take the rest of the marines ashore. Keep them out of sight if possible but cover the landward end of the quay. Monsieur Goriau, I would ask you to take charge of your boat. Take three crewmen and ready her to leave."

"*Oui* ..." Goriau mumbled, with a shrug of his shoulders which said that he believed he had at no time relinquished command of his vessel.

"Take the rest of the men onto *Liberté*, Mister Ludlow, and sit tight until I return. If the shooting starts don't let the men fire until you've broken out our own colours."

"How will we be getting the schooner to sea, *Monsieur*?" Goriau asked.

"I think if the wind stays where it is we can use *Esprit du*

Breese to pull the schooners' head to wind," Ebbs replied.

"It is possible ..." Goriau said hesitantly.

"And you, Smith." I felt the breath catch in my throat. "Come with me," Ebbs snapped. "You had better put that cutlass under your coat," he went on. "You can't walk down the quay sporting that!"

What was he talking about? Why would a sane person want to walk down the quay? My mind was racing. We were in a precarious situation and I had no intention of going sight-seeing, but Ebbs was already on his way down the quayside. My right arm quivered like a leaf as I climbed the rail and jumped onto the quayside.

Ebbs turned. "Catch up, Egan," he hissed.

He used my real name! Was this to be some rite of passage? I felt a little more confident of discovering his plans.

"Where are we going," I asked, as I fell into step alongside him.

"What is that smell?" he said, totally ignoring my question.

"Smell? To the devil with any smell! Why are we walking towards the town when the schooner we came for is moored back there?"

Ebbs stopped abruptly and turned towards me. Anger shone brightly from his eyes as he glared up at me.

"You left me for dead, but I have kept your identity as a mutineer safe all this time." His voice trembled as he spoke. "Don't you dare speak to me in that way, Nathaniel Egan."

His castigation left me flooded with guilt, but I had just enough spirit left for one more question, "But where are we going, Jacob?" I pleaded.

"You told Captain Pearson and I, that you smelt a strange aroma of overly heated tallow on your previous visit to this quayside. I have dwelt upon what you said ever since, and the smell hit me the moment I set foot ashore. The smell of hot tallow is a sure sign of a steam engine, but where is it? I've a notion that we may find a clue downriver."

He pointed straight ahead of us, towards the thin spiral of smoke which I had seen earlier. It was about two hundred yards down the quayside, and there were a couple of tiny figures nearby.

"It seems to be coming from the middle of the river ...," I opined hesitantly.

"It must be in a boat, Nathaniel," Ebbs said, striding downriver once again.

"A steam engine in a boat!"

"Exactly, think on that for a moment or two," Ebbs advised, as I caught him up again. "If the French can power vessels with engines, they can move warships on windless days when we would be powerless to oppose them. It might even make Bonaparte's invasion of England a possibility again!"

"But we have our instructions to cut out a schooner and she lays back there___"

"We must go and look, Nathaniel," he interrupted viciously. "I have to take you with me because you are the only fellow in this expedition, apart from myself, who has the slightest knowledge of steam engines. Captain Pearson can lust for his prize money as much as he wishes, but it is of far greater importance that the Admiralty know of the presence of this steam driven ship: if it exists."

"We should take more men," I suggested, helplessly trying to slow him down and give myself more time to think.

"We need to attract as little attention to ourselves as possible. If anyone should address us leave the speaking to me."

He issued his instructions resolutely and without breaking step, as he walked determinedly down the quayside. The two figures, we could see by the spiralling smoke, steadily grew in size as we approached them. The quay wall curved slowly away from us, and as we neared the men an irksome foreboding, that Ebb's supposition was correct, took hold of me. I caught sight of a slim smokestack, poking up above the quayside. The two men on the quay were talking to someone below them. They paid us no heed, and when we were about sixty paces away they moved away from the quayside, heading towards a wooden hut set back a little way from the river. As they moved, I could clearly see the smokestack, and hear the kind of hissing sounds which I presumed emanated from a steam engine. Ebbs' stride lengthened, and I could sense his eagerness to discover what lay hidden beneath the quay. We hurried the final few yards, to the point where we were able to see beyond the curve in the quay wall and all was revealed to us! A squat, wide hulled ship with an ugly, bluff bow lay before us; I had never laid eyes on anything like it before. Cast metal plates affixed either side of her stem proclaimed that she was named *Titan*. She had a foremast that would fly a small heads'l but no main mast, and in its place there stood a mountain of metal: out of which protruded the thin black smokestack. The beam engine was more compact than the ones I had seen in Birmingham and Portsmouth, but I could recognise that many of the components were the same.

There were four men on the vessel; three were dressed in working apparel, and the fourth was a distinguished looking figure wearing the garb of a gentleman. Two of the crewmen were feverishly shovelling fuel into the furnace, and the third seemed to be battling to adjust the engine's steam governor that was situated to the stern of the ship, by where the well-dressed man was sitting at a portable writing desk with a pen in his hand. A long cavalry sabre was strapped to his waist, the end of which rested on the deck.

We were now standing alongside the strange vessel, which was fully sixty feet in length. The steamboat was a few yards away from the quay wall, and was connected by a stout hawser to two barges: both of which sat low in the water. The beam engine was driving, what looked like, two water mill wheels, one on either side of *Titan*. The paddle wheels were turning slowly and creating waves in the water behind them, but the ship was making little headway. The steam governor was spinning at a terrifying rate, and I deduced from what Ebbs had explained to me in Portsmouth, that it would be closing the steam valve and reducing the engines power. The workman, who was now cowering beneath it, was aiming spasmodic blows at the governor's spindle with a large spanner as the two metal spheres whizzed round above his head.

"Clear that darn thing, it's robbing me of power," the well dressed man shouted at him, as he leapt to his feet, knocking his writing table to the deck. It was a surprise that he spoke to the workman in English. He also had a strange accent, the like of which I had not heard before.

"A Yankee ...," Ebbs observed quietly to himself. (NOTE: *An American, Robert Fulton, had been present at one of William Symington's early trials of the* Charlotte Dundas, *and in August 1803 he demonstrated a steam driven boat of his own design to officers of Bonaparte's staff on the River Seine. By 1809 Fulton had returned to America and it is not known if the man encountered by Egan and Ebbs was an acolyte of Fulton's.*)

The workman's efforts had no effect on the governor, and *Titan* was slewing slowly from side to side as the paddle wheels struggled to pull the barges forwards. The only effect was that the hawser leading the barges came under a terrible strain and started to vibrate.

To my dismay, I heard Ebbs shout down in French to the two workmen who were loading the boiler. I don't know what he said, but I heard the words for *fisherman* and *this morning*. Before they could reply, the American wheeled around and yelled back.

"Go to hell, damn you. I've no time for sightseers."

But Ebbs wasn't to be deflected, and he ignoring the man's anger and continued to ask questions in French. One of the stokers stopped work and looked up at us. He started to say something to Ebbs before the American burst in again.

"Who the hell are you?"

His face was red and his eyes ablaze with rage.

"If you're fishermen from this port you'd have seen *Titan* before. Who's he? Why doesn't he say anything?"

He was pointing a long, accusatory finger in my direction, and that awful, hollow feeling came alive in my guts once again. It was definitely time for us to go, but Ebbs just stood his ground.

"He doesn't speak," Ebbs shouted, in English but mimicking a French accent. I made a feeble attempt to support his story by making a grunting noise and nodding my head, but I was obviously unconvincing because the Yank exploded.

"You're spies!" he yelled. He turned and shouted towards the hut behind the quay, "English spies! Georges, Paul-Henri. *Vite, vite* run to the *soldats… Anglais, Anglais!*"

The urge within me to run was immediate and powerful, but Ebbs stood stock still and I felt an unwanted surge of loyalty to him well up inside me.

"We are not Englishmen," he bawled in his manufactured accent. Unfortunately, as he threw his arms wide apart, as a gesture of incredulity, his coat opened, and the American received a clear sight of his blue navy coat and the butts of the heavy pistols that were sticking out of his belt.

The outcome now seemed inevitable, and I grabbed Ebbs' lapel and tugged him towards me.

"We're found out! We must run, Jacob," I pleaded.

I started to run back up the quayside and hoped that Ebbs was following. The two men, we had seen earlier, came out of the hut. They had obviously heard the Yankee shouting, and the bigger of the two was carrying a short handled sledge hammer. He ran onto the quayside and blocked my path. Instinctively, I cleared my long coat away from my hip so that he would see the cutlass and pistol that had been concealed there. He didn't back away, and seeing that I was armed only seemed to increase his resolve.

I looked over my shoulder for Ebbs, but he was just standing staring at the steamboat. The American was gesticulating wildly and bawling at the other man on the quay to fetch help. I could barely hear him because the engine's boiler had begun shrieking under the pressure of its load. To my horror, Ebbs took a step toward the edge of the quayside. In the next instant, he leapt towards the steamboat. My body turned to stone and a cold sweat broke out down my back, as he flew through the air and crumpled onto the deck planking. Scrambling to his feet, he ran to the stern of the boat and started hacking wildly at the hawser that was towing the barges with his curved naval hanger. The crewmen on the boat were stunned for a moment or two, and then they all rushed towards him. The stoker nearest to him had his shovel raised above his head like a boarding axe. Ebbs drew his pistol with his left hand and fired at the man, who fell to the deck. Under the intense pressure from the steam engine, and the weight of the barges, the hacked hawser disintegrated, and the boat lurched forward. The two crewmen momentarily lost their footing, but they both seemed to be hanging back away from the crazy Englishman. The American had managed to maintain his balance, and with a bestial bellow he ran at Ebbs slashing wildly at him with his sword. The Yank didn't seem to be much of a swordsman, but to face him Ebbs had to turn his back on the other two crewmen. I had no idea what to do; the nearest group of marines were too far away to see what was happening. I hoped they had heard Ebbs' pistol, but there was no movement from farther up the quayside. The Frenchman with the sledge hammer was only a few feet away from me by now, and I tugged my pistol from my belt. Could I shoot him and run back to the *Esprit du Breese*? I turned to look down into the steamboat that was picking up speed as it advanced up the river: no more than six feet from the quay wall. The two stokers were on their feet now and one threw his arm around Ebbs' neck, and the other was trying to restrain his sword arm. Ebbs' face turned up towards me.

"Nathaniel, Nathaniel. Help me! You can't desert me again!"

CHAPTER EIGHTEEN
Pouldavid River – Douarnenez, France – 9th July 1809

"I have just read the project of Citizen Fulton, engineer, which you have sent me much too late, since it is one that may change the face of the world ..."
Extract of a letter from Bonaparte to the State Council, sent from the camp of the Grand Armée at Boulogne, concerning American Engineer Robert Fulton's plan to invade England by towing landing barges across the Channel with steam tugs, July 1804.

Ebbs' voice knifed into my conscience; my body reacted to his plea involuntarily, and I found myself running across the quayside towards him. Within seconds, I was looking down onto the melee that was taking place on the steamboat's deck. It was as if I had been completely overtaken by instinct and my brain no longer exerted the power to control my actions. I answered Ebbs' call as unquestioningly as a collie dog answers his master's whistle. Ebbs had been my friend. He had stood by me, he had protected me, and when I saw him in peril my actions became automatic.

Tugging the pistol from my belt, I fired in the direction of the stoker who had his arm around Ebbs' neck. He was hit somewhere because he yelped and let go his hold. Throwing the empty gun at the other man and, without pausing to think, I launched myself into the air, screaming and drawing my cutlass as I did so. The Yank was poised to thrust at Ebbs' gut, but he was so shocked by the arrival of my yelling figure that he froze: staring in my direction. My legs were running wildly in mid-air as I swung the yard of forged steel in a huge arc and brought it downwards as swiftly and as forcefully as I could. It embedded into the Americans skull with a sickening thud before my feet had even hit the deck. The jarring in my wrist was as hard as if I had swung an axe into green oak, and he reeled away emitting an awful wail. I crashed onto the deck in a heap, my mind oblivious to the horrendousness of my act. I was caught-up in a maelstrom of violence and, in that instant, setting Ebbs free was all that mattered. Looking up, I saw the remaining Frenchman and Ebbs grappling with each other. The Frog was bigger and stronger than Ebbs. With one hand he had a grip of Ebbs' sword hand and with the other he was throttling the Midshipman. I knew that Ebbs would not survive for long if I didn't remove that Frenchman's fingers from his windpipe. As I leapt to my feet, there was a huge crash on the deck, and a heavy sledge-hammer just missed my foot, bounced off the deck timbers and flew into the engine with a loud clang. The man on the quayside had thrown his weapon, but being a big heavy fellow he didn't have the nerve to make the leap from the quayside. He was purging his anger by shouting from above. Ignoring him, I swung my right fist in a gigantic haymaker that smashed into the temple of Ebbs' assailant. Pain shot up my arm from my already damaged wrist, but the man slumped sideways. His fingers slipped from Ebbs' throat as he lost consciousness. Ebbs tore his sword arm free and, with a shocking amount of care and deliberation, slid the curved blade between the man's ribs.

One of the stokers we had shot was obviously only winged because he scuttled to the boat's stern, and pushed the tiller over in an attempt to put us alongside the quay wall. I was suddenly aware that the boat had virtually lost headway, but I knew that the quayside would soon be awash with angry Frenchmen, hell-bent on avenging their fallen comrades. Ebbs reacted before me, and pulling his sword from his victim's chest he ran to the tiller and slashed at the wounded stoker who fell onto the deck. Ebbs then steered us towards mid river.

"Nathaniel!" he yelled. "Open the throttle; we're not moving for God's sake. We've got to get away from the quay wall before we're overrun by Frenchmen."

I quickly cast my eyes across the engine and decided that the stout handle mounted above a butterfly valve would be the throttle, but it already seemed to be open. Grabbing the handle, I violently turned it in both directions but nothing happened. While I stood there bemused, something whistled past my head and rattled angrily amongst the ironworks of the engine, and a second later the same thing happened near my knee. They were musket balls! Three, blue coated militia men had appeared on the quayside and there were several more in the middle distance.

Ebbs yelled again from the tiller, "Nathaniel ... look to the governor!"

I turned to look at the engine's steam governor for the first time since landing on the boat. The Yank's body was careering wildly around the central spindle with the two steel spheres outstretched horizontally either side of his head. When Ebbs had cut the towing cable, the engine would have experienced a massive drop in load, and the governor's spheres would have been forced upwards and outwards by centrifugal force as the engine rapidly accelerated. The American must have staggered backwards in the throes of death, inadvertently jamming the handle of the cutlass, which I had embedded in his skull, between the pivoted link-arms holding one of the spheres.

The shoulder of the ashen-faced cadaver was wedged tightly between the lower set of arms and the sliding throttle valve. In this position, the governor couldn't operate, and the supply of steam for the engine was cut: accounting for our loss of headway. The angry rattle of more musketry came from behind me, and I knew I had to act fast to clear the governor and get steam into the engine. Grabbing the sledge hammer that lay on the deck, I swung wildly at the body's shoulders as it span round like some macabre, fairground game. I missed and the force of my effort made me topple forward. As I struggled to steady myself, a musket ball tore at the heel of my boot. Ebbs screamed at me from the tiller. I swung again, and the hammer sank into the body somewhere between the left shoulder blade and the spine. There was an awful sound of crunching bone, and the cadaver's shoulder was jerked free from where it was pinned by the pivot arms. The governor's two spheres dropped to the open position, restoring power to the engine. The two 'waterwheel-like' paddles on either side of the boat started to turn, and the body fell from its grotesque perch, clattering onto the deck with the cutlass still protruding from its skull.

With power restored, Ebbs steered away from the quayside. We were steadily picking up speed but the militia men on the quay had caught us up. I was expecting another peppering of musketry, when an involuntary yelp of victory escaped from my mouth and I found myself punching the air. Yule and his group of marines were formed up on the quay: about fifty yards ahead of us. There was a belch of smoke as they fired a tidy volley, and two of the French part-timers toppled to the ground. I was fairly certain that we would be out of range by the time the Frenchmen regrouped themselves.

"Nathaniel, take the tiller."

Ebbs ran up the deck.

"Mister Yule," he bellowed in the direction of the quay, "make for the prize. We shall pull her onto the wind."

Yule issued an order we could not hear, and the marines dutifully started to trot back up the quayside with Sergeant Walters keeping order at the back.

"Steer close to *Esprit du Breese*; I need to give instruction," Ebbs barked at me, as he disappeared behind the bulk of the steam engine on his way to the bow.

All my senses were at full alert. Each individual event seemed to take an age, although, somewhere in the back of my mind, I knew that they were passing in fractions of seconds. With Ebbs out of sight, I felt exposed and alone. I tugged at the tiller sending the steamboat as close to *Esprit's* side as I dared. Even with so much else to occupy my mind, it was a strange, unsettling feeling to con a vessel without reference to the wind. In a sailing boat, it would have required much play with the sails, and constant tacking, to make headway into a wind that was blowing, pretty much, straight down the Pouldavid River.

We were drawing close to *Esprit's* stern and Ebbs was bawling instructions.

"Monsieur Goriau you will have to take your boat out as best you can with the three hands that you have."

Goriau was standing at *Esprit's* taff rail, clearly silhouetted against the sky. He was staring at the steamboat with an expression of amazement on his face. I guessed that he had been preparing to take *Esprit* out and was expecting no help from the Navy. Two half-raised headsails were flogging in the wind at her bowsprit. I raised my hand in recognition, but he remained motionless. Suddenly, he gave me a cursory nod, and started to run forward on his boat shouting commands. I had no idea how Ebbs was planning for our escape, and fleetingly wished I was onboard *Esprit*.

"Or you can leave her and make your escape with us on the prize," Ebbs added. Goriau turned his head and glanced at Ebbs, but made no reply. He had heard the suggestion but was wasting no time with it.

Turning his attention to *Liberté*, which lay a short distance further up the harbour wall, Ebbs was already yelling at the top of his voice.

"Make ready with a line, Mister Ludlow. We'll pull your bow to the wind."

Instinctively, I found myself questioning the steamboat's ability to do this but it had pulled two laden barges, and I decided to trust to Ebbs' judgement. By now we were only thirty yards or so from the bow of *Liberté*, and there was frantic activity aboard her as they roused a line forward. By the time we were level with her stem, a crewman had a foot on her cathead with coiled line in his hand.

"Let it go man!" Ebbs shouted, as he made his way back down the boat.

The line arched in the air and flopped across out starboard side, just behind the main bulk of the engine. Ebbs grabbed it and started to pull handfuls of line onto our deck. After a few moments, the thin line gave way to a much heavier rope, and Ebbs' work became far more difficult.

"They've sent an anchor cable," yelled Ebbs in my direction. "Give me a hand to get it on board."

I left the tiller, between us we managed to drag enough of the cable onboard to be able to throw a turn over the heavy cleats at the stern that still held the remnants of the hawser that had pulled the barges.

"Let everything go, Mister Ludlow," yelled Ebbs. "Run up a jib and some stays'ls as fast as you like!"

He then turned to me; "We'll pull her into the wind. Steer across the river, Nathaniel."

I pushed the tiller away and Ebbs ran to the engine. Everything seemed to be running smoothly, and the governors' spheres were spinning at a low level. The slack in the cable tightened quickly, the hemp fibres stretching as the rope reached its maximum tautness. The huge paddles at the side of the boat seemed to spin quicker, but we weren't moving. The spheres on the governor started to climb up the spindle and were spinning quicker than a few moments before. The rope groaned and the boat's bow flicked from starboard to larboard under the strain. And then very, very slowly *Liberté* started moving from the quay wall. At first a few inches, then a foot and then a yard. It would take several minutes at this speed to take the schooner away from the quay, and Yule and the last of the marines were running pell-mell up the quayside. Apart for their shouts and oaths, the scene was remarkably quiet.

Where were the French? There should have been more reaction by now. *Liberté's* bow was slipping through the water at something like walking pace, and her headsails were just starting to flicker in the wind. Another few yards and her sails would start to fill. Once her headsails drew, Ludlow would be able to turn her to windward, and two tacks would see her clear of the river mouth.

I couldn't see Ebbs but I could hear him screaming with glee. From the accompanying sounds, I guessed he was fuelling the furnace. He then appeared at the side of the engine, triumphantly pumping the air with a dirty, short-handled shovel.

"We've done it, Nathaniel. We've taken their war secret!" he yelled. "And we wouldn't have done it if you hadn't freed me. I knew you wouldn't let me down!"

He ran down the boat, his face glowing with victory. He was so elated that he grabbed me in a celebratory embrace. He was behaving as if we were free of danger, but as he was shouting 'we've done, we've done it' the threatening crackle of musketry returned from the quay.

"They're shooting at us, Jacob," I yelled. "We've got to get out of here."

Pushing him away from me, I turned towards the noise and saw that a gaggle of blue-coated soldiers had gathered at the dockside *Liberté* had just vacated. They looked like regulars and I guessed that they had run from the gun battery that jutted out from the sea wall. Ebbs just stood there, totally unconcerned, beaming at me. A couple of small clouds of white smoke blotted out the soldiers as musket balls hummed past us.

"Jacob attend to the engine," I yelled.

"The engine is well primed," he replied unconcerned. "We can't move any faster."

Then he turned his attention on *Liberté* behind us.

"The main stays'l, damn you Ludlow!" he yelled and climbed

onto the taff rail behind me, steadying himself by holding onto the ensign staff. He wanted to be as close to the schooner as possible. "Spread as much fore 'n aft canvas as you can. Sheet everything in hard."

The deck of *Liberté* was pandemonium. As Ludlow disappeared to attend to the sails, Yule poked his head over the bow rail and raised his hand in acknowledgement to Ebbs. Behind him, there were several marines who were still gathering their wits from their dash along the quay. There were volleys of shouting from the deck above us, and in a few seconds halyards quivered and sails rose into the air.

The Frenchmen on the quay were concentrating their fire on the steamboat, and a hunk of timber flew out from the taff rail as one ball smacked home. Ebbs was behaving as if he hadn't noticed the danger, and as I crouched down beside the tiller, he was still standing on the rail, screaming orders to Yule. There was the sound of more musketry, but it was closer this time, and I knew it was coming from our marines on *Liberté*.

The two heads'ls that flew from *Liberté's* bowsprit were beginning to fill and Yule succeeded in pointing her a little way towards the wind: she was underway of her own volition. The cable between the two vessels went slack. The steamboat sped forward, as the dead weight was lifted from her, and jerked the line taught again which pulled the schooner further into the wind. Her flying jib snapped into shape, shortly followed by the fore staysail. *Liberté* was sailing! Now we stood a chance of making our escape! My spirits soared, but the Frenchmen on the quayside were adhering to their task and another brace of musket balls zinging over our starboard quarter kept me crouching behind the cockpit coaming. Ebbs jumped down from the taff rail and walked nonchalantly up the deck. He turned round to study the schooner's progress and stood stock-still in the middle of the afterdeck with his hands behind his back.

"Prepare to drop the cable, Nathaniel," he shouted to me. "The schooner shall be travelling as quickly as us in a moment."

"Get down, Jacob. You're making a fine target of yourself," I yelled back at him, scrabbling beneath the taff rail towards where the cable was cleated behind the tiller.

Peering over the top of the rail, more smoke clouds appeared and obscured the soldiers, who were moving up the quayside. An awful vision of Ebbs crumpled on the deck flashed through my mind; in a panic, I corkscrewed my head to look but he was still standing as indifferent to the danger as before. Several lead balls ricocheted between the heavy metal components of the engine. The Frenchmen didn't have time to shoot again because we slipped behind the hull of the schooner as she moved alongside us. Safe under the lee of the two-master, I stood up and cast off the cable from our stern. As I did so, *Liberté's* hull resounded with a dull thump as one of her guns went off. Yule's head appeared over the rail above us.

"I don't think we'll 'ave any more trouble from they on the quay wall, Sir," he shouted down to Ebbs. "Be we taking that kettle thing back to England?"

"We'll try, Mr Yule," Ebbs yelled back to him. "Stay close-by and keep the jolly boat ready to put over the side in case you have to come and get us."

"Jacob, this is no more than a raft with a heavy engine in the middle of it!" I said anxiously. "She'll never cross the channel."

"We have to try! I'm certain the Admiralty would like to know how this contraption works. Besides, we don't know what sort of keel she has beneath her. I'm hoping that we'll be able to tow her home."

For the first time this morning there was human activity on the Tréboul side of the river. If they had all been at Mass they were out now, and firing *Liberté's* cannon had drawn them to the river wharf. I couldn't see any soldiers only townsfolk, and to be honest, they looked more bemused than angry at what was going on. They must have been used to seeing the steamboat pulling sailing vessels seaward. I steered a course toward them, to give Yule as much water as possible to manoeuvre the schooner. Some of the spectators started to call across to us. Presumably enquiring what the gunfire had been about. Ebbs took to yelling back to them in French, while sporting a huge grim and executing a series of gracious bows. Whatever he said they didn't like, and within a few seconds they began pelting us with stones and any other debris that came to hand. Luckily, *Liberté* had made enough speed for Yule to put the helm over and her bow moved through the wind as she settled on a course that headed for the river mouth. I gladly followed in her wake and turned away from the protesters on the Tréboul bank.

We were nearing the mouth of the river on the full tide: there was a big decision to be made. If we stayed in the main channel, we would have to tack across the wind but would have plenty of water beneath us. There was, of course, the sickening possibility of being blown out of the water by the defensive battery at Tréboul (See Map). The alternative was to reach across the wind and head south of Île Tristan. We would have to slip through the channel, between the sea wall and the rocky shelf south of the island, and we had no real idea as to how deep the water would be. Running the schooner aground would result in death or capture for us all, but I was convinced the gamble was preferable to sailing directly under the guns. Not for the first time on this day I felt panic spreading from the pit of my stomach. What would Ebbs' decision be? Yule was obviously thinking in a similar fashion to me because his head appeared at the taff rail above us and he looked anxiously at Ebbs.

"Bear away, man, bear away!" Ebbs yelled, gesticulating widely to the starboard side. "Head south of the island but keep your canvas hard to the wind."

Ebbs' instructions came as a palpable relief, but I realized we faced grave dangers on this course as well.

The schooner was handsomely underway by now and she responded smartly as her tiller lifted. I followed her round and set us on a course only fifty yards or so from the sea wall. One of *Liberté's* guns roared once again and canister shot peppered the wall's great stones. A cloud of white smoke drifted back from the starboard side of the schooner and hid her from us for a couple of seconds. When the smoke cleared, I saw the schooners sails harden as Yule ordered them sheeted in. *Liberté* was reaching across the wind but by hardening the sails the schooner would heel over and her keel draw less water.

I could see Yule, Ludlow and two crewmen above me fighting at the wheel to hold *Liberté's* course against the hardened sail. Ahead of us, a few of the blue-coated militia men were gathering once again on the wall. With the schooner heeled over to pass through the channel she would not be able to sweep the sea wall again with her guns, but it still felt better to run the gauntlet of muskets than sail under the muzzles of the Tréboul battery on the other side of the island. The militiamen were making ready to fire and I yelled another warning to Ebbs, but he just gazed back at me as nonchalantly as he had done before. Several puffs of smoke appeared from the top of the sea wall, and I was flat on my stomach before I heard the rattling sounds of the muskets. I looked anxiously towards Ebbs, but thankfully, he was still there and just returned my gaze with a mocking gleam in his eye. Hopefully, by the time the militia men had reloaded we could be through the channel and into the bay.

Peering over our bow, I could see scattered whitecaps starting to appear on the tops of the breakers ahead of us in the open waters of Douarnenez Bay. We were nearly beyond the wind shadow of Île Tristan. The schooner was only a few yards ahead of us and, as she emerged from the behind the island, she heeled even further with every foot that she made. Yule had to ease his sheets and *Liberté* began to rise on her keel but thankfully there was a sufficient depth of water for her. With her sails and keel working more efficiently she rapidly picked up speed. On board *Titan*, the steam-engine was clacking away, but it seemed to me that the paddles were finding it harder to find any purchase as the swell increased in size. Within minutes the schooner would be beyond hailing range.

Ebbs must have thought the same because he was in the bow again yelling to Yule: "Spill wind, Mr Yule. We can't keep up!"

I was sure his instructions would be lost on the wind, but within a moment, Yule's head appeared over the taff rail again. He cupped his hands behind his ears to signify that he had not heard his instructions, and Ebbs elaborately mimed the easing of sheets. The burly seaman raised his hand in affirmation and disappeared from view.

We were now out beyond the shadow of the Île Tristan, and our unseaworthy steamboat was yawing on the short waves that were being blown into the bay. It felt as if the boat had been constructed with little or no keel beneath the waterline and we were being thrown about like a toy. The American had obviously been more engineer than boat builder. Ebbs and I exchanged glances; we both knew that any hopes of crossing the English Channel aboard this vessel were sunk.

"We must study the engine carefully, Nathaniel," said Ebbs. "Look for any configurations of the mechanics which look unlike what you have seen before, and try to commit them to your memory."

"I can do better than that; I can sketch them," I replied.

I knew that I had the skill to make a useful reference sketch in a few minutes and was of the opinion that being engaged in some labour was preferable to agonising about the perilous nature of our situation. I glanced behind us; we were drawing away from the sea wall and well out of musket range now. The muzzles of the guns of the sea wall battery were visible a little further down the coast, but we were still at an obtuse angle to them and would have to get quite a way out into the bay before they would be able to be brought to bear upon us.

I ran to where the American's writing desk still lay on the deck. I picked it up and set it on its spindly legs. Throwing open the lid, I searched for pen and paper, but to my delight the desk was full of drawings: high quality engineers drawings, of the steam engine.

"Jacob, we have everything that we need here," I yelled.

Ebbs ran across the deck to me and in his eagerness he snatched the drawings from my hand.

"There are more: many, many more. There are drawings of every facet of the engine and from every angle," I said, feverishly leafing through the contents of the desk.

But Ebbs was too engrossed with what he had to take any notice of me.

"Yes, yes ...," he was mumbling to himself. "I see ... the vertical motion of the machine ... translates into rotary motion through these two cams ..."

As he spoke a breaker hit the steamboat beam on and showered us with salty spray.

"Well, we know for certain that this tub isn't up to the job of hauling warships at sea," I said.

"No. Of course, you're right but we must sink her. We can't allow some Frog the opportunity of developing that Yank's engine. I'd better have Mister Yule come and collect us."

He ran towards the bow shouting for Yule. The schooner had slowed considerably and was still within earshot. I returned to the tiller and fought the boat's tendency to turn side on to the swell. Waves were regularly breaking over the larboard gunwale and the scuppers on that side were steadily filling up. The spray made the boiler hiss and steam from the engine was billowing around me, restricting my sight. I reckoned that there were probably bullet holes in the boiler compounding the problem.

"Can you wrap those drawings up and stuff them into your shirt," Ebbs ordered, as he returned from the bow. "If we can get on board *Liberté* I'll turn her guns on this little devil and she'll soon go down."

"How are we going to get onto *Liberté*?" I asked.

"I'm having Yule heave-to and drop the jollyboat. We have to keep those plans in fine order, Nathaniel. Wrap them in some rags."

In a few minutes Ebbs and I were seated in the stern sheets of *Liberté's* smallest tender watching the boats crew labour against the short, steep waves that were surging up the bay. The steamboat battled on by itself. The paddles were still spinning at maximum velocity but the vessel rode the waves poorly. Every now and then, the swell would pick her up and one of her paddle wheels would spin clear of the water. With no one at the tiller, she showed her natural tendency to broach, and it was not long before she was lying broadside to the swell. The larger waves rolled over her low rail and she was soon listing heavily.

❖ ❖ ❖

Ebbs and I leaped from the jolly boat and onto netting that had been hung over *Liberté's* side. Reaching the relative safety of a sea-worthy ship, heading out into Douarnenez Bay was a huge relief, but I felt totally drained of energy and struggled to clamber over the gunwale. Yule came to my aid and grabbed me by the arm. In contrast, Ebbs was completely invigorated by the success of the mission and he vaulted the gunwale with ease.

"Mister Yule, take great care with that man. I shall be beholden to him for the rest of my life. If he hadn't leapt onto the steam-boat when he did, I wouldn't be enjoying this celebration! I would have been sliced up by that Yank for sure."

"What Yank be that, Sir?" asked Yule.

Ebbs' eyes shone brightly as he burbled out his reply. "On the steamboat ... Didn't you see him? The Yank who built it ... the bastard was about to gut me but Nathaniel jumped upon him and buried a cutlass in his scull."

"You'll need to write a full report for the Captain, Sir," said Yule soothingly to Ebbs, as he lowered me gently to the deck.

"Yes, yes Mister Yule, I shall directly, but I need to tell you everything that occurred. This is quite the proudest day of my life," Ebbs babbled. "We may have failed to capture their secret steamboat, but we have secured the complete plans and specifications of their craft, and I have command of my first prize as well! No Lieutenant can be more blessed than I this day."

Amid the excitement of our escape, I had forgotten that the

American engineer's plans were still stuffed inside my clothes. I undid the few buttons left on my shirt and proffered the now damp drawings up to the big quartermaster.

"There they are Mister Yule, the American's drawings!" Ebbs cried ecstatically. "Why he should be working for the French I have no idea, but Nathaniel put a timely end to his shenanigans. I was overpowered by two of his crew and about to be murdered by the fellow when Nathaniel arrived upon the scene to save my life."

By now *Liberté* was standing out into the Bay of Douarnenez, but we would still need to stay on the same course for quite a while if we wanted to clear the northen tip of Île Tristan easily on our next tack. With Yule's help, I struggled to my feet and surveyed the situation from the rail.

"Permission to make ready to go about, Sir" Yule yelled to Ebbs.

Ebbs was so pumped up that he just waved to the quartermaster in the most casual manner. He was totally engrossed in his success. By taking the channel in front of the sea wall, we had kept away from the main defensive battery on the Tréboul side of the river, but soon we would briefly come under the guns from the smaller battery stationed on the sea wall at Douarnenez. I gazed in their direction, and a tell tail puff of white smoke appeared from the battery, followed by another, and another. Four guns had fired before I heard the resounding dull thud of the first. The retorts were followed by plumes of white water erupting half a cable behind us and off our starboard quarter.

"We must go about or we shall be under their guns, Sir," Yule insisted.

"Very well Mr Yule," replied Ebbs, returning to the here and now. "As we come about order the larboard guns to sink the steamboat. I don't want the Frogs towing her back into harbour."

The steamboat was slewing across the swell. There was another puff of smoke from the distant sea wall. I didn't want to stay in front of that battery any longer than we had to. I would quite happily have left the steamboat to fend for its self, but Ebbs was determined to see it beneath the waves.

"Fire as soon as the guns bear, Mister Yule," he bellowed, and then turned his glowing face towards me. I still had the battery on my mind and I found myself involuntarily crouching below the taff rail.

"You know Nathaniel, that Yank had his great steam engine too far forward in his boat for it to ever be seaworthy. If the weight of the boiler and condenser were better distributed to trim the vessel aft you may have a machine that could be of some use to a naval power. What d'ye thinks?"

He looked at me expectantly. His enthusiasm was driving his brain to think and he had no time for considering his safety. I was happy to leave the re-designing of steam driven boats until we were well out of the line of fire.

"I am glad to see you so content with our little victory but could we not discuss this at a later time," I replied.

"Of course, of course," he replied magnanimously. "I have to thank you again for leaping to my rescue on the steamboat. I had not lost my faith in you Nathanial, but you had sorely tested me at Aix Roads. However, now I will never be able to thank you enough."

"Think nothing of it, Jacob. I feel sure that I know you would have done the same for me if the situation was reversed," I replied, feeling a little stupid as I crouched before him, behind the taff rail.

We looked at each other warmly for the first time since our confrontation in the pinnace at Aix Roads. His forgiveness washed over me. Perhaps it was the first time I had felt at ease with myself since the mutiny? Ebbs reached down and put his hand on my shoulder. I saw another puff of white smoke leave the sea wall. I felt his hand tightly squeeze my shoulder blade, in the next instant there was a terrifying hiss, the like of which I have never heard before, and the world disappeared from my view.

I was lost in a thick, red quagmire. I clawed at my eyes, but all I could feel was a great, gluttonous mess. I scrapped frantically in my eye sockets. Both of my hands filled with wet, soft, warm flesh. I must be dead ... I must be, but I could still feel Ebbs' grip on my shoulder. Clawing handfuls of slop from my face, a glimmer of light appeared to me through a red haze. I wiped my eyes frantically with the backs of my hands, and the deck re-appeared in front of me. I looked up and saw Ebbs standing before me, but he had no head! The wide white lapels of his jacket were coated with blood and gore. My hands were covered with his brains, and I realised what had coated my eyes were the contents of his scull. To my midriff I was drenched in coagulating blood. Ebbs still stood straight and his arms and legs were making little jerking movements. I was driven by a powerful passion to aid him and leapt to my feet: grabbing hold of this living corpse. His stock, around where his neck had been, formed a reservoir of blood and viscera, and they tipped out and splashed over me as we jostled together. His corpse made a staggering step backwards, followed by another, and I rushed forward in an attempt to hold it upright. For a couple of seconds, I was entwined in the most macabre embrace imaginable, and then, in an instant, all movement left him and his cadaver collapsed in a heap onto the deck.

CHAPTER NINETEEN
English Channel – 14th July 1809

I have been authorized to inform Messers Andrew and Nicholas Dobbs, Prize Agents of 41 Green Lane, Hamble, Hampshire that the Lords of the Admiralty shall be releasing the sum of £16,873-18 shillings and nine pence in prize funds to be distributed between the officers and crew of His Majesty's frigate Myrmidon *as final settlement upon auction of, and sale of cargo from, the French vessel* Séverine *captured off the Brittany coast 17th May 1803.*
Extract of a letter from the clerk of Portsmouth Prize Court to Hampshire agents, June 1807.

It was with little concern that I stood outside the Captain's cabin of His Britannic Majesty's Laurel-class frigate, *Tiger*. Yule had shaken me out of my sick bay hammock, saying that Captain Pearson had sent word. He had dragged me onto my feet and directed me straight to the quarterdeck, where the steward bid me to wait at the door to the great cabin. Cocooned in a tortured world of my own, I was very nearly oblivious to the activities around me. I had no idea how long I had been this way, but the last thing I could clearly remember was a puff of white smoke appearing on the sea wall at Douarnenez.

Ever since arriving back in *Tiger*, Yule had relieved me of all duties, which was both good and typical of the man. My behaviour had been so strange that I think he considered me a danger to others on deck and consigned me to the sick bay to sleep. The only problem was that I couldn't sleep; I could only lie on my hammock staring at the timber planking above my head. My mind was alive with distorted memories of the scene on the captured schooner following that fateful puff of smoke. I couldn't shake the awful sensation of scooping Ebbs' dissembled brains out of my eye sockets. I could still feel the fingers of his headless corpse gripping my shoulder, and the gruesome memory of our ghastly dance together was fresh in my mind. It made me squirm inside every time I thought of it, and I thought of nothing else.

"Enter."

Pearson's command pierced my thoughts. What had he demanded my presence for? He must be pleased with himself; he had acquired a captured vessel and a valuable cargo without doing anything. I opened the door and, ducking my head, went into the cabin.

I had not seen Pearson's florid features since the day that Marc Goriau had cajoled him into promising our freedom in return for leading his men into Douarnenez. And then I remembered: I was a free man! Goriau and I had fulfilled our side of the bargain, and we had Pearson's guarantee of release. Or did we? I searched my memory. Who had kept the document? Of course, it was Goriau. But where was he? When had I last seen him? Yes, yes ... I remembered Ebbs shouting to him at the river quay in Douarnenez, and I'd seen *Esprit du Breese* under full sail in the bay. But did it matter where Goriau was? Pearson was a Post-Captain in the Royal Navy; he would have to be true to his word wherever Goriau was: wouldn't he? He must have summoned me to tell me I was now a free man. Perhaps, that was even why he had allowed me to stay off watch? I felt a surge of optimism rise within me, but then I realised I was reporting to an officer and hadn't yet spoken.

"Able Seaman Smith, Sir," I said, touching a knuckle to my forehead.

Captain Pearson was studying a letter and didn't look up at me. He didn't seem to have the mien of a man gleefully calculating his prize money.

"Smith ...er yes," he said distractedly. "Mister Ebbs has left behind a letter, addressed to myself, concerning you."

The statement hit me like a bolt of lightening striking a masthead.

"A letter, Sir?" I mumbled.

What letter? What did it say? Didn't Ebbs trust me after all and he'd left a letter exposing me as a mutineer? Had he told Pearson my history and my real name? Could the man I'd risked my life for have condemned me to swing? Could fate have dealt me such a deadly backhander?

"What does the letter say, Sir?"

I stared hard at Pearson willing him to reply but he said nothing.

"Sir?"

Infuriatingly, he just sat there staring at the damn thing. I felt the familiar icy chill of panic beginning to creep up my spine. I frantically scanned the clutter on Pearson's desk, searching for any clue to the content of Ebbs' letter. The drawings I had taken from the steamboat were scattered about in front of him. My mind grabbed them like a drowning man grasps a straw. Those drawings wouldn't mean anything to someone like Pearson: who would have very little knowledge of steam engines. Perhaps, Ebbs' letter explained that I knew something about the new engineering. That could be it! Pearson needed me to talk him through how the steamboat worked so that he could appear knowledgeable in his report to the Admiralty. Ebbs had remembered I had mentioned the smell of cooked tallow, and he had suspected that some sort of secret engine was in Douarnenez. He might well have mentioned it to Pearson before we left. But if that was the case why didn't Pearson tell me?

He suddenly jerked into life and loudly banged the letter on the desk, his eyes shot up to meet mine. He was angry.

"You're a rich man, Able Seaman Smith," he half-sneered, half-shouted when he said the name 'Smith'.

I hadn't seen that one coming! My feet felt unsteady and I had to take an involuntary step backwards to support myself. It was difficult to imagine anything that Pearson could have said that would have shocked me more.

"W…what, Sir?" I spluttered after a few moments.

"Lieutenant Ebbs has left you his share of the prize *Liberté*," Captain Pearson said. He spoke slowly, deliberately and coldly. "He has also left you a remittance for all his outstanding pay and all his possessions on board which includes his correspondence." Pearson waved his hand across a packet of letters tied together with a black silk ribbon in the middle of his desk. "I understand there to be more letters in his sea chest. Amongst them somewhere is one addressed to you explaining his actions."

"W...what, Sir?"

"You sound like a bloody parrot, man," he yelled. "For reasons only known to himself, Lieutenant Ebbs has set you fair for rest of your damn, worthless existence."

This was too much for me to take in. Why had Ebbs done this? Why had he left his prize money and his pay to me? What about his family?

"Lieutenant Ebbs was owed £16-16 shillings in pay, and I'll have the ship's clerk draw up your right to his captain's share of *Liberté*. You will have to report to the clerk of the prize court in Portsmouth after she has been appraised." (NOTE: *The Admiralty honoured Seaman's Wills from as early as the seventeenth century and Egan would no doubt have seen a few being completed before the Battle of Aix Roads. As the officer commanding Goriau's commandeered vessel, Ebbs would have been due two eighths of the value of* Liberté, *and as the officer who ordered her cutting out, Pearson would have been awarded one eighth.*)

Even in my state of confusion the pure animosity in Pearson's voice took me by surprise. I guessed he was angry because Ebbs would be due a bigger share of the prize than himself. I knew he had gambling debts - Yule had told me that – and money gave him the chance of redeeming his honour, but his malevolence towards me seemed to run deeper than simple jealousy. I could only conclude, that Pearson couldn't understand why a naval officer of noble birth would want to bequeath money to a lowly rating in preference to a 'brother' officer or his family. It was unheard of and it offended his hateful view of social order, but it made me feel proud. I was proud that Ebbs considered me worthy of his patronage and that he had the determination to rise above the class divides. The only positive aspect of Pearson's anger was that if he was upset about sharing prize money, he wasn't planning to renege on his guarantee of my freedom!

"And when will we next land in England, Sir?" I asked with just a little insolence in my voice.

"Oh, don't worry, Smith," he sneered again when he said Smith. "The frog fishing boat is off our starboard beam waiting to take you back to the Scillies. Goriau was not enthusiastic about landing without you; the passport I gave him is in both your names."

So Marc was waiting for me and Pearson was keeping to his

- 234 -

word. That was all I needed to know!

"When can I transfer to *Esprit du Breese*, Sir?"

"All in good time man," he snapped irritably. "Before I let you go, I need you to explain to me everything you understand about these damn drawings."

❖ ❖ ❖

It took a couple of hours to make Pearson understand anything about the mechanics of a steam engine, and evening had turned into night by the time I left his cabin. I was clutching Ebbs' parcel of letters to my chest, and a paper decreeing my right to his share of *Liberté* was safely tucked inside my shirt. There was now no chance of being rowed across to *Esprit du Breese* until the morning, and so I could read them at my ease.

I made my way down the companionway to the gunroom. Pearson had told me, in an off-hand way, that is where I would find the rest of Ebbs' belongings, and I had spoken to Yule who gave me permission to take them to his quarters. I may be a free man, but I still had nowhere on *Tiger* to store possessions.

A removable bulkhead separated the gunroom from the rest of the gun deck and there was a marine sentry on duty. I nodded at the man before rapping smartly on the door. Some sort of muffled cry came from inside and I went in. The gunroom in a single-deck ship like *Tiger* has no stern windows and it took a while for my eyes to grow accustomed to the dimly lit space. The ship's doctor was sitting at the long table in the centre of the room. He was alone and reading a book by the light of a small lantern. There was a wine bottle at his elbow and when he raised his slightly hooded eyes to look at me, I knew he had been entertained in both pursuits for some time. He lost interest in me almost as soon as he was aware of me. When I stated my business and asked the whereabouts of Ebbs' cabin, he just waved an arm generally down the starboard side and returned to his reading.

All the ship's officers shared the gunroom and there were half-a-dozen cabins along either side. The ones nearest the stern were constructed of wood and had doors but the rest were little more than canvas partitions. There had only been two lieutenants on *Tiger* and so I reasoned that one of the wooden cabins would have belonged to Ebbs. I walked to the end of the wardroom and on the door of the last cabin on the starboard side was painted, rather crudely, 'Lieut. J. Ebbs'. I went into the tiny cabin and found it was barely big enough to hang a cot. A huge sea chest occupied most of the floor space and that there was no other furniture. A grubby canvas kit bag lay forlornly on the swinging bed. I was uncertain of what to do. Although I knew his belongings were now mine, it didn't seem right to just walk out with them. I simply stood there for a few minutes wondering how to act.

"What the devil ..."

The door behind me had been forcefully opened, and I was pushed onto the cot. A shock of red hair, sporting Ludlow's cheery face beneath it, entered the room, and I noticed that his long, single-breasted coat no longer bore white collar patches.

"I've come for Mister Ebbs' belongings, Sir," I said, getting up.

"Ah yes! Captain Pearson said that you would be here for his things ... most unusual."

Ludlow was a few years younger than me and his milky skin still bore the spots of adolescence around his mouth and nose, but he had always been considerate to me and I liked him.

"Do I have your permission to ask the marine at the door to help me with the chest, Sir?"

"No need, I can help you," he said.

His offer of help came as some surprise; I wondered what position he thought I now occupied? Did he know I was a free man and a rich free man at that? He just grinned when he saw my bemusement.

"My world is replete, Smith. I am desperately upset about Mister Ebbs' demise, off course, but good for me has arisen from the circumstance, and Captain Pearson has just made me up to acting lieutenant! This is to be my cabin now."

"I am glad for you Mister Ludlow," I replied, feeling a genuine good will towards the youngster. "Perhaps you would like Mister Ebbs' spare uniform and white breaches? They will be of no use to me."

"That is kind of you Smith, I would greatly appreciate them. Here, these candles belonged to Mister Ebbs. They must now be yours."

The youngster took a handful of candles from a small shelf above the cot and handed them to me. Real wax candles were too fine a luxury to be refused.

Ludlow helped me to transport Ebb's chest and kit bag to the quartermaster's cabin near the bow, adjacent to the sail lockers and store cupboards. As I pulled aside the canvas partition that served as a door to the cabin, the dismal light from the lower deck allowed me to see that Yule was lying on his cot. Although he was expecting me, he was surprised to see the acting Lieutenant acting as my bearer. He climbed to his feet and saluted the youngster.

"Relax, Mister Yule. I shall be gone in an instant and leave Mister Smith to your good care," said Ludlow, putting down his end of the chest and nodding good naturedly at us before he let the partition fall closed, and plunged us into near darkness.

"I just can't believe it, Mister Yule," I burbled enthusiastically as soon as the boy was gone. "Mister Ebbs has not only left me his back pay and all his possessions, but also his share of the prize money; I think I shall be quite rich."

"I knew something strange was afoot when the Captain let you lie in the sick bay without complaint," replied Yule.

"How long had I been there?"

"You 'ave been there the best part o' two days. You 'as been in a strange place, Smith. I came and spoke to you on occasion, but I couldn't make you answer me. Your eyes 'ave been open the whole time, but I couldn't rouse your senses."

"Oh ... I had no idea ... I am aware that I have lost some time, but the memory of poor Jacob's head exploding ..."

"Aye lad, I know. It 'aint that surprisin'; you 'ave 'ad a great shock," Yule said soothingly. "I 'ave seen people react like that afore, but what was a shocker wus when Captain Pearson let an able 'and lie in the sickbay and not want a reason why. When I told 'im that you weren't sensible he just shrugged 'is shoulders and walked away."

"He needed me to explain to him about the importance of the steamboat and what happened in Douarnenez," I explained. "He had to wait for my mind to right itself before he could write his report."

"Captain Pearson sent *Liberté* back to England with a prize crew, but he 'as been keepin' Marc Goriau an' his fishin' boat safely nearby," said Yule.

"I'm indebted to Marc that he waited for me: many men would not have."

"Although I'm sure he would 'ave waited for you, he has had no choice in the matter," said Yule. "He came alongside yesterday mornin' to ask about you. He can't sail back to the Scillies without help an' I reckon he'll want an Englishman wit' him when he gets there. The situation there could 'ave changed since we left."

This was an avalanche of information for me to assimilate. I had no idea of what had happened over the last couple of days, or that my mind seemed to have closed down in an effort to protect me. A whirlpool of thought rushed around my head in light of the recent news. Pearson must indeed be preparing to let me leave *Tiger* if he had left me lying senseless for two days, and I was quite sure that Marc would have waited for me regardless. But mainly I thought of Ebbs. What an astonishing thing for him to have done; to decide I was the most important recipient of his money. He must have made his decision before the attack took place, before I ever dreamt of leaping onto the deck of the steam-boat.

"I'm sure Goriau would have waited for me … I am just so proud that a good man like Jacob considered me worthy of his worldly belongings. I thought that I had betrayed his trust too deeply …"

The words just tumbled out of my mouth. I had momentarily forgotten that Yule was there, and I was just talking to myself.

"How be, Smith? As he told me, 'twas you that saved 'is life?"

Yule's question pulled me up short; if he hadn't spoken, I think I would have found myself blurting out the parts that Ebbs and I played in the mutiny.

"Oh … yes, but I … hesitated a few moments on the quayside before I jumped onboard the steam-boat," I replied.

"Don't worry 'bout a few moments, lad. Not when you were responsible for saving an officer's life, and capturin' that secret steam-vessel thing."

I had always hoped that Ebbs would trust me again, but his behaviour after I had joined Tiger left me believing there was no hope of reconciliation. But no, he considered me to be his friend, perhaps his greatest friend, because he had chosen me to be his beneficiary. I had no idea why he had left everything to me, but it made me feel warm and glad that he had. Money would matter so little to the son of an Earl and the master of great estates, but he would have known, only too well, how much it meant to me. He had given me another chance in a life that fate had almost destroyed. I could live anywhere in England I chose to, but thinking of my good fortune also brought back the awful feeling of clawing his brains from my eyes. I felt a burning need to read

Ebbs' letters and find out why he had done this for me.

"Would it be possible for me to sit here in your cabin and read my letters, Mister Yule?"

"Are you so keen to inspect your spoils?"

"I am very anxious, Sir. Captain Pearson said that there are letters in this chest, and I am most keen to try and find out why Mister Ebbs chose me above his family."

"Very well; there be an oil glim an' tinderbox upon that shelf attached to the futtock."

"Thank you, Mister Yule, but I have some candles."

This made Yule raise his eyebrows in awe of my new found wealth. He then nodded to me and pushed his way through the canvas partition.

In my haste to light my candle, I was all fingers and thumbs. I dropped the flint and firesteel, and it took an agonising few moments to find them again. In the back of my mind, optimism was taking wing; I would be able to go back home, and start a business. I could employ father … everything would be the same as it was … only I would be without my poor Mary. My newfound wealth, would mean a new position in society. Perhaps, I would even by allowed to call on Lady Sarah: to thank her for her brother's generosity? My imaginings shot about in as many different directions as a brown hare on a spring pasture.

At last! The charcloth glowed as a steel fragment burnt a hole in it. I frantically blew tiny embers onto the tinder and, in a few moments, the clean light of a real wax candle illuminated the cabin. Feverishly, I pulled the package of Ebb's letters from inside my shirt. I tugged at the black ribbon that bound them and the package sprang open, scattering its contents onto Yule's cot. I quickly leafed my way through them, but I couldn't see anything addressed to me, and so I swung open the lid to the sea chest and searched for more letters amongst the linens and coats. Either Ebbs had not kept his belongings in tidy order or else a third party had been rummaging around in there. His correspondence was not in one place but rather littered throughout the whole chest. The first note that came to hand was signed by First Lieutenant James Taft and attested to the fact that he '*was indebted to Lieutenant Jacob Ebbs the sum of two guineas in lost wagers*'. It wasn't what I was looking for, and I cast the note aside with an inward grin to myself. Two hours ago, I would not have been so flippant about a sum as large as two guineas, and I briefly considered whether I had any chance of collecting the money from the First Luff? I found letters randomly among his shirts and linens. I flicking them open and scanning the first few lines. Some were contained in wrappers and some were just folded pieces of paper, but I could find nothing that seemed to concern me. There were bills for wine and victuals from the gunroom, receipts from the purser and endless letters written in the same characteristically shaky hand which I took to be from one of Ebbs' elderly relatives.

And then I found it!

It was a short note that had been recently written on one piece of folded and sealed paper. Ebbs had even used my real name: this letter was personal. '*For the attention of Nathaniel Egan and him alone*' I read on the outside before breaking away the wax seal that displayed an unfamiliar coat of arms upon it. '*If you are reading this Nathaniel, then you will know that God has taken me to Him. I owe you a great apology and I feel that I shall forever be in your debt*'. What was he talking about? He had written this before we had set out for Douarnenez. '*I have made financial provision for you in the advent of my death, and I have written to Captain Pearson begging he attend to my wishes which include that you receive all my belongings, my back pay and any prize money I have accrued*'. I read on growing more mystified by the second. '*I have explained that your name is Egan and when I entered your name as 'Smith' onto the books of the cutter* Theseus, *I was affording you protection against the possibility of smuggling charges which have since been dismissed due to your agreement with Captain Pearson to take our men into Douarnenez.*

"*I have told nobody in the world of your involvement in the mutiny at Basque Roads, for which I forgive you completely, and at the time, I reported you lost overboard in the struggle. I wish you the best of luck in your future life and pray that you can recover from the misfortunes that you have already suffered. I sincerely wish that you can regard me as your friend. Jacob Ezekiel Ebbs, Second Lieutenant, His Majesty's Frigate* Tiger.

I sat motionless on Yule's cot for a few minutes, and then tucked the note inside my shirt. What it meant I had no idea, but I felt instinctively that no else should read it. What debt could Ebbs owe to me? It was me that owed gratitude to him! He had done his utmost to make my life tolerable when I was impressed; he who had given me the bounty, he who had shielded me from the awful punishments for mutiny.

I turned my attention back to the chest and the search for more letters that might explain what he was thinking. When I had nearly reached the bottom, I was confronted by Ebbs' best dress uniform. I had never seen him wear the long, blue coat with stand up collar and white lapels, but as I pulled it out of the chest, to give to Ludlow, it somehow brought Ebbs back to life. I felt a melancholic pall settle over me, and I stood motionless for a few moments simply staring at the coat. I could feel the wetness of a tear collecting in the corner of my eye, and it took all my resolve to wipe it away and resume my search. I dug down through the relatively ordered pile of breeches and stockings at the bottom of the chest, and came across one last, slightly crumpled, letter.

As I pulled it from the chest, the stiff outside wrapping slipped from my hand and fluttered to the deck. The letter held the faintest trace of scent and was written in a bold but graceful hand. It was headed, '*Alton Court, Hampshire*'; there was something curiously familiar about the address but I couldn't put my finger on it. The correspondence began, '*My beloved Jacob. I am writing to thank-you my dearest brother for the loving attention that you lavished upon your undeserving sister during her stay at Portsmouth Dockyard*'. It was from Lady Sarah! My spirits soared and I instantly wondered whether she would make any mention of me? My fingers were trembling as I read on. '*Henry Stubbings took great care of me in the four-wheeler on the way home, and I was safely returned here before dinner*'. She went on to describe the state of their father's health and her worries for her mother's ability to cope with the inevitable loss of her husband. I started to scan the letter hoping to find a reference to myself, but not really believing I would, and then there it was! '*Do not punish yourself over the difficulties that befell Mister Egan, Dear Jacob. I thought him a good man of honest integrity*'. I felt a warm glow as I read Lady Sarah's description of me. She went on: '*who I am certain would bear you no ill will over what happened. You merely sanctioned a course of action that was already underway.*' Here it was again: what could I possible resent about Jacob? What were they referring to? And then, for some reason, I picked up the wrapper that had fallen onto the deck. I heard myself issue an involuntary exclamation of shock when I read it.

To be delivered to Viscount Alton, presently serving on His

Majesty's ship Tiger *and known as Midshipman Jacob Ezekiel Ebbs.*

Viscount Alton! The man responsible for my being forced from the farm at Lilstock, the man responsible for the death of my wife in Birmingham and ultimately my impressment into the Navy. I heard a smart smack, as the wrapper fell from my dumfounded fingers onto the deck.

Acknowledgements

Primarily, I have to thank Dr Stuart Croskell for his constant encouragement and tireless work editing drafts of Spindrift. I also need to acknowledge the late Jim O'Donoghue, of Oxford University, for his historical input in the early planning of this book.

So many people have been generous with their time in replying to my research enquiries that I think it would be easiest to acknowledge them in a list:

Jack Kirby, *Curator of Birmingham Science Museum.*
Dr David Symons, *Curator of Antiquities and Numismatics, Birmingham Museum and Art Gallery.*
Heather Johnson, *Royal Naval Museum, Portsmouth.*
Richard Garay, *Musée de la Marine, Paris.*
Leticia Ferrer, *The Science Museum, London.*
Lorraine Carpenter, *Naval Base Property Trust, Portsmouth.*
Richard Larn OBE, *Founder of the Shipwreck Heritage Centre,* who provided detailed information about the Isles of Scilly.
Philip Gross, *Professor of Creative Writing, University of South Wales.*
Mawgan Lewis for his invaluable help with designing the front cover and *www.oldbookillustrations.com* for the engine image.
Graham West, for information gleaned from many years sailing England's South West coast and various members of the *History Department of Birmingham University.*

Battle of Aix Roads
11th and 12th April 1809

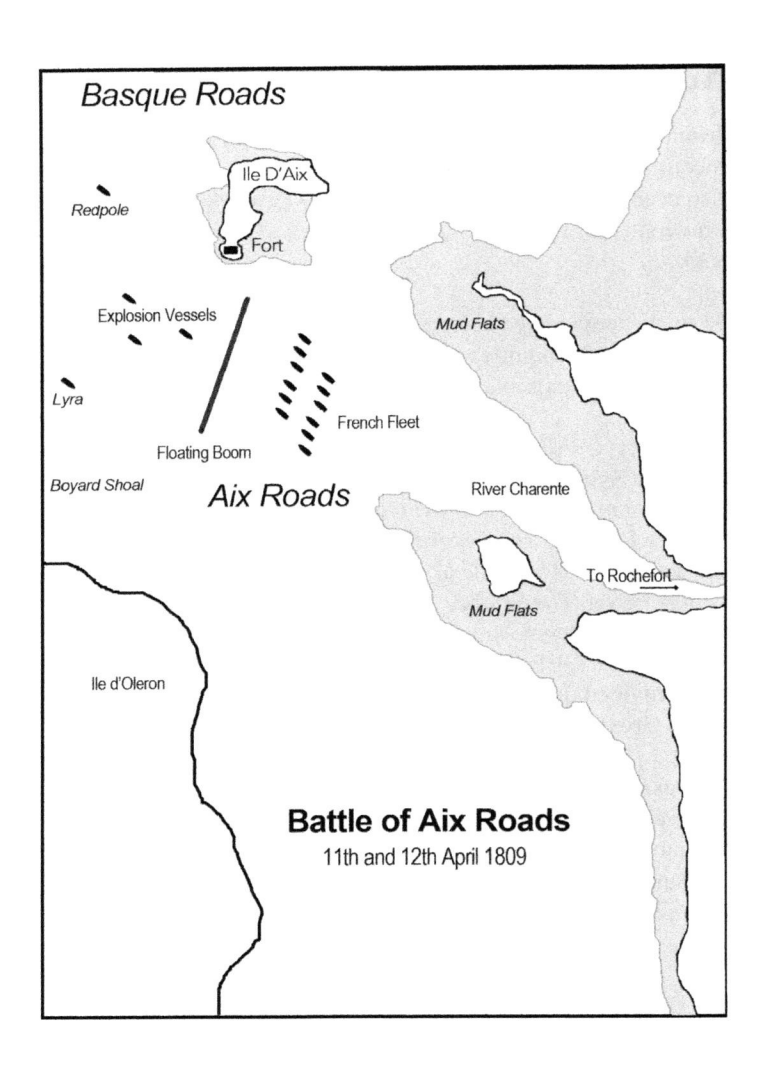

Historical Note

The battle at Aix Roads began on 11th April 1809, very much as described in Spindrift, except that the crews of the explosion vessels would have been smaller than I have described. They also used lightweight gigs to make their escapes rather than the pinnace which I have employed for reasons of later narrative.

In his excellent book *Cochrane: The Life and Exploits of a Fighting Captain* Robert Harvey mentions that the story concerning Cochrane's return to the vessel after the fuses had been lit to rescue the ship's dog, appeared in the press at the time. I have not been able to find any press reports myself or any other references to this taking place. I suppose that we will never know whether this is an extension of the Cochrane myth or a true event!

Author information

Neil Champken is a Fine Art and Art History graduate who spent many years working both as a journalist and running a marketing/design company. He has contributed to many publications in the UK but most notably the *Guardian*, the *Daily Telegraph*, *Country Life* and all the regional newspapers in Somerset, mainly concerning environmental topics.

He lives on the Polden Hills in Somerset, England and makes and retails high quality Somerset Cider Vinegar online. It is also worth saying, that in his youth Neil was a sailing enthusiast and spent ten years on traditionally rigged boats of one sort or another.

Douarnenez and Île Tristan

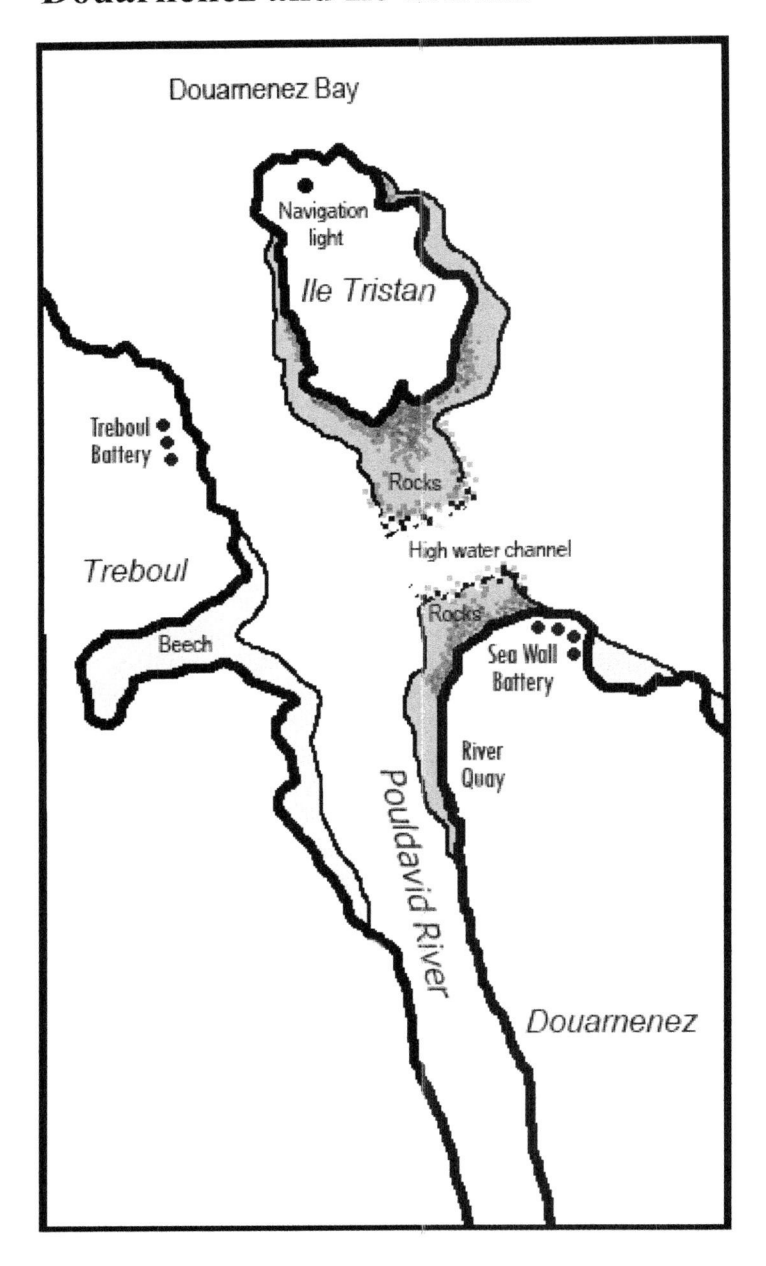

Bibliography

Birmingham: The First Manufacturing Town in the World 1760-1840, *Eric Hopkins, Weidenfeld & Nicolson, 1989.*

Cochrane: The Life and Exploits of a Fighting Captain, *Robert Harvey, Constable & Robinson, 2000.*

The Lunar Men: Five Friends Whose Curiosity Changed the World, *Jenny Uglow, Faber& Faber, 2002.*

Life and Adventures of William Cobbett, *Richard Ingrams, HarperCollins, 2005.*

Smuggling in the Bristol Channel 1700-1850, *Graham Smith, Countryside Books, 1989.*

Forgotten Fruits, The stories behind Britain's traditional fruit and vegetables, *Christopher Stocks, Windmill Books 2008.*

British Birds and their Haunts, *Rev. C. A. Johns, Routledge & Sons, 1909.*

Billy Ruffian: The Bellerophon and the Downfall of Napoleon, *David Cordingly, Bloomsbury, 2003.*

Nelson's Navy, *Brian Conway, Conway Maritime Press, 1989.*

Cochrane the Dauntless, *David Cordingly, Bloomsbury, 2007.*

Britain's Maritime Heritage, *Robert Simper, David & Charles, 1982.*

The Command of the Ocean, *Nicholas Rodger, Penguin, 2004.*

A Note to Readers

Thank-you for reading *Spindrift*. It is a great feeling to create stories, but an even better one to know that other people are enjoying them!

I would like to ask, that if you enjoyed *Spindrift*, could you leave a review on Amazon or share your thoughts on my *Novel Histories* FaceBook page?

Established authors have advertising budgets, editors and public relations teams to support and promote their work, but I, dear readers, only have you!

Printed in Great Britain
by Amazon